**This title is also available from
Simon & Schuster Audio and as an ebook**

"J.A. Jance fans, especially fans of the Ali Reynolds series, will not be disappointed with this new novel. It's a page-turner."

—*Green Valley News and Sun* (AZ)

CRUEL INTENT

"Compelling . . . satisfying."

—*USA Today*

"A fast-paced read with as many twists and turns as a county fair roller coaster."

—*Seattle Post-Intelligencer*

"Jance has honed her talent for writing entertaining, accessible mysteries that readers can zip through."

—*Booklist*

"This veteran has the knack."

—*Kirkus Reviews*

"This is an enjoyable and easy read, which is perfect for a weekend in front of the fireplace."

—*Sacramento Book Review*

"Jance's novel is impressively 'cyber savvy.'"

—*The Tennessean* (Nashville)

HAND OF EVIL

"Entertaining. . . . Jance fits together the many pieces of this literary jigsaw puzzle into a coherent and satisfying whole."

—*The Tennessean* (Nashville)

"Jance at her best, weaving a masterful story of suspense."

—*Sierra Vista Herald* (Bisbee, AZ)

"Like Jance's popular and long-running Joanna Brady series . . . the Ali Reynolds novels boast well-realized characters and make the most of their beautiful Southwest setting."

—*Booklist*

"Jance keeps the entertainment value at a steady level. . . . Ali is a believable, interesting character."

—*South Florida Sun-Sentinel*

"Sparks between Ali and Dave and an upbeat ending keep this latest Ali outing on track."

—*Publishers Weekly*

"Skillfully balances the various plots, giving each its fair share of attention, and intertwines them to a suspenseful climax."

—*Daily Camera* (Boulder, CO)

J. P. BEAUMONT MYSTERIES

WALKER FAMILY MYSTERIES

POETRY

J. A. JANCE

TRIAL BY FIRE

AN ALI REYNOLDS MYSTERY

POCKET BOOKS

NEW YORK LONDON TORONTO SYDNEY NEW DELHI

Pocket Books
An Imprint of Simon & Schuster, Inc.
1230 Avenue of the Americas
New York, NY 10020

This book is a work of fiction. Any references to historical events, real people, or real places are used fictitiously. Other names, characters, places, and events are products of the author's imagination, and any resemblance to actual events or places or persons, living or dead, is entirely coincidental.

This Pocket Books paperback edition January 2020

POCKET and colophon are registered trademarks of Simon & Schuster, Inc.

For information about special discounts for bulk purchases, please contact Simon & Schuster Special Sales at 1-866-506-1949 or business@simonandschuster.com.

The Simon & Schuster Speakers Bureau can bring authors to your live event. For more information or to book an event, contact the Simon & Schuster Speakers Bureau at 1-866-248-3049 or visit our website at www.simonspeakers.com.

Manufactured in the United States of America

10 9 8 7 6 5 4 3 2 1

ISBN 978-1-9821-3188-3
ISBN 978-1-4165-6388-4 (ebook)

TRIAL
BY FIRE

{ PROLOGUE }

She awakened to the sound of roaring flames and to searing heat and lung-choking smoke. Maybe she was already dead and this was hell, but why would she go to hell? What had she done to deserve that? Just then a scorched beam fell across her leg, and she felt the horrifying pain of burning flesh—*her* burning flesh. That's when she knew she wasn't dead. She was still alive. And on fire.

She tried to shake the burning two-by-four off her leg but it was too heavy. It wouldn't budge. She tried shoving it away and managed to move it a little, but in the process her hand caught fire as well. She tried to sit up, desperate to find some avenue of escape, but the floor around her was a sea of flame. She was barefoot. She couldn't bring herself to step into the fire. There was nowhere for her to go, no way to escape. It was hopeless. She was going to die.

Falling back onto the bed, she began screaming and praying and coughing, all at the same time. "Please, God. Let it be quick. Thy will be done on earth as it is in heaven."

Another wooden beam fell. This one didn't land on her directly, but as the hungry flames licked away at it, she knew they were really searching for her. The pain was all around her now. Her whole body was on fire. Somewhere, far beyond the flames, she heard something else—the sound of breaking glass. Was there glass in heaven?

"Hello," a voice called. "Where are you?"

Why is He asking that? she wondered. *God knows everything. He must know where I am.*

Then, unexpectedly, a mysterious figure clothed all in yellow or maybe even orange rose up silently out of the flame and smoke. He was holding his arms stretched out toward her, reaching for her.

Not God after all, she thought despairingly. *Satan. I really am in hell.*

Darkness fell and there was nothing at all.

{ CHAPTER 1 }

On a gorgeous mid-May morning with temperatures still in the seventies, all was right with Ali Reynolds's world. The cobalt blue sky overhead was unblemished by even a single cloud, and Sedona's towering red rocks gleamed in brilliant sunlight.

The seemingly endless remodeling project on Ali's recently purchased Manzanita Hills Road house had finally come to an end. The workers were gone, along with their trucks and their constant noise. Now, seated on her newly refurbished flagstone patio and surrounded by an ancient wisteria in full and glorious bloom, she was enjoying the peace and quiet, as well as a third cup of freshly brewed coffee, while she worked on a speech, a commencement speech actually, that she was due to deliver at not one but two high school graduation ceremonies at the end of the week.

How she had gotten roped into doing two commencement speeches one day apart was a wonder to her still.

A year or so earlier Ali had agreed to take the helm of the Amelia Dougherty Askins Scholarship Fund, a charitable entity that helped provide financial assistance for college expenses to deserving students from schools all over Arizona's Verde Valley. Though she was once an Askins Scholarship winner herself, this was Ali's first year of administering the program. The time-consuming process of searching out and evaluating likely recipients had put her in touch with students, teachers, and administrators from a number of local schools.

Ali's ties to Sedona Red Rock High School had to do with the fact that both her son, Christopher, and her new daughter-in-law, Chris's bride, Athena, taught there. When it came time to cajole Ali into agreeing to speak at commencement, her son and daughter-in-law had known just which strings to pull.

Although Sedona was Ali's hometown, Sedona Red Rock wasn't her actual alma mater, since there had been no high school in Sedona at the time Ali was an eligible student. Instead, Ali and her classmates had been bused to nearby Cottonwood, where they had attended Mingus Union High School and where Ali's favorite teacher had been the head of the English department, a gruff but caring character named Ernie Gabrielson. Once word leaked out that Ali had been scheduled to speak at Sedona's graduation ceremonies, a delegation had been sent requesting that Ali do the same for Mingus. Hence the two separate invitations. The two events, however, required only one speech, and Ali had been working on it for several days.

She wanted her talk to be fun and meaningful. Ali had graduated from high school and gone away to college. After obtaining her degree in journalism, she had gone off to work in the world of television news, first reporting and then anchoring newscasts in Milwaukee, New York City, and finally L.A. She had returned to her hometown in the aftermath of losing both her anchor position and her philandering husband, Paul Grayson. Her initial intention had been to stay in Sedona just long enough to regroup, but now she had settled back into small-town life and was reveling in it. She was glad to be out of the constant hustle and bustle and traffic of L.A., and she was enjoying living close to her parents and her son.

That was part of what she wanted to say to the graduates later this week, on Thursday evening in Sedona and on Friday in Cottonwood—that it was fine for students to leave home in order to further their educations and make their marks in the big, wide world— but she also wanted to tell them that it was fine for them to stay at home or to come back home eventually, bringing with them the benefit of both their education and their hard-won experience, which they could then apply to problems and opportunities that existed in their own backyards.

Lost in thought and concentrating on the work at hand, Ali was surprised when her majordomo, Leland Brooks, cleared his throat and announced, "Excuse me, madam, but you have a visitor."

For the better part of fifty years, Leland had managed the house on Manzanita Hills Road, first for the previous owner, Arabella Ashcroft, and for her mother. Now he did the same thing for the new owner. During Ali's massive remodeling project he had served as the on-site supervisor. Now he mostly supervised Ali. She didn't require much supervision, but she'd grown too fond of Leland Brooks to consider putting him out to pasture.

Ali looked up in time to realize that the guest in question, Gordon Maxwell, had followed Leland onto the patio. Maxwell was sheriff of Yavapai County, and he certainly looked the part. He was dressed in a crisply starched khaki uniform and held a white Stetson gripped in one hand. A loaded pistol, a 9-millimeter Smith and Wesson M&P in its molded scabbard, was strapped to his right hip. Weaponry aside, he looked like a man who could handle himself.

For one thing, he was large. The heels on his highly polished snakeskin cowboy boots added an extra inch or so to his barefoot height of six foot six. Ali estimated him to be somewhere in his early sixties, but he had the physique and carriage of a much younger man. If he had worn the Stetson instead of carrying it around, it would have completed the impression of youthfulness by covering his bald head. On his chest was a silver star and a name tag that said *Sheriff Maxwell*. The presence of that white hat, worn or not, served notice to one and all that Gordon Maxwell was one of the good guys.

"Morning, ma'am," he drawled in greeting. "Hope you don't mind my dropping by unannounced like this."

Ali could tell from the disapproving frown on Leland's forehead that her butler most certainly minded. In Leland Brooks's world, well-mannered guests never dropped by uninvited; it simply wasn't done. Sheriff Maxwell, however, had apparently failed to get that particular memo. Ali knew that since the sheriff lived miles away in Prescott, the county seat, he couldn't exactly claim that he was simply in the neighborhood and decided to drop in. No, he had come to

see Ali on purpose, and he hadn't called in advance
because he was worried she might try to dodge him.

"No," Ali said at once, clearing her laptop out of the
way. "Of course not. Please have a seat. Would you
care for coffee?"

"Yes, ma'am," Maxwell said. "A cup of coffee would
be greatly appreciated." With that he eased his lanky
frame into one of the empty patio chairs and then set
his hat carefully, with the crown down, on the seat of
another.

Ali nodded in Leland's direction. With only the
smallest disapproving shake of his head, the butler
picked up Ali's empty mug and bustled off to fetch
coffee while Ali turned to her visitor.

"To what do I owe this honor?" she asked.

Sheriff Maxwell looked both thoughtful and
uncomfortable at the same time. "It's to whom," he
said finally, with the kind of carefully chosen grammar
that would have done Mr. Gabrielson proud. "Not to
what. And the real answer to your question would be
your friend Detective Holman. I suppose he's told you
that my department has been through a bit of a rough
patch recently."

It was true that Dave Holman had mentioned the
sheriff's department's difficulties, but so had everyone else. The story had been the talk of the town,
from the Sedona post office to the lunch counter at
the Sugarloaf Cafe, a neighborhood diner run by Ali's
parents, Bob and Edie Larson.

According to local gossip, a longtime evidence clerk
named Sally Harrison had come under suspicion of
hijacking some of the drugs that had been left in her
charge. When the alleged thefts finally became known,

her boyfriend, Devon Ryan, a deputy who not only happened to be the department's media information officer but was also still married to someone else at the time, had decked an overly inquisitive reporter from the Flagstaff daily newspaper, the *Coconino Courier*. Oscar Reyes, the reporter in question, had turned up at a press conference with plenty of questions about the alleged thefts, but also with pointed questions about the couple's illicit affair. The press conference altercation had gone from verbal to physical. Now both the evidence clerk and the media relations officer were off work on administrative leave while the reporter, more outraged than physically hurt, was supposedly in the process of filing suit against Devon Ryan as well as the Yavapai County Sheriff's Department.

"So I've heard," was all Ali said.

Maxwell nodded. "I'm afraid that reporter from Flagstaff isn't the only one with a black eye over this. The county attorney is hinting around about making a settlement with him. If that happens, the voters will have my balls." Suddenly aware of his slip, he said, "Oops, please excuse my blunt language. The truth is, both Harrison and Ryan were working for the department long before I was elected to office, but that's not going to count in my favor. As far as people in the county are concerned, riding herd on my employees is my responsibility. They'll say I wasn't supervising them properly."

Ali knew that was true as well. It was exactly what people around town were already saying, including Ali's mother, Edie Larson; but that bit of gossip didn't explain why Sheriff Maxwell was here on Ali's patio, staring off across the valley at some of Sedona's most spectacular red rocks.

Before anything more could be said, Leland Brooks marched onto the flagstone patio carrying a fully laden tray. Ali noticed at once that Leland was taking a butler's revenge on their impromptu guest: rather than the casual everyday dishes, he had loaded the tray with a pair of tiny, carefully ironed napkins and Ali's good Limoges Bélème-pattern china. Ali knew at once that the oversized fingers on Sheriff Maxwell's meaty paws would barely fit inside the handles of those delicately shaped cups.

Without a word, Leland unloaded the tray, depositing napkins, bread plates, and silverware along with a platter of freshly baked cookies onto the patio table's glass top. Then, after serving the coffee, he returned to the house.

Maxwell watched him go with a bemused expression on his face. "Didn't he used to work for Arabella Ashcroft, and for her mother?" Maxwell asked as he stirred a pair of sugar cubes into his coffee.

"He works for me now," Ali replied civilly, but she wasn't about to reveal any more than that about her domestic arrangements. Besides, Leland Brooks wasn't the only one who was more than a little put out by Sheriff Maxwell's taking the liberty of dropping by her place uninvited, especially when she was impatient to get back to work on her speech. If the man's visit had a point, he had yet to set about making it, and Ali thought it was high time he did.

"Why exactly are you here?" she asked.

Maxwell shifted in his chair. He reached for his Stetson as if considering holding it in front of him as a shield. Then, sighing heavily, he left the hat where it was.

"My two miscreants—Sally Harrison and Devon Ryan—are off on administrative leave right now. They'll stay that way as long as the charges against them are being investigated. That leaves my department shorthanded, but I can't hire permanent replacements until the situation has been resolved. If it goes the way I think it will, they'll both get their walking papers."

Listening to him, Ali still wondered what any of this had to do with her.

"I've got someone on my staff who can take up the slack in the evidence room," Maxwell continued, "but the media relations problem is a white horse of a different color. Ryan made quite a mess of it, and our recent history with the press is such that no one inside the department is willing to step up to the plate."

Ali was beginning to get the picture, and she was astonished. "Are you asking me to take on the media relations job?"

Maxwell nodded and then took a sip of his coffee. Hanging on to the tiny cup with one pinky finger poking out in the air made him look as silly as Leland Brooks had intended. Finally he gave up and engulfed the tiny cup in one massive hand.

"On a temporary basis," Maxwell added, after carefully returning the cup to its matching saucer. "Of course, we can't pay you nearly what you earned when you were a television news anchor out in California, but you used to be a reporter, Ali. You know how those people think. You know what they want, and you'll know how to handle them."

"I'm not a cop," Ali said. "Never have been."

Maxwell gave her the smallest grin. "There have

been several times the last couple of years when you could have fooled me."

It was true. Since returning to her hometown, Ali Reynolds had found herself in one scrape after another, sometimes dealing with some very bad people. The previous winter she and her mother had helped bring down a serial killer, but that had all come about through her being in the wrong place at the wrong time.

"I'm forty-seven years old," she said. "I haven't been thinking of starting a new career. Besides, back in the day I did a couple of stories on the L.A. County Sheriff's Department Police Academy. It struck me as being pretty intense. I don't think I could hack it."

"No one is asking you to go through police academy training," Maxwell said. "This would be on a temporary basis only, until we can officially give Ryan the boot and appoint someone else to the position permanently. Please believe me when I say this. I certainly wouldn't expect you to go around mixing it up with any bad guys, although I know you've done that on your own account on occasion. I also understand that you have a concealed-weapon permit and that you're fairly handy with both your Glock and your Taser. 'Armed and dangerous' is the way Dave Holman put it."

"He would," Ali said. *And so would my dad,* she thought ruefully. Bob Larson had yet to resign himself to the fact that his wife, Edie, now carried her own pink metallic Taser with her wherever she went. As for Ali's Glock? He disapproved of that as well.

"So we need someone who can help us smooth things over with the media in the meantime," Maxwell said. "Dave thought you might be just the person to fill that bill."

The voice in Ali's laptop chose that moment to speak up. *You are now running on reserve power,* it announced, which brought Ali back to the words she had been writing at the time Sheriff Maxwell had appeared. Her message had been all about encouraging local students to go off into the world and then come back home, bringing whatever expertise they had gained on the outside to help out the home team. Did Ali mean those words? Or were they just meaningless rhetorical flourishes on her part—a case of "Do as I say, not as I do"?

Then there was the fact that with the complex remodeling job finally over, Ali had been at loose ends, casting about and wondering what she would do with the rest of her life.

It wasn't as though she needed to discuss her decision with anyone or ask for anyone's permission or opinion. That's one of the things that went with the territory of being single at her age. Ali knew without asking that her mother would be thrilled. Her father, on the other hand, would disapprove—mostly because he wouldn't want his little girl putting herself in some kind of "pressure-cooker job." Christopher and Athena might swing either way on the subject, most likely down the same division as her parents, with Christopher advising caution and Athena saying, "Go for it." Leland Brooks would back Ali's decision to the hilt regardless of what it was. As for Dave Holman? From what Sheriff Maxwell was saying, Dave had already made his position on the matter quite clear.

"I like my life at the moment," Ali said. "I got out of the habit of punching a time clock a long time ago."

"There won't be any call for time clocks," Maxwell said. "I'd be hiring you as a media consultant."

"With no benefits, I presume," Ali put in.

Maxwell nodded. "That's the best way for me to walk this past the Board of Supervisors. Besides, by doing it this way I can offer quite a bit more money than I could otherwise. Most of the time you could operate out of the Village of Oak Creek substation, but I'd need you to come in to the office in Prescott some of the time—especially early on, so I can brief you on some of our policies and procedures and bring you up to speed with what we've got going at the moment. There are the usual press issues—when we're dealing with the Board of Supervisors, for example, or seeing to it that routine police matters make it into the media—but there are times when we'll need to be able to call you out if there are emergency situations that need to be handled."

"Company car?" Ali asked.

Maxwell grinned at her again. He knew she wouldn't be asking that question if she hadn't already made up her mind to take him up on his offer. What they were doing now was negotiating terms.

"I saw that nifty blue Porsche Cayenne of yours as I came up the driveway," he said. "Your helper was in the process of detailing it. Believe me, none of the vehicles in the department's fleet would measure up to that. I'm afraid you'd need to use your own wheels and settle for a car allowance. You'll need to keep track of your mileage."

"Of course," Ali said. "What about a radio?"

"It'll take some time, but we'll set you up with the same kind of communications equipment our plainclothes people use, although you may not want a radio permanently installed in your vehicle. We'll also equip you with a Kevlar vest, which will need to be worn at all times when you're working for us—except when you're in the office, that is. Oh, and you'll need a complete contact list."

Will need, Ali noted. *Not would need.*

In other words, Maxwell knew that he had hooked her. Now he was going for the assumed close.

"When would I start?" Ali asked.

Sheriff Maxwell looked enormously relieved, as though a huge weight had been lifted from his broad shoulders. "Anytime," he said, getting to his feet and donning his Stetson. "The sooner the better."

He left then, sauntering away across the patio. Watching him go, Ali had no idea how much her life had just changed—in ways she could never have envisioned.

{ CHAPTER 2 }

In the end, Ali's cheering section sorted itself out in exactly the way she had expected. She went to the Sugarloaf that very afternoon to give her parents the news. Edie Larson was thrilled.

"Will you have your own badge?" she wanted to know.

"I suppose," Ali said. "An employee ID badge to wear in the office and a wallet with a badge and another ID to carry in my purse."

"It's a good thing you already have your Glock and your Taser," Edie continued. "I'm really proud of you. This is great."

Ali's dad, Bob Larson, wasn't nearly as happy to hear it. Looking aggrieved, he folded both hands across his chest—including the one that still held a spatula.

"I don't get it," he said. "You were such a sensible kid growing up. What I can't understand is why, as an adult, you're always dead set on getting yourself into all kinds of hot water. Why can't you be as levelheaded as your mother?"

Ali almost laughed aloud at that one. Her father was the levelheaded one. Her mother was not.

After calling first to make sure it was okay for her to stop by, Ali went next to Chris and Athena's house—her old house on Andante Drive—to tell the kids her news.

Chris reacted stoically. "Are you sure this is what you want to do, Mom?" he asked.

"Yes," Ali answered with a nod. "I'm sure."

"Then go for it," Chris said.

Athena's enthusiasm mirrored Edie Larson's. "You'll be great," she said. "And from what I've heard, that Devon guy is a real piece of work. Sally Harrison isn't the only ladylove he has on the side. With any kind of luck he'll be going down the road on a permanent basis."

As for Dave Holman? Ali called and invited him to stop by for dinner that very night. He arrived holding a somewhat forlorn bouquet he had snagged from what was left in the flower section of Safeway. He had gone there to raid the deli section so he could make a single-dad dinner for his two school-aged daughters.

"You're not mad at me, are you?" Dave asked warily as he handed Ali the flowers. "For interfering in your life, I mean?"

Ali handed the flowers over to Leland, who gave them a disparaging look and then set off for the kitchen with the bedraggled bouquet in hand. No doubt he'd get rid of the faded flowers and sort the rest into something a bit more appealing.

"I take it you've already heard the news?" Ali returned.

Dave nodded. "Gordy was delighted—and relieved."

"Gordy?" Ali repeated. "That's what you call Sheriff Maxwell?"

"Not to his face," Dave admitted. "But he's not getting a fair shake on this one. The previous administration left him encumbered with a pile of deadwood—Devon Ryan being the worst case in point. Due to civil service rules he can't just dump the guy, but Sheriff Maxwell needs some help cleaning up the mess—someone from the outside, and someone with a little class."

"Namely me?" Ali asked.

Dave grinned. "Absolutely."

He poured two glasses from the opened bottle of Coppola claret Leland had liberated from the *vin ordinaire* section of her ex-husband, Paul Grayson's, extensive wine collection. Taking their wineglasses with them, Dave and Ali retreated to the patio while Leland finished cooking.

"So when do you start?" Dave asked.

"Next week," she said. "In the meantime I have those two commencement speeches to give. I'm still working on them."

"What are you going to say?"

"To the graduates?" Ali asked.

Dave nodded.

"That regardless of what their high school experience may have been, unqualified success or miserable failure, the world beyond high school is entirely different. They should go out into that world and explore it—see what there is to be seen and get their education. But eventually I hope some of them will feel compelled to come back home with whatever they've learned."

Dave took a thoughtful sip of his wine. "After all," Ali added, "that's what you did."

"I suppose," he said.

"That's also the real reason I had to say yes when Sheriff Maxwell asked me to help out," she said. "Either that or face the fact that I'm a complete hypocrite."

"You wouldn't be a hypocrite even if you'd turned Sheriff Maxwell down cold," Dave said. "That's not who you are."

"Thanks," Ali said, smiling and accepting the compliment. "But what's it going to be like? He says he wants me to shadow him next week and get an idea of what's going on—sort of like one of those new waiters who follow the old ones around, smiling a lot but never touching a plate. I'm not looking forward to that. I have a feeling the people who are there already won't exactly welcome me with open arms."

"They don't have a leg to stand on," Dave pointed out. "None of them was willing to step up and take on the job, even when it was offered. Besides, you're a consultant, remember? That word alone conceals a multitude of sins. You'll be fine."

"I'm not so sure," Ali said, but Leland appeared in the doorway just then to announce that dinner was served. Since there was no point in agonizing over what might or might not happen in the future, Ali stood up and led the way into the house.

"Let's go eat," she said. "No sense letting it get cold."

That night, long after Dave left, Ali lay awake and thought about the twists and turns of her life. She had been devastated when her television broadcast career had been ended without warning. She had walked away from her marriage to an adulterous spouse expecting to leave with her dignity and a reasonable property settlement. Her financial situation had changed remarkably when Paul Grayson was murdered prior to finalizing their divorce. As Paul's surviving spouse, Ali had been left with far more financial security than she had ever expected. It wasn't really necessary for her to go looking for work, but it seemed that, in this case, work had come looking for her.

On Thursday of that week, she delivered the commencement address at Sedona Red Rock High School. After giving what Ali hoped was a motivational speech, she watched with pride as one of her scholarship winners, Marissa Dvorak, rolled her wheelchair across the stage to accept her diploma. The Askins Scholarship award would enable Marissa to attend the University of Arizona, where she hoped to earn a degree that would allow her to work in the field of medical research.

As the Sedona High graduating class filed across the stage in alphabetical order, Ali noticed that the school's second runner-up for the Askins Scholarship, a boy named Ricky Farraday, wasn't listed in the program. Ali had scratched him from the list when she had learned, through Leland's efforts, that Ricky had scammed his way into a large financial settlement by staging a phony hate crime. The school district had paid up, but Ali wondered if Ricky had transferred to another school or simply dropped out. He was bright enough, but if other people in the community had caught on to his shenanigans, the kids at school, along with the teachers, might have made life miserable for him—and in Ali's opinion, deservedly so.

After the ceremony, Ali posed for photos with Marissa and her adoptive and very proud parents. Then she went home and read through another hundred pages in a book called *Street Legal,* a textbook on criminal investigative procedures written by a guy named Ken Wallentine. In her previous existence as a television news anchor, she had always believed in being prepared before she did an interview.

Now, faced with the prospect of being on the other side of the news process—the one being interviewed as opposed to the one doing the interviewing—Ali thought it reasonable to prepare in the same way. That's where the textbook came in, giving her a crash course in pretrial criminal procedure. Then, on Friday, after reading for most of the day, she gave the commencement address for Mingus Union High.

When Ali's speech was over, she watched with undisguised pride as the other of her two scholarship winners received her high school diploma. Haley Marsh, looking confident and determined, strode across the stage in her cap and gown with her almost three-year-old son, Liam, perched on one hip.

When Ali first met her, months earlier, Haley had seemed defeated and close to giving up. She had enrolled at Mingus Union High as a sophomore—a very pregnant and unmarried sophomore. She and her grandmother had moved to Cottonwood from Oklahoma in the aftermath of the vicious rape that had resulted in Haley's unintended pregnancy.

Predictably, Haley's well-established schoolmates at Mingus Union had treated the new arrival as a social pariah. For the next three years, Haley had soldiered on, persisting in being a good student if not an outstanding one. With her grandmother's help, she had managed to eke out a decent GPA while also caring for her baby. By Haley's senior year, however, the strain had taken its toll, and Haley had all but given up on her ambition of becoming a nurse. Her family's straitened financial situation and her less than top-drawer grades made going on to college seem impossible. Instead, she had expected to use her high school diploma to help her land full-time work at a local discount store.

Ali's appearance on the scene and her offer of an Askins Scholarship had changed all that. Suddenly, the possibility of Haley's attending college was back on the table. By graduation night, Haley's transformation was a wonder to behold. When Haley reached the principal, who was holding her diploma, she set Liam down beside her long enough to accept it. Taking the leather-bound document in hand, she passed it along to her bow tie–wearing son for him to hold during the principal's congratulating handshake. While her son opened the diploma and seemed to try to read it, Haley blew a kiss to her beaming grandmother. Haley exited the stage as Liam's self-possessed performance elicited some good-natured laughter from the crowd, as well as sporadic applause.

Ali was again drafted into a postgraduation photo session. The process was barely under way, however, when Marissa Dvorak rolled into the middle of it. With a squeal of joy, Liam abandoned his mother and raced over to Marissa, then clambered up into her lap.

The previous November, shortly after the two scholarship winners had been announced, Ali had arranged for Haley and Marissa to meet. That meeting of the two girls, both of them considered social misfits in their own schools, had proved to be an unqualified success. In the ensuing months the two girls had formed an unlikely but close friendship. They had both been accepted for the fall term at the University of Arizona, in Tucson, where Leland Brooks had succeeded in locating a wheelchair-accessible apartment that would suit them both. And Liam, too, apparently.

"You have no idea what a blessing Marissa is in our lives," Haley's grandmother, Nelda, said, appearing suddenly at Ali's elbow. "Haley's never had a friend like that, not a really close friend, not even back home in Oklahoma."

"They look like they're having fun," Ali said.

Nelda nodded. "You should hear them. Those two girls are on the phone every night, making plans, talking about what they're going to do once they get to Tucson. And as you can see, Liam's crazy about Marissa, too."

"That's clear enough," Ali agreed with a laugh.

Shortly thereafter, she and Nelda were summoned both to take pictures and to pose in them as well. When the celebration was over, Ali went back home to Sedona to hit the books—or rather, to hit the book. Now that she and Sheriff Maxwell had come to terms about her salary arrangements, she was due to show up for her first staff meeting on Monday, where her temporary position with the Yavapai County Sheriff's Department would be announced.

It was true that she would be receiving far less than she was accustomed to being paid in the California media world. *But this is Arizona,* she reminded herself. *I'm doing this for my hometown.*

On Monday morning she was up and out. She left the house at six, a good half hour earlier than she needed to depart in order to make the 8 a.m. briefing at the Yavapai County Sheriff's Department on East

Gurley Street in Prescott. She was tempted to stop by the Sugarloaf so her mother could wish her luck but, concerned about the long, slow construction zone between Sedona and the Village of Oak Creek, she headed immediately in that direction.

Ali was on edge during the drive, but that was hardly surprising. She had always been nervous when it came time to start a new job. The trick was to over-prepare and then not let anyone else know that she was anything other than ten feet tall and bulletproof.

Before getting on the freeway, she stopped long enough to shuffle through her music selections—including her Aunt Evie's extensive collection of musi-cals. Then, singing along with "I Whistle a Happy Tune" from *The King and I,* Ali turned south toward Highway 169.

Part of Ali's overpreparation plan, beyond studying the police procedure textbook, meant that she had also spent hours learning what she could about the Yavapai sheriff's office. She knew, for example, that the eight-thousand-plus-square-mile county was divided into three command centers. The main office and jail complex were located in Prescott, but there were also substations scattered throughout the far-reaching jurisdiction that stretched from the outskirts of Peoria, near Phoenix, on the south; to Seligman, to the north; and to Wickenburg, on the west.

According to what she read, the Media Relations area came under the heading of Technical Services, where it was lumped in with Dispatch. That, too, was headquartered in Prescott. From what Ali read online, she wasn't able to fathom why Sheriff Maxwell had wanted to bring in an outsider, someone with no law enforcement experience, even on a temporary basis. Ali somehow suspected that there was more behind the move than the purported reason she had been given—that she was being asked to pinch-hit while a long-term and possibly disgraced officer was off on paid administrative leave.

What's really at work here? Ali wondered. Sheriff Maxwell was glad she was signing on, and so, evidently, was Dave Holman, but what about everyone else?

Once she reached Prescott, she parked outside the two-story, modern-looking sheriff's office on East Gurley Street, then walked into the public lobby of the sheriff's office.

"I'm Ali Reynolds," she said to a clerk stationed behind a glass partition. "I believe Sheriff Maxwell is expecting me."

"Just a minute, please. I'll see if he can see you."

The clerk's words were polite enough, but they were accompanied by such a cold-eyed, dragon-lady stare that Ali found herself wondering if she had spilled coffee down the front of her blazer.

The one-minute wait turned into several. A full ten minutes later—and five minutes after Ali had been told to arrive—a young woman finally emerged through a door at the far end of the lobby.

"Hi," she said, holding out her hand in greeting. "I'm Carol Hillyard, Sheriff Maxwell's secretary. You must be Alison Reynolds. He asked me to come find you and bring you back to the staff meeting."

That was what she called it—a staff meeting—but when Ali walked into the crowded conference room a few minutes later, the chilly reception made her think she had wandered into a refrigerator.

She walked into the room to find Sheriff Maxwell standing at a lectern in front of an assembled group of officers and other personnel. "Ah, yes," he said, nodding in her direction. "Here she is. I'd like to introduce Ali Reynolds, the media consultant I was telling you about. I know some of you are less than thrilled by my decision to temporarily outsource our public information functions, but I think giving ourselves a complete break with the past is the best strategy to allow the department to move forward."

"Yes," an unidentified voice grumbled from the back of the room. "Let's start by reinventing the wheel."

If Sheriff Maxwell heard the sarcastic muttering, he chose to ignore it and continued. "Ms. Reynolds lives in Sedona. As I mentioned earlier, since this is a temporary assignment, I see no need for her to work out of this office on a daily basis, especially considering the ease of communications we have these days—teleconferencing, e-mail, cell phones, and the like. I've assigned her office space in the substation at the Village of Oak Creek.

"She'll be spending the next few days traveling with me, seeing how we do things, and meeting all of you. Please be so kind as to introduce yourselves to her and let her know what part you play in the big picture. I'm going to expect your complete cooperation in all this. It's one thing to do the job we do, but our constituents need to hear about it.

"Ali," he added. "Would you care to add a few words?"

There was nothing Ali wanted less. Clearly the people in the room weren't thrilled to see her, and she doubted they'd care to hear what she had to say, either. But since Sheriff Maxwell was motioning her to join him at the lectern, she did. Other than Sheriff Maxwell and Dave Holman, who was seated in the far back corner, none of the people seated in the conference room seemed familiar to her, but the general air of disapproval seemed to echo the reaction of the growling gatekeeper out in the front lobby. Ali didn't think there was anything she could say that would bring these folks around, but she had to try.

"Good morning," she said cheerily. "As Sheriff Maxwell said, I'm Ali Reynolds. I'm a Yavapai County native. I grew up in Sedona, where my parents still own and operate the Sugarloaf Cafe. I attended high school at Mingus Cottonwood and NAU in Flagstaff before spending several years working in television news both on the East Coast and in California.

"As you probably know, I have no background whatsoever in law enforcement. That means I'm coming to this job knowing a lot about the news broadcasting side of the street and very little about yours. And so I'm going to need your help. I'll probably be asking plenty of questions as I learn the ropes, and I hope you'll be patient with me. As Sheriff Maxwell said, my job will be to help get the word out about everything this department is doing to promote public safety. It's your responsibility to do a good job, and it's my responsibility to make sure the people in our various communities know about it."

As Ali stepped away from the microphone someone started a halfhearted round of applause that followed her as she took a vacant seat in the front row next to Sheriff Maxwell, who stood up and returned to the lectern. Ali suspected that Dave Holman had started the polite clapping, but she couldn't be sure. What was clear enough was that it sure as hell wasn't a standing ovation. Most of the people in the room regarded her as an interloper and didn't want her there.

She was forced to sit through the remainder of the interminable meeting, in which a woman from the county human resources department offered a long, tedious discussion about the open-enrollment period for the county's redesigned health insurance program, as well as a detailed explanation of new benefits. None of that had anything at all to do with Ali; since she was a consultant rather than a permanent employee, she wasn't a qualified participant.

When the meeting finally ended, the room emptied quickly. Before leaving, Sheriff Maxwell stopped long enough to introduce Ali to his three sector commanders as well as the sergeant in charge of Technical Services. Ali did her best to catalog the names and faces, but she knew that would take time. A few other people stopped off to introduce themselves before they, too, drifted out of the room. Once they were gone, the last man standing was Dave Holman.

She looked at him and shook her head. "That was fun," she said. "Thanks for tossing me into the lions' den. What's really going on here?"

"A bit of a range war, actually," he said. "Some of the younger guys are trying to decertify the old union, Arizona Peace Officer and Employee Local 76, and put in a new one, International Union of Deputy Sheriffs, which would represent sworn officers only and leave the other employees out in the cold. Devon Ryan, the former public information officer, and Sally Harrison, his gal pal, were both officers in the old union, which claims they were put on leave in order to make decertification easier."

"Which is why no one is willing to take the job," Ali concluded. "Because anyone who takes it will be considered a union-busting scab by one side or the other. What does that make me, and which side are you on?"

"Arizona is a right to work state," Dave explained. "I don't belong to either of the unions because I don't have to. But Gordy's a good guy and I could see that the two sides are in the process of tearing him apart, like a pair of dogs worrying a bone."

As small business owners, Ali's parents had never belonged to unions of any kind. Neither had their long-term employees. In her previous career Ali had joined unions because membership had been a prerequisite to taking a job in some places, but she understood Dave's take on the situation. It was pretty much her own.

"You could have told me about all this up front," Ali said.

"I suppose so," Dave said, "but if I had, would you have signed on?"

"Probably not," Ali said.

Dave grinned at her. "See there? It's a lot harder to back out now that you've been introduced to a roomful of people. So how about it? Can I drag you down to Kate's and buy Yavapai County's new public information officer a cup of coffee?"

Ali relented. "I guess so," she agreed with a laugh. "But the operant word here is 'temporary,' not 'new.'"

"Right," Dave agreed. "I stand corrected."

"Don't you have something better to do?"

"Actually, I don't," Dave said. "Since I'm not a member of either camp, Sheriff Maxwell asked me to take charge of you. You need to be decked out in your own Kevlar vest, one that you can wear under civilian clothes. You also need working ID badges that'll let you in and out of the department as well as in and out of this end of the building. That way you won't have to call down and ask for an escort."

"Which reminds me," Ali said. "Who is the sour-puss behind the partition out in the public lobby? She acted like she was ready to bite my head off."

"A younger woman, but not all that good-looking?" Dave asked. "She wears glasses and sort of resembles a horned toad?"

Ali couldn't quite suppress a giggle. Dave's incredibly uncomplimentary description was also on the money.

"Yes," she said. "That's the one."

"That's Holly Mesina, Sally Harrison's best friend. The two of them go way back."

"I take it she's not too happy about any of what's going on," Ali said, "and most especially my showing up on the scene?"

"That's right," Dave said. "She thinks it's all a witch hunt on Gordy's part."

"As in, any friend of my enemy is my enemy," Ali added.

"You've got it," Dave agreed. "Now, how about that cup of coffee? Then we'll take care of the Kevlar vest, not that you're ever going to need it."

{ CHAPTER 3 }

It was a grueling week. On the days Ali had to go all the way to Prescott, the three-hour round-trip made her think she was back to doing a southern California commute, except for the fact that there was a lot less traffic. And far more varied terrain.

On Friday, to reach the sheriff's Seligman substation, she'd had to pass through Flagstaff and a vast ponderosa forest. Today, on her way to visit the substation in Congress, she had to drive through Prescott and then down Yarnell Hill, passing from pine to piñon to prickly pear and yucca and finally to saguaro.

When Ali had worked on the East Coast, she had discovered there were plenty of people there who assumed that Arizona was all saguaros all the time, but that wasn't true. Saguaros are picky about where they grow, and they like to grow together. No matter how many times Ali drove down to the desert valleys that surrounded Sedona, she always watched for the first sentinel saguaro. In this case, the first one was at the top of a cliff near milepost 274. Soon there were dozens more.

Shortly after passing that outpost saguaro, she ran into a road-widening project. When a flagger stopped her to wait for the return of a pilot car, Ali leaned back in her seat, closed her eyes, and thought about what she was doing.

Right, she thought. *Something for the home team.*

It was ironic to think that the inspiring words Ali had delivered so cheerfully to the graduating seniors a week earlier were now coming back to haunt her. Other than Dave Holman and Sheriff Maxwell himself, no one else on the sheriff's office "home team" had been what you could call welcoming of the new arrival.

The previous Monday, when Gordon Maxwell had introduced her at the staff meeting, Ali had assumed that the surly greeting she had received from Holly Mesina, the clerk in the outer office, had been an aberration. A week and a day later, Ali understood that Dave's reaction was the exception, while Holly Mesina's was the rule.

During the remainder of the week Ali had followed Sheriff Maxwell on his round of duties around the office as well as out in the community. She had also visited the various substations scattered around the huge county. At each stop along the way, Ali had grown accustomed to the idea that departmental employees would put on their happy faces with her as long as the sheriff was present, but the moment Maxwell's back was turned and the boss was out of earshot, their skin-deep civility toward Ali vanished.

Their reactions made her position in the culture of the Yavapai County Sheriff's Department blatantly clear—Ali Reynolds was the ultimate outsider.

Sort of like what happened to Haley Marsh when

she first showed up at Mingus Union High School, Ali thought ruefully. *Of course, there's a difference. I could quit. Haley couldn't.*

Ali had told her father that very thing the previous afternoon toward the end of a Memorial Day cookout at Chris and Athena's house, where the newlyweds had marked the six-month anniversary of their wedding by hosting a shakedown test hamburger fry on Chris's new gas barbecue.

"So how are things?" Bob Larson had asked his daughter as the two of them sat on the small patio next to the driveway, enjoying the afternoon sun. "You look glum—not at all your usual self. Is it work?"

Ali nodded. "Don't tell Mom," she said.

"I don't have to," Bob observed cheerfully. "I'm pretty sure she already knows."

"Great," Ali muttered. "I suppose that means I'll get the third degree from her, too."

"Not necessarily," Bob said. "How about if you tell me and I tell her? What's going on?"

"It turns out your daughter is a pawn, caught between two feuding unions. When I walk into a room—it doesn't matter if it's the break room, an office, or a lobby—people simply stop talking. When I try to interact with them, they answer direct questions only. The other day somebody left a paper Burger King crown on the seat of my desk down at Village of Oak Creek, and on Friday, when I drove up to Ash Fork and Seligman to introduce myself to the folks up there, someone let the air out of three of my tires."

"So the people you have to work with all think you're stuck-up, and as far as the tires are concerned, no one saw a thing," Bob said. "Right?"

"Right," Ali agreed.

"So how many more of these introductory substation visits do you have to do?"

"I have to drive down to Congress tomorrow. That's it."

Just then Athena had emerged from the house carrying a pitcher of iced tea. "Refills, anybody?" she asked.

Athena, an Iraq war veteran, had returned from her national guard deployment minus two limbs—her right arm below the elbow and her right leg below the knee. She had become amazingly proficient at using her two high-tech prosthetic limbs, but she had also made great progress on becoming a lefty. She wielded the full pitcher without any problems or spills.

Ali's father waited until Athena went back inside before he spoke again. "What those guys are doing is hazing you."

Ali laughed. "Do you think?"

"And they're watching to see how you react."

"Correct."

"So don't give them the satisfaction," Bob said. "Besides, you know what your aunt Evie would say."

For years, until her death from a massive stroke, Ali's aunt Evie, Edie Larson's twin sister, had been partners with Ali's parents in the Sugarloaf Cafe, a restaurant started originally by Ali's grandmother. Aunt Evie had always been considered the wild one in the family. She had also been one of the most positive people Ali knew.

"I'm sure she'd say, 'Brighten the corner where you are,'" Ali said with a laugh, remembering some of her aunt Evie's Auntie Mame antics. That particular line had come from one of Aunt Evie's favorite hymns, and it had been her personal watchword.

"Exactly," Bob said.

"What do you say?" Ali asked. She liked her parents and was interested in their opinions.

"If there's a rattler in your yard, wouldn't you rather know where he is?"

Ali nodded.

"So make friends with your enemies," Bob advised. "It'll surprise the hell out of them."

When the barbecue ended, Ali went home to her new place on Manzanita Hills Road. She had taken a crumbling jewel of midcentury modern architecture that had never been updated and brought it into the twenty-first century. She had invested money, time, and effort in the process. Leland, who had more or less come with the house, had fought the remodeling war at her side. Now he and Ali were both enjoying the fruits of their labors—a job well done.

Leland had taken Memorial Day weekend off, and the house seemed impossibly quiet without him. Ali went from room to room, turning on lights and music. She settled into one of the comfy armchairs in the library and picked up the textbook she was still studying. A few minutes later she was joined by Samantha, her sixteen-pound one-eyed, one-eared tabby cat. Sam clambered up into the matching chair, circled three times, then sank down silently to wait for bedtime.

Ali hadn't made it through two whole pages when the phone rang. Checking caller ID, she answered with a smile in her voice.

"Hi, Mom," she said. "What's up?"

Ali already knew that once the barbecue ended, Bob Larson would have immediately reported the gist of his conversation with Ali to his wife.

"You should have told us about all this the minute it started," Edie scolded.

"I didn't want to worry you," Ali said.

"Worry? Of course we're worried," Edie said. "One of those practical jokes could go way too far. Your father is right. You need to make friends of your enemies. Who's the worst one of the bunch?"

Not a hard question to answer, Ali thought.

"That would be Holly Mesina," she said. "She's a clerk in the public office over in Prescott. She's also best friends with the evidence clerk who's out on administrative leave."

"With Sally Harrison?" Edie Larson asked.

It came as no surprise to Ali that her mother would be tuned in to all the sheriff's department's goings-on. Ali sometimes wondered if running the Sugarloaf Cafe wasn't merely a cover for Edie Larson's real job of keeping track of everyone else's business. She had an impressive network of unnamed sources, and her up-to-the-minute intelligence was often uncannily accurate.

"Didn't Sally go to school with you?" Edie asked now. "I thought she graduated a year or so after you did."

"I don't remember anyone named Sally Harrison," Ali replied.

Edie sighed. "Don't be silly. Harrison is her married name. I believe her maiden name was Laird. That's right. Sally Laird. Her father drove a dairy truck, for Shamrock. He was just as proud of his little girl as he could be. Never stopped talking about her, especially when she got elected homecoming queen."

Given her mother's hint, Ali did remember. The

name Sally Laird made more sense than Sally Harrison did.

A cute little blond, Ali thought, *Right about now,
her father's probably not nearly so proud of his darling
daughter.*

"Dad says you have to drive down to Congress
tomorrow," Edie continued. "What time are you planning to leave?"

Ali was somewhat taken aback by the seemingly
abrupt change of subject.

"I'll probably head out a little after eight," Ali said.
"I expect to drive down through Prescott. There's road
construction on Yarnell Hill, so I may come back home
the long way around, through Wickenburg and over to
I-17."

"All right, then," Edie said. "Stop by the restaurant
on your way out of town. I'm going to make a couple
of extra trays of sweet rolls for you to drop off at the
sheriff's office in Prescott on your way through."

Working together day after day, Edie and Bob Larson squabbled a lot, but they were definitely of a mind
on most things, especially anything concerning their
daughter. Clearly the two of them had decided that
helping fix Ali's difficulties at work was a project worthy of a team effort. Sugarloaf Cafe sweet rolls were
legendary throughout the Verde Valley, where they
routinely placed first when it came time to tally the
votes in annual Best of Sedona contests. Ali knew that
passing some of her mother's rolls around the office
would be a very effective tactic for keeping her departmental enemies close.

"I'll also put my ear to the ground," Edie Larson
promised. "I may be able to learn something useful.

But right now I'd better hit the hay. Since I'm doing extra batches of sweet rolls in the morning, I'll need to get an early start."

Ali knew Edie was usually in the restaurant baking rolls by four o'clock in the morning. "Thanks, Mom," she said. "I'll stop by and pick them up."

"Kill 'em with kindness," Edie added. "That's what I always say."

Ali put down the phone. Leaving the book she had been reading facedown on the side table, she walked over to the shelf that held her yearbooks. Family finances had been so tough her senior year in high school that Ali hadn't been able to buy one of her own, and she never expected to have one. Two years earlier, however, her best childhood friend, Reenie Bernard, had died tragically. In the aftermath of her death, Reenie's less-than-grieving husband and his girlfriend had packed up all of Reenie's worldly possessions and shipped them off to Goodwill. Fortunately, one of Ali's friends had intervened and intercepted the castoffs before they could be unpacked and sold.

Reenie's kids, eleven-year-old Matthew and eight-year-old Julie, had been sent to live with Reenie's parents in Cottonwood. Since the kids' grandfather was allergic to cats, their overweight kitty, the incredibly ugly Samantha, who had been mauled by a raccoon long before she came to live with Reenie's kids, had been pawned off on Ali, supposedly on a temporary basis. Two years after the fact, that temporary arrangement was pretty much permanent. Sam had adjusted. So had Ali.

Months after their mother's death, Ali had invited Reenie's orphaned kids to spend the weekend at her house. They had spent the better part of three days going through the boxes of their mother's goods, sorting out and repacking what they wanted to keep and getting rid of the rest. One of the boxes of reject books had held Reenie's complete four-year collection of yearbooks.

The last evening of the three, Ali and Reenie's kids had gone through the yearbooks one by one, with Ali recounting stories about things she and Reenie had done together back then, laughing at their exploits and the weird clothing and the even weirder hairdos.

"Until I saw this, I had forgotten all about that Halloween party our senior year," Ali said, studying a photo in which she and Reenie had been dressed in sheets turned into Roman attire. Or maybe Greek.

"How come?" Matt had asked. "Don't you have a book like this?"

Matt, the older of Reenie's two kids, was red-haired, while his sister was blond. She was a lighthearted whirling dervish of a child. Matt was more reserved and serious, their mother's death still weighed heavily on his spindly shoulders. Ali didn't want to add anything more to his burden by mentioning how poor her family had been back then.

"I think I must have lost mine somewhere along the way," Ali had lied.

"Why don't you take this one then?" Matt asked. "I think Mom would like you to have it."

It was true. Reenie would have loved for her best friend to have it, and Ali had been overwhelmed by the little boy's instinctive generosity.

"Thank you," she had said, brushing away a tear. "That's very kind of you, but if you and Julie ever want it back, you'll know where to find it."

With night falling outside the library windows, Ali had returned to her chair with the yearbook in one hand. On the way past the other chair, she paused long enough to scratch Sam's furrowed brows. Sam opened her one good eye, blinked, and then closed it again.

Back in her own chair, Ali browsed through the book, paying close attention to the photos of the people who had been seniors with her and trying to make sense of what she knew had become of some of them in the intervening years.

She paused for a long time over the smiling photo of her best friend, Irene Holzer. It was difficult to comprehend that less than twenty years later, Irene's loving presence would have disappeared from the earth. Reenie had died in a horrific nighttime car wreck in a vehicle that plunged off a snow-covered mountain road. For a time, officials had ruled Reenie's death a suicide. They maintained that her recent ALS diagnosis had caused her to decide to end it all as opposed to putting herself and her loved ones through the devastating progression of Lou Gehrig's disease. Only Ali's dogged persistence had proved Reenie's supposed suicide to be something else entirely.

Leaving the senior class behind, Ali paged on through the remainder of the book. She recognized some of the underclassmen by both name and face, but she didn't know as many of them and had no idea what had become of most of them either during high school or after.

Halfway through the freshman class roster, Ali located the first photo of Sally Laird. Even in a low-budget, badly lit school photo, Sally was a knock-out, with a straight-toothed smile and a halo of naturally blond hair.

Several pages later, Sally Laird was pictured again. This time she was posed in a tight-fitting and revealing uniform as a member of the junior varsity cheerleading squad. The third and final photo showed Sally as that year's homecoming queen. Dressed in a formal gown and wearing a rhinestone tiara, she managed to assume a regal pose while clinging to the arm of a beefy uniformed football player listed as Carston Harrison.

Carston was someone Ali remembered. He had been a senior along with Ali and Reenie when Sally had been a freshman. Ali had been in a couple of classes with Carston over the years. He had been a less than exemplary student, long on brawn and athletic ability. He had scraped by with average to below-average grades while lettering in four different sports.

That homecoming photo notwithstanding, Ali didn't remember Sally and Carston being an ongoing item during the remainder of that year, but she now realized they must have been. Having a jock like Carston supporting her candidacy and lobbying in her favor could go a long way toward explaining how Sally Laird had packed off the homecoming queen title as a lowly freshman.

As Ali closed the book, it occurred to her that Sally and Carston must have peaked early, and she wondered if anything the couple had done later on had matched their successes in high school.

The next morning Ali had gone straight to the Sugarloaf to pick up the promised sweet rolls. By the time she got there, the restaurant was in full breakfast mode, so there wasn't much opportunity to visit with her mother. She grabbed the sweet rolls and a cup of coffee and headed for Prescott, where she hoped Edie Larson's delectable treats would make Ali Reynolds the hit of the break room, if not the department. Mindful of her father's advice about keeping her enemies close, Ali drafted none other than a grudging Holly Mesina to help carry the trays of rolls from the car, through the lobby, and into the break room.

The construction flagger now came over and tapped on Ali's window, startling her out of her long reverie. "Pilot car's here," he said, pointing. "Get moving."

When Ali finally arrived at the Congress substation, both of the deputies she had been scheduled to meet—Deputies Camacho and Fairwood—were nowhere around. The only person in attendance was a clerk named Yolanda, who looked so young that Ali wondered if she was even out of high school. The clerk may have been young, but when Ali introduced herself, Yolanda had the good grace to look embarrassed.

"Are you kidding?" she asked. "When they left, I reminded them you were coming today. They said they'd call and let you know they'd been called out and that you probably shouldn't bother."

Ali understood that it wasn't Yolanda's fault that the two deputies she was stuck working with happened to be a pair of jerks who had deliberately stood Ali up.

"They probably got busy and forgot," Ali said easily, excusing them and thereby letting Yolanda off the hook. "Don't worry about it. But since I'm here anyway, where did they go?"

"A rancher busted some cactus smugglers down along the Hassayampa River a few miles north of Wickenburg," Yolanda answered. "We have a lot of that around here. It takes a long time to grow saguaros—like a hundred years or so. That's why people try to steal them."

"Tell you what," Ali said. "Why don't you get their location for me? This sounds like something that would make an interesting press release."

She wasn't sure that releasing information about a cactus-rustling ring would do much to bolster Sheriff Maxwell's image in the community, but it was a start. While Yolanda waited for information from Dispatch, Ali put on a winning smile and plied her for more information.

"When did all this go down?" she asked. "And how did it happen?"

"Earlier this morning. The rancher is an old guy named Richard Mitchell. His deeded ranch is up by Fools Canyon, but he leases a lot more BLM land to run his cattle.

"Anyways, he was out checking fence lines on his Bureau of Land Management lease this morning and came across two guys in a rental truck loaded with cactus. He told them to stop, but they didn't. When they tried to make a run for it, they, like, ended up getting stuck in the middle of the river."

Ali thought about her days working in the east. People unfamiliar with the desert southwest might have jumped to an immediate and erroneous conclusion at hearing the term "middle of the river." If you grew up near the Mississippi or the Missouri rivers, for example, you would most likely assume that someone "stuck" in the middle of any river would be over their head in water and swimming for dear life.

That wasn't true for the Hassayampa. As the sheriff

had said a day or two ago, "It's a white horse of a different color." For one thing, most of the time the riverbed was bone dry. There was no water in it—not any. A few times a year, during the summer monsoon season or during winter rainstorms, the river would run for a while. If it rained long enough or hard enough, occasional flash floods coursed downstream, liquifying the sand and filling the entire riverbed with fast-moving water that swept away everything in its path. People in Arizona understood that their very lives depended on heeding warning signs that cautioned, *Do Not Enter When Flooded.*

On the other hand, when longtime Arizonans saw the highway sign in Wickenburg that stated, *No Fishing from Bridge,* they understood that was an in-crowd joke, because there hadn't been fish in the bed of the Hassayampa for eons.

In this instance, six weeks or so from the first summer rainstorms, Ali knew that the term "middle of the river" really meant "middle of the sand." No one would be drowning, but in the heat of the day, if people had ventured into the desert with an insufficient supply of water, they could very well be dying of thirst.

"Anyways," Yolanda said again, warming to her story and losing track of her grammar in the process. "Mr. Mitchell chased after them. Once they were stuck, he hauled out his shotgun and held 'em at gunpoint. Then he used his cell phone to call for help."

Picturing the action in her head, Ali couldn't resist allowing herself a tiny smile. In the old days, and probably faced with cattle rustlers rather than cactus rustlers, Mr. Mitchell would have been left on his own to deal with the bad guys. Now, through the magic of cell phones, he could run up the flag and call for help when he was miles away from the nearest landline phone.

A radio transmission came in from Dispatch and Yolanda jotted down a note. "Okay," she said. "Got it." When she finished writing, she handed the note to Ali and then turned to a nearby file drawer, where she retrieved another piece of paper, which turned out to be a map. Using a blue felt-tipped pen, she outlined the route Ali would need to follow.

"Here's a detailed map of the area," Yolanda added, pointing. "Just follow the blue lines. According to Dispatch, they're right here where this little road crosses the river. The bad guys are in custody, but the deputies are waiting for a tow truck to come drag the rustlers' rented truck out of the sand."

"Good," Ali said. "If you happen to talk to one of the deputies, you might let them know that I'm on my way."

As she started for the door, Yolanda seemed to reconsider. "Maybe you shouldn't drive there. It's rough country. What if you get stuck, too?"

"I have four-wheel drive," Ali told her. "I can manage."

She had to drive almost all the way into Wickenburg before she found the narrow dirt track that led back out to the river and the stalled rental truck. The intersection was easy to find because she arrived at the junction at the same time the summoned tow truck did. All Ali had to do was follow the truck with its red lights flashing, and that's exactly what she did, keeping back just far enough so her Cayenne wasn't engulfed in the billowing cloud of dust kicked up by the vehicle.

The tow truck ran down into a dip and came to a

stop on the edge of a trackless desert wasteland. Ali stopped, too. When she did so, a uniformed police officer sauntered up to her SUV. She opened the window and let the early summer heat engulf her.

"You'll have to move along," the officer told her brusquely as she rolled down the window. "You need to go back the way you came. We've got an incident playing out here," he continued. "We can't have civilians involved."

The name tag on his uniform read F. *Camacho*. Ali had done her homework. That would be Deputy Fernando Camacho, a six-year veteran in the sheriff's office.

"I'm not a civilian, Deputy Camacho," she answered, flashing her own official sheriff's office name tag in his direction. "I believe we had an appointment earlier. I'm your department's new public information officer. What's going on here?"

The deputy straightened. "Glad to meet you," he said with obvious insincerity. "Sorry about not letting you know. We had an emergency call out and didn't have time."

That, of course, was a lie. From the information on Yolanda's note, Ali knew exactly when the call came in. They could have contacted Ali while she was still in Prescott. Traveling between the substation and here they would have had time enough to make a dozen separate calls. The deputies had done this on purpose, to inconvenience Ali and make her look stupid.

"I guess you've been drinking the water, then?" she asked innocently.

"Water?" Deputy Camacho repeated blankly, looking off across the half-mile-wide expanse of sand. A quarter of a mile away, a U-Haul truck sat mired hubcap-deep in fine, hot sand. "What water are you talking about?"

"The water in the river," Ali answered. "According to legend, people who drink water from the Hassayampa never tell the truth again."

Deputy Camacho was lying. Ali knew he was lying, and he knew she knew he was lying. As far as evening the score, that was a good place to start. "So how about you tell me what's going on?" she said.

Just then, a gnarled old man carrying a shotgun and accompanied by a white-faced blue heeler came walking up to the Cayenne. Sinewy and tough, he didn't look the part of crime victim. Neither did his equally grizzled dog.

"Hey, lady," Richard Mitchell called. "Is this here deputy giving you a hard time?"

"Not at all," Ali returned. She gave Deputy Camacho a winning smile. "This looks like Mr. Mitchell himself," she said, opening her car door and stepping out. "If you don't mind, I believe I'll have a word with him."

Deputy Camacho did mind, and he looked as though he was about to object. Then, thinking better of it, he backed off.

"Be my guest," he said gruffly. "Knock yourself out."

{ CHAPTER 4 }

Ali made it back to Prescott by two, in time to jot off a press release about the incident along the Hassayampa. It turned out that the alleged cactus rustlers had warrants and were working for a landscaping company in Phoenix that was helping finish up a cut-rate remodel on a once thriving hotel in downtown Scottsdale. Now under new ownership, some of the hotel's former reputation remained, but Ali suspected that the contractor's use of illegal saguaros wasn't the only corner that had been cut in the makeover process.

Remind me never to stay there, she told herself, *and don't encourage anyone else to stay there, either.*

In the break room the two baking sheets were empty—empty of rolls but still dirty. Even though there was a kitchen sink only a few steps away, no one had bothered to rinse out the mess. Ali cleaned the trays herself using dish detergent she found under the sink and drying them with a handful of paper towels. Then, for good measure, she wiped down the tables and countertops.

Her DNA dictated that she leave the kitchen spotless. That's what her father did for her mother every day before he finished his afternoon shift at the Sugarloaf.

Ali was rearranging the chairs around the tables when Sheriff Maxwell himself showed up in the break room doorway and leaned against the frame. At five foot ten, Ali had always thought herself tall. Gordon Maxwell made her feel downright petite.

"You really believe in pitching in, don't you," Maxwell observed affably. "When Dave Holman first mentioned you as a candidate for this job, I was afraid you'd turn out to be stuck-up. You're not."

You might consider mentioning that to some of my coworkers, Ali thought.

"That was a great piece you sent out about the incident down along the Hassayampa. Did any of the media outlets bite on it?"

"Not so far," Ali told him, "but it's early days. They probably have this evening's broadcasts racked up and ready to go. Maybe tomorrow."

"I don't suppose following up on cactus rustlers was what you thought you'd be doing when you signed on."

"No, I didn't," Ali agreed, "but I loved meeting Richard Mitchell and his blue heeler wonder dog, Trixie."

Sheriff Maxwell grinned. "Ol' Rich is one of a kind, all right," he said. "They don't make 'em like that anymore. Those guys would have been well advised to pick on someone a little less self-sufficient. They're lucky he called us. Twenty years ago Rich would have handled it on his own, and the devil take the hindmost."

"As in shoot first and call for help later?" Ali asked.

"You got it." Then, nodding in the direction of the

baking trays, he added, "Were those your mother's
sweet rolls?"

"Yes," Ali said.

"Tell her thanks from me. I helped myself to one
before they all disappeared. Pure heaven."

"I'll let Mom know you liked them," Ali said.

Ali had headed home to Sedona a little past three-
thirty. Once there, she changed into jeans and headed
to the library for another session of hitting the books.
When it was time for dinner, she ventured into the
kitchen. In the fridge she discovered the artfully
arranged plate of Caprese salad Leland had left her.
The sliced tomatoes were plump and fresh, the mozza-
rella smooth and creamy, and the fresh basil delightfully
tart, especially once they were doused with a generous
helping of balsamic vinegar and olive oil. Ali wasn't sure
where in Sedona Leland Brooks managed to find such
wonderful produce, but he did so day after day and
week after week. For that Ali was incredibly grateful.

She had settled back in for what she had anticipated to be a long, quiet evening of reading. When
her phone rang at nine, she thought it might be Chris
or Athena, but caller ID said *Restricted*. That meant it
was more likely to be an aluminum siding salesman.

"Ms. Reynolds?"

"Yes."

"This is Frances Lawless with Yavapai County Dispatch."

Ali felt her heartbeat quicken.

"There's a serious house fire burning just south of
Camp Verde. Fire crews and deputies have been dispatched to the scene, but Sheriff Maxwell said you
should be summoned as well."

"Yes, of course," Ali said. She was already kicking off her slippers and shedding her jeans. On her first media relations on-camera appearance, she couldn't risk showing up looking Friday casual.

"Do you need directions?" Frances was asking.

"Just give me the address," Ali said. "The GPS should be able to find it."

"Probably not," Frances replied "Verde View Estates is a new development. The fire hydrants aren't hooked up yet. They're having to truck water to the fires in Camp Verde's old pumpers."

Fires, Ali thought. *As in more than one.* "Directions then, please," she said aloud.

"Take the General Crook exit," Frances said. "Cross under the freeway, then turn north on the frontage road."

"Got it," Ali said. "General Crook exit, north on the frontage road."

Her Kevlar vest was now an essential piece of daily attire. She needed to be safe, but she also needed clothing that made her look businesslike. Finding blouses and blazers that worked with the vest was a challenge.

As Ali dressed, she noticed her hands were shaking. She wasn't sure if that was from fear or stage fright or a combination of the two, but it made buttoning the last button on her blouse particularly challenging. She grabbed a navy blue pantsuit out of her closet, remembering Aunt Evie's advice as she did so.

"You have to dress the part," her always fashionably dressed aunt Evelyn had often told her niece. "You only have one chance to make a good first impression."

Expecting uneven footing, Ali opted for penny loafers instead of heels. Then she spent a few seconds in her bathroom retouching her makeup. On her way out of the bedroom she paused for a quick examination of her reflection in front of a full-length mirror.

Maybe not ready for prime time in L.A., she told herself critically, *but good enough for late-night Yavapai County.*

Out in the garage, she stuck the blue emergency bubble light on top of the Cayenne and headed out. Even with the flashing light encouraging other drivers to get out of the way, it seemed to take forever to get through the construction zone and out to I-17.

Driving south, Ali caught sight of the fire from several miles away across the Verde Valley. At first glance it appeared as little more than a pinprick of light, but as she came closer, that one pinprick became two separate ones. Both blazes roared skyward, and surrounding them on all sides were the flashing lights from clots of emergency vehicles. Clouds of smoke, dotted with flaming embers, billowed skyward as well. It was dark, but as Ali approached, she noticed that the once black smoke was now a lighter smudge against a much darker sky. She knew enough about fires to understand that if the color of the smoke was changing from black to gray or even white, the fire crews must be making some headway in their fight against the two separate blazes.

As Frances Lawless had directed, Ali took the General Crook Trail exit and drove under the freeway. Signaling for the left turn onto the frontage road, she caught sight of an ambulance speeding toward her with red lights flashing and siren blaring.

Someone's hurt, she thought. *Is it a firefighter, or is it someone else?*

Pulling over onto the shoulder, Ali stayed out of the way until the lumbering emergency vehicle roared around the corner and under the freeway. Once there, the ambulance turned south toward Phoenix, with its big urban hospitals and specialized medical practices. That probably meant bad news for the person inside, someone who was right that minute strapped on a stretcher and being rushed headlong through some kind of medical maelstrom.

Ali was about to move back into the roadway but she again had to wait for oncoming traffic as an arriving fire truck came roaring up behind her with its lights flashing. As it sped past, she noticed the City of Sedona decal on the passenger door.

Ali wasn't surprised to see a Sedona-based fire crew so far outside the city limits. If the now four-alarm fire managed to spread from the burning structures to surrounding grass and brush, it would pose far more of a hazard to life and property, especially to the town of Camp Verde, itself a little to the north. That was no doubt why crews from other fire districts had been called in to supplement the locals.

With the GPS firmly telling her that the frontage road she was driving didn't exist and that she was *Off Road,* Ali drove to the scene. At the first police barricade, Ali flashed the credentials she had been issued by the Yavapai County Sheriff's Department. The officer examined her ID. Then, after directing her to an appropriate place to park, he stepped aside and let her through. Ali was relieved to see there were no reporters or cameras milling around so far. She had beaten them to the scene by arriving while emergency equipment was still en route. They would be coming soon, however, and Ali needed to be ready.

Turning off the Cayenne's engine, Ali opened the door and stepped out into a world of noisy, smoke-filled chaos. Shouted orders flew back and forth over the roar of the flames. Pulsing strobelike flashes from emergency lights punctuated the darkness, while bright beams directed at the fires helped the firefighters who were battling the two separate blazes to see what they were doing.

Ali removed the blue emergency beacon from the top of the car, switched it off, and then stood for a moment, taking in the scene. Both houses appeared to be completely engulfed. In fact, just as she shut her car door, the burning roof of one of the houses collapsed in a loud *whoosh,* sending another cloud of embers skyward like a dangerous volley of Fourth of July fireworks. Firefighters hurried after the glowing trail of embers, trying to find and extinguish them before they set fire to something else.

Even without the roof, one wall of the collapsed building was still standing. Peering through the eye-watering smoke, Ali was able to make out one chilling detail. Scrawled in yard-tall spray-painted letters on the plywood walls were three letters—*ELF.*

The Earth Liberation Front, Ali thought. *America's own special brand of homegrown terrorists.*

Dave Holman came up behind her just then. "Hey, Ali," he said. "Are you okay?"

She nodded.

"Nothing like a trial by fire for your first time out," he added.

"An ambulance was leaving just as I got here," she said. "Was someone hurt?"

Dave nodded. "Since the houses were under construction, no one expected them to be occupied, but then one of the Camp Verde firefighters heard her screaming. He went in and brought her out."

"Her," Ali confirmed. "A woman? Who is she? What was she doing there?"

"I have no idea."

"What's her condition, and where are they taking her?" Ali asked. When reporters arrived on the scene, those were some of the details they would want to know. Ali would need to have answers at the ready.

"She's evidently badly hurt," Dave answered, "but I have no idea where they're taking her."

"Do you know the name of the firefighter who rescued her?"

"Nope," Dave said. "Sorry. For that you'll need to check with the Camp Verde Fire Department."

Someone summoned Dave and he was gone, disappearing into the smoke-filled night.

Squaring her shoulders, Ali followed Dave's lead and set off to gather as much information as possible. She knew that in an hour or so, when she found herself standing in front of an assembled group of reporters for the very first time, they'd be looking to her for all available information—for answers to those pesky *who, what, where,* and *why* questions that were the news media's real bread and butter.

One bit at a time Ali gathered the necessary information. The first 9-1-1 call had come in at 8:29. Arriving on the scene, the Camp Verde Volunteer Fire Department had assessed the situation and had radioed to request additional help, some of which had arrived at almost the same time Ali did.

Following the chain of command upward, she finally located Captain Carlos Figueroa of the Camp Verde Fire Department, who was directing the action from a vehicle parked across the street. He wasn't thrilled when Ali introduced herself, but he grudgingly agreed to answer her questions.

"Lieutenant Caleb Moore is the guy who dragged her out of there," Figueroa said. "He never should have gone in—too dangerous—but he did. I'll have some serious words with him about that once we get him back from the hospital."

"He's hurt then, too?" Ali asked.

Figueroa nodded. "Not too bad, I hope, but he swallowed enough smoke that we need to have him checked out."

"What about the woman?" Ali asked.

Captain Figueroa shrugged. "Who knows?" he returned. "Maybe she'll make it; maybe she won't."

Just then a firefighter raced up to the car, dragged along by an immense German shepherd. "We got a hit, Captain," he said. "Out here on the street, between the two houses."

"What kind of hit?" Ali asked.

"You didn't hear that," Figueroa said. "But the dog is Sparks, our accelerant-sniffing dog. The guy with him is his handler. Sparks doesn't need to wait for the fire to cool down to investigate if the perp was dumb enough to leave tracks for him outside on the street."

"So it is arson, then?" Ali asked.

"Most likely," Figueroa said, "but don't quote me on that. It's not for public consumption at this time."

Ali's cell phone rang at ten forty-five. "I understand

there's a whole slew of reporters waiting just inside the entrance to Verde View Estates," Frances Lawless from Dispatch told her. "Any idea when you'll be there to brief them?"

"Give me a couple of minutes," Ali said.

She went back to the Cayenne, grabbed her computer, and spent the next ten minutes typing up a brief summary of everything she had learned. She'd be able to cover more ground if she started with a prepared statement before opening up for questions. Finally she closed her computer and headed back down the hill.

Don't be nervous, she told herself on the way. *They're doing their jobs. All you have to do is yours.*

When she reached the first van-cam, she stuck the Cayenne in park, turned it off, and then went to face the milling group of reporters, who immediately clustered around her, shouting questions at her and vying for her attention. She felt a momentary glitch in her gut. Once she had been one of the yellers. Now she was their target.

"All right," she said, fixing a steady smile on her face and shouting back in order to be heard over the din. "Good evening, everyone. Could I have your attention, please? I am Alison Reynolds, public information consultant for the Yavapai County Sherrif's Department. Hold on. I'll give you what information I can."

She opened her computer and said, "A call came in to the 9-1-1 emergency operators in Prescott at eight twenty-nine p.m. reporting a house fire at Verde View Estates. Firefighters from the Camp Verde Volunteer Fire Department responded with two trucks. When they realized that they were dealing with two separate house fires rather than just one, they requested further assistance. Two additional fire trucks and crews were dispatched to the scene from the City of Sedona. Because Verde View Estates is located on unincorporated land, several officers from the Yavapai County Sheriff's Department were dispatched to the scene as well and will be part of the ongoing investigation. It appears that both structures are a total loss.

"The houses were under construction and were thought to be vacant. Unfortunately, that wasn't true. Soon after the first Camp Verde fire crew arrived, a firefighter, Lieutenant Caleb Moore, a six-year veteran of the Camp Verde Volunteer Fire Department, entered one of the burning buildings, where he located and rescued one person. The victim, an unidentified female, is in the process of being transported to a Phoenix-area hospital. Lieutenant Moore was also injured, but it's my understanding that his injuries are not considered life-threatening.

"The fires are currently considered to be contained if not controlled, but crews expect to remain on the scene through the night, extinguishing hot spots and making sure smoldering embers from the affected houses don't spread to any other structures or to the surrounding grass and brush. Now, are there any questions?"

Ali paused and tried to look around. Blinded by the lights from the cameras, she found it impossible to tell how many people were there. From the noise they made it could have been a dozen or more.

"Is this arson?"

"That would be pure speculation at this time." Ali answered carefully, remembering Captain Figueroa's cautioning words. "No determination on that can occur until after the fire cools down and a full investigation can be mounted."

She herself had seen the blaring, bright red ELF tag that had been sprayed on one wall. It seemed clear enough that if the Earth Liberation Front was claiming responsibility for this incident, the cause of the fires would most likely turn out to be arson. Still, her on-the-scene comments had to be circumspect. Captain Figueroa had told her that, and so had Sheriff Maxwell.

"When it comes to ongoing investigations, don't give away anything you don't have to," Maxwell had told her. "What the media people want to know and what we can tell them are two different things."

"You said an unidentified victim left here by ambulance," a male reporter observed. "Is that person suspected of starting the fire?"

Ali had clearly said that it was too soon to suspect arson, but some of the reporters, and this one in particular, were already presupposing arson to be the cause. They would no doubt couch their stories in that same fashion. For now, Ali needed to steer them away from arson.

"As I said earlier," she told them, "we have no word as to the identity of the victim or what relationship she might have to either the fire or Verde View Estates. She could have been a member of a work crew. She might also be someone who is in the process of purchasing one of the homes."

"What about someone who's homeless?" another reporter asked. "Is it possible a bum broke in after the workmen left, looking for a place to stay?"

"Anything is possible," Ali said.

"What's the median price tag on homes here?" another voice asked. "I heard some of the firefighters talking about ELF. Don't they usually target more upscale places?"

Ali wished she knew which of the firefighters were blabbing to reporters. As for the reporters? She also wished she could see the faces of her questioners. She needed to have some idea of who they were and where they came from. Once she had a personal connection with some of them, this would be easier, but that wasn't going to happen tonight.

It's like dealing with recalcitrant two-year-olds, Ali told herself. *You have to say the same thing over and over. Was I this dim when I was a reporter? Was I this rude?*

"As I said before," she told them firmly, "it's too early in the investigation to declare this incident to be arson. It will be some time before we can determine the cause of the fire."

"What about the victim? Was it a man or woman?"

"A woman."

"How old is she?"

"No word on that at this time."

"Do you know where the victim was taken?"

"She was taken by ambulance to a private airstrip east of Camp Verde. Once there, she was transferred to a medevac helicopter and flown to a Phoenix-area hospital."

"To the burn unit at Saint Gregory's?"

Since the burn unit at Saint Gregory's Hospital on Camelback treated burn victims from all over the region, that was a reasonable guess, but it wasn't something Ali could confirm.

"That I don't know," she told them.

"Wasn't the last ELF fire in the area up near Prescott a couple of years ago?"

Ali recognized the voice. It was the same male reporter who had posed the earlier ELF question, but this one stumped her.

"I personally have no knowledge about any other incident, so you've got me there," she answered. "As I said earlier, there has not yet been a determination as to the cause of this fire. Attributing it to any one individual or group of individuals at this time would be premature."

Behind her, the engine of one of the fire trucks rumbled down the road. As it went past, she saw that it was one of the crews from Sedona. If the crew was returning to base, that probably meant that the fire situation here was considered fairly well under control.

Once again Ali addressed the reporters. "As you can see, some of the crews here are being released. When we have word on the progress of the investigation, I'm sure Sheriff Maxwell will let you know, or you can contact me. My contact information is on the Web site for the Yavapai County Sheriff's Department, listed under Media Relations. When any additional media briefings are scheduled, I'll send out announcements to the contact list I have. I'll also post that information on the Web site. If I don't have your contact information and you want to be on the list, please let me know before you leave. Now, is there anything else?"

"Hey, Ali," someone called. "This is a new gig for you. How does it feel to be on the wrong side of the cameras?"

She knew the assembled reporters were taking her measure, just as fellow employees in the department were doing. To do her media relations job effectively, Ali had to walk a fine line between serious and not so serious. She couldn't afford to be seen as a light-weight, but if she tried too hard, everyone would know it, and so would she.

"First off," Ali said, "cameras don't have wrong sides. People on both sides of them—the ones pointing them and the ones being photographed—have work to do. When people turn on their radios and television sets or pick up a newspaper in the morning, they're going to want to know what went on here tonight. It's our job to tell them.

"Yes, this is a new gig, as you call it. I can tell you right now that in a news studio, the lighting is a lot better. Makeup and wardrobe are better, too. I always got to choose which side of the news desk to sit on, and guess what? I always chose to have my good side face the camera. Out here you're going to have to take me lumps and all. Anything else?"

"Are you glad to be back home in Arizona?"

"Yes," Ali said. "I am glad to be back in Arizona, but this isn't about me. Sheriff Maxwell has asked me to help out in media relations on a temporary basis, and that's what I'm doing. So if there are no other questions about tonight's incident—"

"How long is temporary?"

"I would imagine that depends on how well I do."

"To say nothing about how long it takes for Internal Affairs to finish looking through the situation with Deputy Devon Ryan. Isn't he still on paid administrative leave?"

"Look," Ali said firmly. "I'm here tonight to discuss this specific incident. How about if we stick to that? Now, are there more questions about the fire?"

Eventually the lights went off and the cameras disappeared. Several people stopped long enough to give Ali their contact information before disappearing into their separate vehicles, where they'd be able to write and file their stories using wireless uploads.

As Ali turned back to the scene of the fire, Sheriff Maxwell appeared out of the darkness. She had no idea when he had arrived or how long he had been standing there listening.

"Good job," he said.

"You were watching?" Ali asked. "Why didn't you come talk to them?"

"Because I wanted to see how you'd handle yourself," he replied. "You did fine."

"About that ELF stuff," she continued. "I didn't know anything about that previous fire. The one up near Prescott."

Maxwell nodded. "Right," he said. "That happened several years ago. They burned down a Street of Dreams project. Four nearly completed houses, each of them worth more than a million bucks. They were supposedly being built with all kinds of green technology inside. Why ELF went after them is more than I can understand. I mean, green is green, right?"

"What about these houses?" Ali asked.

"With the current housing crisis, they're not worth nearly that much. Probably three fifty to four hundred thou. Maybe ELF has decided to go downscale rather than up."

"What about the wall?" Ali asked. "The one with the ELF tagline."

"That's still standing," he said. "Once the sun comes up tomorrow morning, anybody with a pair of binoculars will know this was arson. We know it, too, thanks to Camp Verde's accelerant-sniffing dog."

"I saw Sparks," Ali told him, but the sheriff's comment left Ali second-guessing her actions. "Should I have announced it was arson tonight?"

"Hell, no. You did exactly what I wanted you to do. I'll make the arson announcement myself first thing tomorrow. Let's say nine a.m. on the courthouse steps in Prescott. If you could send out a notice about that between now and then, I'd appreciate it."

"I'm still not sure why we didn't make the announcement tonight."

"That's easy," Sheriff Maxwell said with a sardonic smile. "You can't hand over every little detail all at once. Got to dribble it out a little at a time and give those yahoos reason to come back. That also gives them a reason to write two stories instead of just one. That's good for them and good for us. How else am I going to keep my name out there in public?"

He started to walk away, then paused. "By the way," he added, "the guy who asked about the ELF thing is named Kelly Green."

"What kind of a name is Kelly Green?" Ali asked. "Is that some kind of joke?"

"His real name was the joke. His given name was Oswald. He changed it to Kelly a few years ago."

"I guess I would have changed it, too," Ali said.

"Mr. Green likes to think of himself as the *Arizona Reporter*'s star investigative reporter. He's also a royal pain in the butt, but he was one of Devon's favorites, so watch your back around him."

"Favorites?" Ali asked.

"As in feeding him scoops before information went to any of the other media outlets."

"Got it," Ali said.

Gordon Maxwell walked away then. Watching him go, Ali understood a whole lot more about Sheriff Maxwell than she had before. He was a politician and a canny operator. Yes, the man was caught in a war between rival union factions at work, but he was also an elected official who, in order to win reelection, needed to show the workings of his department in the best possible light. Sheriff Maxwell was using Ali Reynolds as part of his own charm offensive in the same way Edie Larson used her sweet rolls.

Dave Holman drove up behind her, stopped, and came over to where Ali was standing. "How'd you do?" he asked.

"All right, I guess," she said. "Sheriff Maxwell seemed pleased."

"You aren't?"

After a short-lived romance, Ali and Dave had fallen back into their longtime friendship. It was nonetheless disconcerting for Ali to realize that Dave sometimes knew her better than she would have liked.

"One of the reporters nailed me with a gotcha question about an ELF-related fire up near Prescott a few years ago. He acted like I should have known all about it."

"I remember that one," Dave said. "It happened right after I came back from deployment—a fire that turned a Street of Dreams into a Street of Nightmares. The houses—expensive one-of-a-kind homes—were close to completion when they were burned to the ground. What the insurance settlement paid wasn't enough to make the developer whole, and he ended up going bust. The poor guy walked away, and the project was abandoned."

"What happened then?" Ali asked.

"They brought in an army of bulldozers and front-end loaders and carted away the debris. As far as I know, the property sits empty to this day. The trees were cut down to make way for construction. Now the trees aren't there and neither are the houses. I believe ELF did claim responsibility for the fire, but no one was ever charged or arrested, to say nothing of tried and convicted."

"In other words," Ali said, "what ELF got for their trouble is one poor guy who's been driven out of business and a beautiful piece of real estate that's permanently wrecked."

"That's right," Dave agreed. "It also means the terrorists won that round."

"So far," Ali said. "Maybe this time we'll catch them."

"We?" Dave repeated with a smile. "That sounds like you're taking this investigation personally. I'm not so sure that's just a consultant talking."

Ali laughed. "I'm not so sure, either. Now, tell me about the victim. Do we know anything?"

Dave's smile disappeared. "Before they hauled her away in the ambulance, I talked to Caleb Moore, the guy who brought the burn victim out. He's really broken up about it. He says she's badly hurt and isn't likely to make it."

"He has no idea who she is?"

"None, but I doubt she was the one setting the fire," Dave said. "For one thing, she was stark naked and trapped on a stack of drywall piled in the middle of a sea of flames. I've come up against arsonists from time to time, but never one who went around setting fires buck naked."

"A vagrant then?" Ali asked.

"Could be, but not likely," Dave answered. "Even though it's May, it can still get plenty cold overnight. These houses were under construction. That means there was no heat inside, and it makes no sense that she'd be there without any clothes on."

"Young or old?" Ali asked.

"Caleb said he couldn't tell exactly, but an older woman—mid-sixties to seventies. It's unlikely that a grandmotherly type like that would be going around setting fires."

A radio transmission came through summoning Dave back to the scene of the fire. Shaking her head, Ali climbed into the Cayenne and headed home.

Once the remodeling process on her own home had been completed and there were no longer workers coming and going at all hours, Ali had installed an electronically operated gate as well as an intercom at the bottom of the driveway. The gate closed automatically at 6 p.m. She and Leland both had gate openers in their vehicles. Overnight, anyone else had to call and ask for permission to enter.

When Ali came up the driveway, she noted that the lights were off in Leland's fifth-wheel trailer, parked on the far side of the house.

"I don't see why you don't move back inside now that the house is finished," Ali had said to Leland Brooks. "You're more than welcome to stay in your old room."

Leland had lived in the house for years, looking after both the troubled Arabella Ashcroft and her mother. He had moved into a fifth-wheel during the long months of remodeling.

"I'm quite accustomed to having my own place now," he had responded cheerfully. "It's tidy and small, and it gives us both some privacy."

In case either of us ever needs any, Ali had thought.

Her brief romance with Dave Holman had ended even if their friendship hadn't, and Leland's long-term relationship with Yavapai County Superior Court judge Patrick Macey had also run its course.

Ali had let Leland's housing decision stand without any further discussion, and in truth she was enjoying having the house all to herself. She had loved having Chris around in the house on Andante Drive, but it was also nice to be completely on her own and in her own place. There had been no question that the Beverly Hills mansion where she had lived with her second husband, Paul Grayson, had been his before she arrived, while she lived there, and after she left. And in many ways, the house on Andante Drive still bore the stamp of Ali's aunt Evie, who had bequeathed it to her niece.

This home was Ali's. It was far smaller than Paul's but larger than Aunt Evie's. That went for everything from furniture to appliances to the radiant heat in the floors.

Ali parked in the garage and then let herself into the house through the kitchen door. She wasn't completely on her own, however; Sam showed up immediately, wrapping her body around Ali's leg and complaining vociferously, as only cats can, for having been abandoned. This was all a lie, since Ali knew without a doubt that Leland would have fed Sam much earlier in the evening.

"You're a terrible liar," Ali told the cat aloud. "I know good and well that you've already been fed, and I'm not falling for your phony claims to the contrary."

Ali was tired, but she was also wound up from her long night's work. Knowing she wouldn't be able to sleep right away, she stopped in the kitchen long enough to make herself a cup of hot cocoa. While there, she wrote a note for Leland,

"Have to be in Prescott between eight-thirty and nine," she told him. "Don't worry about breakfast."

Once in her bedroom, she pulled off the clothing she had worn and wasn't the least surprised that it smelled of smoke. A closer examination showed several places where falling embers had charred the material. The pantsuit had been expensive when she bought it and now it was ruined. She dropped it on the floor in front of her closet.

Maybe I should ask Sheriff Maxwell for a uniform allowance, she thought.

On that note she headed into her spacious marble-tiled bath for a luxurious shower. Afterward, dressed in a nightgown and robe, she took her cocoa and her computer into the small study next to her bedroom.

Time to do some homework, she told herself.

Opening her computer, she added the new names and addresses to her media contact list and then sent out an announcement about the press briefing scheduled for the courthouse steps the next morning. She intended to do some background studying on the Earth Liberation Front, but soon found herself nodding off over her computer keyboard.

Finally, without even finishing her cup of cocoa, Ali gave up. She closed her computer and crawled into bed. It took no time for her to fall asleep. Not surprisingly, while sleeping, she had one recurring nightmare after another. They weren't all exactly alike, but they were similar.

In each one, Ali was trapped in a locked room—a room with no windows or doors. Sometimes the room was familiar, sometimes not; but in each dream, one thing was the same: someone—some unseen person—was coming after her, intent on doing her harm. In each instance she knew her attacker was armed and dangerous. She also knew there was no escape.

{ CHAPTER 5 }

The ICU nurse picked up the phone and called out to the nurses' station. "The patient seems to be stirring," she said in a voice inaudible to the woman lying in the bed on the far side of the room. "Let Sister Anselm know."

The patient struggled awake, emerging from the horrible nightmare of being caught in a fire, but found that even though the dream was gone, the heat was still there. She was drifting in a cocoon of pure pain. Excruciating pain. Agonizing pain.

She tried to move her head but could not. She tried to move her lips to cry out, but she couldn't do that, either. She was unable to speak or move, but she could see, and she tried desperately to make sense of what she was seeing.

Gradually she became aware that there were people moving around her—people who spoke in hushed voices, with the sounds of their words barely audible above the steady *beep, beep, beep* of some kind of machine that was just outside her line of vision. The sound resembled the warning backup *beep* on a piece of heavy equipment, but that made no sense. How could there be something backing up in here? It was clear that she was inside a building somewhere—inside a brightly lit room.

She strained to hear and understand what the voices were saying. A man's voice said something about damage to lungs and something about keeping up the . . . something that seemed to start with an O. Osmosis, maybe. And something else that sounded like a ringer, or maybe a wringer. What was that? Someone else spoke about keeping the morphine levels high enough to keep her from going into shock.

"We'll do all we can, all that's reasonable." It was the man's voice again. "The problem is, without a next of kin or a durable power of attorney, we can't pull the plug."

Who are these people, she wondered, *and who are they talking about? Do they mean me? Are they talking about pulling my plug?*

She tried again, desperately trying to move her lips, but no sound came out.

Someone else in the room spoke, and her welcome words were far more easily understood.

"Looks like it's time for another dose."

A woman—a nurse, most likely—dressed in a brightly colored, flowered tunic appeared briefly in her line of vision and began working with something beside the bed. Because it was a bed, she realized, but a strange kind of bed. She was in it and the nurse was doing something to an IV tree that stood next to the bed. She seemed to be adding something to the IV drip. Maybe what the man had said at first was a lie. Maybe they were about to pull the plug and she was going to die.

Don't, she wanted to scream aloud. *Please don't. I'm here. I'm alive and awake. Please don't.*

But she couldn't say any of those things. She could hear herself screaming the desperate words in her head, but her lips still wouldn't move. Her voice was lodged somewhere deep in her chest.

Gradually, the appalling pain seemed to lessen. The brightly lit room dissolved around her, and so did the voices. As she drifted away into nothingness, she hoped the dream wouldn't come again, but she knew it would.

She understood that the moment she closed her eyes, the flames would be there again, waiting to consume her.

By the time Ali made it to Prescott the next morning, Gurley Street, from the sheriff's department to Whiskey Row, was full of news-media vehicles. The arson story, confirmed or not, complete with suspected ELF-involvement (officially unconfirmed ELF-involvement), was evidently out in the world in a big way. News outlets from all over the state, and some national outlets as well, were apparently paying attention and in attendance.

Welcome to the three-ring circus, Ali thought as she searched for a parking place. *And I'm the newbie ringmaster with no assigned parking.*

She finally found a spot on the street three blocks away. When she stepped out of her Cayenne, someone was waiting for her. "Nice ride," he said admiringly.

Ali recognized the voice at once—the ELF-centric reporter from the previous evening. "Thank you," she said and then added, "good morning, Mr. Green."

He seemed a little surprised that she knew his name—surprised and pleased. He wouldn't be nearly as pleased if he knew she knew the Oswald part, but then again, for someone with properly moussed hair, perfect clothes, a perfect tan, and perfect teeth, that was only to be expected. It came with the territory; it was only his just due.

The man gave her what was supposed to be a disarming smile. Ali wasn't disarmed. She wanted to ask him straight out what he needed, but she didn't bother. She already knew the answer. Mr. Green was accustomed to receiving special treatment from Devon Ryan. No doubt he hoped to establish the same kind of cozy relationship with her.

Don't hold your breath, she thought.

"What can I do for you?" she asked.

"I was wondering if I could have a word."

"Sure," she said agreeably. "For one word there's no extra charge."

Pausing slightly, he blinked at that comment, then he went on. "So you get to do the whole nine yards, the lighthearted stuff and the tough stuff, the cactus rustlers and the fires?"

If this is his way of winning me over, it isn't working.

"That's right," she said. "I get to do it all. I'm a one-woman media relations phenomenon."

He smiled again, letting her know he got the joke. "I want to apologize for putting you on the spot last night about that ELF fire up in Prescott," he continued more seriously. "Someone told me later that you weren't even living here at the time, so it's completely understandable that you wouldn't know about it."

"I know about it now," Ali told him. "I understand they call it Street of Dreams gone bad."

"Now the same folks are back and doing it again," he said.

Ali saw the trap and dodged it. Kelly Green had come to her looking for more than a private word. What he really wanted was a premature arson confirmation.

"You should probably see what Sheriff Maxwell has to say on that subject." She glanced pointedly at her watch. "If I'm not mistaken, he's about to start."

"You couldn't give me a little preview?"

Ali needed to put Kelly Green on notice that things had changed. "No," she said firmly. "I don't think so. Better you should get that information from the horse's mouth."

"You're nicer looking."

"I'm also late."

While they had been talking, they had been walking toward the courthouse. Speeding up, Ali moved away from him and then shouldered her way through the throng of reporters waiting on the steps, sidewalk, and grass outside the courthouse. The building's portico with its soaring columns provided a suitable background. A lectern, positioned front and center, was surrounded by a sea of microphones. Using her badge, Ali made her way to the top step and stood off to one side. She set her briefcase down at her feet just as Sheriff Maxwell and another man emerged through the glass door. The man stopped and stood beside Ali while the sheriff stepped up to the microphones, where he tapped noisily on one in particular, making sure that the loudspeakers parked on the courthouse steps were turned on and in good working order.

"Good morning, ladies and gentlemen," he said.

"Thank you for coming. As I'm sure you're all aware, we're here this morning due to the incident that occurred outside the Camp Verde city limits last night," he began. "Before I give you the particulars, I'd like to take this opportunity to welcome Agent Richard Donnelley and his team from the ATF field office in Phoenix, who will be assisting local authorities in this investigation."

A murmur ran through the crowd. The presence of Alcohol, Tobacco, Firearms and Explosives meant that arson was definitely on the table. Once the talk subsided, the reporters, with cameras and recorders running, settled in to listen while Sheriff Maxwell read from a prepared statement. Listening in the background, Ali found that the sheriff's prepared text added little to what she had already said to a much smaller group of reporters the night before.

Sheriff Maxwell's down-home delivery was peppered with bits of humor, including a bit about the accelerant-sniffing dog, Sparks, who was credited with making the first definitive arson confirmation. The gathered reporters responded to that bit of news with titters of laughter, and the sheriff waited in his genial delivery long enough for the laughter to filter through his audience before continuing. Ali could see that Maxwell was a commanding presence and totally at ease in front of the cameras. She also suspected that his easygoing affability and good-old-boy style of delivery would play well for television viewers watching the evening news.

Why does he need me? Ali wondered.

"As of this morning, some hot spots remain," he continued. "What we're hoping for now is assistance from the public. Whoever started these fires had to get to the site, and they had to leave it. Believe me, they weren't dropped off by a helicopter, and Scotty didn't beam them up, either."

That line was good for another bit of general laughter.

"Our hope is that while they were driving to or from the incident, someone may have seen them. If you noticed any unusual activity or unusual vehicles in or around the Camp Verde area yesterday evening, please let us know. Call the information in to our Crime Stoppers hotline." He read off the Crime Stoppers number twice before continuing. "We need to catch whoever did this. We need to put them out of business. With your help, we'll do exactly that.

"Now please allow me to introduce my counterpart from the ATF, Phoenix Agent in Charge Richard Donnelley. Dick."

Donnelley took Sheriff Maxwell's place at the lectern. The differences between them were immediate and striking. Sheriff Maxwell, in his starched khaki uniform as well as his signature boots, stood in stark contrast to Agent Donnelley's full-court-press business attire—suit, tie, white shirt.

Not just any suit and tie, Ali told herself, *and they didn't come off the rack at Men's Wearhouse, either.*

Ali immediately identified Donnelley's impeccably tailored gray suit as an Ermenegildo Zegna that probably came from Saks for two thousand bucks plus some change, rather than a Zegna Bespoke that would have gone for twice that. Donnelley's silk repp tie was red-and-blue striped. It was harder to tell about the highly polished shoes, but Ali suspected they were most likely Johnston & Murphy.

In other words, Ali thought, *Donnelley's not just dressed for success. He's really out to impress the unwashed masses as well as those who know their high-end designer clothing.*

Sheriff Maxwell had maintained a low-key approach with a few touches of homespun humor that had made him seem like one of the folks. Donnelley had apparently ridden into town on a high horse. His remarks were all business all the time, dry as a bone, and totally devoid of humor.

"Thank you, Max," Donnelley said, moving forward and taking the sheriff's place at the microphones.

That in itself was a faux pas. Sheriff Gordon Maxwell was Gordy to his friends but most definitely Sheriff Maxwell when it came to doing his job. As far as Ali knew, no one at all referred to him as Max. Ever. In other words, Donnelley's one attempt at making nice had turned into a belly flop. His version of events added little to what Ali and most of the listening reporters already knew, but with two agencies jockeying for position it was only natural that both head guys needed to have their say.

Once Donnelley ended his official presentation, the two men fielded questions together. During the Q&A, Ali took mental notes of the reporters who were gathered there, cataloging their names and faces and trying to keep track of which outlets they represented. This briefing was better attended than hers had been. She understood that these were people she would be working with on a regular basis. To be effective, she needed to know who they were.

There were plenty of local print, radio, and TV reporters from Phoenix, Flagstaff, Sedona, and Prescott, as well as a couple of out-of-towners. Ali recognized Raymond Martin, a West Coast stringer for Fox News. Another, Alicia Hughes, hailed from truTV. The presence of the last two in particular implied that the possibility of ELF involvement had put the incident at Camp Verde on the national media map.

Of all the people there, Kelly Green was the one who kept pressing the ELF button over and over. The tone of his questions implied that he was under the impression that he knew far more on the topic than anyone else in the audience—Sheriff Maxwell and Agent Donnelley included. Green wanted everyone else to defer to his supposed brilliance.

In Ali's previous life, guys like that had been a dime a dozen, and she hadn't much liked them, especially when they regarded themselves as God's gift to the opposite sex, as Mr. Green seemed to do.

After the briefing ended, Ali made a point of introducing herself to the two correspondents with national connections. After collecting contact information for both Raymond Martin and Alicia Hughes, Ali took her laptop-loaded briefcase and hiked the two blocks back to the sheriff's office on Gurley. Once there, she made her way to the broom closet–sized office Sheriff Maxwell had designated as her Prescott headquarters.

Logging on to her computer, she found a mountain of e-mail. The subject line of most of them showed they were requesting information on the Camp Verde fires. One of them, with the subject line "Hassayampa," came from the editor of the *Wickenburg Weekly*. He wanted more details about the cactus-rustling situation. The rest of the world might be focused on ecoterrorism with a capital *E,* but small-town newspapers still thrived on small-town events and people, with an emphasis on names.

Ali replied by suggesting the editor contact the rancher in question, Richard Mitchell. Smiling to herself, Ali also typed in the contact information for the Congress substation. Deputies Camacho and Fairwood wouldn't be able to give out any more information about an ongoing investigation than she could. She wondered if they'd actually report the request to her.

Ali had just punched Send and was starting to deal with the other messages when Sheriff Maxwell popped his head inside her office. "Busy?" he asked.

"I am," Ali said, "but what do you need?"

"I just had a call from Jake Whitman, the administrator of Saint Gregory's Hospital down in Phoenix. They're dealing with the same kind of media frenzy we are. They've got a clot of reporters parked in their lobby wanting information on our unidentified victim, who might or might not turn out to be an unidentified suspect. Mr. Whitman wanted to know what I'm going to do about it. I told him I'd ask you if you'd be willing to go down to the hospital and hold the fort for a while. Would you mind?"

"Not at all," she responded. "If that's what you need me to do, of course I will. How long do you think you'll need me to be there?"

"Today for sure," Sheriff Maxwell said. "Maybe tomorrow, too. If you need to stay overnight, book yourself a hotel room and expense it."

"What if it turns out to be longer than overnight?" Ali asked.

Looking uncomfortable, Sheriff Maxwell hesitated

momentarily before he answered. "According to the EMTs, the woman has second- and third-degree burns on her legs, hands, and arms—close to fifty percent of her body. With burns like that as well as smoke-inhalation injuries, chances are she won't last much longer than that."

"You really want me to be down there that long, just to take charge of the media during a death vigil?" Ali asked. "With everything else that's going on, wouldn't you be better off with me here?"

"Actually," he said, "there's one more thing you might do."

"What's that?"

"I've hammered out an agreement with Donnelley that his folks will be the ones tracking the victim's identity. Truth be known, in dealing with a major incident like this I don't have enough detectives to cover all the bases. So I'm hoping you'll keep your ear to the ground while you're down there. If you hear anything about an ID on the victim, or anything else at all, I want you to let me know—ASAP."

"Wait a minute," Ali said. "You just told me that the ATF would be working on identifying the victim. Shouldn't they be the ones keeping you apprised of everything they've learned?"

Sheriff Maxwell gave a mirthless chuckle. "My poor little honey lamb," he said, shaking his head. "You really are new at all this, and you don't know how things work."

"What do you mean?" Ali asked.

"It's like this," Maxwell said. "Of course Agent Donnelley and I stood up together in front of all those cameras and microphones and acted like we were the very best of pals, long-lost friends, or maybe even blood brothers. Don't believe it for a minute. That was strictly a public relations performance, and it's also a big wad of B.S. His people aren't gonna tell me or my people a damned thing they don't have to. The reverse is also true. You tell them nothing without checking with me first. Got it?"

"Understood," Ali said. "As plain as my woolly little butt."

Half an hour later, Ali turned off her computer and repacked her briefcase. On the way out, she stopped by the front office to let them know that she would be gone from the office for an unspecified time. Holly Mesina seemed downright thrilled to hear the news.

The only thing she'd like better, Ali thought, *was if she'd heard I'd been run over by a bus.*

The media folks had disappeared. Now there was plenty of parking on the street, but when Ali made her way back to the Cayenne she was surprised to see a rect-angular piece of paper stuck under the windshield wiper.

That's just what I need, Ali thought, *a parking ticket.*

Except when she plucked the paper off the wind-shield, it wasn't a parking ticket at all. It was an unsigned note with a Prescott area phone number. "Please call me," it read.

Ali got into the driver's seat, put her briefcase on the floor next to her, and dialed the number in question. "This is Ali Reynolds calling. Who's 'me'?" she asked when a woman answered.

The person on the other end of the line hesitated for a moment, then said, "I'm surprised. I didn't think you'd call me back."

If you'd said who you were, I might not have, Ali thought.

"You asked me to call," she said aloud. "Who is this?"

"It's Sally," the woman said. "Sally Harrison. I used to be Sally Laird. I was afraid that with everything that's happened, if I left my name, you wouldn't return the call."

"But I am returning it," Ali pointed out a trifle impatiently. "I'm calling, as you asked. What can I do for you?"

"I wanted to talk to you. I wanted to tell you my side."

If this was going to be a rehash of the union situation, Ali didn't want to be involved.

"Look," she said, "I'm working media relations for Sheriff Maxwell. I'm not at all concerned with events that occurred around here before I arrived on the scene. Those things don't really matter to me, especially not right now. After what happened at Camp Verde last night, I have my hands full."

"I didn't do it," Sally said.

"Didn't do what?"

"I didn't take drugs from the evidence room. Ever."

The fervor in her voice made Ali pause. "Why are you telling me this?" she asked. "I'm a temporary consultant. Shouldn't you be saying that to someone inside the department?"

Like Internal Affairs, Ali thought. *Or maybe a defense attorney?*

"Don't make me laugh," Sally replied. "I'm off on administrative leave, but that's only temporary. Once they have a chance, I'm gone. The problem is, I can't afford to lose this job."

"As I said," Ali told her, "this has nothing to do with me."

"Yes, it does," Sally insisted. "You're in the middle."

Exactly, Ali thought, *and I need to stay that way.*

"Have you met Devon Ryan yet?" Sally asked.

"I haven't had the pleasure."

"He's good-looking," Sally said. "He's smart and funny, and he's messed up my life. I'm about to lose my job. My marriage is on the rocks. Carston and I are in counseling to see if we can pull things back together. They're saying it's all about 'conduct unbecoming,' but that's bogus. Devon's slept around before, and so have other people in the department. What they're after me for is evidence-room theft—that I didn't do."

"You're saying someone's framing you?" Ali asked.

"Yes, and it's working."

"Who would be doing that?" Ali wanted to know. "Why?"

"To get rid of me, maybe?" Sally returned. "I can't let that happen. If I get laid off or fired, we lose our health benefits. Carston works as a bartender. Our health insurance is through my job, not his. He doesn't have any, and with our daughter . . ."

She stopped talking abruptly and seemed to be trying to get herself under control.

"What about your daughter?" Ali asked.

"Our youngest daughter," Sally answered finally. "Bridget. She's only thirteen, but she was born with a heart defect. She had a dozen different surgeries before her first birthday. We're on the waiting list for a heart transplant, but if I change insurance carriers, it probably won't be covered because they'll call it a preexisting condition. So you can see that I can't lose this job. Do you understand?"

Ali did understand, but it seemed unlikely she could do anything about it.

"Look," she said, "I'm on my way out of town right now, and things are really hectic at the moment. I still don't see why—"

"It's all about the union," Sally interrupted. "The old one and the new one. That's why they're getting rid of me."

"I've heard a little about this," Ali admitted, "but it sounds like something you should be taking up with your shop steward so he or she can go to bat for you. What about Devon Ryan? Isn't he in the same boat?"

Sally laughed outright at that. "Are you kidding?" she asked.

"Why would I be kidding?"

"He's a guy," Sally replied. "He's also a sworn officer. All they have him up for is the conduct charge. If they really gave a damn, they'd be bringing up the names of all the other women he's screwed around with over the years, but they won't. He won't lose his job or his benefits. They probably won't let him back in Media Relations, but regardless of which union is elected, he'll be part of it—one of the movers and shakers. I'm staff. I'm expendable, so I'm the one they're throwing to the wolves."

Ali glanced at her watch. Sheriff Maxwell had wanted her in Phoenix sooner rather than later.

"Sally," she said, "I'm really sympathetic about your situation, but I'm in a rush right now. I really don't see that I can do anything to help."

"I just need to know that someone there knows the real story, that someone is on my side."

"What about Holly Mesina?" Ali asked. "I thought she was your friend."

"So did I," Sally said bleakly.

She sounded so lost and alone that Ali's heart went out to her, but she couldn't delay any longer.

"I'm sorry, Sally," Ali said. "I really have to go now." The line went dead. Sally Harrison had already gone.

Ali had planned to drive back home to pack before heading for Phoenix. Now that her departure had been delayed, that no longer seemed feasible.

Connecting to her Bluetooth, she called home, where Leland Brooks answered. "I'm just now leaving Prescott," she said. "I need to go down to Phoenix for a couple of days."

"Would you like me to pack up a few things and meet you at Cordes Junction?" he asked. "That way you wouldn't have to come all the way back here."

That was something Ali had learned to appreciate about Leland Brooks—he always seemed to know exactly what was needed without ever having to be asked.

"Where will you be working?" Leland wanted to know. "How long will you be gone?"

"I'm going to Saint Gregory's Hospital," Ali answered. "Maybe one day, maybe two."

"That's at Sixteenth and Camelback, isn't it?"

"Yes," Ali answered.

"Very well then," Leland said. "I'll meet you in Cordes Junction as quickly as I can. At the Burger King."

Ali smiled at that. Her former associates in L.A. would have been appalled. "Great," she said. "See you there, and thank you."

{ CHAPTER 6 }

Her eyes blinked open, fighting the light. A woman's face, partially concealed by a white surgical mask, swam across her line of vision, hazy and out of focus. She fought to make her eyes work, searching for details that might help clarify the situation.

The eyes peering at her from behind a pair of gold-rimmed glasses brimmed with kindness and compassion. The woman attached to the eyes wore green surgical scrubs with a matching green cap perched on the top of her head. Over that she wore a gauzy-looking material that rustled like paper when she moved. Barely visible beneath it was a simple gold cross that hung on a chain around her neck.

The woman—was she a nurse? it was hard to tell— spoke then, her words soothing and quiet, while the patient strained to listen and make sense of any of this.

"There was a fire," the nurse was saying. "A terrible fire."

Yes, she thought. *The fire. I remember that—all of it.*

She had witnessed the fire from every angle, from inside the fire and from above it. She knew that what she had first thought to be a bed was really a stack of Sheet-rock. The house had been unfinished, all studs and wires and pipes. That much she knew. The rest was a mystery.

Whose house was it? she wondered. *What was I doing there? How did I get there? Why wasn't I wearing any clothes?*

Speaking softly, the woman continued her explanation. "A firefighter found you inside a burning house and carried you out. You were transported to a hospital here in Phoenix—Saint Gregory's. Until we're able to locate relatives, I've been asked to serve as your patient advocate."

Phoenix, she thought. *That sounds familiar. But where is it, and what am I doing there? Or here, if there is here? And what's a patient advocate? I thought she was a nurse. Why not a nurse?*

"You have second- and third-degree burns over fifty percent of your body," the woman said. "You're being treated in the burn unit at Saint Gregory's."

Never heard of it. Saint what?

"The kinds of injuries you have sustained are very serious and very painful. We're keeping you heavily sedated due to the pain."

She thinks I don't know about the pain? Is she nuts?

"You're on a ventilator because you also suffered inhalation injuries. You're being given fluids as well as being treated with a morphine drip. Most patients are able to adjust their own pain-management requirements by pressing the pump and upping the dosage as needed, but the injuries to your arms and hands make managing your own pain impossible. That's one of the reasons I'm here—to help with your palliative care. My name is Sister Anselm."

Pal what? she wondered. *What's that? And Anselm. Isn't that a man's name?*

"I'm a Sister of Providence," Sister Anselm said patiently. "I'll be monitoring your vital signs twenty-four hours a day. If I see warning signs that the pain is getting to be too severe, I'll be able to increase the dosage. Do you understand?"

Yes, I understand. Of course I understand. There's a button that I can't push. I need to push it now. Because the pain is coming back. It's coming.

"We need to find a way to communicate," Sister Anselm continued. "Do you need pain medication now? If so, blink once for yes."

Yes! Yes! Yes!

She was trying to blink with every fiber of her being. Trying. Trying. Trying. But nothing happened. Nothing.

Sister Anselm gazed at her face for a very long time. Eons. Ages, while the pain rose up and engulfed her. Finally the nun sighed and said, as if to someone else in the room, "Nothing. It's too soon, I guess, and maybe that's just as well."

Even so, the nun must have pushed the button on the pump, because shortly after that the welcome cotton cocoon began to descend around her. The room retreated.

In those few moments between waking and sleeping, between the arrival of oblivion and the return of the flaming nightmare, she had time for one last realization.

Sister Anselm may not be a nurse, she thought, *but she's my guardian angel.*

On the drive to Cordes Junction from Prescott, Ali thought long and hard about her situation. When

Sheriff Maxwell had shown up on her doorstep a few weeks earlier, it had seemed to her that the man had practically begged her to take the job he was offering, that he had really needed her to come and handle his department's media relations concerns. The Camp Verde fires constituted a major media relations event.

So why's he sending me to the sidelines? she wondered. *What's going on with that?*

She met up with Leland Brooks at the Burger King in Cordes Junction. He was waiting for her inside, seated in a booth. He had ordered two Whoppers and two coffees, one each for both of them. Raised in the Sugarloaf Cafe and out of loyalty to her parents, Ali had a hard time setting foot in fast-food joints. When the need arose, however, Leland Brooks had no such compunction.

"You skipped breakfast," he explained, pushing one of the Whoppers in her direction. "That's not good for you."

Ali had never had an uncle, but if one had existed she imagined he would be a lot like Leland Brooks— bossy, understanding, solicitous, exasperating, and terrific, all at the same time. Her parents, her father especially, had questioned her keeping Leland Brooks on the payroll.

"What does a single woman like you need with a butler?" Bob had grumbled. "It seems like you'd have better things to do with your money."

The truth was, thanks to Paul Grayson's death, Ali had plenty of money. Keeping Leland Brooks on the payroll had been a conscious decision on her part. His loyalty to her in the face of very real danger had made a big impression.

She had told him at the time, while he was still under a doctor's care, that as long as he wanted to work, he had a place with her. Her parents' opinions notwithstanding, Ali expected to keep her end of that bargain. She suspected that not working would have killed the man. Besides, Ali enjoyed Leland's unassuming company and his efficient way of managing things—her included. And on a day like today, it was his presence at the house—looking after the place and taking care of Sam—that made it possible for her to leave home on a moment's notice for an unspecified period of time.

"I booked you into the Ritz," he was saying now. "Suite three oh one. That's the room where Arabella liked to stay on those rare occasions when she went to Phoenix."

Having pled guilty by reason of insanity to three separate homicides and one attempted homicide, Arabella Ashcroft was now permanently confined to a state-run facility for the criminally insane. Ali felt a momentary flash of sympathy for the woman.

Her room now probably isn't nearly up to Ritz standards, Ali thought.

"The hotel is located at Twenty-fourth and Camelback," Leland continued. "The concierge tells me that's quite close to the hospital."

"Somehow I don't think my per diem is going to cover a suite at the Ritz," Ali said with a laugh.

"You'll simply have to pay the difference," Leland returned, brooking no argument. "Being in the suite will give you a decent place to sleep and some room to work as well. You need both, you know."

"All right," Ali conceded. "A suite it is."

Once lunch was over, they went outside, where Leland transferred two pieces of luggage—a suitcase and a makeup case—from his Mazda 4x4 into Ali's Cayenne.

"This one is primarily clothing," he explained. "The other one is toiletries. I didn't want anything to spill and wreck your clothes."

"You do think of everything," she said.

He nodded seriously. "I try, madam," he said. "I certainly do try."

Ali arrived in Phoenix a little past one. Thinking it was probably too early to check in at the Ritz, she drove straight to the hospital rather than stopping at the hotel first. When she opened the car door in the parking garage, the oppressive early-summer heat was like a physical assault. Sedona was a good twenty degrees cooler than this, and she wasn't acclimated.

She hurried into the hospital. In the elevator lobby, she caught sight of the milling group of reporters that seemed to have taken over one end of the hospital lobby. They were easy to spot, but she didn't make any effort to engage them right then. Instead, following Sheriff Maxwell's directions, she made her way to the hospital administration section on the third floor.

"Mr. Whitman is very busy this afternoon," a receptionist told her. "May I say what this is about?"

Ali handed over one of the cards the sheriff had printed up with her Yavapai County information. "It's about the victim from last night's fire in Camp Verde," she said. "I believe Mr. Whitman is expecting me."

Indeed he was. Moments later, the receptionist stood up and motioned for Ali to follow. She was led into a spacious office that would have done most any

Hollywood mogul proud. An immense window on the far side of the room framed Camelback Mountain.

Jake Whitman, complete with a power suit and tie that rivaled Agent Donnelley's, rose from his desk and stepped forward with his hand outstretched in greeting. He seemed genuinely happy to see her.

"Thank you for coming," he said. "Sheriff Maxwell told me he was sending someone, but I didn't expect it would be someone quite so . . . well . . . attractive." He paused, giving her an appraising look and frowning slightly.

Ali understood the unspoken implication. Since Whitman found her attractive, he assumed she was a wimp and/or stupid. As a five-foot-ten natural blond with curves in all the right places, Ali Reynolds had endured a lifetime's worth of blond jokes.

Fortunately, Whitman let it go at that and led Ali to a chair. Once she was seated, he sat down next to her. The gesture was a clear indication that the man wanted her help, and that the two of them were on the same side.

"I have a pack of ravening wolves camped out in the lobby downstairs," he said. "I hope you're up to handling them."

"I'm tougher than I look," she assured him. "And since I used to be a member in good standing of that same pack, I should be able to manage."

"You used to be a reporter?" Whitman asked.

Ali nodded. "In L.A."

"Isn't doing this job a lot like changing sides?"

Here was someone else who had arrived at the conclusion that cops and members of the media had to be at loggerheads.

"We're all here to serve the public," she reminded him. "If the reporters downstairs are in some way disrupting the workings of your hospital—"

"You're right," Whitman said. "Their presence is a disruption. When people are here seeking treatment, they have an expectation of privacy, which we take very seriously. We've told those folks in plain English that no information concerning that patient will be forthcoming, but they're hanging around anyway. I suppose they're hoping to pick up some snippet from a visiting relative."

"What visiting relative?" Ali asked.

"Exactly," Whitman answered. "Since we have no idea who the patient is, there are no relatives, and she's in no condition to supply the names of any. But I'm happy to say that those people are now your problem. I want you to get rid of the reporters—all of them."

It's your hospital, Ali thought. *Why don't you do it yourself, or have your people do it?*

After a moment's reflection she knew the answer to that. The group in the lobby might well include local media people that the hospital couldn't afford to offend. It would be far better for Jake Whitman's next hospital fund-raising effort if someone else was the bad guy here.

Especially if the bad guy happens to be from someplace out of town, she thought.

"Most of the time I'm expected to dispense information rather than quash it," she said, "but I'll be glad to take care of this for you."

"Thank you," Whitman said with a smile. "If you manage to get rid of the reporters in the lobby, you might want to hang out in the burn-unit waiting room on the eighth floor just in case. I wouldn't put it past some of them to try sneaking up there as well." Standing up, he glanced at his watch. "Now, if you don't mind, I have a meeting to go to."

Ali took the hint. She collected her briefcase and headed for the lobby, where she found that a security guard had isolated the group of reporters by herding them into a small seating area just outside the latte stand. She walked over to them and raised her hand to get their attention.

"Good afternoon," she said. "My name is Alison Reynolds. I'm the media relations officer with the Yavapai County Sheriff's Department. We have no additional information to give you at this time. The hospital administration is asking that you vacate the premises. If you'll leave me your contact information, I'll be sure you receive all pertinent information once it becomes available."

"I saw the Angel of Death come in a little while ago," one of the female reporters said. "Is she here because of the burn victim?"

"Excuse me?" Ali asked. "The what?"

"Sister Anselm," the woman replied. "She's a nun, a Sister of Providence. She's often called in to minister to dying patients, especially unidentified ones. If that's why she's here, it's probably bad news."

"I'm sorry," Ali said. "I know nothing at all about that, and I would advise against any speculation in that regard."

That response was followed by a chorus of questions.

"What can you tell us?"

"Do you know who she is?"

"What was she doing in the house?"

"Is she suspected of being the arsonist?"

Ali held up her hand once more, silencing the questions. "I can tell you that the burn victim from the Camp Verde fires was transported here last night and is being treated here. I have no information about her identity. You'll need to contact Sheriff Maxwell's office up in Prescott for details about the ongoing investigation."

"Talk about passing the buck," one of the men groused. "I already tried that. The sheriff's department told me to contact the local ATF office. They in turn told me to piss up a rope. 'No comment at this time.'"

His words were greeted with a spate of knowing and derisive laughter from his fellow reporters. While Ali waited for the group to quiet down, she finally had an inkling of what was really going on. Sheriff Maxwell had brokered a media relations truce with Agent Donnelley, which meant that media folks from the ATF would be in charge of dispensing any and all information concerning the investigation. By sending Ali to Phoenix, they had seen to it that she was safely out of the way, not so much demoted as remoted.

The idea of sticking Sheriff Maxwell with a bill for a suite at the Ritz was sounding more appealing by the moment.

Finally Ali was able to continue. "I understand that you're all trying to do your jobs, but right now your presence here is interfering with the workings of the hospital. Once again, leave me with your contact information, and then be on your way. If anything breaks, I'll be in touch, or someone from the ATF will be."

Grumbling and muttering about it, they began to

comply, gathering their laptops and recording equipment. Several stopped to give Ali contact information to add to her distribution list. The last of those was Sadie Morris, the woman who had mentioned the Angel of Death.

"Tell me about Sister Anselm," Ali said. "What's this about her being an Angel of Death?"

"She calls herself a patient advocate," Sadie explained. "She's usually brought into play when hospitals have seriously injured unidentified patients. Like after some coyote's speeding Suburban goes rolling end over end and spills undocumented aliens in every direction. Sister Anselm evidently speaks several languages, and she works with the patients by standing in for family members until authorities are able to locate next of kin. She claims that her mission is as much about healing relationships as it is about healing bodies."

"How do you know about this?" Ali asked.

"Someone wrote a feature about her a few months ago. It appeared in the *Arizona Sun,* I believe. Just Google 'Angel of Death.' The article should pop right up."

"I'll do that the first chance I get," Ali said. "Thanks."

Once the reporters moved on, so did Ali. She made her way up to the burn unit on the eighth floor. A plaque on the wall opposite the elevator doors laid out the visitation rules. Only authorized visitors were allowed to enter patients' rooms, where proper sanitary gear, including face masks, was to be worn at all times. Sanitary gear was to be deposited in the proper containers upon leaving patient rooms. Bottles of hand-sanitizing foam were mounted on the wall outside each door, and all visitors were exhorted to use it before entering.

Since Ali wasn't a relative, she didn't want to draw attention to herself by speaking to any of the nurses. If pressed for identification, Ali had no doubt that her ID, with the words *Media Relations* written on it, would be enough for her to be sent packing. Ali ducked past the nurses' station and made for the burn unit's small waiting room.

Furniture there consisted of several worn but reasonably comfortable-looking chairs, a matching couch, a somewhat battle-scarred coffee table, a pair of bedraggled fake ficus trees, and two regular round tables surrounded by several molded-plastic, not-so-comfortable chairs. One of the tables was half covered with a partially worked jigsaw puzzle.

For Ali Reynolds, the place came with an all-pervading air of hopelessness that was far too familiar. Years earlier, when Ali's first husband, Dean Reynolds, had been diagnosed with glioblastoma, she had spent months that had seemed like a lifetime in tired little rooms just like this one. Even now she still felt the same kind of overwhelming despair leaking into her soul. She was glad there were no other people around just then.

Three of the rooms she had passed as she walked from the elevator were empty, making her hope that perhaps this was a slow season for burn victims. Right at that moment, there were no other family members or friends around, but they would show up soon enough. Ali knew she would have to steel herself in order to deal with them. She understood that hearing their stories and encountering their heartache would bring back those same feelings in her as well. Some of the time—in fact most of the time—she managed to keep Dean's death in the distant background of her life. But hospital settings always brought those bad old days to the foreground. At least this time she was here to do a specific job, and she needed to keep that idea firmly in mind.

Trying to shake off the unwelcome memories, she chose one of the easy chairs with access to the coffee table as well as a convenient power outlet for her computer. Then, with her computer on her lap, she logged on to the Internet. Her mailbox was full of requests for current information on the investigation—information she didn't happen to have access to at that moment.

She pulled out her cell phone and punched in Sheriff Maxwell's number. He answered on the second ring.

"I'm here at the hospital," she said curtly. "I sent the reporters packing. Now what? I have a dozen requests for information sitting here in my computer and since I have no information to provide, what would you like me to do? Maybe the best thing would be to tender my resignation."

"Look," Maxwell said, "I can tell you're pissed, but please don't do that. Don't quit on me. Donnelley had my nuts in a vise on this."

And you threw me under the bus, Ali thought.

"How can that be?" she asked. "You're the sheriff. It's your department, isn't it?"

"It may be my department, but I've also been given my marching orders," he said. "Have you ever heard the term 'Homeland Security'?"

"What does that have to do with anything?" Ali asked.

"That's the thing," Maxwell told her. "The domestic terrorism aspect of this case trumps anything and everyone else. The feds are taking charge. They expect to have all available assets—theirs and mine—focused on the fire investigation. They also want their media guy to be in charge of disseminating any and all material that goes out on this."

I called that shot, Ali thought. She said aloud, "Including the requests for information that I have on hand right now?"

"Yes," Maxwell said. "Please. I'll text you his address information in a moment."

"From what you're saying, I could just as well pack it in here and come home," Ali said. "I haven't checked into my hotel yet. Maybe I should call and cancel the reservation."

"No," he said hurriedly. "Don't do that. I want you there at the hospital as much as possible for the next several days."

"Why? You sent me here to scare away the reporters. I did that."

"As I said, the domestic terrorism aspects of this case take precedence over everything else. Donnelley is running that show, and he's conscripted most of my available manpower into working the investigation as he sees fit. What that means in a nutshell is that while they're out shaking every tree to see if ELF falls out of it, our attempted homicide is taking a backseat—a back backseat.

"We need to know who that unidentified victim is," Sheriff Maxwell continued. "If she comes around, we need to have someone there to ask her what she knows. Once her family members show up, we need to ask them what they know."

"Wouldn't you be better off having a detective ask those questions?"

"Yes, we would," Maxwell conceded. "Of course we would, but I can't send one of my sworn officers because, if they're available, Donnelley is running them. You're not on my official roster, Ali. Agent Donnelley was adamant that you be out of the picture so his folks could handle media issues. My sending you to Phoenix lets us both get what we want: Donnelley has the conn as far as what information is given to the media, and I have another asset in place, someone I can trust, who can keep an eye on how things are going down there."

Ali thought about that for a minute. "What do you want me to do?"

"According to what Dave tells me, you're a fairly respectable investigator in your own right. The first step in this investigation is to identify our victim."

"I thought you told me earlier that Donnelley's people were going to be doing that."

"Maybe they are," Maxwell allowed, "but who's to say they're not doing that in a half-baked way? Besides," he added, "there's no rule that says we can't duplicate their effort, and maybe even go them one better. Do you know Holly, who works out in the front office?"

Unfortunately, I do, Ali thought. "Yes," she said. "We've met."

"I have her keeping an eye on all missing persons reports that are coming in on a statewide basis. If she comes across anything that looks promising, she's to let you know."

I wouldn't hold my breath, Ali thought.

"That doesn't seem right somehow," she said. "You

sent me down here to get rid of the reporters who were hanging around the hospital, trying to find out whatever they could about the victim. Now they're gone, but you're asking me to do the same thing—find out about the victim."

"Yes," Sheriff Maxwell agreed, "but there's a big difference. They were nosing around in the hope of finding information that would fill up empty airtime and newspaper columns. You're doing it—we're doing it—in the hope of finding out who tried to kill that poor woman. Whether she lives or dies, it's our responsibility to bring her attacker to justice."

Ali thought about that, but not for long.

"I'll do what I can," she said.

"Excellent," Sheriff Maxwell said. "There's one more thing."

"What's that?"

"I know you have a concealed weapons permit. I also know that you carry a Glock. Just don't use it, especially not in Maricopa County. Please. That would set off another whole set of problems that I don't have time to deal with right now."

Before Ali could frame a suitable response, one of the doors farther down the hallway swung open and a tall, angular woman stepped into the hallway. She stood for a moment, peeling off an outer layer of protective paperlike clothing and leaving behind a pair of green scrubs. Her hair was steel gray and cut short.

Ali knew without being told that she was seeing the woman called Angel of Death. She had wanted to Google the article on Sister Anselm and read up on her before encountering the woman in person, but that wouldn't be possible now, not with the nun walking straight toward her.

"I've got to go," Ali told the sheriff abruptly. Closing her phone, she stood up and walked down the hall. "Sister Anselm?" she asked.

The woman frowned and peered at Ali through gold rimmed glasses. "Yes," she said. "Do I know you?"

"No, you don't, but someone told me about you and about your 'mission,' I believe she called it." Ali handed over one of her newly printed business cards. "My name is Alison Reynolds. I'm the media relations consultant for the Yavapai County Sheriff's Department. Yavapai is the next county north of here."

"I'm familiar with Yavapai County," Sister Anselm said firmly. "My home convent happens to be in Jerome. What are you doing here in the burn unit? I thought I made it quite clear to Mr. Whitman that no reporters were to be allowed access to this floor."

"I'm not a reporter," Ali said quickly. "Please don't be misled by what it says on the card. In my case it's more like a case of media nonrelations. It turns out I was dispatched by both Mr. Whitman and my department to break up the gaggle of reporters who were gathered downstairs in the lobby. Which I did. I sent them all packing."

"Thank you for that, and good riddance," Sister Anselm said, glancing briefly at the card and then slipping it into her pocket. "Then I suppose you'll be leaving as well?"

"Not exactly," Ali said. "Sheriff Maxwell wants me to stay around and make sure none of the reporters comes prowling around up here."

"That shouldn't be necessary," Sister Anselm said. "I

don't have any say about lobby issues, but here on the unit my wishes do carry some weight, especially as far as the welfare of my patients is concerned. If any of those reporters turns up here, I'm perfectly capable of giving him or her the boot myself."

Ali was thinking about what she'd been told earlier, that the so-called Angel of Death was often involved in trying to reconnect unidentified victims with their missing loved ones.

"Sheriff Maxwell is hoping I may be able to offer you some assistance in identifying the victim."

From the quick flash of interest that crossed the nun's weathered face, Ali knew she had scored a hit.

"How do you propose to do that?" Sister Anselm asked.

"By monitoring any information that may be reported concerning recently reported missing persons cases. One of those may match up with the woman down the hall."

"You can do that from here?"

Ali sat down in front of her computer and patted it. "Yes, I can," she said. "I have a portable broadband connection."

Nodding thoughtfully, Sister Anselm sank down in the chair opposite Ali. "I suppose having access to official information could prove to be very helpful. There have been instances in the past where law enforcement personnel were, shall we say, less than interested."

She pulled an electronic device of some kind out of her pocket, studied it for a moment, and then slipped it back away. Leaning back in her chair, she studied Ali's face for some time before she spoke again, and Ali did the same.

Sister Anselm's countenance was kind and totally devoid of makeup. She wore two pieces of jewelry with her green scrubs—a small gold cross on a chain around her neck and a simple wedding band on the ring finger of her left hand.

"You mentioned that you had heard about me," Sister Anselm said. "From whom? One of the reporters downstairs?"

Ali nodded and Sister Anselm sighed.

"I suppose it was more of that Angel of Death nonsense," she said gloomily. "I do wish they'd stop citing that article. I didn't want to do that interview to begin with, but the bishop insisted. When it came out, Reverend Mother was not amused. She thought it gave the order a bad name. But you know how newspapers are—if it bleeds, it leads."

Ali smiled at the unexpected comment. "That's journalism for you," she said. "But I don't understand the bad-name part. The woman who mentioned you to me said that you specialize in caring for unidentified and critically injured folks, and that you often work to reunite them with their families."

"That's exactly what I do," Sister Anselm said. "Unfortunately, many of the patients I work with do die. Modern medicine can do miracles, but only with the patient's full participation. When seriously injured people are isolated and alone, they often can't find any reason to fight back."

"Because they have no one to get well for and, as a consequence, no reason to live?" Ali asked.

Sister Anselm nodded. "Without the will to live it's not surprising that many of them die."

"That makes sense to me," Ali said.

"Not to Ms. Hazelett," Sister Anselm said. "According to her, once a hospital requests my participation, it's a sign that they've given up on the patient and that he or she is on his or her way out."

"Hence the Angel of Death moniker?" Ali asked.

"Yes," Sister Anselm said. "Unfortunately, that name stuck. I doubt most people remember anything else about the article other than that. Ms. Hazelett didn't come right out and blame me, of course. She didn't imply that I was somehow responsible for the deaths that occurred, but she made it clear that once I showed up on the scene, death was sure to follow."

"Wait a minute," Ali objected. "Even when a patient dies, if you manage to locate the victim's missing family members, you're at least giving the family someone to bury. You're also giving them closure and answers. I should think the family members would be most appreciative."

"Most of the time they are," Sister Anselm agreed. "Unfortunately that wasn't the focus of the article. But your reasoning is understandable since you don't appear to be a Goth."

"A Goth?" Ali asked. "Who's a Goth?"

"That's how Nadine Hazelett refers to herself in her Facebook entry. From the looks of her photos she wears all black clothing, and even black lipstick. I should have checked her entry prior to doing the interview. Once the article came out, however, it was too late."

Ali liked the fact that Sister Anselm was computer literate and that she noticed things like lipstick colors.

"Having a Goth interview a nun doesn't sound like a good fit to me," Ali said. "Who came up with that brilliant idea?"

"I don't know, but I'm quite sure the article that was published wasn't what Bishop Gillespie had in mind."

"He was looking for some positive publicity?" Ali asked.

Sister Anselm nodded. "He ended up with something else entirely. I thought we should seek legal recourse, but Reverend Mother's take on the situation was that we should let it go. No one wrote irate letters to the editor or anything like that, but the sisters at the convent pray for Ms. Hazelett every day."

"They pray for her soul?" Ali asked.

"No," Sister Anselm said with a smile. "We pray that she'll find enlightenment. It's not quite turning the other cheek, but it's close."

There was a small buzzing sound, an electronic alert of some kind. Sister Anselm pulled the small device from her pocket again. She did something to it, and the sound was silenced.

"Duty calls," she said, rising to her feet. "I enjoyed chatting with you, Ms. Reynolds. If you come up with any information on the identity of my patient, I would be most grateful."

"Of course," Ali said. "I'll let you know. Immediately."

Sister Anselm started to walk away. Then she stopped and turned back. "If you have a chance, you might want to stop by the nurses' station. Tell them you need to sign into my logbook. They'll know what you mean."

For a time after the nun disappeared behind the closed door, Ali sat staring after her. It seemed that she and Sister Anselm were working opposite sides of the same coin. The people from the Yavapai County

Sheriff's Department wanted to identify the victim to track down the woman's would-be killer.

Sister Anselm wanted to do the same thing—to save the woman's immortal soul.

Very different goals, Ali told herself. *But maybe we can work the problem together.*

{ CHAPTER 7 }

Sheriff Maxwell's text message came through, giving Ali the name and contact information for the ATF media relations officer in Phoenix. Still provoked by the sheriff's parting comment about Ali and her Glock, she could easily have delayed passing along the media requests she had collected, but she didn't. She sat there for some time, dutifully forwarding the information. Only when she finished did she step over to the nurses' station.

"Excuse me," she said, when the attendant looked up from a phone call. "Sister Anselm says I need to sign the logbook."

Nodding, the attendant handed over a small spiral notebook. The cover was blank other than a self-adhesive tag with the number 814 handwritten in ink. When she opened it, the first page had marked spaces that called for name, date, phone number, and message. Ali looked up from the page and aimed a questioning look at the attendant.

"What am I supposed to do with this?" Ali asked.

"Just fill it out," the woman said with a shrug.

"Sister Anselm likes to keep a record of visitors for the patients and their families. That way they have some idea of who came by to visit, and why."

"What's the reason for doing that?" Ali asked.

"For many family members it's a comfort to know that someone cared—that at the very least their loved one wasn't all alone here in the hospital, alone and forgotten."

Returning to her chair, Ali opened the notebook to the first page and jotted down her name, department, and contact information. Writing those snippets of official information was the easy part. After that she spent several minutes staring off into space and trying to decide what else to write.

If she told the actual truth, she would be obliged to say something to the effect that she was the injured woman's sole visitor because there was a turf war brewing between the Bureau of Alcohol, Tobacco, Firearms and Explosives and the Yavapai County Sheriff's Department. Family members reading those words after the fact weren't likely to find much comfort or solace in them. Finally, after several long moments of consideration, Ali took up her pen and continued:

> *I witnessed the fire the other night. It's a miracle anyone survived. Sheriff Maxwell asked me to come here to handle any Phoenix-area media concerns regarding the unidentified patient or the hospital.*

When she finished, Ali read through what she had written. It wasn't much, but it was close enough to the truth to pass muster.

If a grieving family member read it later, she hoped they might find comfort in knowing Sheriff Maxwell had seen fit to dispatch a representative from his office, someone who was there in person. And even though Ali was in the burn unit in an official capacity, she was also a legitimate visitor.

Closing the book, Ali returned it to the nurses' station. Then she went back to her chair and opened her laptop. While she waited for her computer to boot up, a text message came in on her cell phone from her friend and homegrown cyber security guru, Bartholomew Simpson. Cursed with sharing his name with a cartoon character and teased mercilessly about it by his classmates, B. Simpson had abandoned his given name by the time he reached junior high. He had also dropped out of high school and thrown himself into the world of computer science. He had put his natural genius and self-taught computer skills to work in Seattle's computer-gaming world, where he had made a name for himself as well as a fortune.

In the aftermath of a tough divorce, B., like Ali, had returned to his hometown roots in Sedona, where he started a computer-security company called High Noon Enterprises. Months after Ali had signed on to become one of his clients, he had come to her rescue when she had been the subject of a cyber-stalking event. Her computer had been hacked by a serial killer who used an Internet dating service to target and harass unsuspecting victims. B. Simpson had played an integral part in taking the bad guy down.

In the months since then, High Noon Enterprises had become wildly successful. B. had, in fact, spent the last three weeks in Washington, D.C., doing something he couldn't discuss, with someone at Homeland Security whose name was classified and couldn't be mentioned.

While B. had been gone, he had sent the occasional text message, several of them hinting that when he got back, he would like to look into the possibility of their being more than friends. That was another issue entirely. Ali had kept her responses breezy and noncommittal. Admittedly, she was attracted to the man. Why wouldn't she be? He was smart and had plenty of money and a disposition that reminded her of a gentle giant (he towered over her at six foot five). Ali liked him, her parents adored him, and Chris thought B. was slick. As far as Ali was concerned, however, the difficulty lay in the difference in their ages. She couldn't quite get beyond the fact that B. Simpson was closer in age to Christopher and Athena than he was to Ali.

That disparity seemed to have no effect at all on B.'s apparent interest in her. She scanned through his text message:

Bak n Sed. Bfast @ SLC. Prnts say u r in PHX. Kno u r workn 4 Sheriff Max, PHX in June! R U NUTS?

Smiling, Ali texted him back:

Nuts R U!

The elevator door swished open. Ali looked up from her cell phone in time to see a stocky young man step into the hallway and stride purposefully toward the nurses' station.

"I'm here about the burn victim from Camp Verde," he announced.

Ali was suddenly all ears. Closing her phone, she turned her attention to what was happening at the nurses' station.

"Are you a relative?" the charge nurse asked.

"No," the man said impatiently, pulling out his wallet and displaying his identification. "My name is Caleb Moore, and I'm with the Camp Verde Fire Department. I'm the one who carried the victim out of the burning house."

The nurse glanced at his ID. Ali more than half expected that the man would be given the bum's rush. Before the nurse could do so, Caleb rushed on.

"I already know that you can't give me any information about her condition. You probably can't even confirm she's here, not officially anyway, but I know this is where the helicopter brought her. I know that nun is here, too. You know, the one who takes care of dying patients. So I'd like to sign the logbook, please—the one Sister Anselm keeps. I want to let the woman and her family know that I was here and that I was thinking about them."

If Ali was surprised that Caleb Moore knew of the existence of Sister Anselm's logbook, the charge nurse was not. Without a word, she handed over the notebook.

While Ali watched curiously, Caleb Moore clutched the notebook to his chest and marched past her to a table in the far corner of the room. Tossing the notebook onto the table, he settled heavily into a chair, removed a pen from his shirt pocket, and began to write.

Oblivious to everyone else in the room, he hunched over the notebook with an air of painstaking concentration, like a student dealing with difficult questions on a final exam. He wrote slowly and carefully, as though the words he put on paper would be judged as much for penmanship as for content.

Had Caleb glanced up from his task, he might have seen Ali studying him. She realized then that she might have caught a glimpse of him the night before at the fire, but the scene had been chaotic, so she wasn't sure. The man she had seen in full firefighting regalia had been hustled into an ambulance. Today, clad in ordinary jeans and a dark blue golf shirt rather than his firefighting garb, and with his crewcut brown hair, Lieutenant Moore looked perfectly ordinary, like a young neighbor who might stop by in the hope of borrowing a lawn mower or a rake.

Halfway down the page, he paused long enough to cough a horribly wracking cough. When he turned to cough into his armpit, Ali noticed the hospital identification bracelet he wore on his arm. Ali had assumed that the injured firefighter had suffered burns as well. Now she realized that his injuries were more likely related to smoke inhalation. He had been admitted and treated. Now, after being released, he had come straight to the burn unit.

Unwilling to interrupt his process, Ali waited until Caleb finished writing. Then she sat and watched while he read over what he had written. Only when he seemed satisfied with the result and started to return the notebook to the nurses' station did Ali move to intercept him.

"Mr. Moore?" she asked. "Do you have a moment?"

He turned to face her as if noticing her presence for

the first time. "Who the hell are you and what do you want?" he demanded. "How do you know who I am?"

Startled by his apparent anger, Ali held up her sheriff's department ID. "I overheard you give your name to the nurse. I'm Ali Reynolds," she explained. "I was at the scene of last night's fire."

He looked up from examining her ID with an expression of ill-concealed fury on his face.

"Media Relations?" he demanded. "I'm not interested in talking to someone from the media. Not at all!"

"I'm not a reporter," Ali said quickly. "My job right now is to keep reporters away from everyone involved, including you, but I do want to offer my personal congratulations about what you did last night. Your efforts to save the woman were wonderful . . ."

He tossed the book onto the counter and then whirled to face Ali. "You think what I did was wonderful?" he demanded with a bitter snort. "Pardon the hell out of me if I beg to disagree. It would have been wonderful if we had gotten there sooner and I'd been able to carry her out of that burning building before the fire got to her instead of after the fact. Wonderful my ass!"

With that he turned and marched away, carrying his own burden of undeserved anguish with him and leaving Ali with the half-uttered compliment still stuck in her throat.

The rest of the world might regard Lieutenant Caleb Moore as a hero, but that wasn't how he saw himself. Despite his valiant efforts to save her, to him the unidentified burn-unit patient in room 814 represented a terrible failure on his part. As far as he was concerned, what he and the rest of the Camp Verde

Fire Department had done on her behalf was much
too little and way too late.

Ali turned back to the nurses' station. The charge
nurse shook her head sadly as the elevator doors
closed behind him.

"That's not unusual," she explained in response
to Ali's unspoken question. "Firefighters tend to take
their losses very personally."

"Could I see that book again for a moment?" Ali asked.

With a shrug, the nurse handed over the notebook
and then turned away to answer a ringing telephone.
Ali took the logbook back to her chair and opened the
journal to the second entry.

> *My name is Caleb Moore. I'm a volunteer firefighter*
> *for the Camp Verde Volunteer Fire Department. I'm*
> *the one who carried you out of the burning house*
> *last night.*
>
> *Thirty years ago, when I was little, my younger*
> *brother, Benjamin, and I were playing with matches.*
> *His clothing caught fire. I was only two years older*
> *than he was. I didn't know enough to roll him*
> *around on the ground to put out the fire. All I could*
> *do was stand there and watch. I have nightmares*
> *about that to this day. I wake up in a cold sweat*
> *still hearing his screams. He was burned over ninety*
> *percent of his body. An ambulance came and took*
> *him to the hospital, where he died two days later.*
>
> *My parents forgave me but I have never forgiven*
> *myself, and I've never forgotten it, either. Everyone*
> *tried to tell me that what happened to Benjy wasn't*
> *my fault, but I know better. I was four. He was only*

two. I'm the one who got the matches down from the cupboard. I'm the one who lit the first one.

I've spent my whole life trying to make up for what I did. That's one of the reasons I joined the fire department. I'm here to tell you how sorry I am that we didn't come to help you sooner. I hope they catch whoever did this to you.

You and your family will be in my prayers every day. I wish I knew your name, but God knows it even if I don't. If there's anything I can do to help, beyond donating blood and praying, please let me know.

I'm leaving my card here with a phone number. If you or someone in your family would like to talk to me, please feel free to call anytime, day or night.

Sincerely,
Caleb Moore

Fighting back tears, Ali closed the logbook. Then she walked back over to the nurses' station and deposited it on the counter.

"Are you all right?" the charge nurse asked.

"I'm okay," Ali answered.

But she wasn't okay. Not really. Over the years, and especially in the aftermath of September 11, she had found herself wondering what kind of person would walk into a burning building in the hope of saving another. Now she had met one, a real American hero. She knew she was lucky to have done so, and so was the woman in room 814.

Regardless of whether the patient lived or died, she

and her unknown family owed a huge debt to a man who, despite his personal history or maybe because of It, had chosen to become a firefighter, placing himself in a position where he would have to face his worst fears on a daily basis.

Maybe Caleb Moore's previous night's rescue attempt hadn't lived up to his own high expectations, but Ali couldn't help but admire the man's raw courage and his continuing effort to right an unrightable wrong.

Once more she emerged from a drugged sleep into a world of impossible pain. Unbelievable pain. She looked around, hoping to see the woman—the nun or the sister or the nurse—and hoping she would come and push the button.

Who was she again? Right then, she couldn't remember the woman's name or what it was she had called herself. Not a nurse or doctor. Something else, but the pain blotted out any memory of those words just as it blotted out everything else. Everything.

With some dismay she realized that beyond the fire—beyond the world of flame that should have been hell but wasn't—she remembered nothing. The fire was all she could recall. Only the fire. It was as though she had come into existence in the fire. Before that she had been nothing.

Who am I? she wondered. *Where am I from? Why can't I remember?*

The pain was brutal, beyond anything she could imagine. She wanted to howl in agony, but the ventilator stifled her ability to make any sound other than a muffled whimper.

Suddenly the nun's concerned countenance appeared above her. Seeming to sense her distress, the sister punched the invisible button that magically released the sweet narcotics into her veins. She knew that in a few moments the painkillers would push back against the pain. Once again she would drift into a state of welcome oblivion.

Before that happened, however, she realized the nun was speaking to her directly.

"Do you know who did this to you?" she asked. "Do you have any idea who left you in that building? Blink once for yes. Blink twice for no."

It seemed that she had been asked to do that once before, but blinking her eyes seemed like a very complicated concept. The idea that some person had placed her in that building and then set fire to it made no sense. Why? Had someone been trying to kill her? But who? Who in the world hated her that much?

"Do you have any idea about who is responsible for what happened to you?" the nun insisted. "We don't have much time before the drugs take over. Please blink once for yes. Twice for no."

She blinked twice for no because she had no idea.

If the nun was disappointed in her answer, she didn't show it. "Where do you live? Are you from Arizona? Again, blink once for yes. Twice for no."

She thought about that, too, as the narcotics began to seep into her body, dulling the pain and dulling her mind as well. Was she from Arizona? The word "Arizona" sounded familiar somehow, as though she ought to know it, but she didn't, not for sure.

"Again," the nun reminded her, "one blink for yes. Two for no."

The answer should be perfectly simple, but it wasn't. She didn't know who she was or where she came from. One blink or two wouldn't work for that. She blinked several times in rapid succession, and the nun got it.

"Does that mean you don't know?" she asked.

She blinked once. Yes, for I don't know. Yes, for I have no idea. None. As the painkillers gradually erased her pain, unanswerable questions tumbled through the falling curtain of drug-induced fog.

One prospect was too terrible to consider—that no one else had done it, that she alone was responsible. That was the final despairing thought that surfaced as the narcotics took over. Maybe her previous life had been so bad that she could no longer tolerate it. Maybe no one else had put her in the house. Maybe she had walked into the house on her own, started the fire on her own.

Somewhere in the far, dark reaches of her mind she understood that if that was true, if she had attempted to commit suicide, then she was damned. Forever. She really would go to hell.

And even Sister Anselm . . . Yes, that was her name. She could remember the name now that the pain was less and when she no longer needed to know it. If that was the case, Sister Anselm, too, would desert her.

She would be left alone—alone and helpless. Alone and in pain. Alone and unable to push the button.

Drifting back into the searing flames of her ever-present nightmare, she heard someone screaming.

The awful noise went on and on and on. Eventually she knew whose voice it was because in the nightmare there was no ventilator.

"Help me," she begged aloud in the dream. "For the love of God, please help me."

Ali wasn't eager to place the call to Holly Mesina, but remembering the other charge she'd been given by Sheriff Maxwell, and after thinking about it for a while, she finally shaped up and picked up the phone. Holly's voice was cheerful enough when she first answered, but the cheer drained away once she learned Ali was on the line.

"Right," she said curtly. "I'm looking into it, but as you can imagine, we're buried around here today. I'll have to get back to you on that."

Holly hung up without bothering to say good-bye and without asking for Ali's number, either. In other words, it would be a cold day in hell before she deigned to call back with information of any kind.

Yes, Sheriff Maxwell had asked Holly to work with Ali on the missing persons situation, but that wasn't going to happen. Maxwell was enough of a politician to have won a countywide election, and he was smart enough to sort his way through dealings with the ATF, but Ali suspected that some of the political wrangling inside his department had so far escaped his notice.

Ali was still wondering what to do about that when the eighth floor of Saint Gregory's Hospital came alive with activity. A gurney pushed by two ER attendants came racing down the corridor. Before the two attendants shoved the loaded gurney into the open door of room 816, Ali caught sight of the sedated patient lying there—a dark-haired young man, a teenager by the looks of him.

The room's door swung shut, and the elevator doors opened. Two separate groups of people hustled into the waiting room. Ali soon realized that although the people had arrived in two elevator loads, they were all members of the same group—the distressed loved ones of the young man, who had just disappeared into room 816.

As the new arrivals talked excitedly among themselves, Ali was able to gather that the boy, James, had accidentally set fire to his jeans in the garage at his home while working on the fuel line of an old Ford F-150 pickup he'd been given for his sixteenth birthday.

One especially distraught middle-aged woman, the boy's mother most likely, hurried over to the door of room 816. While she donned the required antibacterial clothing, other concerned relatives—a grandmother, two aunts, a stray uncle, and two sisters, along with two not yet school-age younger children—settled into chairs in the waiting room, filling it with chatter and with a series of cell phone calls that would no doubt summon more relatives to come and join the vigil.

The difference between the two patients—the boy in room 816 and the unidentified woman in 814—was remarkable. The young man's arrival was accompanied by a whole retinue of care and concern. His presence filled the waiting room with people who were worried about his welfare.

The woman in 814 was alone. Other than Caleb Moore, Sister Anselm, and Ali Reynolds, that nameless patient had no one. That thought had barely registered in Ali's head when the situation suddenly changed. The elevator opened again, and this time a man in a gray business suit stepped out into the noisy room. Ignoring the clutch of James's worried relatives, the newcomer made straight for the nurses' station.

Ali didn't know the man's name, but she immediately recognized him for who he was and what he represented. He was a fed. He pulled out an identification packet and thrust it toward the charge nurse.

"Agent Gary Robson," he announced perfunctorily. "I'm here to see the patient who was brought from Camp Verde last night."

Robson may have expected everyone to jump to his tune, but the charge nurse wasn't impressed. "I'm sorry," she said, holding up the logbook. "The patient's condition is such that she can't see anyone right now. You're welcome to make an entry in the visitors' logbook."

Unaccustomed to being told no, Agent Robson ignored the proffered book and raised his voice several notches.

"Apparently you don't understand," he said. "I'm an officer of the law, and I'm investigating last night's fire. I need to speak to the patient immediately. If she's not available right now, perhaps I could speak to whoever is in charge of her care so we can get some idea as to when she *will* be available. Speaking to her is of the utmost importance."

"Hold on a minute," the charge nurse said. "I'll see what I can do." She picked up a phone and dialed a number. "Someone to see you," she said.

Seconds later, the door to room 814 swung open and Sister Anselm appeared. "May I help you?" she asked.

Robson swung around to face her. "I'm here about the Camp Verde fire victim. Are you in charge of her care?"

She gave him what was clearly a reproving smile. "I doubt that," she said. "I prefer to believe that God is in charge. What exactly do you require?"

The rest of the room fell silent as James's relatives tuned in to the confrontation.

Agent Robson held up his identification, which Sister Anselm pointedly ignored. Instead, she kept her eyes focused on his face while placing her body squarely between him and the door to room 814.

Realizing that his attempt to bully her wasn't working, Agent Robson tried turning on the charm. "My sentiments exactly," he said smoothly. The words were accompanied by what was intended to be a disarming smile. "God is definitely in charge. At least that's what my mother always taught me."

From the bemused expression on Sister Anselm's face, Ali understood that the nun recognized B.S. when she heard it, and she wasn't buying any of it.

"I'm with the ATF," Agent Robson said finally. "That's Alcohol, Tobacco, and Firearms and Explosives." With that, he pocketed his ID wallet and pulled out a business card, which he passed to Sister Anselm. She slipped it into her own pocket without comment and without examining it, either.

Definitely not buying, Ali thought.

"Our agency is in charge of the investigation," he continued pompously. "We have reason to believe this may be a case of domestic terrorism, one with possibly national implications. Since it's likely this woman, your patient, is our only real witness, we urgently need to speak with her. If you could let me know when she'll be available for questioning, I'd be most appreciative. I'm sure you can see this is a matter of some importance, and I trust you'll agree that the sooner we can speak to her, the better."

Ali noticed that Agent Robson's account of things conveniently airbrushed Sheriff Maxwell's department out of the picture. For a long time, Sister Anselm regarded the man with an an unsmiling, wordless gaze. Finally she turned toward the nurses' station.

"I'll take the logbook, please," she said. When the charge nurse handed it over, Sister Anselm in turn offered it to Agent Robson.

"What's that?" he asked, even though he'd already been told.

"A visitors' log," Sister Anselm explained. "For right now, if you'd be so good as to jot down your name and contact information—"

"I'm not here to sign someone's guest book," he declared. "I don't think you understand. This is a critical investigation. I need to know when I can talk to her. In person."

"And you don't seem to understand this is a hospital," Sister Anselm returned coolly. "Our job here is to care for our patients to the best of our ability, which includes protecting them from any unwanted intrusions, official or not. On this floor especially, we limit visitors to people who are directly related to the patient. No exceptions."

"So where are her relatives, then?" Robson said. "Let me speak to one of them."

Sister Anselm did smile at that. "I'm sure you're entirely aware that the patient in question has yet to be identified. Until she is, we have no way of contacting her relatives. Perhaps you could assist us with that part of the equation."

"I doubt that," Agent Robson said. "Not without some quid pro quo."

"Then you and I have nothing more to say to each other." Sister Anselm returned the logbook to the nurse and turned away. Going back the way she had come, she disappeared beyond the door to room 814, which she closed firmly behind her. She didn't bother posting a *No Visitors* sign. It wasn't necessary.

For a moment, Agent Robson stared after her. Then, turning, he stalked off toward the elevator. The waiting room remained mostly quiet until the doors to the elevator slid shut. Only then did the tension in the room evaporate as James's assembled relatives resumed their conversations. Unnoticed by everyone else, Ali threaded her way to the counter. "Could I have the logbook, please?"

"Again?"

"I forgot something," Ali said.

Taking the book back to her chair, she opened it again. On the first blank page beyond Caleb Moore's carefully written words, Ali added the following entry:

> *Agent Robson of the local ATF office stopped by with the expectation of interrogating you about the events at Camp Verde. Sister Anselm refused to give him access.*
>
> *When requested to do so, he declined to write in the logbook. This entry is written by Alison Reynolds, Yavapai County Sheriff's Department.*

Returning the book to the nurses' station, Ali went back to her chair, where she sat quietly for a few moments, holding her computer on her lap. The conversation ebbed and flowed around her while she thought about what had just happened. Both Caleb Moore and Agent Robson had come to the burn unit with full confidence that the woman they were looking for was to be found there. So had the reporters who had shown up in the hospital lobby earlier that day.

Sister Anselm seemed to be concerned about locating her patient's relatives in the hope of repairing whatever damage might have occurred in those relationships, but Ali knew that identifying those relatives would pose its own risk, because Ali understood the grim reality of homicide. In most cases, victims perish at the hands of someone they know and love—an estranged lover or partner, an angry spouse, a distraught or overwhelmed parent. From the time children are old enough to be warned about such things, everyone is on the lookout for "stranger danger." Few people give any thought to some of the very dangerous folk who are much closer at hand.

Once the woman's relatives arrived in the waiting room to mingle with James's concerned family members, there was a very good possibility that her attempted killer, the person who had set the fire, would be there as well.

He or she would use a mask of concern to disappear into the background while waiting for an opportunity to finish what had been started. Since only relatives were allowed inside burn-unit rooms, that meant there was a good chance the helpless woman would end up being left alone and at the mercy of her attempted killer.

The very idea filled Ali with a sense of dread. Identifying the woman had seemed like a good idea right up until it turned deadly. Feeling sick over the apparent contradiction, Ali still tried to do what Sheriff Maxwell had asked her to do—identify the victim.

It was plain enough that Holly Mesina wasn't going to get back to her with anything useful, so Ali attempted to search out the missing persons information on her own.

She knew from personal experience that, with some exceptions, taking missing person reports about adults is a very low priority in most law enforcement jurisdictions. Immediate reports were taken with regard to missing children and for adults who were considered to be at risk due to dementia or other medical issues. When it came to adults who weren't at risk? Forget it. Adults were supposedly free to come and go at will. Their worried relatives were encouraged to behave like the boy in that old country tune who was advised to "take an old cold tater and wait." They were expected to wait until enough time had passed that an official report was deemed warranted.

In the old days, concerned relatives would have had to accept that official line as the gospel. Other than going around their neighborhoods and tacking flyers and photos on telephone poles, there hadn't been much they could do in the meantime. Ali Reynolds understood better than most that the Internet had changed that dynamic. The Internet didn't come with a twenty-four-hour mandatory waiting period.

Ali knew that her only hope of staving off disaster was to be there first—to identify the woman and find her would-be killer before the would-be killer found them. With that in mind, Ali opened her computer again and logged on.

{ CHAPTER 8 }

Ali's initial Internet search went nowhere. Checking on an Arizona missing persons list she found only one possible prospect. The woman was in her nineties and much older than Dave's "sixty or seventy" estimate, but she had disappeared from an adult day-care facility in Chandler around the right time—midafternoon of the previous day. When Ali called for more information, she struck out. The woman who answered the phone apologized profusely; her mother had been found in the early evening hours only a few blocks away from the facility. In all the hubbub the daughter had forgotten to remove the posting but she said she would do so immediately.

Frustrated but with nothing else to do just then, Ali absently googled "Angel of Death." She found the *Arizona Sun* profile of Sister Anselm as the third item down on the first search page.

THE ANGEL OF DEATH
by Nadine Hazelett

When Marta Esperanza Mendoza was found in the desert near Tucson in August of last year, she was near death. The illegal immigrant had suffered a combination of sunstroke and dehydration. She was airlifted to Tucson Medical Center, where she was hospitalized in critical condition.

Abandoned by the group of smugglers who had brought her across the border, she had no documents, no insurance, no family in attendance. The fact that she spoke only Spanish made communicating with her doctors and nurses cumbersome.

Enter the Angel of Death—Sister Anselm Becker, a Sister of Providence. For the past five years she has been summoned to help out with similar cases throughout Arizona. Dubbed a "patient advocate," Sister Anselm has traveled the state providing comfort and counsel to gravely injured people who might otherwise have had no one in their corner. Her work is sponsored by an anonymous donor under the auspices of the Catholic Diocese of Phoenix.

Trained as both a palliative nurse and a psychologist, and fluent in several languages, Sister Anselm is summoned from her home convent in Jerome by area hospitals when they have need of her services. She often works with gravely injured patients who have difficulty communicating with medical care providers. In the case of undocumented aliens, all that may be necessary is a skilled translator who can cross the language barrier

and explain the medical aspects of the situation to the
various patients as well as to their families.

"Doctors and nurses provide treatment," Sister
Anselm said, "but they're not necessarily good at
communicating, primarily because they don't have
time. That's what I bring to the table—time, and the
ability to explain to patients and their loved ones
what's going on.

"Occasionally my job requires me to outline the various procedures and inform the patient of the attendant
risks arising out of that care. People who find themselves in those kinds of circumstances are often isolated from their families. If and when family members
are located, I explain those things to them as well."

Often, one of Sister Anselm's primary goals is to
reunite critically injured patients with their loved ones.
"With comatose patients, the arrival of a loved one
sometimes may stimulate them enough to awaken,
but communicating with severely injured patients in
short questions that require only yes-or-no blinks takes
time. Again, that's the gift my mission brings to the
process—time. I don't punch a time clock. I have all
the time in the world."

When asked how often she succeeded in reuniting
patients with their loved ones, Sister Anselm admitted that is seldom the case. Many of her patients
succumb to their injuries long before relatives can be
located. That's what happened with twenty-six-year-old
Ms. Mendoza.

Sunstroke left Mendoza paralyzed, unable to speak,
and close to death. Doctors were unable to reverse the
effects of her stroke as well as of her severe dehydration. Eventually she died, but Sister Anselm's efforts

didn't end with the woman's death. The self-styled patient advocate continued to search for the young woman's family and eventually managed to locate them in the city of Guadalupe Victoria, Sinaloa, Mexico. When Alfreda Ruidosa came to Arizona to retrieve her daughter's remains, all Sister Anselm had to offer the woman was a logbook that documented all the people who had interacted with her daughter in her last days.

Contacted at her home in Mexico last week and speaking through a translator, Alfreda Ruidosa said that she keeps her daughter's logbook with her family Bible. "At least I know my Marta didn't die alone," she said.

Unfortunately, however, that's how things turn out in most of the cases that involve Sister Anselm. Because she is often summoned to deal with only the most severely injured, it's not too surprising that many of those patients don't survive. Hospital personnel who often welcome Sister Anselm's help in those instances are also the ones who have dubbed her the Angel of Death, since once she's involved with a patient, death often follows.

Hospitals who make use of Sister Anselm's services dodge liability issues by signing a waiver that allows her to function as a contractor, a private-duty care provider. To date no legal actions have been pursued against hospitals in relation to their use of Sister Anselm's services.

Ali stopped reading and stared off into space. How had Nadine Hazelett come up with those kinds of statistics? Surely the hospital records shouldn't have been made available to a journalist—but they evidently had been. No wonder Sister Anselm's mother superior had been bent out of shape about it. The diocese probably wasn't too happy, either, since that last sentence was nothing short of an open invitation for some personal-injury lawyer to come charging into the situation and make life miserable for everyone.

Ali's phone rang. A glance at the readout told her the caller was Edie Larson. "Hi, Mom," Ali said.

"B. stopped by the restaurant earlier," Edie said. "I told him you're down in Phoenix at the hospital with that woman from the fire."

Like Nadine Hazelett, Ali's mother seemed to have access to information she probably shouldn't have.

"Is she going to live?" Edie asked.

"I don't know," Ali answered. "No information has been released about that so far."

"But you're the public information officer," Edie objected.

"That's true," Ali said, "but no information about that has been released to me, either."

"Oh," Edie said.

She sounded disappointed. No doubt she had expected to have an inside track as far as the investigation was concerned. After all, what was the point of having her daughter work for the sheriff's department if Edie wasn't allowed first dibs on news about whatever was happening?

"What's all that noise in the background?" Edie asked.

The small waiting room was jammed with James's collection of relatives, several of whom were arguing noisily among themselves.

"I'm in a waiting room," Ali explained. "Another patient came in a little while ago. Several of his family members are here now, too."

"Are you coming back tonight?" Edie asked.

"I'm not sure," Ali said. "I've reserved a hotel room, but I haven't checked in yet. I came straight to the hospital instead."

"But you'll have a room if you need one," Edie said, sounding relieved. "I don't like the idea of your driving up and down the Black Canyon Highway all by yourself at all hours of the day and night. Not after what happened in Camp Verde. There are all kinds of nutcases out and about. I worry about you, you know."

That's the real reason for the call, Ali thought. *She's worried.*

"I can take care of myself, Mom," Ali said reassuringly. "I have my Taser."

Over her husband's objections, Edie Larson had handed out Taser C2s to everyone for Christmas that year. A previous misadventure with a serial killer had turned Edie Larson into a militant Taser enthusiast. Tasers and accompanying training videos were what had been wrapped and placed under the tree for Ali, Christopher, and Athena to open on Christmas morning. Since Ali's father was still adamantly opposed to all things Taser, his prettily wrapped box of the same size and shape had contained a lump of coal.

"Good," Edie said. "I'm glad you have it with you."

Ali was also carrying her Glock, but she didn't mention that. Edie was a lot less open-minded when it came to actual handguns.

"Are you staying at a decent place?" Edie continued. "I hope it's not one of those dodgy hotels your dad is always choosing."

Ali was relatively sure that her father had never willingly set foot inside a Ritz-Carlton, certainly not as a paying customer, but there was no reason to rub that in.

"No," Ali told her mother. "It's a very nice place. I'll be fine."

Edie rang off after that, leaving Ali to consider that mothers continue to be mothers no matter how old their children. She was about to go back to reading the article when someone spoke to her. "Ms. Reynolds?"

Ali looked up to find a very tall black man standing in front of her. The name on his badge said *Roscoe Bailey, RN*, but his tall, thin frame suggested basketball player far more than it did nurse.

"Yes," Ali answered. "That's me."

"Sister Anselm would like a word," he said. "This way, please."

It was more a command than a request. Closing her computer, Ali stood and followed him down the hall. She was surprised to find that while she had been reading the article, a security guard—an armed security guard—had been seated on a chair just outside room 814. Sister Anselm stood at the end of the hallway, looking out a window at Camelback Mountain, looming red in the afternoon sun. It was much the same view as from Jake Whitman's administrative office, but from a higher floor.

The nun glanced away from the window at Ali's approach. "I've always loved the desert," she said. "For many newcomers, Arizona seems desolate. Not for me. When I see this mountain especially, I know I'm home."

Ali understood what she meant. During her own years of East Coast exile and while she had lived in California, she had often flown home via Phoenix's Sky Harbor Airport. She, too, had always searched eagerly out the windows for that first welcoming glimpse of Camelback.

"You wanted to see me?" Ali asked.

"I'd like to talk to you," Sister Anselm said, "but not here at the hospital. Are you familiar with the area?"

"Pretty much."

"Do you know where the Ritz-Carlton is?"

Ali smiled. "I have a room there. Why?"

"That makes sense," Sister Anselm said. "It's the closest hotel. I often stay there myself when I'm here at Saint Gregory's. They serve a marvelous afternoon tea in the lobby. My patient is sleeping. I probably have an hour or two before I'm needed again. Would you care to join me for tea?"

At first Ali was taken aback by the news that Sister Anselm also stayed at the Ritz, but then Ali recalled what she had read in the article about the anonymous benefactor who bankrolled Sister Anselm's mission.

"Of course," Ali said. "My car is down in the garage. If you'd like a ride—"

"No," Sister Anselm said at once. "That won't do. We shouldn't be seen leaving the hospital together. Too many people nosing about. You go there and get a table. I'll join you in fifteen minutes or so."

Ali got the hint. Sister Anselm wanted to speak to her privately, and in a place where their conferring would be less noticeable than it would be on the grounds of the hospital. Besides, the chance to be briefed by Sister Anselm seemed like a good enough reason to abandon her post in the waiting room.

Fifteen minutes later, Ali was checked into the hotel. Her luggage had been taken up to her room, and she was ensconced at a small table for two just to the right of the entrance to the dining room. The room was alive with people having tea, including a noisy corner spot where several tables had been pushed together to accommodate a lively group of Red Hat Ladies.

By the time Sister Anselm entered the lobby, she had ditched the green scrubs in favor of a dark charcoal-gray pantsuit. The pinstriped outfit looked far more like formal business attire than it did a nun's habit. Ali noticed that as Sister Anselm walked through the lobby she was greeted warmly and by name by both the concierge and the hostess.

Once she was seated at the table, the waitress hurried over. "The usual?" she asked.

Sister Anselm's seemingly severe features rearranged themselves into a grateful smile. "Yes, please, Cynthia," she replied. Ali noticed that Sister Anselm recalled the waitress's name without having to resort to checking her name badge. "That would be wonderful."

Cynthia turned to Ali. "What can I get you?" she asked.

Ali had yet to study her menu, and the question caught her off guard. "I'll have what she's having," she said, nodding in Sister Anselm's direction.

"My pleasure," Cynthia said, backing away.

Once she was gone, Ali turned to face the woman seated across from her. Ali estimated Sister Anselm's age to be somewhere around seventy. Her skin had the appearance of someone who had spent long hours in the sun. Liver spots dotted the backs of her hands, but there was no hint of arthritis in the long tapered fingers that could have belonged to a concert pianist.

To Ali's wonderment, despite what must have been a brisk walk in raging afternoon heat, Sister Anselm showed no sign of being overheated. No sweat beaded her brow. Her face wasn't red. She wasn't huffing and puffing.

Sister Anselm leaned back in her armchair and studied Ali with the same kind of concentration. Behind gold-framed glasses, her bright blue eyes gleamed with intelligence.

"I suppose you're a bit baffled by all this cloak-and-dagger business," she said. "About my not being willing to talk to you at the hospital."

"I'm sure you have your reasons."

Sister Anselm smiled and nodded. "Yes, I do," she said.

Cynthia bustled over with two pots of tea. "You may want to let it steep for a few minutes," she said. "Your scones and sandwiches will be right up."

After she left, Sister Anselm dropped three cubes of sugar into her teacup to await the steeping tea. "Nuns aren't perfect," she said thoughtfully. "We're expected to forgive those who trespass against us, and I do my best, but I'm afraid sometimes I come up short in that regard, especially when people overstep. I believe it's safe to say that Agent Robson brought out the worst in me."

Ali couldn't help smiling. "He did the same for me," she said. "You merely sent him packing; I wanted to smack him. I've never quite mastered the art of turning the other cheek."

It was Sister Anselm's turn to smile. She poured her tea and then stirred it carefully, dissolving the sugar.

"I noticed that he claimed his agency, the ATF, is in charge of the investigation," she said, "as though your department had nothing to do with it."

"Funniest thing," Ali replied. "I noticed that as well. I think that would be news to Sheriff Maxwell, too."

"Which means Mr. Robson is not above adjusting

the truth a little when it suits him," Sister Anselm observed. "But then it wouldn't do for me to throw stones, since I'm not, either."

That last admission came as something of a surprise. Ali said nothing.

"Have you ever heard the term 'HIPAA'?" Sister Anselm asked.

"I've heard of it, even though I don't remember exactly what each letter stands for," Ali said. "I believe it means that health care providers are prohibited from releasing information on any patient in their care unless they have been given express permission to do so by the patient him- or herself."

Sister Anselm nodded. "That's correct. The Health Insurance Portability and Accountability Act. It amounts to federally mandated requirements of confidentiality. I suppose some of the time it's necessary. There are other times when I think of it as so much federally mandated foolishness."

Sipping her own tea, hot and strong, the way Leland Brooks always served it, Ali wondered where this conversation was going. Cynthia appeared again, carrying a tray covered with scones and freshly made finger sandwiches.

"In other words," Sister Anselm said thoughtfully after Cynthia left, "by even mentioning any of this to you, I'm in violation of HIPAA. That's one of the reasons I didn't want to be seen speaking to you in the hospital. I need some help here, Ms. Reynolds." She paused long enough to lift a cucumber sandwich from the tray. "I would have asked Agent Robson for assistance if he hadn't been such an overbearing, unpleasant individual," she continued. "Now I'm asking you for help instead, and violating federal law in doing so—what you might call doing wrong to do right."

"What kind of help do you need?" Ali asked.

"Information," Sister Anselm answered. "My patient is an unidentified woman. Someone tried to murder her by leaving her unconscious and helpless in a burning building. I need to know who she is, but I also need to know who it was who tried to kill her, in case they decide to come back and attempt to finish the job."

Ali was a little surprised that Sister Anselm had arrived at much the same conclusion she had. Instead of commenting, she simply nodded while Sister Anselm continued.

"Often the patients I deal with turn out to be non-English-speaking illegal immigrants."

"Like Marta Mendoza?" Ali asked.

"I suppose you've read the *Sun* article, then?" Sister Anselm asked.

"Yes," Ali answered. "Part of it, anyway."

"That's not the case here," Sister Anselm told her. "This woman speaks English fluently, and she doesn't appear to be Hispanic, either. I suspect she's from somewhere around here. The problem is, she has no idea who she is or where she's from."

"She has amnesia?" Ali asked.

Sister Anselm nodded. "Telling you, that counts as another HIPAA violation, by the way," she said, "but you're correct. She has no memory of the attack, or of anything else, either."

"She doesn't know who she is?" Ali asked.

"Or how she got to Camp Verde," Sister Anselm said. "Her X-rays show that she suffered a vicious blow to the head, probably sometime prior to the fire. Presumably whoever left her there and set the house on fire never expected her to regain consciousness in time to call for help. And they certainly didn't foresee someone walking into that burning building to save her."

"Does she remember anything at all?" Ali asked.

"Only the fire. Apparently that's all she remembers—the fire itself. Nothing before that. Not her name, or where she lived. Nothing."

"Including who is responsible for her injuries," Ali added.

"Yes," Sister Anselm agreed. "She has no idea about that, either, but I do. Women of a certain age aren't likely to run around naked, not willingly at any rate. I suspect that there's some malice aforethought at work here. Whoever did it wasn't just trying to kill her. Her attacker was making a statement by robbing her of her dignity as well as her life, all of which leads me to believe that the perpetrator may be someone quite close to her, a relative or a loved one—using the term loosely, of course."

"I'm thinking the same thing," Ali said.

Sister Anselm paused long enough to butter a scone and slather on some strawberry jam. "Good," she said. "I'm glad we're on the same page."

"Is she going to live?"

Sister Anselm's expression darkened as she bit into her buttered scone. "Do you have any experience with burn patients?"

Ali shook her head. "No," she admitted.

"Generally speaking, patients with severe burns over fifty percent of their bodies don't survive."

"You're saying she's going to die?"

"We're all going to die, Ms. Reynolds," Sister Anselm said with a smile. "As for the patient, I think it's likely that she'll be gone sooner than later. I could be wrong, of course. Miracles do happen occasionally. The point is, she's alive right now—highly sedated, but alive. Over the next few days, we'll most likely have to up the dosage of pain medications. Eventually, I suspect her organs will shut down and she'll be gone."

"When that happens this will become a murder investigation."

Sister Anselm nodded. "Yes," she said. "Indeed it will."

"You still haven't mentioned what kind of help you need," Ali said. "I've been trying to work the missing persons angle, but so far I've come up empty. If she's from somewhere here in Arizona, I have yet to find any report that comes close to matching."

"If you can identify her, that will certainly be useful, but it could also place her in more danger."

"Because the person who tried to do her harm is likely to show up here, along with everyone else."

"Correct," Sister Anselm said. "Whoever did this is going to be very anxious about her condition. They probably already know that she survived the fire, but they won't want to show up here until after they've been officially notified. Showing up too soon would give away the game, but they'll be desperate for information about her condition. They'll be worried about whether she has been able to identify her attacker."

"If this person happens to be a close relative, he or she may very well be granted access to the victim's room," Ali said.

"Yes," Sister Anselm said.

"I can see all that," Ali added. "I get it, and I'm sure that's why you posted a security guard at her door

before you left the hospital. What I still don't understand is how I can be of help."

"I need feet on the ground," Sister Anselm said. "As
I said earlier, it would have made sense to ask Agent
Robson for help, but I could see right away that wasn't
going to fly. I doubt he would have been amenable to
taking suggestions from me."

"You think I am?" Ali asked.

"I believe so, yes."

"You've given me confidential information about
your patient, information I shouldn't legally have
access to. Why did you do that?" Ali asked. "What
makes you think you can trust me?"

"I can, can't I?" Sister Anselm asked.

"Yes, but—" Ali began.

"Agent Robson's first priority is solving his case,"
Sister Anselm interrupted. "He's far less concerned
about our patient's welfare. Now tell me what you
know about James."

Our patient? Ali thought, but for a moment Sister
Anselm's request left her baffled. "James who?" she
asked aloud.

"The young man in the room next door, the patient
in room eight sixteen."

Ali thought about that. "Let's see. He suffered
burns over thirty percent of his body. Face, hands, and
legs, mostly. He's in serious condition, not critical."

"Did you happen to learn about his condition from
one of the nurses?" Sister Anselm asked.

"No," Ali said. "Of course not. From what his relatives said among themselves."

"Right," Sister Anselm said. "What else?"

"Let's see," Ali said, pausing to remember what

had been said. "James is sixteen. He's the youngest, the baby of the family. He has two older sisters. His mother's name is Lisa. His father's name is Max. His parents are divorced. The father gave him a car for his birthday, against his mother's wishes. He was doing something mechanical on the car without being properly supervised when it caught fire. The accident evidently happened at the father's house, in the garage."

"So the mother was unhappy about that?" Sister Anselm asked.

"Very. The father showed up a little while ago, quite a bit later than everyone else. He's a truck driver and was on his route driving freight to Flagstaff when all this happened. It took him some time to drop off his load and drive back down here. When the father came into the waiting room, the other grandparents gave him hell about the car thing. So did the mother a few minutes later. She had to come out of the room so the father could go in to see his son. It was pretty ugly."

"Who are all the people out in the waiting room?"

"His parents, both sets of grandparents, various aunts and uncles—mostly on the mother's side—James's two older sisters, and a niece and nephew."

"Did anyone from the family actually speak to you?"

"No," Ali said. "Not at all. I was working on my computer. They left me completely alone."

"You see?" Sister Anselm said. "Sitting there with your computer open rendered you completely invisible to everyone else in the room. Although you may have been working on that computer, you were also listening, and not just with your ears, either. I believe you were listening with your heart. It turns out that's exactly the kind of help I'm looking for. Most of the time I'll be in the patient's room. What I want you to do is spend as much time as you can in the waiting room. If you're there when the patient's relatives start arriving, my guess is they won't even notice you. As you've just learned about James's family, what people say to one another when they're in crisis is likely to be quite unguarded."

"You expect me to function as some kind of undercover operative?"

Sister Anselm beamed at her. "Exactly," she said.

"You do know I'm not a trained police officer," Ali said.

"I don't think that will matter." Sister Anselm reached into her purse and extracted an iPhone, which she waved in Ali's direction. "While you've been reading up on me, I've been checking you out as well. From the sound of it, you're quite capable of handling yourself in any number of difficult situations, including one very spectacular shoot-out in a hospital waiting room right here in Phoenix."

The longer Ali spoke to Sister Anselm, the less surprising it seemed that the seventy-something nun would have been surfing the Net.

"You can't believe everything you read," Ali said.

"Fair enough, as long as you do me the same favor as far as what Ms. Hazelett wrote about me, all that Angel of Death nonsense. As a nonbeliever, Ms. Hazelett gave short shrift to Saint Michael, the real Angel of Death. In a manner of speaking she's right, of course. I often find myself shepherding people and giving them comfort at the ends of their journeys. That being the case, I'm hoping you may be willing to join me in this particular endeavor, and yes, if you were operating undercover, that might be best for all concerned."

"What about the people at the nurses' station?" Ali

asked. "I've spoken to several of them in the past couple of hours. They all know who I am and that I'm associated with the Yavapai County Sheriff's Department. For that matter, what about the killer? No doubt he or she has been following press coverage of the incident with avid interest. If that's the case, the perp might very well have seen me on TV during that initial press conference. Aside from all that, what about the two entries I made in the visitors' logbook?"

Sister Anselm leaned down and pawed through the contents of her large purse before emerging with two pieces of jagged-edged notebook paper.

"You mean these?" she asked, handing them over.

When Ali examined the papers, she saw that they were indeed her handwritten entries from the visitors' log. "You pulled them?" she asked.

"Yes, I did," Sister Anselm admitted with a smile. "I can always reinsert them later, but for right now it's a good idea for them to disappear. As I said, Agent Robson isn't the only person around here who's willing to adjust the truth when it's deemed necessary."

For a long time, Ali said nothing.

"You're still not convinced, are you?" Sister Anselm said.

"No," Ali agreed. "I guess not. Not enough to try to persuade Sheriff Maxwell to go along with this."

Sister Anselm sighed and nodded. "I suppose I'd best tell you the rest of the story then," she said, "but that's going to require another round of tea." She raised her hand and caught Cynthia's eye.

"My guest requires further convincing," she said when Cynthia approached the table. "Hit us again, please. We'll both have some more of your wonderful tea."

{ CHAPTER 9 }

By the time the second pots of tea came, most of the scones and sandwiches were gone.

"Have you ever heard of displaced persons?" Sister Anselm asked.

"In conjunction with World War Two, or from some other war?" Ali asked.

"World War Two," Sister Anselm said.

"I've heard about them," Ali replied. "They were people set adrift in Europe in the aftermath of the war. Often they were people whose homes and livelihoods had been destroyed. In some cases their very countries had disappeared, or if the country remained, they had no way of getting back there."

"That's my history in a nutshell," Sister Anselm said with a sad smile.

"How is that possible?" Ali returned. "You're an American, aren't you?"

"I was born an American," Sister Anselm said. "And I'm an American now, but that wasn't always the case. My mother was born and raised in Milwaukee. My father was born in Germany, but he immigrated to this

country in the mid-thirties. I suppose you've heard of
the Japanese war-relocation centers that were operated in this country during World War Two."

"Yes," Ali said with a nod.

"Are you aware there were German war-relocation
centers as well?"

"I never heard of them," Ali said.

"You and everybody else," Sister Anselm said, "but
they did exist. My father, Hans Becker, was a printer
working for a German-language newspaper in Milwaukee when he met and became engaged to my
mother, Sophia Krueger. Her parents disapproved of
the match, but Hans and Sophia married anyway and
had two children—my older sister, Rebecca, and me.
Everything was fine for a while, but then the Japanese
attacked Pearl Harbor.

"December seventh is my birthday. On that day in
1941, Becka was twelve and I turned ten. We were
supposed to have a party. Instead, officers from the
INS showed up at our front door, arrested my father,
and took him into custody. They led him away in hand-
cuffs. For most of the next year he was held in an INS
facility in Wisconsin."

Ali had guessed Sister Anselm to be somewhere in
her early seventies. Listening to the story, she realized
that the nun was older than she had originally thought.

"So there was my mother. She was left with no husband, no income, and two children. When we could
no longer afford to live in the apartment, we moved
in with our grandparents. I believe they thought that
by taking us in, they would have a chance to extri-
cate their daughter from what they considered to be a
disastrous marriage.

"My grandmother was not a nice woman. She was vindictive and mean. She tried her best to turn Becka and me against our father. One day she let slip to Becka that she and our grandfather were the ones who had set the authorities on our father. My mother never spoke to her mother again."

"Even while you were living in their house?"

"Even then," Sister Anselm nodded. "For a long time after that, Becka and I carried notes back and forth between our grandparents and our mother. Finally we heard that Father was going to be transferred to a newly established relocation camp in Crystal City, Texas. By then he had developed TB and was desperately ill. When Mother learned there was virtually no medical care at the camp, she asked to accompany him. The Justice Department told her that the only way that would be permitted would be if she renounced her citizenship."

"That's what she did?" Ali asked.

"Yes," Sister Anselm said. "As far as my mother was concerned, living with her parents was more onerous than living in a prison camp. But when she renounced her citizenship, it turned out she renounced ours as well. We packed everything we could carry into suitcases, and off we went to Texas on the train."

"What happened to your grandparents?"

Sister Anselm shrugged. "I never saw them again. After the war, I tried to contact them. My letters were returned unopened. But that's getting ahead of the story. We went to Texas. Our father was very ill. Mother took care of him and worked for chits at the German mercantile store. Becka and I went to school. She hated the camp. I loved it. There were lots of

families whose circumstances were similar to ours—
Japanese, German, and Italian. The guards did their
best to keep the groups separate, but that didn't work
for the kids at school. I made friends with all of them.
My father had taught us to speak German at home,
but I learned to speak Japanese and Italian, too."

*No wonder Sister Anselm is concerned about broken
relationships,* Ali thought. She said, "You still haven't
told me how you became a displaced person."

"I'm coming to that," Sister Anselm said. "By early
1943, the prisoners at the Crystal City facility were
being repatriated, but because Mother had renounced
her U.S. citizenship, we were sent 'back' to Germany
with our father, even though my mother, my sister, and
I had never set foot outside the United States.

"In the dead of winter, we were shipped to New
York City by train and put on the Swedish ocean liner
Gripsholm. After a stormy crossing the ship finally
docked in Marseilles. From there we were supposed
to be taken first to Switzerland and then, finally, on to
a prisoner exchange in Germany, but by the time we
landed in Marseilles, Father was too ill to travel. He
was transported to a nearby hospital, where he died a
few days later."

"So there you were, stuck in France," Ali said.

Sister Anselm smiled. "That was bad enough. We
were penniless. We had no connections there, just as
we had no connections in Germany, and none of us
spoke French. Not only that, by then Mother, too, had
developed TB. Eventually she was moved to a sanatorium outside Paris that was operated by the Sisters of
Providence."

"What about you and your sister?" Ali asked.

"Since we had nowhere else to go and no one to look after us, we went there, too. While our mother was dying in the sanatorium, Becka and I lived in a Sisters of Providence convent adjacent to the hospital, one that housed the nuns who worked as nurses in the sanatorium.

"By the time Mother died, Becka was a rebellious teenager. She hated the convent just like she had hated the camp in Texas. She thought she had exchanged one prison for another. She ran away, lived on the streets for a while, and was stabbed to death in an alley in Paris before she turned seventeen."

"What about you?" Ali asked.

"I stayed on at the convent," Sister Anselm said. "I loved the nuns, and they loved me. They took care of me and saw to my schooling. When I turned eighteen, I could have exercised my right to return to America as a citizen. Instead, the little Lutheran girl named Judith Becker from Milwaukee, Wisconsin, converted to Catholicism and became a nun. For the next twenty-five years I lived and worked mostly in France. In the seventies, I was offered the chance to come home to America, and that's what I did." Sister Anselm paused and smiled. "So there you have it, the real background on that whole Angel of Death thing."

"That's why you do what you do?" Ali asked.

"Yes, it is," Sister Anselm answered. "Even if my mother had survived, I don't believe the breach with her family ever would have healed. So often, the people who come under my care are in similar circumstances to what happened to us in France. They're lost and alone, sick or hurt, and far from home. Usually they're dirt poor, and often they don't speak the language. Not all of that applies to the woman in room 814, but she does seem to be alone in the world. No one has reported her missing. No one seems to be looking for her."

"Except for the person who tried to kill her."

Sister Anselm nodded. "And you and I may be the only people standing between her and her would-be killer. That's why I need your help."

That was supposition on Sister Anselm's part, but Ali happened to agree. "Doing what exactly?" she asked.

"Listening and watching," Sister Anselm said. "If she has visitors, I want you to keep track of who they are, what they do and say, how they comport themselves."

"I can't do anything of the kind without checking with Sheriff Maxwell first," Ali said. "I can't imagine he'll be in favor of it."

"Don't worry about that," Sister Anselm said with a confident smile that waved aside Ali's objection. "It's all in what you say and how you say it. Just be sure to let him know that if he says no, I'll be obliged to turn to Agent Robson for help. That should fix it." She gave Ali an appraising look. "You're right, of course," she said. "The killer may well have seen you in that first news conference. I think we need to change your looks a little, and also your name. For some strange reason you look like a Cecelia to me. Yes, Cecelia should do very nicely, but Cecelia what? Let's see. How about Cecelia McCann? With a name like that, I think you'd be better off having red hair. That would certainly change your appearance."

Ali was stunned. "You want me to dye my hair?"

"Certainly not," Sister Anselm declared. "There's a wig shop in that new shopping center right across the street from the hospital, Biltmore Commons. That shop in particular specializes in providing wigs for cancer patients, but I'm sure you'll be able to find what you need."

Sister Anselm pawed in her purse again, extracted her iPhone, and fiddled with it for several long moments. "Ah, yes," she said. "Here it is. It's called Hair Again. If you go over there shopping, you might want to pick up some other footwear, something more comfortable. Heels aren't good for hiking around hospitals. I'll be changing back into my running shoes before I head back."

Sister Anselm raised her hand and summoned Cynthia.

"Would you like to bill this to your room?" the waitress asked.

"Yes, please," Sister Anselm said.

"You're staying here, too?" Ali asked.

"Oh, yes. I suspect that the benefactor for this program has some connection to the hotel business. I often stay in upscale hotels, not that I spend much time in my rooms, but it's good to have a place to go to decompress if I need to."

"I could have bought my own tea," Ali said as the nun signed the check and handed it back to Cynthia.

Sister Anselm smiled. "Think of it as a bribe, my dear, and there's no reason to feel guilty. I have an idea my benefactor has deeper pockets than yours. Nevertheless, I would like you to contact Sheriff Maxwell, the man who, according to Mr. Robson, isn't the least bit involved in this case. Please let him know that you and I both have some concerns about our patient's safety. We should probably refer to her as Ms. Smith for the time being—Ms Mary Smith. Ask him if he can spare someone else to come here and help make sure no one gains unauthorized access to her room. My first priority is to make certain that whoever committed this heinous crime doesn't have a chance to finish it."

Ali already knew that Sheriff Maxwell had no one to spare—except for a certain stray media relations consultant—but she didn't say that aloud.

"Of course," Ali told Sister Anselm. "I'll get in touch with him right away, but let me call for my car. I can give you a ride back to the hospital."

"No," Sister Anselm said. "It's only a few blocks. I'm more than capable of walking that far."

"But the heat . . ."

"I'm fine, and the less the two of us are seen together, the better."

They exchanged telephone numbers. Just then the electronic device Ali had heard before sounded again. "Ms. Smith's vitals," Sister Anselm said, plucking it out of her purse and studying the face of it. "She's starting to come around again. I need to go."

With that, Sister Anselm picked up her purse and was gone. Ali waited until she exited the lobby, heading for the bank of elevators. When that happened, Ali picked up her phone and speed-dialed Sheriff Maxwell's number.

"He's very busy right now," Carol Hillyard, the sheriff's secretary, said. "Who's calling, please? Is this important?"

"It's Ali Reynolds," she said, "and yes, it's important."

Three long minutes later Sheriff Maxwell finally came on the line.

"Ali, glad you're checking in. I assume you've heard about the missing persons report?"

"What missing persons report?"

"I asked Holly to give you a call about it. She must have been too busy, or maybe she couldn't get through."

I'm sure, Ali thought. She said, "This is the first I'm hearing about it."

"The call came in to the Fountain Hills Marshal Office a little over an hour ago. The missing woman's name is Mimi Cooper. She's seventy-one, about the estimated age of our victim. Her husband is a pilot for Northwest Airlines. He came home from a trip this afternoon and said that his wife has evidently been gone since sometime yesterday. Her car is missing, and so is she."

"Any sign of a struggle?" Ali asked.

"Nope, but she didn't leave a note, either. Dave Holman is on his way to meet with the Fountain Hills authorities and maybe, depending on what he learns, with the spouse as well. At this point we don't know for sure that this Cooper woman is our victim. It's really a wild guess on the husband's part. What we do know is that so far hers is the only missing persons report statewide that fits in with our time frame as well as with the victim's approximate age."

"What do we know about her?"

"Not much. Mimi Cooper must be reasonably well-to-do. You can tell that from the Fountain Hills address. Married, with a couple of grown kids. Once Dave has more details, I expect he'll call them in, especially if it looks like Mimi might turn out to be our victim. If you're not calling about that, though, what's up?"

With a sigh, Ali launched into the story of Sister Anselm's scheme to turn her into an undercover agent, Cecelia McCann. Sheriff Maxwell's initial reaction was exactly what Ali had expected—not just no, but hell no! Until she mentioned Agent Robson and Sister Anselm's intention to cut the ATF agent out of the picture. Just as Sister Anselm had predicted, Sheriff Maxwell grabbed the ball and ran with it.

"Hell of a good idea," he said. "Sounds like you and Sister Anselm are a good duo. You two do what you can. I, for one, am all for it. Dave probably will be, too, as long as you're not out mixing it up with any bad guys. And just in case Dave drops by the hospital, what's the name you'll be going by again?"

"Cecelia. Cecelia McCann. Tell him to act like he doesn't know me."

"Will do," Sheriff Maxwell said. "It wouldn't do for him to blow your cover."

Knowing there was a tentative identification on the horizon, Ali reasoned that things might start happening sooner than later. She sent a text message to that effect to Sister Anselm.

The nun's text response showed up almost immediately: "Get here when you can. Once you're in the waiting room, if you need me, remember to text, don't talk."

Ali had never imagined that she'd be texting a seventy-something nun toting the latest in phone gadgetry, but then she had never imagined that her mother would be routinely packing a weapon, either. Edie carried her pink and black Taser C2 in her purse at all times, right along with her compact and lipstick.

Thinking of those two remarkable women, Sister Anselm and Edie Larson, made Ali smile. Edie was a generation younger than the nun, but they were certainly of a piece—women of a certain age who had found ways to live and thrive by embracing modern technology rather than dodging it.

Ali went up to her room and checked her suitcase. Fortunately, Leland had included a selection of outfits, one of which was a bright pink jogging suit, and some of her favorite workout shorts. The jogging suit wasn't exactly designer wear, but she figured that, along with some running shoes, it would allow her to blend into the waiting room crowd a little better than the knit skirt, blazer, and heels she'd worn when she had left home for Prescott much earlier that morning.

Ali drove her car as far as the hospital, left it with the valet, and then walked across the street to the newly redeveloped shopping mall, Biltmore Commons. The sun had dropped behind the western skyline, but it was still incredibly hot—well over a hundred degrees. In the time it took her to cross Camelback and find the store, the tracksuit became drenched with sweat.

How does Sister Anselm hike back and forth in this heat? Ali wondered.

When she finally located the wig shop, Ali was relieved to slip into Hair Again's frigidly cool interior. Sister Anselm had told her that the ladies who worked there specialized in dealing with the beauty needs of cancer patients, but they were more than happy to help Ali find a reasonably attractive wig. Within minutes, she was staring at a reflection in the mirror that didn't look anything at all like the Ali Reynolds she knew. The carrot-topped wig was a long way from Ali's own blond hair.

The bright pink suit clashed with her new hair color. After all, the idea of Ali undergoing a sudden hair color change wasn't something even the seemingly all-knowing Leland could have anticipated.

At least it fits, Ali thought as she made her way back across Camelback to the hospital entrance. *And the less it looks like me the better.*

She walked into the hospital through the main entrance. As Ali headed for the bank of elevators, she caught sight of a few media folks still lingering in the lobby. Some of them were people she had spoken to much earlier, but none of them recognized her or gave her so much as a second glance. Obviously the tracksuit and her bright red tresses were doing their job.

Ali was in the elevator, trying to get her head around who she was supposed to be, when her phone rang. "Ali?" Athena said.

Calls to Ali from Chris were far more commonplace than calls from her daughter-in-law, but Ali was delighted to hear from her.

"Yes," Ali said. "How are you? Where are you?"

"I'm on my way to Tempe," Athena said. "I'm bringing down a load of stuff for the apartment."

Athena and Chris were working on master's degrees to keep their teaching credentials up-to-date. They had sublet an apartment in Tempe so they could attend both sessions of summer school, but the first session wasn't set to start for a week.

"Wait," Ali said. "I thought you and Chris were going to fly to Minnesota this week to see your grandmother and your folks."

Having just heard about Sister Anselm's troubled early life, Ali couldn't help comparing Athena's situation with that. When Athena's first husband divorced her, her parents—for reasons known only to themselves—had stuck with their former son-in-law, his new wife, and their new baby. It had saddened Ali to realize that Athena's folks had turned away from their own daughter. Only one member of Athena's family had deigned to attend her wedding to Chris. Ali had been glad to hear they planned to make a brief visit to Minnesota prior to the start of summer school. She was hoping that breach, like the one that had long existed between Ali and Chris's paternal grandparents, could also be repaired.

"We're not going," Athena said. "I changed my mind."

Ali was smart enough not to ask why. "I'm sure you had your reasons," she said.

"Yes," Athena said. "I do, and I'd like to talk to you about it."

Heading into the waiting room as a supposedly undercover operative, Ali was in no position to play hostess to Athena, but she didn't want to turn her down, either.

"I'm working right now," she said. "Could I meet up with you later this evening? Are you staying over in Tempe tonight, or going back to Sedona?"

"I'm staying," Athena said. "Give me a call when you're available."

Closing her phone and exiting the elevator, Ali saw that the waiting room was even more crowded than it had been earlier. As far as Ali could tell, all the visitors in attendance were there for James rather than for the woman in room 814.

In Ali's absence, James's two sets of still-feuding

relatives seemed to have taken possession of most of the furniture in the room, leaving a chair-free no-man's-land between them. A group of teenagers, presumably James's friends, had invaded that space. Using a collection of backpacks to mark their territory and to provide backrests, they sat on the highly polished tile floor and talked quietly among themselves.

Ali pulled one of the few unoccupied chairs into what appeared to be neutral territory. Settling into it, she opened her computer. While she waited for her AirCard to connect, she listened to the talk buzzing around her. Sister Anselm was right. It was as though the presence of the computer rendered her invisible.

The kids may have been there because of James, but they weren't talking about him. They were more concerned with other issues—who had flunked which class and was having to go to summer school; who had dropped out and was going to get a GED; who had gotten tossed out of a local movie theater for fighting; and whose parents had kicked someone out of the house when they had figured out at the last minute that he wasn't going to graduate.

Listening to that, Ali reminded herself to be grateful that Chris had been such an easy kid to raise. She was also thankful that Chris and Athena were the ones dealing with teaching high school–aged kids like these on a daily basis. After enduring a solid nine months of doing that, a vacation should have been in order. Ali couldn't help wondering why Athena and Chris had abruptly canceled their plans to visit Athena's family.

Settling into a chair, Ali tuned in to what James's relatives were saying. It was more of the same. When they had first trooped into the waiting room, Ali had marveled at their apparent solidarity, their show of support and love for James, but they had also brought along a history of petty grievances.

It was shocking to see how completely what she had thought of as a united front had shattered in a few hours' time. A woman Ali had determined to be James's grandmother on his mother's side was still mad that his daddy had gotten drunk and disrupted Thanksgiving dinner—two years earlier. James's older sister, the one with the two now hungry and cranky kids in tow, was firmly aligned on her mother's side of the grievance list, while the younger sister stuck with her dad's group. The father's relatives had their own list of complaints. At some point in the past, one of the father's former brothers-in-law had borrowed a truck and wrecked it. That incident was still up for discussion, as were noisy arguments about child support and visitation.

Ali was more than a little taken aback by the casual way in which these folks dragged their private battles into the public arena, and she knew that Sister Anselm was right to place someone in the waiting room. If family members showed up to keep a vigil for the patient in 814, any fractures in their relationships were bound to show up as well.

To say nothing of ours, Ali thought ruefully.

Whatever was going on between Chris and Athena didn't sound good.

CHAPTER 10

U pon opening her computer, Ali's first instinct was to log on and track down the Mimi Cooper missing persons information on her own, but knowing she also needed to put the Holly Mesina issue to rest, she decided to deal with that.

First things first, Ali thought.

She walked down the hall, far enough to be out of earshot, and called Holly's extension, leaving a cheery message. "Sheriff Maxwell just called and told me there's a missing persons report from Fountain Hills that could be relevant. I need the details. Please give me a call when you can."

She left her number. That was enough. The message served notice to Holly that Ali was aware that she was withholding information. By invoking Sheriff Maxwell's name, Ali was also letting Holly know that she would be called to account for not doing what she had been told to do.

Ali had closed her phone and was returning to the waiting room when the elevator door opened and a distraught man in a rumpled airline uniform rushed off and headed for the nurses' station.

Is this the woman's husband, Ali wondered, *or is it her son?* He looked to be a good twenty years younger than Ali would have expected.

"I'm here about my wife," he said urgently to the woman behind the counter. "Her name is Mimi Cooper. I need to see her."

"I'm afraid we have no one here by that name—" the attendant began.

"Don't you understand?" he demanded. "That's what I'm here for—to give you her name. It's that woman from the fire in Camp Verde last night. She may be my wife. I came home from a trip and found out Mimi is missing. When I called the marshal's office in Fountain Hills, the person I spoke to there suggested that I check here."

"One moment," the attendant said calmly. "Let me see if her attendant is available."

"I don't want to see her attendant," the man insisted. "I want to see my wife, and I want to see her now."

It was almost the same thing Agent Robson had said, but with far better reason.

Within moments, Sister Anselm emerged from room 814. When she stripped off her paper gown Ali saw that the green scrubs had been replaced by a set of floral-patterned ones.

"May I help you?" Sister Anselm asked calmly, addressing the agitated man who was pacing back and forth in front of the counter. He stopped in midstride.

"Are you Mimi's doctor?" he demanded. "Is she going to be all right?"

"I'm Sister Anselm," the nun responded, "and no, I'm not a physician. I'm what's called a patient advocate. I'm assigned to care for the patient in room eight fourteen. I don't believe I caught your name. What was it again?"

"Cooper," he said. "Hal Cooper. My wife's name is Mimi. Mimi is short for Madeline—Mimi Cooper."

"What makes you think she's here?"

"My wife is missing," he declared. "When I talked to the cops over in Fountain Hills, one of them suggested that I come here. She had seen something on the news this morning about an unidentified victim of a fire. She wondered if the two incidents might be connected."

"Tell me about your wife," Sister Anselm said solicitously. She collected a pair of chairs, set them fairly close to Ali, and then guided Hal Cooper into one of them. "How long has she been gone?"

Before taking a seat next to him, Sister Anselm nodded slightly in Ali's direction. Taking the hint, Ali understood what was expected. This was turning into an interrogation of sorts, and Ali would be transcribing it. Opening her computer screen to a new document, she began to type.

"That's the thing," Hal said quickly. "I don't really know how long ago she left. I came home from a trip this afternoon and she was gone."

"She didn't give you any idea about where she was going, or why?"

"No," he said with a sigh. "We had a big argument before I left. A serious argument. I thought she'd get over it, but the whole time I was out of town, she wouldn't take my calls. I left one message after another. She never picked up, and she never called me back, either."

"How long were you gone?" Sister Anselm asked.

"A week," he said. "I'm a pilot for Northwest," he added unnecessarily; his rumpled uniform made that obvious. "When I'm scheduled to do international flights I'm usually gone for about five days at a time. This time I was away for two extra days. I stopped off in Michigan to see my mother. When I came home this morning, Mimi's car wasn't in the garage, and she was gone. I found both her cell phone and her purse in the bedroom. That really worried me—Mimi doesn't go anywhere without those. But other than that, there was nothing out of place, and no sign of a struggle. The painting was gone, but I didn't notice that until later."

"What painting?" Sister Anselm asked.

Hal shook his head. "This incredibly ugly thing that looks like somebody's bad idea of a patchwork quilt. I never liked it. Mimi's first husband gave it to her as an anniversary present. She's always said it was worth a ton of money, but you couldn't prove it by me. She'd been talking about selling it for the past year or so. I thought maybe she'd gone ahead with that, or maybe she had sent it to the gallery on consignment."

"Does Mimi have a vehicle of her own?" Sister Anselm asked.

"She certainly does," Hal answered. "An Infiniti G37. Like I said, it should have been parked in the garage, but it wasn't. That's what our fight was about. I gave her strict orders that she wasn't allowed to drive it while I was gone."

"Why not?"

"Because she's due to have cataract surgery ten days from now. I told her it was too dangerous for her to be out driving on her own, especially at night, when she can't see worth a damn.

"Once I left town I even called her daughter—well, I tried calling her daughter. Serenity wasn't in but I left a message with Donna—that's Donna Carson, Serenity's personal assistant. She said that Serenity would be out of town part of the week as well, but Donna assured me that between the two of them, they'd look in on Mimi and make sure she was okay.

"So the next day when I arrived in Frankfurt I called Serenity's office. She wasn't in—she was doing a spa week down in Tucson somewhere—but Donna said they'd both been stopping by to see Mimi. Donna said that when she was there yesterday morning, everything was fine and it didn't look like the car had been moved. She's the one who suggested I call the cops."

"Did you?"

"Yes, of course I did, but the guy I talked to wasn't very sympathetic. He kept hinting around that maybe Mimi had left on her own because I was some kind of heavy-handed bozo. Stuff like, was it possible that Mimi had taken off because I was giving her too hard a time? He made it sound like maybe she was the victim of domestic violence or something. That made me mad as hell. I finally hung up on the guy. After I got off the phone with him, I started calling hospitals—every single hospital here in the Valley, including this one, but they all told me the same thing. None of them had a patient named Mimi Cooper.

"Making those calls took the better part of an hour. About the time I finished was when I finally noticed that the painting was gone. I doubt it was stolen because, as far as I can tell, nothing else is missing. Still, I thought I should call the cops back and let them know about it, just in case it had been stolen."

"Did you?" Sister Anselm asked.

"Yes, but that time the jerk detective I had spoken to earlier was busy or on a break or something. I ended up talking to someone else, a woman. She took down the information about the painting. She also seemed to really listen to everything I said. She's the one who mentioned the incident in Camp Verde last night. Once I heard that an unidentified, critically injured woman had been brought here from the fire, it was like an alarm went off in my heart. I'm sure it's Mimi. It has to be."

"Does your wife have any connection to Camp Verde?" Sister Anselm asked.

"None at all," Hal answered decisively. "As far as I know she's never set foot in the place, and why on earth would she go there at night? She hates going out at night, even when I'm driving, because the glare from the headlights bothers her eyes. Even so, I have a feeling this has to be her. Now please let me see her."

Sister Anselm leaned over and placed a quieting hand on his shoulder. "I know you're anxious and upset right now, and I don't blame you. This woman may well turn out to be your wife, but she's asleep right now. You can't see her."

"Couldn't I look in on her even if she's asleep?" Hal argued. "I promise I won't be a bother. If it's not Mimi, I'll just walk away, and if it is . . ."

His voice faded into silence. He sat there shaking his head as he contemplated two appalling alternatives.

Patiently Sister Anselm explained the realities of the HIPAA regulations, including the fact that only visitors expressly authorized by the patient would be allowed access. These rules were clearly news to Hal Cooper, and, just as clearly, Sister Anselm had no intention of bending them.

"What can you tell me about your wife?" Sister Anselm's question gently but firmly changed the subject. "How old is she?"

"Seventy-one, but she doesn't look a day over sixty," Hal declared. "Some people might say she's frail, but she's not. She's tiny. Size six."

"Does she have any distinguishing features?"

"When cops ask that question, they're usually asking about scars or tattoos—that kind of thing," Hal said. "Believe me, Mimi wouldn't have a tattoo if her life depended on it, but she does have a mole on her left shoulder—on the back of her left shoulder."

Ali noted the small frown that flitted briefly across Sister Anselm's face, as though the presence of the mole said something to her—something important. While the nun said nothing, Hal rushed on.

"Dental records?" Sister Anselm asked.

"I can get those for you with no problem. Her dentist is in Scottsdale. Mimi's had a couple of implants, but they're mostly her own teeth."

"Could you tell what clothing she might have been wearing?"

"No. She has three closets full of clothing. No way for me to tell that. But I do know about her jewelry. She had two diamond rings, one on each hand. The big one she called her no-divorce ring, or else her no-promises-kept ring. That's Mimi's sense of humor, by the way. That one is a two-carat rock. She was thinking about divorcing her first husband. Before she had a chance to call it quits, he died on her. She told me she made out far better as a widow than she would have as a divorcée. The other one, the smaller one, is the one I gave her a year ago when we got married."

Hal broke off. His lips trembled. He cleared his throat and pawed at his eyes with the back of his hand. "A year next Tuesday," he added. "We got married in San Francisco at a park overlooking the Golden Gate Bridge. With the surgery coming up, I figured we'd take an anniversary trip back there after she'd had a chance to recover."

Ali had noticed that in the beginning James's family members had tuned in and listened avidly to what Hal Cooper had to say. Now, though, losing interest in someone else's drama, they were back to focusing on their own issues and squabbling among themselves. As Hal paused momentarily to regain control, Ali's fingers sped over the keyboard, catching up with the last of both Sister Anselm's questions and Hal's answers.

Thank you, Miss Willis, she thought.

Miss Augusta Willis had been Ali's typing teacher at Cottonwood's Mingus Union High, where, during her junior year, Ali had been one of only two students to achieve the coveted seventy-five words per minute that made for an A in Typing II.

"Where did you say you live?" Sister Anselm asked.

"Fountain Hills. Northeast of Scottsdale. It's a very safe neighborhood. At least it's supposed to be safe. That's what the Realtor told us when we bought the place."

"There was no sign of a break-in?"

"No," Hal said. "No forced entry. Nothing like that."

"Do you have an alarm?"

"We have one, but Mimi doesn't like turning it on.

A couple of times the alarm got tripped by accident. That turned into a big hassle."

"But if the painting was valuable—" Sister Anselm began.

"I'm really not worried about the painting," he interrupted. "It's a watercolor, but it's ugly as all get-out. It looks like one of my grandmother's old patchwork quilts. Donna didn't know if Mimi had decided to sell it. Or if she knows, she wouldn't say. For all I know, Serenity may have already located a buyer, not that she'd tell me about it. As far as she's concerned, her mother's art collection is none of my business."

"I take it you and Mimi's daughter don't get along very well," Sister Anselm concluded.

"With Serenity? Are you kidding? Except for Donna, her P.A., no one gets along with Serenity. She doesn't get along with me, not with her brother, and not with her mother, either. Especially not her mother. Her dearly departed daddy could do no wrong, but everyone else comes up short in her book. At the time we got married, Mimi worried that the kids might be a problem. I thought, *How bad could it be?* Turns out Mimi was right. Serenity has been badmouthing me to anyone who will listen. Despite her name, she specializes in creating discord."

So Mimi Cooper's relatives aren't that much different from James's, Ali thought.

"The name on Serenity's birth certificate is listed as Sandra Jean," Hal continued. "With her father's approval and help, she went to court and changed it on the day she turned eighteen. Why wouldn't she? Anything that came from her mother, including her name, is automatically suspect. I've mostly tried to stay out of her way and not rock the boat. I thought long and hard before I called her to lend a hand while I was gone this last time, but with the surgery coming up and since Mimi's her mother . . ." He shrugged and sighed. "That's what I did—I called."

"You didn't call her son?" Sister Anselm asked.

"There's no point. For one thing, Winston Junior lives in California. He couldn't have afforded to come look after his mom. He's gone through a whole series of sales jobs in the last few years. He's working again now, but they're just barely making ends meet. His wife, Amy, is pregnant. The two of them would be out on the street if Mimi hadn't taken pity on them. They live rent-free in a town house Mimi owns in California. Mimi asked Serenity to put him in charge of the Langley Gallery in Santa Barbara, but Serenity wouldn't hear of it. Fortunately he found work some-where else."

Suddenly the pieces all came together in Ali's head as the names finally registered. Winston Langley Gal-leries. She remembered Winston Langley Sr. as some-one whose path she had crossed occasionally during her time in California. Langley had been a strikingly handsome man with a high-flying art gallery empire that included branch galleries in Santa Barbara, Palm Springs, Scottsdale, Santa Fe, and Sedona.

Hal had already mentioned that Mimi had been estranged from her husband at the time of his death. Ali seemed to recall that Winston Langley had died several years earlier, and that his death had been sud-den—from a heart attack, or maybe a stroke. Now it looked to Ali as though, after Winston Senior's death, his widow had taken up with a much younger man.

No wonder her kids were annoyed about Hal Cooper. It seemed likely that he wasn't much older than his stepchildren.

Ali also remembered what Sister Anselm had said about the estrangements in families that made showing up in a hospital injured and alone somehow more likely. From the sound of it, the Cooper/Langley entourage was suitably screwed up. If the patient in room 814 did turn out to be Hal's wife, Sister Anselm would have some relationship healing to do here as well.

Ali's phone rang just then. Taking her hands from the keyboard, she checked the readout. Caller ID said it was Holly Mesina returning her call. "I can't talk right now," she said abruptly into the phone. "I'll have to call you back."

"But—" Holly began.

Ali simply ended the call. As she put her phone away, she heard the buzzing sound of Sister Anselm's alarm— the one that gave her a readout of the patient's vitals.

"I'm sorry," she said, standing up. "I need to tend to my patient. If she's willing to see you, I'll come back and get you."

"If she's awake, can't I see her now?"

"No," Sister Anselm said. "Not yet. Not until I check with her. Sorry."

As she walked down the hallway toward the room, Hal Cooper turned to Ali. Evidently the sound of her tapping on the keyboard had penetrated his consciousness.

"You can type like crazy," he said. "What are you doing, writing a book?"

Ali was taken aback by his scrutiny. She didn't want to lie, but she couldn't very well be honest, either.

"Something like that," she said.

"So you're here with someone, too?"

Same person you're here for, she thought.

"No," she said, thinking on her feet. "I'm doing a special project. For the burn unit."

If he had asked more questions, Ali wasn't sure she would have been able to answer, but it turned out Hal Cooper was only interested in his own sad story and not in anyone else's.

"I just wish Mimi would have taken my phone calls while I was gone," Hal said, talking more to himself than to anyone else. "That way I would have known what was going on with her. I know why it happened. Mimi spent thirty-five years being bossed around by her first husband. When I told her not to drive, she went ballistic. In a way I don't blame her, but what will I do if the last memory I have of the two of us together is of standing in the middle of the kitchen yelling at each other?"

With that he buried his face in his hands and began to sob. Just then the elevator door opened and Dave Holman stepped into the waiting room. He stood for a second surveying the room. Then, without so much as a glance in Ali's direction, he stepped up to Hal Cooper and opened his ID wallet.

"Mr. Cooper?" he asked when Hal finally removed his hands from his face long enough to notice the pair of shoes standing in front of him. "I'm Detective Dave Holman with the Yavapai County Sheriff's Department. I'm here about your missing persons report. Could I have a word?"

Hal Cooper looked up at him gratefully. "I'm glad to know that someone else is worried about it, too—that I'm not the only one. Of course you can have a word."

Dave looked around the room. Again his eyes passed over Ali with no sign of recognition. The rest of the people in the room had fallen silent as all of them paid attention to this new arrival.

"Maybe we could go down the hall to someplace a little more private," Dave suggested.

Hal immediately nixed that idea. "I'm not leaving here," he said. "Not until I know for sure if my wife is in that room down the hall."

"For privacy's sake—"

"I don't need privacy," Hal declared. "I need to know that my wife is okay. If you want to talk with me, talk here. Otherwise, go away and leave me alone."

Shaking his head, Dave pocketed his ID, then pulled up a chair and sat down.

She fought her way back through the flames. Even in the dream, she knew if she could get back somehow, the room would be there waiting for her with the odd but reassuring steady beep of all those machines that told her she wasn't dead.

She was grateful to know she was still alive, and she hoped that the nun would be there, too. The nun with the magic finger that could press the button and take away the pain, the pain that was even now howling at her. Screaming at her. And she would have been screaming, too, if it hadn't been for the ventilator. That's what it was called, she realized. The thing in her throat that made it so she couldn't speak was a ventilator.

But where was the nun? The woman with a face that was stern and calm and kind. Maybe this time, Sister Anselm wouldn't be here. Maybe this time she wasn't aware that her help was needed, but it was. The pain was roaring back, overwhelming her.

Just then Sister Anselm's steadying face reappeared over the bed, filling the patient with a sense of wonder. Was she an answer to a prayer? How did she know she was needed? What made her come into view at just the right time? Maybe she didn't go away at all. Maybe she was there in the room the whole time, close but somewhere out of sight.

This time, though, Sister Anselm didn't push the button, not right away.

"Does the name Mimi Cooper mean anything to you?" she asked urgently. "Blink once for yes and twice for no."

She tried to gather her thoughts. She tried to concentrate on the name. Mimi Cooper. Was that who she was? Was it possible she was that woman? But the name didn't seem familiar to her. Not at all. There was no part of the name Mimi that resonated in her head. Shouldn't your name go with you no matter what? Isn't that the one thing about yourself that you would always know and remember? Well, maybe not if you had that disease, that old people's disease—what was it called again? She couldn't remember the name of that, either, even though it was right on the tip of—well, not on the tip of her tongue. Because she couldn't talk.

"Blink once for yes and twice for no," Sister Anselm commanded.

She blinked twice. The name Mimi meant nothing to her. She couldn't be a Mimi. That sounded like a silly name. A stupid name. Surely that wasn't hers.

Sister Anselm was speaking again. "There's a man outside," she said. "A man who thinks he know you.

He says his name is Hal Cooper. Do you know him? Blink once for yes. Twice for no."

I'm not stupid! she wanted to shout. *I know the code. You don't have to keep telling me over and over.*

"Do you know him?" Sister Anselm insisted.

I don't know. Maybe. Maybe that name sounds familiar even if Mimi doesn't, but I'm not sure. How can I be sure?

She blinked several times in rapid succession. That was part of the code, too. Many blinks for "I have no idea."

"He would like to see you," Sister Anselm said. "So he can know for sure, but I'll only allow him to come into your room if you want to see him. You don't have to. You're under no obligation."

Someone wants to see me? Someone who thinks he knows me? What do I look like? I must look awful. I know I look awful. My hair isn't combed. Do I even have hair? She would have touched her head to check, but of course she couldn't move her hands.

"Blink once for yes, twice for no," Sister Anselm commanded.

She thought about that while trying to hold the pain at bay. She wanted to beg the nun to push the button and send her back into oblivion, but another part of her wanted to know.

If this man knows who I am, if he can give me back my name, I need to know that, too.

It took an extraordinary effort on her part. She had to battle back at the pain and concentrate long and hard before she was finally able to blink. Once only.

Once for yes.

{ CHAPTER 11 }

Dave pulled a waiting room chair close to Hal. Then he removed a tiny tape recorder from his pocket, switched it on, and placed it on a nearby table.

"I'll need to ask you a few questions," he said. "In case the woman down the hall does turn out to be your wife."

"Sure," Hal said. "I'll answer any questions you want. Whatever you need."

The teenagers seated nearby were transfixed by this process, but Ali knew what was going on. As long as Hal hadn't been identified as an official suspect, Dave was free to ask him anything he wanted without having to read the man his rights. That would change if, at a later time, Hal Cooper was moved onto the list of declared suspects. At that point, he would be read his rights, and any statements made in the course of any "official" interview would be checked for consistency with this first, presumably "unofficial" one.

Ali understood that was the basic premise behind all interrogations. Crooks lie, and catching them in a small lie often leads to catching them in bigger ones. Damning ones.

For her part, Ali continued to listen in on the conversation, all the while tapping away on her keyboard, taking notes for her own benefit as well as for Sister Anselm's.

Initially, during their first few minutes together, the information Hal Cooper gave Dave was much the same as he had given Sister Anselm earlier. He did, however, add a few embellishments, including the fact that, at age fifty-six, he was fifteen years younger than his wife.

That detail caught Ali's attention. *He's as much younger than Mimi as B. is younger than I am,* she thought.

"You want to hear something funny? It's how Mimi and I met," Hal admitted. "She bought me at an auction."

"Excuse me?" Dave asked.

"It was a charity bachelor auction to benefit the symphony two years ago last spring," Hal explained. "It was a big, splashy event. Mimi was one of the cochairs. It was her first big social venture out after her first husband died. She bought me for top dollar, thinking she'd found a foolproof way of fixing her daughter up with somebody nice."

"I take it that didn't work out too well?" Dave asked.

Hal laughed aloud at that comment. "Are you kidding? Serenity despised me on sight. She told her mother that airline pilots were nothing but a bunch of glorified bus drivers. She also said that I was way too old for her. Mimi told her, 'Well, he looks pretty good to me. If you won't go out with him, I will. I paid a lot of money for him, and for a donated dinner at Vincent's, and I'm not going to waste either one.'"

"So you ended up with the mother instead of the daughter?" Dave asked.

"Yup," Hal said. "Mimi and I went out on the charity date, and then we went out again. We had one great time and then another. The rest is history. Next week we'll be celebrating our first anniversary. It's great for us, but maybe not so great for her kids, for her son and daughter, Winston Langley Junior and Serenity. They both think I'm far too old for Serenity but much too young for their mother. They think I'm some gigolo type who came sniffing around after Mimi's money, but that's not it at all. Never was. I love her."

"It's safe to assume you're not on good terms with either of Mimi's kids?"

"No. Not especially."

"How would the children fare as far as their mother's estate is concerned if Mimi were to predecease you?"

Hal gave Dave an appraising look. "Before Mimi and I got married, I volunteered to sign a prenup. I've been an airline pilot for years. I'm not exactly on poverty row, so I thought a prenup between us might settle some of Serenity's hash, but Mimi wouldn't hear of it. She told me, 'I spent thirty-five years putting up with Winston Langley's womanizing shenanigans. The kids got their fair share of their father's estate, but I paid for mine the hard way—by being married to the bastard. I don't tell them what they should or shouldn't do with their money, and I'll be damned if Serenity or Junior is going to tell me what to do with mine.' Those may not be her exact words, but you get the idea."

Dave nodded. "In other words, if your wife dies first, you'd be her primary beneficiary."

"Correct," Hal answered. "The only beneficiary. When I die, whatever's left after that goes to her kids in equal shares, but you need to know Mimi's money isn't what I wanted, and it's not what I want now. I'm hoping and praying that I'll be able to get my wife back someday, alive and well."

"Of course," Dave said soothingly. "I understand."

Sitting and listening, however, Ali wasn't convinced Dave was buying Hal's story, and his next question confirmed that opinion.

"When did you leave town again?" Dave asked.

Hal would have to have been dumb as a stump not to realize that he was already under suspicion, stated or not, but he answered readily enough, repeating much of what he had already told Sister Anselm about his being out of town. It seemed to Ali that Hal Cooper was being cooperative and more than forthcoming, but she also realized, as Dave did, that when a wealthy woman became a victim of foul play, most of the time a greedy husband turned out to be the culprit.

Sister Anselm emerged from room 814. Hal rose and hurried toward her. "Will she see me?"

"Yes," the nun said with a nod. "She will, if now is a good time."

Hal Cooper breathed a relieved sigh while Dave switched off the recorder.

"She's awake at the moment," Sister Anselm told him. "She's due more pain meds very soon, so I'm afraid if this is Mimi, you won't have much time."

Nodding in agreement, Hal started for the door, but Sister Anselm stopped him before he could enter.

"I must warn you, Mr. Cooper," the nun cautioned.

"This woman has been severely injured. Even if she turns out to be your wife, she may not recognize you."

Hal stopped abruptly. "Are you saying Mimi may not know who I am?"

Sister Anselm nodded. "That's correct. She's suffering from some degree of amnesia. She's also on a ventilator due to smoke inhalation. If you try speaking to her, you need to know that she won't be able to respond in anything other than yes or no answers. One blink for yes; two for no."

"All right then—"

"One more thing," Sister Anselm interrupted. "Have you ever been around a patient who has suffered major burn injuries?"

"No, but—"

"Do you play poker, Mr. Cooper?"

"Some," he said, frowning at her. "Why would you ask that?"

"Because I'm hoping you'll be able to put on a poker face. What you'll be seeing in that room will be nothing short of shocking. If this is Mimi, she's not the same woman you left behind a week ago. Up to now, I don't think she's given much thought as to how she looks, but it's important that when you see her, you try to hold your reactions in check."

Hal paled a little and swallowed hard. "Don't worry about me," he said. "I was in the military. No matter what, I'll be fine."

"Excellent," Sister Anselm said briskly. "I'm glad to hear it. Come along."

Once again the pain was swirling around her. It was too much. She couldn't stand it. Couldn't bear it.

Where was the button? And where the hell was that nun? Why didn't Sister Anselm come? Wasn't she supposed to be here? Wasn't that her job?

Suddenly she was aware of some other presence beside her bed. Not Sister Anselm. Not one of the nurses. Someone else was standing there next to her. Then a face appeared above hers—a man's face, contorted with something that was half sob and half smile.

"Hello, there, honey bun," he managed. His voice shook as he spoke. Tears sprang from his eyes. "How's my Mimi girl?"

Suddenly, over the pain and somehow above it, she heard the words and recognized the gentle voice. She knew the grayish-blue eyes peering down at her, and the strained features on his shockingly pale face.

Hal! she thought. *He's found me at last. He's here!*

Just as suddenly she felt overjoyed. She knew Hal's name. She recognized his face. At least she remembered that much.

"Sorry," he muttered. "That wasn't a yes or no question. I can see how you are. You're hurt, damn it. Do you know who I am?"

Yes! One blink. One very long blink.

"Do you know I love you?"

Another blink. *Yes, I do know.*

Then she heard Sister Anselm's voice speaking to both of them as if from a great distance.

"You look a bit pale, Mr. Cooper. Are you sure you're all right? If you need to sit down or go back outside . . ."

"No," he answered. "I'm fine. I'll stay."

Hal didn't sound fine at all but the soft cotton cloud was already descending around her.

Mimi. He called me Mimi! The name still seemed strange and foreign somehow, and she regarded it with no little astonishment. *If Mimi really is my name, how could I have forgotten it?*

She tried to fight the cloud, but Sister Anselm had already pushed the button. She wanted the pain to go away, but she didn't want to fall asleep again.

I want to be here, she thought. *I want to be here with Hal. I want to be able to see his face and hear his voice. I want to know that when I open my eyes, he'll be here beside me. I want to know that he won't go away and leave me again. I want him here. With me.*

Even as she formed those thoughts, she was already drifting away from him, slipping away into some other space and time, but this time she was able to pick out a few details in the room that she hadn't noticed before. The walls of the room were very white, and she was surprised to see that on the wall above his shoulder was a simple wooden cross.

Has that cross been hanging here the whole time? she wondered. *If so, why didn't I see it before?*

Much closer at hand, she studied Hal's face. He looked incredibly tired—as though he hadn't slept for days. His cheek was rough—covered with a five o'clock shadow of stubble. That wasn't at all like him. Then, as she watched, a solitary tear coursed down his cheek and dripped off his chin.

He looks awful, she thought. *Why is he crying? Doesn't he know how glad I am to see him? Why doesn't he ask me that? Am I glad?*

Oh, yes. Please ask me. One blink for yes.

He leaned over her. He was wearing one of those paper gowns like the one Sister Anselm wore. It rustled when he moved.

"I'm right here," he said. "I won't leave. I promise."

Those words were like a balm to her tortured soul. She could feel herself sliding steadily into unconsciousness, but this time no flames awaited. The air around her was soft and moist and cool. For a disorienting moment she couldn't imagine where she was. She noticed there was grass underfoot and fog all around, wrapping them both in an eerie embrace. In the distance she heard the sound of a foghorn.

The foghorn. Of course. In San Francisco. How could she have forgotten that? Where they had stood on a hillside in front of the justice of the peace and said they would be together, loving and honoring each other, in sickness and health, until death do us part.

"Go to sleep, Mimi," he whispered hoarsely. "I'll be right here."

The next blast of the foghorn was followed by another sound—the disturbing sound of a grown man weeping.

"Come, Mr. Cooper," Sister Anselm said several minutes later. "You really shouldn't stay here much longer. We should go now, and let her sleep. Leave me a number. If you're not in the waiting room, I'll call you when she's waking up so you can be here when she does."

As Hal Cooper left the waiting room, Dave turned to Ali. "Wait a minute," he said in a performance worthy of an Academy Award. "Don't I know you? Didn't we have an art history class together at ASU a few years ago?"

This was nothing short of an outrageous lie, since Ali Reynolds had never set foot on the Arizona State University campus. Obviously Dave had known who Ali was all along, but he had been careful not to show it

"Yes," she said, smiling back at him, holding out her hand and carrying her own part of the charade. "Cecelia McCann," she said. "How nice to see you again."

"Dave," he answered. "Dave Holman. Yavapai County Sheriff's Department. How about you?"

"I'm a consultant," she said quickly. "Doing a project for the hospital."

He gave her a quick wink, one that she hoped none of the other people in the room noticed.

Ali wondered how long she and Dave and Sister Anselm could keep up the fiction that they knew one another but didn't have a close working relationship.

The elevator door opened and a woman stepped into the room. She was blond, mid-thirties, and definitely dressed for success. She stopped and surveyed the waiting room before going over to the nurses' station. "My name is Donna Carson," she said. "I'm looking for Hal Cooper."

Ah-ha, Ali thought. *The daughter's personal assistant.*

There was an attendant behind the desk, someone who hadn't been privy to all the earlier discussions

"I'm sorry," she said at once. "We don't have anyone here by that name."

"He's a visitor, not a patient," Donna said impatiently. "He came to see about his wife."

One of the lolling teenagers spoke up. "That guy's down the hall," he explained. "Visiting in one of the rooms."

"Which one? I need to talk to him."

"Are you a relative?" the attendant asked.

"No, but—"

"Only authorized relatives are allowed access to the patients' rooms. You'll have to take a seat."

"It is his wife, then?" Donna asked. "It is Mimi Cooper?"

The attendant didn't budge. "I'm not at liberty to disclose any information whatsoever," she said. "If you'll be good enough to sit down—"

"But I spoke to Mimi's daughter, Serenity Langley. She sent me here to find out what's going on," Donna argued. "If her mother has been injured, I need to let her know."

"Please," the attendant said. "I'm sure you'll know in good time."

That response evidently wasn't good enough. Donna had already punched a button and was holding the phone to her ear.

"The people who work here won't tell me anything, not a word," she whined into the phone when someone answered.

A few of James's relatives had decamped for the evening, leaving behind a couple of unoccupied chairs. Donna Carson chose one of those and dropped into it.

"One of the other visitors told me that Hal is here right now. He's in one of the rooms, but they won't tell me which one. I'm guessing that means it's bad news. Yes," she added after a pause. "You'd probably better head home. I'm at Saint Gregory's. On the eighth floor, in the burn unit. Do you want me to call your brother? Okay. It's probably better if you do that, and if I happen to see Cooper, I'll let him know you're on your way."

Just then the door to room 814 opened and Sister

Anselm emerged, leading a sobbing Hal Cooper. Dave left Ali behind and hurried to meet them. "It's her?" he asked.

Hal nodded wordlessly.

"Perhaps you'd be so good as to come with me, Mr. Cooper," Dave said, taking Hal by the arm and leading him toward the elevator. "We need to put you in touch with investigators from the ATF, and from the marshal's office in Fountain Hills. We're all going to need to ask you some questions."

Donna jumped up and hurried over to them. "Is it Mimi?" she wanted to know. "Is she going to be all right?"

Hal shook his head numbly. "I don't know," he managed. "It's too soon to tell."

"Are you saying she's going to die?" Donna sounded stunned.

Before Hal could say anything more, the elevator door closed.

Dave and Hal disappeared. Once the door shut, Donna again opened her phone and dialed.

"It is your mother," she confirmed when someone answered. "She's here in the burn unit at Saint Gregory's in Phoenix. Yes, the one on Camelback. You'd better get here as soon as you can." There was a pause. "How bad is it?" Donna Carson shook her head. "I don't know, but I'd say it's pretty bad."

Across the room Ali opened her phone and sent a text message to Sheriff Maxwell.

> Victim IDed. Mimi Cooper. Dave is taking the husband to meet with ATF and Fountain Hills marshals.

Sheriff Maxwell's response came back in less than a minute.

> Good work. Richard Donnelley's gonna crap his britches over that one. I don't think the agent in charge will like being showed up like that. They'll need to do a crime scene investigation in Fountain Hills. Does that nun still need you?

Ali looked up. Down the hall, Sister Anselm was standing at her favorite window, looking out at the nighttime city. Without responding to the sheriff's message, Ali sent a text message to her.

> Can we talk?

Sister Anselm glanced at her phone. Then, smiling, she beckoned for Ali to join her at the window.

"Sheriff Maxwell was just asking me if I thought you still needed me."

"Oh, yes," Sister Anselm said. "I certainly need you here tomorrow."

Ali nodded. "All right. I'll be here. But did she recognize her husband?"

"Absolutely," Sister Anselm said. "Her response to him was a wonder to behold. She's resting more peacefully now than she has all day."

"She still doesn't know who's responsible for setting her on fire?" Ali asked.

"No, and just because Mimi was glad to see Mr. Cooper doesn't mean he had nothing to do with all this. I intend to keep a close eye on him."

Which meant, Ali concluded, that Sister Anselm didn't trust the man and was unprepared to leave Hal Cooper alone with his injured wife.

Ali was about to text a response to Sheriff Maxwell when her phone rang. A glance at caller ID told her that this wasn't the sheriff calling back. It was Athena.

"My daughter-in-law," Ali explained to Sister Anselm. "She's in town and was hoping we could get together."

"Of course," Sister Anselm said. "I think things are under control for tonight."

"You'll call if you need me?"

"Absolutely."

By then Ali's phone had stopped ringing, so she punched Redial. "Sorry I couldn't answer before. I'm leaving the hospital right now. Where are you?"

"At the apartment," Athena said. "Just off Apache in Tempe."

It sounded like Athena was sniffling. June in Phoenix was hardly the time to come down with a cold or sinus infection. Ali wondered if she had been crying.

"What about grabbing something to eat? I'm starving," Ali said. "Do you want to meet me somewhere?"

"Not really," Athena said. "I'd rather you came here."

Ali's gut gave an ominous twist. Athena Reynolds was boundlessly enthusiastic, and always ready for whatever. This didn't sound like her.

"Tell you what," Ali said. "I'll pick up something on the way. Give me your address so I can program it into the GPS."

On her way down to the hospital lobby, Ali called her hotel, spoke to room service, and asked them to box up some food—fries and two burgers—that she could take with her. At the hotel, she left the car in the driveway and hurried upstairs to shed the red wig.

Ali knew instinctively that whatever was going on

between Athena and Chris needed to be handled by Ali Reynolds rather than Cecelia McCann.

The Desert Dunes apartment complex had little to recommend it other than its proximity to the ASU campus. It was a grim-looking three-story place built around a courtyard with a few scraggly palm trees for landscaping. It looked as though the courtyard might once have included a pool. That was gone, filled in and covered over by a tiny basketball court where no one was shooting hoops through baskets missing their nets.

Ali followed Athena's directions up two flights of stairs and down a long breezeway—a breezeway with no breeze on this hot summer night. The doorbell outside apartment 310 was covered with a three-by-five card reading *Out of Order,* so Ali knocked on the metal hollow-core door. Seconds later, Athena flung the door open.

Ali could tell at a glance that her earlier assumption was correct. Athena had been crying.

"I come bearing food," Ali said, presenting Athena with the room-service burgers.

"Come in," Athena said. With a notable lack of enthusiasm she took the bag and ushered Ali into the room. "It's not much, but it's cheap, and we're only here for summer session."

Surprisingly enough, the apartment was nicer inside than Ali would have expected. Someone—maybe an assistant professor rather than a grad student—had gone to the trouble of assembling a collection of good-quality secondhand furniture. Nothing matched, but the chairs covered with faded chintz were comfortable, and the end tables and bookshelves were sturdy if old-fashioned. The artwork on the walls was anything but old-fashioned. The unframed canvases provided explosions of splashy color on the otherwise landlord-bland taupe interior.

"Art student?" Ali asked.

Athena nodded on her way toward the galley kitchen. While Athena busied herself with setting out plates and glassware on the fifties-era Formica tabletop, Ali forced herself to take a seat and keep her mouth shut. She was dying to ask what the problem was, but she knew she needed to let Athena tell her at her own speed.

"I'm pregnant," Athena said bluntly, once they were seated.

I'm pregnant, Ali noted. *Not we're pregnant.*

Still, of all the news Athena might have given her, news of an expected grandchild was something Ali welcomed wholeheartedly.

"That's wonderful," she said. "I'm thrilled. What does Chris think?"

"I haven't exactly told him," Athena admitted.

"Why not?" Ali asked. "It's his baby, too."

"We didn't plan on getting pregnant," Athena said. "At least not so soon. Actually, I didn't expect to get pregnant at all, but I got careless. I forgot a couple of pills. Now this has happened, and I don't know what to do."

Ali was mystified. Surely Athena wasn't thinking about having an abortion.

"You're married," Ali said quietly. "You and Chris love each other. You tell him you're pregnant, and the two of you deal with it together. What's so hard about that?"

"My father never wanted me to join the military," Athena said.

This seemed like changing the subject, but Ali suspected it wasn't. "So?"

"And when I got hurt, he said I'd wrecked his chances of being a grandfather. That since I was a cripple, even if I had a baby, how would I take care of one with this?"

Athena held up her prosthetic arm and hand and stared at them as though she'd never seen them before. Ali understood that there must be a lot more to the story than what she'd heard so far. For one thing, Athena's parents hadn't come to the wedding. As far as Ali knew they had been invited but had declined to attend.

"Your father called you that?" Ali asked. "A cripple? Sounds like he doesn't know you very well. It sounds to me as though he's the one who's decided to take a pass on the grandfather bit."

"What if he's right?" Athena murmured. "Maybe I *am* a cripple. How do I hold a baby with this? How do I change one?"

"Wait a minute," Ali said. "You're tough enough to go to war in Iraq, tough enough to almost die from an IED, tough enough to live through Walter Reed and do all the rehab, and you're tough enough to spend all day, every day teaching high school kids. You expect me to believe that you're scared of changing a baby?"

"Not just changing it," Athena said. "Feeding it, bathing it. I just keep thinking of all the things mothers do—all the things mothers have to do. What if I can't do them? What if my child grows up thinking his mother's a freak?"

"But you *are* a freak," Ali said with a reassuring smile. "You play basketball, and you're evidently very good at it, even one-handed."

"That's not what I mean," Athena said.

"Kids always think their parents are freaks," Ali said. "For instance, Chris thought I was a freak because I was on TV. As far as he knew, none of the other mothers did that."

Athena, staring at her untouched hamburger, said nothing.

"Is this why you called off the trip to Minnesota?" Ali asked.

"Yes," Athena said. "I told Chris I'm not ready to deal with my parents yet, and it's true. I'm not."

"Look," Ali said. "I get it that you don't have perfect parents. Nobody has perfect parents, but I can tell you from personal experience that throwing a grandchild into the mix can help resolve a lot of old, lingering problems. Look what happened with me and Chris's other grandparents at the wedding. As I recall, you're the one who made that happen."

"Yes, but . . ."

"But what?"

"Those were Chris's relatives, not mine, so it wasn't as big a deal for me. My parents are a big deal. Besides, what if they're right, and I'm not cut out to be a mother?"

"Because of your missing hand and leg," Ali asked, "or is it for some other reason that you're not mentioning?"

Again Athena said nothing. For almost a minute she and Ali sat in silence at the table while their untouched hamburgers turned stone-cold.

"Look," Ali said finally. "I can tell you there hasn't ever been a woman who found out she was pregnant who didn't worry about being up to the task, but Athena, I happen to know *you* are. You and Chris together will be great parents. If he somehow thinks he's got a pass from changing poopy diapers, then I'll be happy to set him straight. And if I can't make a believer of him, my parents will."

"You think it will be all right then?" Athena asked uncertainly.

"It'll be more than all right," Ali said. "It's going to be wonderful. Yes, I know bringing home a new little baby and having its health and well-being entirely on your shoulders is scary. Tiny babies and grown ones, too, require a lot of care, but you'll grow into the job as the baby grows. So will Chris."

"Even with this?" Again, Athena held up her prosthetic hand.

Ali had always been impressed by Athena's determination to never let her missing limbs keep her from doing anything she wanted to do. Yet the daunting prospect of caring for a baby seemed to be more than she could handle. Ali was touched that Athena had come to her looking for reassurance.

"Until the baby is born," Ali went on, "yours is the voice that child will hear and know—your heartbeat, your breathing. Kids are adaptable. They love the people who love them. They love what's familiar. Someday this child may notice that other kids' mothers have two arms, but as far as this little kid is concerned—as far as *your* little kid is concerned—mothers with two arms will be the odd ones out."

"So you think I should call Chris?" Athena asked.

"Over the telephone? Of course not. You don't have classes in the morning, and if you leave now, you can be home in two hours. Go home and tell Chris this wonderful news. Celebrate this miracle in person and together."

"You're sure?" Athena asked.

Ali laughed aloud. "Yes, I'm sure. And once Chris knows, you'd better be sure everyone else knows as well—my parents; Chris's other grandparents; your grandmother; and, yes, your parents, too. Uncancel that airline cancellation, Athena," Ali advised. "Go to Minnesota after all, sooner rather than later. Who knows? Maybe your father will change his stripes and stop being such a jackass."

For the first time, Athena smiled. "I doubt that," she said.

"Try it," Ali said. "He might just surprise you."

{ CHAPTER 12 }

Upon returning to the hotel, Ali fell into bed. The idea of being a grandmother thrilled her. The only thing that saddened her was that Dean hadn't lived to see the arrival of this new person and to watch him or her grow into adulthood.

Ali was glad it was far too late to call her parents. Otherwise she might have been tempted, but this was Chris and Athena's news to deliver, and they were the ones who needed to do the telling.

Ali fell asleep almost instantly. When she woke up at six-thirty the next morning, she bounded out of bed with a happy heart. Yes, she had to go to the hospital, where people were dealing with life-and-death matters, but for right now, Ali's cup was brimming.

Not so her suitcase. The other clothing Leland had packed for her was more formal than the jogging suit, and she knew it wouldn't blend into the burn-unit waiting room background. Instead, Ali did a rerun of the pink jogging suit, topped off with her wig. Once dressed, she hurried down to the lobby to grab a cup of coffee. The temperature outside at this hour was

surprisingly pleasant—cool enough that she decided
to leave the car where it was and walk to the hospital.

On the eighth floor, Ali found the waiting room
area relatively quiet, and there were only two people
in the waiting room. James's father was dozing in a
chair. That most likely meant that his former wife
was in the room with their son. The only other occu-
pant was one of the teenagers, who had moved from
the middle of the room to one of the chairs, which
were now back in their original positions.

There was an attendant at the nurses' station. "Is
Sister Anselm here?" Ali asked.

"Yes," the woman said, "but she's currently unavail-
able. If you'll take a seat . . ."

Ali did so. A few moments later the teenager rose
to his feet, yawned, and stretched his lanky frame. "Is
that lady in room eight fourteen a friend of yours?" he
asked.

The kid was lean and tough and looked to be seventeen or eighteen years old. If Ali had met him on a dark
street, she might have been worried, but since he had
clearly spent the whole night in the waiting room, she
couldn't help being impressed by his apparent loyalty
to his injured friend.

"Sort of," Ali replied. "I know her."

"Her son got here a little while ago," the young man
volunteered. "He drove over from California last night,
and her daughter is here now, too. They just went
downstairs to get some breakfast."

Ali appreciated knowing that tidbit. "Thanks for the
info," she said. "What about her husband?"

The young man nodded. "He's still in the room,
along with that nun. He's been in there off and on most

of the night. The doctors came through on rounds a little while ago. Nobody else has been allowed inside."

The nurse had said Sister Anselm wasn't taking calls, but maybe texting was all right. Ali opened her phone and sent a message.

I'm back. Outside. In the w8ing rm.

Ali's phone rang before there was any chance of a text response. "Are you still down in Phoenix?" Edie Larson wanted to know.

"Yes, I am."

"I have some good news," Edie announced. Ali glanced at her watch. This was the time of day when her mother often made phone calls, after the Sugarloaf's baking was done and before the breakfast crowd descended.

Chris and Athena must have called her after all, Ali thought.

"I wanted to tell you about this yesterday," Edie continued, "but I didn't have a chance. You'll never guess who came in for lunch yesterday."

"You're right, Mom," Ali agreed. "I have no idea."

"Bryan Forester and those two adorable little girls of his," Edie replied. "And you won't believe who was with him."

Ali hadn't known Bryan's twin daughters, Lindsey and Lacy, until after their mother's brutal murder. Both of them were smart, blond, and cute, but in terms of personality, they were very different.

Lindsey was vivacious and talkative; her sister was quiet and withdrawn. Ali suspected that Lacy suffered from Asperger's syndrome. The child was shy to the point of being spookily quiet and was content to let her sister do most of the communicating. Lindsey was easygoing and impetuous, while Lacy was silently observant. No odd details escaped her attention. At the time of their mother's murder, Lacy had been the one who had noticed an out-of-place vehicle and remembered the license plate number. That had been the telling clue that had helped clear her father's name. Edie Larson had long since adjusted to the idea that if the twins came to the Sugarloaf, Lacy would need a separate plate for each kind of food, lest her hash browns, toast, bacon, and eggs somehow come in contact with one another.

Edie continued, "Mindy Farber, that's who. The four of them were all having a great time. In fact, I actually heard Lacy laugh out loud for the first time ever. I didn't know she could."

Mindy Farber had been one of Athena's roommates prior to the wedding. She had also been Lindsey and Lacy's second-grade teacher. At the time of their mother's murder, Mindy had come to the girls' rescue when their father was led off in the back of a patrol car.

"I'm glad to hear that," Ali said. "Glad to know they're having fun."

Ali knew that out of concern for his children, Bryan Forester had stayed in a loveless marriage for years before his wife's murder. Ali liked to think that in Mindy he might have found someone who was capable of loving him back.

"Mark my words," Edie said. "From the way they were all carrying on, I wouldn't be surprised if Mindy turns up sporting an engagement ring one of these days."

"I hope so," Ali said. "They're both nice people."

That was one of the things Ali loved about being

back in her hometown after years of exile—everybody knew everybody else. Most of the time that was comforting, but there were times when having everyone know everyone else's business drove her nuts. She knew that her off-again, on-again romance with Dave Holman had sparked plenty of gossip. And if she started going out with B. Simpson? Ali didn't even want to go there. People around town would have them engaged after one or two dates, which, now that she thought about it, might well be what was happening with Bryan Forester and Mindy Farber.

"So?" Edie asked impatiently, "what do you think?"

Ali's mind had been wandering. Since she hadn't been listening, her mother's question caught her off guard.

"Sorry, Mom," she said. "Something was going on at this end. I wasn't listening."

"For Father's Day," Edie said. "Do you think your dad would like one of those big gas barbecues, like the one Chris and Athena have?"

When Edie had hinted about this before, Ali had avoided taking a stand. Getting a barbecue outfit for a guy who cooked eight hours a day, seven days a week was a lot like getting a yard guy a new lawn mower.

Since Edie had asked directly, however, Ali felt obliged to answer. "I think he'd rather have a big-screen TV. Have you talked to him about it?"

"Of course not!" Edie returned indignantly. "It's supposed to be a surprise. If I have to ask him what he wants, it won't be."

Better to ask and get him the right thing than surprise him with something he doesn't want.

"Suit yourself, Mom," Ali said. "You know him better than anyone."

Except for the years Bob Larson had been in the service, Ali's parents had worked together behind the counter of the Sugarloaf Cafe for their entire adult lives. Part of that time, they had been in partnership with Edie's twin sister, Evelyn. With Aunt Evie gone now, it was just the two of them and a couple of long-term waitresses. During their many daily hours in and around the cafe's small but immaculate kitchen, they argued with each other often, but mostly without rancor. They also tended to finish each other's sentences. They knew each other about as well as two people could.

Ali's phone buzzed. A glance at the readout told her Dave was calling. "Mom," she said, "I have to go. I've got another call."

She switched over to the other line. "Hey, Dave." She had yet to open her briefcase, so she picked it up and carried it down the hallway so they could speak in relative privacy.

"Where are you?" he asked.

"Back at the hospital. I got here just a few minutes ago."

"How's it going?"

"Quiet so far," Ali said. "Sister Anselm's still in Mimi's room. So is Hal Cooper."

"What about Mimi's kids?" Dave asked. "Have either of them showed up?"

"Reportedly yes," Ali replied. "Both of them. I haven't seen them or spoken to them. I was told they're down at breakfast. What's going on with you?"

"I'm still here in Phoenix," he said. "I stayed at a Best Western, but I'm an employee rather than a consultant."

Ali ignored the dig. "How did the interview go?"

"With Hal? All right. When he started talking about Maggie, I thought at first she might be a girlfriend. Turns out she's a cockapoo. He had left her with a neighbor, but when I took him by the crime scene so he could pick up some clothes, he picked the dog up, as well. They're at the Ritz, too, since that's the hotel nearest the hospital."

"What did you think about him?" Ali asked.

"About him staying at the Ritz?"

"No, about whether he did this."

"He fielded questions from several of us all at once, and his story never wavered," Dave said. "He also provided plenty of documentation. The marshals are checking into those, and so far they all check out.

"Oh," Dave added, "I thought you'd want to know that we've located Mimi Cooper's car, or rather the highway patrol did. Her Infiniti was parked in a vacant lot just outside Gilbert with a *For Sale* sign plastered on the front window. It's been there for at least twenty-four hours, stuck in among several other for-sale-by-owner vehicles."

"That would mean that if Hal was involved, he'd need to have at least two accomplices," Ali said. "One to drop off the vehicle, and another one to pick up the driver."

"That's how it looks," Dave agreed. "Someone saw the Infiniti sitting there and wanted to buy it. He called the phone number listed for the seller. When that turned out to be a nonworking number, the guy got suspicious and called the cops. When someone finally got around to running the plates, they traced it to Mimi Cooper. The highway patrol towed the vehicle to their crime lab impound lot. Once they saw what was inside the trunk, they notified the ATF. As of now the ATF guys are all over it."

"Have they found anything?" Ali asked.

"Plenty," Dave answered. "Naturally Donnelley is trying to keep a tight lid on the flow of information, but one of the guys who works at the lab is a good buddy of mine. He told me they found three empty gas cans, along with a partially used roll of duct tape and some women's clothing—a bright blue pantsuit, a bra, a pair of panties, and a pair of gold sandals."

"Sounds like pretty much the full-meal deal as far as Mimi's clothing is concerned," Ali said.

"That's right," Dave agreed. "It's also my understanding that someone from the ATF may be dropping by the hospital sometime this morning. They're hoping Hal Cooper will be able to identify the clothing as belonging to his wife."

Ali remembered that Hal had told him Mimi had two rings—her wedding ring and her no-wedding ring.

"Did they mention finding any jewelry in the car?" she asked.

"Nope," Dave answered. "No sign of that, at least not so far. I'm sure the crime lab is going over it inch by inch, looking for prints and any other trace evidence. Donnelley is still determined this all leads back to ELF. I happen to think he's nuts, but that's just me. As it turns out, however, it's no longer any of my concern. For right now, I'm off the case. Sheriff Maxwell just called. With the ATF taking the lead on the investigation, he wants me back in Prescott, pronto. I have a court appearance scheduled for this afternoon on another case. The county attorney was going to ask for a continuance. Now he doesn't need to, I'm on my way there instead."

"Did Sheriff Maxwell say anything about wanting me back home as well?" Ali asked.

"Not to me," Dave answered. "I think he's still hoping you'll be able to keep an eye on whatever the ATF is up to down here. He remains convinced that Donnelley and his people won't be sharing any more information with us than is absolutely necessary."

Great, Ali thought. *Now I'm working undercover for both Sister Anselm and Sheriff Maxwell.*

In a sudden flurry of activity, two people—a man and a woman—stepped off the elevator. The woman, a tall, willowy brunette, was complaining loudly to someone on her cell phone. The close family resemblance suggested that the man was her brother.

"I've been here for hours," she said. "My poor brother drove all night to get here, but we have yet to be allowed inside the room. Hal is in there, and so is that busybody nurse or nun or whatever. The two of them come and go as they wish, but we can't? It's a pile of crap!"

"I believe Mimi's son and daughter just got off the elevator," Ali said. "I should go."

"Don't speak to them," Dave advised. "Do the same thing you did yesterday. If you sit there with your computer on your lap, you'll disappear into the wood-work. No one will know you're there. In the mean-time, I'm on my way north, but after hearing Hal's description of Mimi's two offspring, I'll be interested in knowing what they have to say for themselves. Let me know if they mention anything about Mimi's miss-ing painting. I've been told it's plug ugly, but it's also worth a ton of money. It's by someone named Klee. That's spelled K-L-E-E, but it's evidently pronounced like C-L-A-Y. I've never heard of the guy. Have you?"

Ali was stunned. "Do you mean Paul Klee?" she asked.

"Right. That's the one."

"Mimi Cooper had an original Paul Klee hanging over her fireplace in a house that didn't have so much as a burglar alarm?"

"Oh, they had an alarm, all right," Dave said, "but according to Hal, Maggie kept tripping the motion detector and triggering false alarms. They figured that since they had the dog, they didn't need to turn on the alarm when they were home."

"Wrong," Ali said.

"Yes," Dave agreed. "They're not the only people to make that mistake."

"Tell me about the painting," Ali said.

"Winston, Mimi's first husband, evidently gave her the painting as an anniversary present. I'm not sure how he came to have it. He said that holding on to the painting was like money in the bank, and much better than a savings account since it would grow with inflation.

"When Mimi was getting ready to divorce him, though, Winston wanted the painting to be included in their community property settlement. Had the divorce become final, Mimi might have lost it. From a financial point of view, Winston Langley did her a huge favor by dying first. Sound familiar?"

It was all too familiar. "Don't remind me," she said.

"Sorry," Dave said. "Back to the painting. Hal says it looks like a paper mat little kids make sometimes

TRIAL BY FIRE 211

by weaving strips of paper together, only this one is done with paint, Hal Cooper doesn't like it much. He claims it's nothing but a bunch of colored squares."

"That fits," Ali said, trying to remember what she had learned in her long ago humanities class. "I believe Klee was a cubist, among other things. From Switzerland originally. I think he died sometime around the beginning of World War Two."

"How do you know all this stuff?" Dave asked.

"I'm a liberal arts major, remember," she returned with a laugh. "My head is full of all kinds of useless information—cotton, hay, and rags, as Lerner and Lowe would say. Which reminds me, what made you come up with that phony art history class story yesterday? It was brilliant."

"The Marine Corps isn't long on art history," Dave replied. "I've always thought about taking a class in it. I just never got around to it."

The sound of raised voices near the nurses' station caught Ali's attention. "Something's going on down the hall," she told him. "I need to go and assume the position."

"Okay," Dave said. "Talk to you later."

Ali closed her phone and went back down the hall. While she'd been speaking to Dave, Agent Robson had arrived and had planted himself in front of the counter, where he was arguing with the charge nurse and the ward clerk. Unobserved by either of them, Ali quietly took a seat.

"If I can't see Mimi Cooper, then I want to talk with her husband, or with that other woman," Robson declared. "You know the one I mean, the woman who was here yesterday. She's a nun or a nurse, I'm not sure which."

"That would be Sister Anselm. She's Ms. Cooper's patient advocate."

"Call her, then," Robson ordered. "Tell her Agent Gary Robson with the ATF needs to see her. Immediately."

"I'm sorry, that's not possible," the charge nurse said.

It was the same nurse who had dealt with Robson the day before. If he recognized her, he gave no sign of it, but Ali was sure the charge nurse knew exactly who he was, and she also had his number. Her "sorry" didn't sound sorry at all.

"You'll have to wait until Sister Anselm comes out," the nurse said. "We've been advised that we're not to put through any calls at this time."

Sister Anselm hadn't responded to Ali's earlier text message, but she was sure it had gone through.

"I really must speak to her," Robson insisted.

Ali opened her phone and sent a second message.

Robson's here. In w8ing rm. Wants to see you.
Mimi's kids r here, 2.

This time Sister Anselm's response was immediate.

Thanks. B rt there.

Ali opened her briefcase and booted up her computer. It turned out she had forgotten to charge the battery the night before. When she pulled out a power cord and started looking around for an electrical outlet, James's friend came to her rescue. Taking the plug end of the cord from her, he moved a chair aside and plugged it into a wall socket.

"Thank you," Ali said. "What's your name?"

"Mark," he said. "Mark Levy. James is my best friend."

"He's lucky to have you," Ali said.

Mark ducked his head self-consciously when she said the words. Ali suspected he was hiding a tear, but a moment later he squared his shoulders and faced her again.

"I'm going down to get something from the cafeteria. Do you want anything?"

"I'd love some coffee."

Ali fumbled a five-dollar bill out of her purse and handed it to him.

"Cream and sugar?"

"No. Black."

By the time the elevator door opened, Robson had given up arguing with the nurse. He had taken a seat and was reaching for his cell phone when the brunette approached him with her hand outstretched.

"I'm Serenity Langley," she said. "This is my brother, Win, short for Winston Junior. Mimi Cooper is our mother. We've been here for hours. My mother's husband and that Sister Anselm won't let us into Mother's room, either."

A frown of annoyance had flashed across Robson's face at the idea of being interrupted. Once he realized who Serenity was, however, the frown was immediately replaced by a more appropriate expression. Standing to accept her proffered handshake, Robson left his phone and plucked an ID wallet out of his pocket.

"I'm Agent Gary Robson," he said, displaying his badge to both of them. "I'm with the Bureau of Alcohol, Tobacco, Firearms and Explosives. Sorry to meet under such difficult circumstances, but our agency has been charged with investigating the incident in which your mother was injured."

"It's true, then?" Serenity asked.

"What's true?"

"What they said in this morning's paper—that you guys are investigating what happened to her instead of the local sheriff. The article claimed the fire is suspected of being some kind of domestic terrorism."

Robson peered around the room. The charge nurse had disappeared from the nurses' station. James's father appeared to be sound asleep. Ali focused her eyes on her computer screen and began to type. For a time, the father's quiet snoring and the clatter of Ali's keyboard were the only sounds in the room.

Satisfied that no one was paying attention, Robson turned his attention to Serenity. "Yes," he said. "That's true, although you'll understand I'm not at liberty to discuss details of an ongoing investigation with anyone."

"Yes, of course." Serenity nodded. "We understand."

"Perhaps you could help by giving us some general information about your mother," Robson said, withdrawing a small notebook from his jacket pocket. "As you can see, we've been unable to speak to her directly."

"Win and I will do whatever we can to help," Serenity said. "Tell us what you need."

In the dream Mimi was young again, young and beautiful and living in California with Winston. They had just moved into a new house, a beautiful place overlooking Santa Barbara. Winston was so very proud of it. "I love it," he said, "and I love you."

The shock of hearing those words again, and hearing them from him, caused her eyes to pop open. Yes, he had said them once, but had he ever meant them?

For a disorienting moment, Mimi couldn't figure out where she was. Then she saw the cross hanging on the wall and knew she was in a hospital, a hospital somewhere in Phoenix.

She was afraid Hal would have disappeared somehow. Her eyes darted quickly to the right, but there he was, dozing in the same chair where he'd been sitting wide awake the last time she had drifted into a drug-induced sleep. His chin had fallen to his chest; his hands lay loose and open in his lap. His clothes were wrinkled, his hair rumpled. Had he been sitting in that chair watching over her all night long? He must have been.

Already the pain was knocking at the edge of her consciousness, but her heart was filled with gratitude. Hal was here. She knew he loved her in a way Winston never had. She wanted to tell him that, but of course she couldn't, not with the ventilator in her throat.

Sister Anselm appeared. She looked tired, too. She walked over to Hal and shook his shoulder. "Mimi's awake," she said.

Hal jolted upright. He looked around wildly for a moment, as if he didn't quite understand where he was or who Sister Anselm might be. Then he nodded. "Thanks," he said.

He stood up stiffly and came over to the side of the bed. When he looked down at her, his face looked so haggard and worn that Mimi wanted nothing more than to reach up and touch him and tell him thank you.

"Good morning, Mimi girl," he said. "How's my honey bun? Did you have sweet dreams?"

How could she answer that with one blink or two? The dream about Winston hadn't been sweet at all, but it was far better than the other nightmare, the one about the fire. The one where she was on fire. That dream had mercifully ceased for good once she saw Hal's face and knew he was there beside her.

She understood what Hal was really doing in asking about her dreams—stating his hopes for her. He was praying that in spite of the machines and the pain she really was okay; that she was comfortable; that she was sleeping peacefully. And so she answered his question by responding instead to all the things he didn't say, and when she answered those unasked questions, she lied. She blinked once for yes.

"Sister Anselm showed me how to push the button," he said. "Do you need me to do that?"

That was easy. She wanted to stay with him as long as she could, looking up into his loving eyes and bearing the pain for as long as she could. She blinked twice for no. *No, not yet. Please not yet.*

He was silent for a long time. He seemed to be building up to asking something or saying something. Maybe he was about to tell her that he had to leave again. How long had she been here? Days? Weeks? Maybe it was time for him to do another flight. She didn't want him to go, but he might have to. He had a job that he loved. She couldn't ask him to give it up so he could stay here with her.

What? she wanted to say to him. *What are you going to say?*

"It's about the picture," he said finally.

What picture? she wondered. *What's he talking about?*

"The one over the fireplace," he explained. "The one that looks like a patchwork quilt."

The Klee, she thought. *What about it? What's wrong?*

"It's missing," he said, answering her unspoken question. "When I came home from my trip, you were gone and so was the painting. I know you had talked about selling it. Did you send it out on consignment?"

The Klee? My Klee? What on earth is he talking about? Why would I sell it? I've been saving it all this time for my old age.

Two blinks for no. For: *Of course I didn't send it out on consignment.*

But it's gone? Where could it be? Did someone steal it? When? When could they? How could that happen?

She was always careful about keeping the doors locked. Had someone broken into the house?

He was talking to her again. Asking another question. With her own thoughts whirling around and with the pain trying to surge back over her like an overwhelming wave, Mimi had to concentrate on his words with every fiber of her being.

"Do you know who did this?"

Two blinks. No.

"Do you remember what happened?"

Two more blinks.

"Donna Carson says she came by to check on you that afternoon after work. She said you were fine—that she offered to go to the store for you or to take you there. You said you didn't need anything. Do you remember that?"

Two blinks. No. *I don't remember.*

"Maybe someone came to the door after that. Maybe you opened it and let them in. Is that possible?"

It's possible, but I can't imagine doing anything that stupid. Many blinks. *I don't know. I have no idea.*

But if someone came there, if they got into the house and took my painting, what about Maggie? Is she all right, or did they hurt her, too? Why doesn't he tell me about Maggie? I need to know if she's okay or not. Oh, God, please tell me they didn't put sweet little Maggie into the fire with me. If they had, wouldn't I have heard? Wouldn't I have known?

All the while the pain was looming closer. She knew that soon she wouldn't be able to stand it any longer. *I'll want him to push the button. I'll need him to push it and send me away.*

What? What's Hal saying now? His voice seems very far away. Is it my hearing, or is he whispering?

"I love you," he said. "You're the best thing that ever happened to me. Don't leave me. Please don't leave me."

I'm not going to leave him. Of course not, but I do need him to push the button. Please push the button. Now.

Sister Anselm appeared beside him. "I'm sorry," she said. "It's time for more morphine."

I don't know if he's the one who presses the button or if she does, but I know the button has been pressed. I know about how long it takes from the time the button is pushed until the soft cottony feeling begins to creep over me, pushing the pain away.

I want to tell him how much I love him. Quick. Please ask me if I love you so I can blink one blink for yes, but he doesn't ask. As Hal melts into the background, I notice that he's crying again, with tears slipping down over the half-grown stubble on his cheek.

{ CHAPTER 13 }

Mark Levy returned to the waiting room carrying a cup of coffee, a soda, and two very sticky Rice Krispies Treats from the latte stand in the lobby.

"I thought maybe you were hungry," he said. "If you don't want it, I'll eat yours."

It turned out Ali did want it. She had eaten only half the hamburger she had taken to Athena's place the night before, and that bit of sandwich had long since disappeared.

"Thank you," she said. "I'm starved."

She had been listening in on Agent Robson's interview for some time. All three of them—Robson, Serenity, and Winston Junior—turned to look as Mark delivered his purchases, and then they looked away. As they resumed their conversation, Ali realized Mark had done her a very real favor. Now the three of them most likely assumed that Ali was there with him—that she was part of James's entourage. That belief rendered her all the more invisible, but eating the Rice Krispies Treat left her fingers too sticky to type. For a time she simply listened.

Robson had evidently been off somewhere over-night tracking the elusive ELF possibility and had not participated in the interview with Hal. Some of the information Ali had already gleaned from Dave, Rob-son was hearing for the first time.

When Agent Robson raised the ELF question with Win and Serenity, both of them took the position that whatever had happened to Mimi was personal, not political. Robson's suggestion of Mimi's possible involvement with environmental issues was met with eye-rolling derision.

"Are you kidding?" Serenity returned. "Mother has enough fur in her closets to send an environut into a spasm. Same goes for global warming. She thinks that's a load of bull."

"You don't believe your mother would have been involved in any form of environmental activism?"

"Absolutely not," Serenity said.

Her conclusive response made Agent Robson back-pedal. "Maybe I'm looking at this from the wrong direction," he said with a frown. "Maybe the situation is the reverse of what I was thinking. Is it possible she had taken some kind of public stand in opposition to environmental activism? Maybe she wrote a letter to the editor or signed on with some anticonservation group, and that's what brought her to the attention of some nutcase."

"My mother isn't political," Serenity declared. "As far as I know, she's never written a letter to the editor in her life. She supports the symphony. She supports the Friends of the Library, but I don't think she's ever taken up with any environmental groups, on either side of that question."

"What about her husband?" Robson asked.

"Exactly," Serenity said. "What about him?"

"Would he be involved in some kind of environmental activism?"

"No. Hal Cooper is interested in money. Period. He came sniffing around my mother because he figured out she was loaded. If she dies, he'll walk away with a fortune."

"What about a prenup?" Robson asked.

"There wasn't one," Serenity said. "If Mother dies first, he gets the whole thing, unless he happens to get sent up for murdering her, right?"

Dave had said that Hal had stood up well under questioning the night before. If Agent Robson knew that, too, he didn't let on.

"It's true," he agreed. "Convicted killers generally aren't allowed to profit from their crimes. Just how much money are we talking about here?"

"When my father died, the galleries were worth about ten million," she said. "There was only enough insurance for me to buy up Mother's half. Winston and I split the rest. I'm paying Win off over time."

"Five million, then?" Robson asked.

"More than that," Serenity said. "There were a couple of houses, and some rental properties. She sold the houses to buy the new one in Fountain Hills. I believe she owns that one free and clear."

"It's more money than I thought," Robson conceded. "People have certainly been murdered for a lot less. What can you tell me about your stepfather? Do you know anything about his personal leanings?"

"I have zero idea about his 'personal leanings,' as you put it," Serenity replied. "The less I know about the man, the better. He's my mother's husband, but he sure as hell is not my stepfather. The only person Hal Cooper is looking out for is Hal Cooper, and nobody else."

Robson jotted a few words in his notebook. It seemed as though the news that Hal Cooper would benefit greatly from his wife's demise was causing the ATF agent to at least think twice about the possibility that the attempt on Mimi's life might be a murder-for-profit plot as opposed to some kind of bizarre political statement.

"We'll certainly be examining all of Mr. Cooper's associations," Robson assured Serenity as he finished making a series of notes. "We'll also be looking into the possibility that regardless of the motivation in your mother's attack, the person responsible is actively involved with the Earth Liberation Front.

"The fire in Camp Verde certainly resembles other ELF-related incidents we've investigated. It's not textbook, but close enough to make us think they're all of a piece. What we need to sort out is your mother's connection to those people. It's possible she somehow got too close to an ELF operative and, as a consequence, needed to be gotten rid of before she had a chance to pass any information along. That's why it's so important that we talk to her immediately."

"No," Hal Cooper declared from the far side of the room. "You're not going to talk to her. Mimi's in no condition to speak to anyone."

Ali had seen Hal emerge from his wife's room and step into the hallway. After stripping off his layer of antibacterial clothing, he had come silently down the hall to the entrance of the waiting room, where he had stood for some time, listening. Agent Robson hadn't noticed him, and neither had Serenity and Winston.

"I've asked Mimi about what happened," Hal continued. "So has Sister Anselm. She has suffered a serious head injury. She doesn't remember anything at all."

"What if she's lying about that," Serenity shot back, "or what if you are? You've got everything to gain. Why would you tell the truth about any of it? I want Mother to be able to talk to someone besides you and that nun. What about Agent Robson here? Why not let him talk to her?"

"No!" Hal's second no was immediate and far more emphatic. "Mimi is not going to spend her last few lucid moments on this earth being interrogated by a cop."

"Last few moments?" Serenity repeated. "Are you saying she's dying?"

Hal Cooper met and held his stepdaughter's questioning gaze. "Yes," he said finally. "That's exactly what I'm saying. That's what the doctors told me this morning when they did rounds. Her organs are gradually shutting down. We're going to lose her. It's just a matter of time."

Serenity was the first to look away. She plucked her cell phone out of her pocket, and the whole roomful of onlookers waited while she placed a call.

"It's me," she said finally into what was evidently an answering machine. "I thought you'd be here by now. Mother's worse. I had several appointments scheduled for today and tomorrow down in Tucson. They're in the calendar on the network. If you're not coming here, you might want to drop by the office and cancel them for me."

While she was speaking, Agent Robson stood up and stepped toward Hal Cooper, flashing his badge. "I'm sorry to hear that distressing news, Mr. Cooper," he murmured comfortingly. "Believe me, my agency is totally committed to finding out who did this, and why. If we could have access to any information your wife may have given you, or if I could speak with her—"

"I already told you, I'm not giving you access to anything," Hal responded. "Not to her, and not to me, either. I heard what you said a moment ago about looking into my "associations," as you call them. I take that to mean I'm now under suspicion."

Robson said nothing, so Hal continued.

"You're welcome to your opinion. If you think I did it, fine. Do your worst to try to prove it, but since I was somewhere mid-Atlantic when all this went down, you'll have a tough time pinning any of it on me. For right now, though, I'm not saying another word to you without an attorney present."

Serenity had gone pale. "I want to see Mother," she said. "If she's dying, I need to see her. It's not fair for you to lock us out."

Hal focused his attention on Serenity and Winston. "You're right," he said. "I'm not going to deny Mimi the chance to see you, if that's what she wants. The next time she comes out of the morphine fog, I'll ask her. It's entirely up to her. If she's agreeable, I'll let you come into the room for a few minutes, but I'm warning you. If either of you hassles her in any way—if you give her any kind of grief—out you'll go, and you'll have me to deal with. Understand?"

Winston nodded while his sister stared back at Hal

with disdainful defiance. "But we're her children!" she objected. "You have no right to deny us access to her."

"I'm not denying you access," Hal replied, "but I am stating the conditions under which that access will be granted. The decision to see you or not is entirely up to your mother, but once you step inside her room, it's my call. If you say or do anything to upset her, I'll send you packing."

Ali was impressed by Hal's forbearance and his ability to hold his temper in check in the face of Serenity's hostility.

Up to now, Winston, apparently the weakest link in this family squabble, had been content to let his sister do all the talking. Now he voiced his own objection. "I was told Mother is on a ventilator. How can she tell you anything about who she wants to see and who she doesn't want to see, to say nothing of what she remembers?"

"She can answer yes or no questions," Hal replied. "That's it." With that, he turned to the nurses' station. "I need to go by the hotel to walk my dog," he said. "I've left word with Sister Anselm that no one is to be allowed in my wife's room until I get back. I'm telling you that, too. That's an order."

"Absolutely, Mr. Cooper," the charge nurse said.

With that Hal walked over to the elevator and pushed the Down button. While he waited for the elevator to arrive, he turned back to the room. "About that missing painting, Serenity," he said, addressing his stepdaughter directly. "The Klee that was over the fireplace. Mimi has no intention of selling it at this time. If you have it, you'd by God better return it. If I find out that you've sold it without being authorized to do so, I'll sue you within an inch of your life."

Serenity looked genuinely stunned. "Mother's Klee is gone? Are you kidding? That thing is worth a fortune."

"Yes," Hal agreed. "It *is* worth a fortune. I know that and you know that. It's also very interesting to note that one painting is the only thing missing from the house."

The elevator door opened. Hal Cooper stepped into it and was gone.

"What painting?" Agent Robson asked. "Something's missing from the house? What is it, and why am I hearing about it now for the first time?"

Ali knew that the missing painting had been mentioned several times, but since a possible art theft didn't fit in with Agent Robson's preconceived notion about the crime, he had most likely disregarded it.

"I've been telling Mother for years that painting belonged in a museum somewhere and not in her living room," Serenity fumed. "Most especially in the living room of a house where they leave the alarm off as often as it's turned on."

"What painting?" Robson asked again. "Is it valuable?"

Serenity gave him a scathing look. "It's a Paul Klee," she told him disdainfully. "Of course it's valuable. It's been in the family for years."

"What's a Paul Klee?" Robson asked.

Shaking her head impatiently at his apparent stupidity, Serenity continued. "Klee was a well-known Swiss-born painter—a cubist. He was born in the late nineteenth century and died in the early forties."

"Never heard of him," Robson said.

"He taught art at the Bauhaus," Serenity added, warming to the topic. "Mother's picture is one of his so-called *Static-Dynamic Gradations*. He did several during his years of teaching. The best known one is dated 1923. It's in the Metropolitan Museum of Art. Mother's version is somewhat earlier than that. For some reason, he wasn't thrilled with it. He signed it and then gave it to one of his students, an American girl named Phoebe Pankhurst."

"Your parents bought it from her?" Robson asked, making notes as he tried to follow the story.

"More or less," Serenity allowed. "That happened years later. Phoebe's widowed mother became ill. Phoebe had to drop out of school and return to California to care for her. The mother eventually died, and Phoebe spent the next fifty years living alone in what had been her parents' home and teaching art to generations of kids.

"Her house in Santa Barbara had a glassed-in sunporch. That's where she taught her art lessons. For years and years, no one ventured any farther into her house than that sunporch area. When she died, her only living cousin flew out from New York to attend the funeral. He went to the house and was shocked by what he found there. Every room was piled shoulder-high with old newspapers, books, and garbage. The load was so heavy the floor was in danger of collapsing. The cousin had no idea where to start on cleaning up the mess.

"That's when my father stepped in. My grandfather was a banker. He and my dad offered to buy the house and all its contents as is, with no contingencies. They also agreed that they would be responsible for all necessary cleaning. The cousin was delighted. He didn't want to be stuck overseeing the work, much less doing it. He took what they offered, washed his hands of the whole mess, and flew back to New York as soon as the funeral was over. My father told me later that buying Phoebe Pankhurst's house was the best investment he ever made."

"Why was that?" Robson asked.

"Cleaning it out was a challenge," Serenity said. "Daddy had to look through every single book and newspaper. Phoebe's art students had always paid in cash. She had a fortune in ten- and twenty-dollar bills tucked away everywhere, but the money was the least of it."

"The painting?" Robson asked.

Serenity nodded. "That one and several others," she said. "There was a Degas sketch, a Renoir, a Matisse, and a few others I don't remember—all of them originals. Dad told me he got enough cash from selling those, and from selling Phoebe's house, to bankroll his first gallery. He kept the Klee, though. He gave it to my mother and told her it was a little bank account."

"How much is it worth?" Robson asked.

Serenity shrugged. "I believe it's insured for seven hundred thousand, but it's probably worth more than that. As I said before, it belongs in a museum somewhere. If it were to go on sale, however, it might provoke a bidding war, which is why it's so ridiculous that my mother left it hanging over her damned fireplace for everyone to see. And now it's gone. I can't believe it."

Ali was struck by the fact that Serenity Langley seemed far more concerned about the missing painting than she was about her dying mother. It was easy to see why Hal Cooper regarded his stepdaughter with such contempt.

James's mother exited her son's room and came into the waiting room. Walking past the others, she made her way to her still sleeping former husband, sat down next to him, and gently touched his shoulder. He came awake with a start.

"What is it?" he wanted to know. "What's happened?"

"One of the doctors just called the room," she said. "They want to talk to us about—"

Breaking off, she leaned against his shoulder and sobbed.

"What?" he said. "They need to talk to us about what?"

"About scheduling surgery." She choked on the words. "Surgery and skin grafts. He's going to be scarred for life, Max. Our poor handsome boy." With that, she began weeping, while he gave her heaving shoulder a series of awkward but comforting pats.

For the better part of two days, the warring couple had waged a very public battle. For now hostilities seemed to have subsided.

"It's okay, Lisa," he murmured over and over. "It's okay. We'll get through it somehow."

For a time their family drama took center stage. When Ali looked away, Serenity was back on her phone.

"It's me again," she said. "My mother's Klee seems to have gone missing. See if you can find out if anyone is offering a new *Static-Dynamic Gradations* for sale. Whatever's become of our Russian friend, Yarnov? He's a great fan of Klee and he's not fussy about provenance."

As in someone willing to buy stolen goods? Ali thought as she typed the name Yarnov.

Serenity was clearly upset to learn that her mother's painting had disappeared, but Ali couldn't help wondering if the woman didn't know far more about it than she was letting on. The painting had come into the family under less than honest circumstances. Serenity had no qualms about what her father and grandfather had done in cheating Phoebe Pankhurst's relatives—to say nothing of the IRS—out of what was rightfully theirs. Ali suspected that Serenity Langley had firsthand knowledge about Mr. Yarnov's lack of concern about provenance.

James's mother had finally quit crying. Once she dried her tears, she and her husband went to confer with their son's physician. For a time after they left the only sound in the room was the clatter of Ali's keyboard. Suddenly, Winston turned around and glared at Ali over his shoulder.

"What the hell are you doing?" he demanded. "It sounds like you're writing down everything we say. Are you?"

Caught red-handed, Ali was groping for an appropriate response when Sister Anselm arrived at the waiting room entrance and came to Ali's rescue.

"She's working for me," the nun explained. "I'm tired of having other people write whatever they want about me. I asked the diocese for permission for an authorized biography, and I've asked Miss McCann to write it. I find it convenient to have her come to the various hospitals when I'm in the city. That way she can interview me during my off-hours, and we save a fortune in long-distance telephone charges."

Having thus quashed the Ali discussion, Sister Anselm looked around the waiting room. "Has anyone seen Mr. Cooper? I expected him back by now."

As if on cue, the elevator door opened and Hal stepped off. "There you are," Sister Anselm said. "Your wife is starting to wake up again. If she's going to see her son and daughter, now would probably be a good time."

Hal nodded. "I'll see what she wants me to do. And thanks for your suggestion. The concierge says not to worry. He'll send a bellman up to the room every couple of hours to take Maggie for a walk, and they'll feed her later this afternoon. I'd hate to be gone when . . ."

He left the rest of the sentence unsaid. Setting his jaw, he marched past Agent Robson and his stepchildren and made straight for Mimi's room, followed by Sister Anselm.

His arrival had been enough to take the focus off Ali and her computer.

"Can you think of anything else?" Agent Robson asked Serenity.

She shook her head.

"What about you, Mr. Langley?"

"Nothing to add," Winston Junior responded. "I think that just about covers it."

"All right, then," Robson said, pocketing his notebook. "I need to make a few calls, but if your mother is able to give you any information . . ."

Serenity patted the pocket where she had stowed the business card Agent Robson had given her. "Yes," she said. "We'll call you immediately."

Ducking her head, Ali resumed typing.

———

Before, she had fought desperately to wake up. Early on, opening her eyes was the only thing that had allowed her to escape the nightmare of flames. Now, though, she would have preferred to stay dreaming and asleep instead of having to return to this stark hospital room with its humming machinery and this strange bed.

This time Mimi had found herself walking along a sandy beach with her mother. Moments later her mother disappeared from the beach, but Mimi was still there, playing ball with her dog, her first dog, Rover. That had to be more than sixty years ago now, but in her dream, her bluetick hound had been alive once more, bringing the grubby sand-covered tennis ball back to her time and again so she could throw it. When he looked up at her with his soulful brown eyes, Mimi stretched out her hand to pet him. His long black ears were soft and silky to the touch, just the way she remembered them.

"Mimi," Hal said from somewhere close at hand. "Are you awake?"

She was awake and yet she wasn't. She didn't want to leave Rover behind. Would she ever see him again?

But Hal was speaking to her insistently, and she needed to listen. She needed to pay attention. Struggling, she finally managed to open her eyes. Hal stood above her, smiling. He looked a little better. His hair was combed. He had shaved.

"I just got back from feeding Maggie," he was saying. "If I'm gone for very long, the concierge says he'll make sure someone walks her and feeds her."

The concierge. What concierge? Our house doesn't have a concierge. What is he thinking? But Maggie? If

*someone is walking her and feeding her, that must mean
she's all right. That means she didn't die. They didn't
hurt her. Thank you, God. Thank you.*

Hal was speaking to her again. She concentrated
on the words coming out of his mouth, trying to make
sense of them.

"Win and Serenity are outside," he was saying. "Do
you want to see them?"

See them? Of course she wanted to see them.
Serenity could be a bitch at times, and there were
occasions when Win looked and sounded so much
like his father that she wanted to haul off and hit him.
She sometimes wondered if he was like his father in
other ways besides looks and voice. Was Win faithful
to his new wife, or did he cheat on her the same way
his father had cheated on Mimi? And what was her
daughter-in-law's name again?

Try as she might, Mimi couldn't quite dredge it
up. She knew the two of them were expecting a baby
sometime soon, and that the baby was a boy—would
be a boy. This would be Mimi's very first grandchild,
but she still couldn't remember Win's wife's name.

Why are names so tricky? Why was it she knew
Rover's name so well, but not her daughter-in-law's or,
for a time, not even her own?

But yes, these were Mimi's children, warts and
all. Despite Serenity's and Win's shortcomings and
despite their disagreements, she still loved them. She
wanted to see them. One blink for yes. One blink for
yes, absolutely.

"Sister Anselm says it might be better if you see
them together," Hal went on. "She's afraid seeing them
one at a time will tire you too much. I'm worried about

that, too. So is it all right to have them both in at the same time?"

What Mimi wanted to do right then was to close her eyes and listen to the comforting sound of Hal's voice. She loved his voice. Sometimes he sang in the shower, and she liked that, too. His solid baritone. Maybe he would sing to her here, if she could just ask him.

But he wasn't singing right now. He was patiently asking the same question in a different fashion. A yes or no fashion. "Together?" he repeated.

One blink for yes. For together. Because after that, after they left, Hal would still be here, talking to her and pushing the button. Because Mimi knew it was almost time for that. She knew it and so did he. She wasn't sure how. It had something to do with that little thing that Sister Anselm carried around in her pocket. When it made that funny noise, they all knew it was time for someone to push the button.

"All right, then," Hal said. "I'll go get them. It'll take a moment for them to get dressed. Don't go away."

Was he kidding? Where would she go? Of course she wouldn't go away. How could she?

Mimi drifted for a time. The pain was there and getting stronger and pulling her toward it. Into it. They needed to hurry, otherwise . . .

She heard the door swing open. Win came first. She saw the shocked expression on his face. *It must be terrible for them to have to see me this way.*

Mimi's son made a brave attempt at a cheerful smile. "Hi, Mom," he said. "How're you doing?"

Mimi couldn't answer. It wasn't a yes or no question. She wanted to say that she was fine, even though she wasn't. That's what you told your kids—that you were fine, even if you were dying. Suddenly that idea came home to her. Maybe that's what this was all about. Maybe she was dying. If that was the case, would someone tell her, or would they leave her to figure it out on her own?

But she couldn't tell Win that she was fine.

Win stepped to one side and Sandra . . . *Not Sandra,* Mimi reminded herself firmly. *Serenity. We're supposed to call her Serenity now!* . . . Serenity moved into Mimi's field of vision. The horrified look on her daughter's face didn't leave much to the imagination.

"Oh, Mother," she wailed, and then she turned away, collapsing, sobbing, into Hal's arms. Mimi saw the momentary shock on Hal's face; then he put his arms around Serenity's quaking shoulders and led her from the room.

That's good, Mimi thought. The fact that Serenity had turned to Hal for help surprised her. Pleased her. But what was even more surprising was how very much Serenity had looked like her grandmother just then. She could have been a twin to the woman Mimi had been walking with on the beach a little while before Hal woke her up.

Serenity was what, thirty-nine now? Forty? However old she was, she looked like her grandmother, *And probably like me, too,* Mimi thought.

"Amy sends her love," Win said.

Amy. That was Win's wife's name—Amy. Win stood there looking down at her, as if he was waiting for Mimi to say something, waiting for her to respond.

Someone needs to give him the code, Mimi thought. One blink. Two blinks. But if Win didn't know the code of yes and no, had anyone told him about the button? It was almost time now. Mimi wanted it. She needed it.

Then Hal was back, standing looking at her over Win's shoulder. "She'll be all right," he said.

At first Mimi thought he was talking about her— that she would be all right—but then she realized that wasn't true. Hal was talking about Serenity. She would be all right. Mimi would not.

"Do you want me to push the button?" he asked.

Now he was talking to her. About her. One blink for yes. One blink for push the button.

Please.

For a moment after Hal led Serenity and Win Langley into their mother's room, the waiting room was perfectly quiet. It seemed to Ali that she had the place all to herself. Then Mark spoke up. James's friend was sitting behind her and off to one side, just out of her line of vision.

"He's right, isn't he?" Mark said accusingly. "That is what you're doing—you're taking down everything they say."

Ali had paid the bill, but she still owed the young man something for the kindness of that cup of coffee and the Rice Krispies Treat, so she told him the truth.

"Yes, I am," she admitted quietly, "but don't tell them that."

"Why?" Mark asked. "Is it because you and that nun think one of them did this?"

Obviously Ali wasn't the only person in the room who had taken an interest in what was going on around him. Ali turned to face him. At first she wasn't going to answer, but then she did.

She nodded. "Maybe," she said.

"That's what I'm thinking, too," Mark Levy said. "I was listening the whole time that cop was asking them questions. That woman seemed a lot more upset about someone stealing her mother's painting than she was about what happened to her mother."

That had been Ali's impression as well. Just then the door to Mimi Cooper's room swung open, and Hal led Serenity out into the waiting room. She was leaning against him and sobbing hysterically. He eased her into a chair.

While Hal went in search of a box of tissues, Ali wondered if Serenity's tears were real or if this was more a performance than anything else.

Ali glanced from Serenity back to Mark. He replied to that look with a small shake of his head that seemed to confirm that, he, too, thought Serenity's tears were entirely fake. And why would Serenity pretend to be grief-stricken if she wasn't?

Maybe she knows more than she's telling, Ali concluded.

For a time Ali sat there with her computer open on her lap and thought about what she was feeling. She was suspicious about Serenity, but there was nothing more to it than that—suspicion. There was no solid information Ali could pass along to either Sheriff Maxwell or Dave Holman. With Dave involved in a criminal trial, Ali was sure if she ran up the flag to the sheriff, he'd most likely pass her off to someone else—like Holly Mesina, for example.

What Ali needed was another kind of help. She punched in a text message to B.

Anyone available to do some discreet hacking today?

B.'s response was immediate:

Always. What's up?

So was hers:

Not texting. I'll call in a few minutes.

Again, only seconds passed before he responded:

Sounds serious.

Over in her chair, Serenity Langley was still sobbing. Closing the screen and leaving her computer where it was, Ali took her phone and walked down the hall to Sister Anselm's favorite window. There, looking out on Camelback Mountain, Ali punched in B. Simpson's number.

"What's going on?" B. asked at once, sounding concerned. "Are you all right?"

"I'm fine," Ali said, "but there's a woman at a hospital here in Phoenix who isn't fine. Before I say anything to Sheriff Maxwell or Dave Holman about this, I'd like to know a little more about her. You know, get my ducks in a row and all that kind of thing."

"I'm great at lining up ducks," B. told her with a laugh. "Just tell me what you need."

"Nothing illegal," Ali said quickly. "Nothing that would require a search warrant, and no information that isn't readily available in public records. It seems likely that you know a lot more about where to search than I do."

"What?" he asked.

"Everything there is to know about Winston Langley Galleries."

"With an S?" B. returned. "As in 'galleries,' plural?"

"Yes. I'd also like to take a look at whatever you can find on Serenity Langley, Winston's daughter," Ali told him. "And also on Winston's son, Winston Junior. The daughter lives in Phoenix. I believe the son is from Santa Barbara."

"Anything else?" B. asked.

"Yes, I'd like to know what you can find out about a Russian guy named Yarnov who's into art in a big way. I'd also like to know when the last time a Paul Klee painting went on sale, and what one would most likely be worth in today's market."

"I'll send you the information as I get it," B. said. "How soon do you need it?"

"The woman I told you about is dying," Ali said urgently. "The sooner the better."

{ CHAPTER 14 }

By the time Ali returned to the waiting room, Serenity Langley had stopped crying. When her brother emerged from their mother's room a few minutes later, Serenity had dried her tears, fixed her face, and opened her phone.

"I don't know where the hell you are this morning, Donna. I'm tired of talking to your answering machine. Call me."

"Mom's asleep again," Win announced, settling down on a chair next to his sister's. "Hal punched the button on her morphine drip and she was out like a light. They have to give her smaller doses more often. Otherwise it'll be too much for her system."

"She looks awful!" Serenity declared. "I couldn't stand it. Just looking at her made me sick to my stomach."

It's a good thing Hal Cooper isn't so squeamish, Ali thought.

"Who do you think took the painting?" Win asked.

He was as concerned about his mother's missing piece of artwork as his sister was.

"Let's hope it's someone who knows what it's

worth," Serenity said. "If someone tries to put it on the market, we'll know about it. No reputable art dealer is going to touch it."

"What about the not-so-reputable ones?" Win asked.

Serenity shrugged. "Then it's lost," she said. "Except since it's insured, Hal will still end up with the money, damn him." She sent a dark look in the direction of room 814. "It was Daddy's," she said. "Hal Cooper is the last person in the world who should benefit from it."

Win looked puzzled. "Maybe you're wrong about him," he ventured. "It looks like he really cares about her."

"Don't be stupid," Serenity said. "Hal Cooper cares about money. The sooner she dies, the better off he'll be, and the hospital bill will be that much lower. For all we know, he's giving that button an extra shove every time he doses her."

Behind her, Mark Levy had evidently heard enough. With an exaggerated sigh of disgust, he tossed a magazine onto an end table, where it landed with a resounding slap. "I need some air," he announced to Ali on his way past. "Do you want anything from downstairs?"

"Nothing, thanks," Ali said. "I'm fine."

Mark punched the elevator button. When the door opened, Donna Carson, Serenity's personal assistant, stepped past him into the waiting room.

"There you are," Serenity said. "I've been trying to reach you all morning."

"I got your message," Donna said. She nodded in Win's direction and then took a seat next to Serenity. "How are you holding up?"

Saying nothing, Serenity shook her head.

"I stopped by the gallery on my way here and canceled those appointments. Do you want me to tell the managers that under the circumstances, we'll be skipping this week's gallery walk?"

"Good idea," Serenity said. "I hadn't thought of that, but you're right."

Seeing the two women seated side by side, Ali noticed that their mannerisms were surprisingly similar. They spoke for several more minutes, with Serenity issuing orders and with Donna jotting them down in a leather-bound notebook.

Shortly after that Sister Anselm emerged from Mimi's room. She looked weary beyond words. "Mr. Cooper will stay here for the time being, Ms. McCann," Sister Anselm said. "I believe I'm going to return to the hotel for a nap. We'll have another go at the interview a little later," she added. "I'd also like to take a look at what you've written so far."

Yes, Ali thought, *Sister Anselm is very good at adjusting the truth.*

On her way past, Sister Anselm stopped in front of Win and Serenity Langley. "Has anyone asked you to sign your mother's visitor logbook?" she asked. "I like to keep them for the families of my patients."

"We *are* her family," Serenity replied pointedly. "We don't need a notebook to tell us so."

"Very well," Sister Anselm said, walking away. "As you wish."

"In all the time you've spent with her, has she said anything at all about who did this?" Serenity asked. "Does she remember anything at all?"

Sister Anselm looked at Serenity and shook her

head. "My patients tell me things in strictest confidence," she said.

With that, Sister Anselm left the waiting room. A few minutes later, so did Donna. Once the room was empty, Ali expected Serenity and Win would go right on talking. Instead, Win slouched down in his chair and dozed off. Since he had probably spent most of the night driving from Santa Barbara to Phoenix, that was hardly surprising. With Serenity busy sending off a series of text messages, Ali was startled when her own phone rang.

"Leland here," Brooks announced, although Ali had surmised as much by looking at her phone. "Do you have any idea when you'll be returning? I'm going out to buy groceries and was wondering if you'd be home this weekend, and whether you were expecting any company."

"I can't say," she said. "I really don't have an answer about that."

"All right. I can get perishables at the last minute anyway," he said. "What about your room at the hotel? Is it satisfactory?"

There was no doubt about that. "Absolutely," she said. "How's Sam?"

"She appears to be managing without you, madam," Leland said, "but I believe she's a bit lonely. She even ventured into the kitchen this morning while I was making breakfast."

"Obviously you're winning her over," Ali said.

"I hope so."

"If you'd like for me to bring anything down to you," Brooks added, "all you need to do is call. I can be at the hotel within a matter of hours."

"Thanks," Ali said. "If I need anything, I'll let you know."

A text message came in from B.

Check your e-mail.

"I need to go," Ali told Leland. "Thanks for staying in touch." She logged in to her e-mail account and found a new message from B. Simpson.

This is too much to text. And I'm going to give you a summary rather than sending you to all the sites I used—proprietary information and all that.

There hasn't been a Paul Klee available in the open market for a number of years. If it's signed and in good condition, it would probably be worth well over a million bucks.

Winston Langley Galleries seems to be in a world of hurt. Two of the locations are running in arrears on rent and utilities. Serenity seems to have an IRS problem as well, so having access to money from the sale of her mother's painting might help bail her out of her financial troubles.

Winston Langley Jr. looks like something of a cipher. Can't seem to keep a job or a wife. He's on marriage number three at the moment. Foreclosed on his last house. Lives in a town house owned by his

mother and stepfather. Drives a four-year-
old oar that was his mother's.

So far nothing on that art collector, but I'm
still looking.

Both Serenity, née Sandra Jean, and
Winston Junior received money from their
father's estate, all of which seems to have
disappeared. I think Junior had a gambling
problem. I'm not sure about Serenity, but I
think it's safe to say that she didn't put any
of her share back into the business.

You might mention some of this to Dave.
Seems to me that taking a good look at
where the son and daughter were at the
time of the incident might not be such a
bad bet.

All for now. Hope this helps. If you need
anything more, call. I'm at your service.
And if you'd like me to be at your service
closer at hand, all you have to do is say
the word.

                                                    B.

That last aside made Ali smile. Despite being
turned down, B. was still hanging around and letting
her know he was available. Obviously he hadn't taken
her most recent no as her final answer on the subject.

She sent off an immediate reply.

> Thanks. This is a great help. If I need
> more, I'll get back to you.

The information B. had given her was more than interesting. Nothing in Serenity Langley's demeanor had hinted that she was having any kind of financial difficulty, but running behind on rent for her various galleries was not a good sign.

Ali took the time to scroll back through her notes to verify what she had been told before. Yes, there it was. According to what Serenity had said, Winston Langley Sr. had been worth a cool ten million bucks at the time of his death. Presumably half of that had gone to Mimi, and a quarter each to Winston's two children.

Much of Mimi Cooper's portion of that estate was evidently still intact. Upon her death, five million more or less, with or without the missing painting, would go to Hal Cooper. Upon Hal's death, whatever remained would go to the two children, and Hal was still a relatively young man.

No wonder Serenity despised Hal so. As far as she was concerned, he had waltzed onto the scene and was in the process of making off with half of her birthright.

It was while Ali was reviewing her notes that she noticed something odd. Hal had clearly mentioned the missing painting to Donna Carson, Serenity's personal assistant, but today, when he had mentioned the Klee's disappearance to Serenity, she had acted as though it was all news to her.

Ali had regarded Serenity's hysterics after leaving Mimi's room as phony and over the top. Was this more of the same? Had she been putting on a show about the painting's having gone missing when she already knew exactly where it was and what had happened to it?

The other possibility was that Donna had either forgotten to mention it or had deliberately neglected to pass that information along to her boss. Why would she do that?

Ali was sure that by now any number of officers would have interviewed Donna to see what, if anything, she knew. After all, since she had stopped by the house on the day Mimi disappeared, that meant Donna was one of the last people to see her. Had she noticed anything out of the ordinary at Hal and Mimi's Fountain Hills home? Had she seen someone hanging around who didn't belong there? Ali wished she could have somehow been privy to that interview, but she wasn't. Most likely no one else at the Yavapai County Sheriff's Department had been informed about it, either.

Then there was Serenity's mysterious client, Mr. Yarnov. Ali had been unable to provide B. with any pertinent information other than the man's last name. Consequently, it was hardly surprising that B. had come up empty, but the Mr. Yarnov in question had to be worth big bucks. Obviously Serenity had a clear idea of exactly how much the missing Klee was worth, but she also seemed to think it might well be within Mr. Yarnov's price range. That meant the guy had plenty of spare change—petro-dollars, perhaps?—clinking around in his pockets. Although Yarnov seemed like a common enough name, Ali doubted there were all that many Yarnovs running around with art money to burn.

Ali did some Google searching of her own but came

up empty as well. None of the Yarnovs she found seemed likely to be art collector types. Gradually the room filled up as James's assortment of concerned relatives reassembled. Ali recognized some of them, but not all. Since Lisa and Max had buried the hatchet for the time being, the relatives did the same. This time they didn't divide up into warring camps, but in the midst of all that activity, Win Langley continued to sit in the center of the room, sound asleep and snoring.

Time passed, and finally Win awakened. After a brief discussion, he and Serenity decided to go to lunch. Ali was thinking about the possibility of lunch herself when Mark Levy returned. He dropped a small rectangular box on the table in front of Ali. Inside she found two pieces of pepperoni pizza.

"Hope you like pepperoni," Mark said.

"Thank you," Ali said, gratefully grabbing one of the slices. "I adore pepperoni. Can I pay you for this?"

"No," he said, shaking his head. "I couldn't stand to listen to any more of their B.S." Mark nodded toward the two empty chairs where Win and Serenity had been sitting. "I had to go sit in the lobby for a while just to cool off. With their mother in the other room dying, you'd think those jerks would start to figure out what's important. Besides," he added, "I think they're wrong. That Hal guy loves his wife. I don't think he gives a damn about the money."

It was interesting that both Mark and Ali had sat on the sidelines in the waiting room and had come away with the same impressions—that Mimi's kids were a pair of greedy opportunists while Hal Cooper was the genuine article. Sister Anselm, too, seemed to be of a similar opinion.

Ali was just finishing the second piece of pizza when a nurse stopped in front of Mimi's door long enough to post a bright red sign. Ali didn't need to be told what it was—a DNR designation. *Do Not Resuscitate.* That meant that somewhere along the line Mimi Cooper had drafted a living will. Hal had most likely asked the attorney's office to fax it over to the hospital.

Moments later a new patient arrived, an older woman. As the burn-unit staff swung into action, the gurney was wheeled into room 812. The door had barely closed when her relatives churned out of the elevator and into the waiting room.

"I told Carol a thousand times that those damned cigarettes would be the death of her!"

The speaker was a silver-haired lady who moved with the aid of a walker and had to be well into her eighties.

"She told me over and over to mind my own business. Now look what's happened. I'll never be able to forgive myself."

She burst into tears and sank into the nearest chair, the one formerly occupied by Serenity Langley. She reached into a large purse that was perched in a basket between the handles of the walker. Pulling out a lace-edged hanky, she gave her nose a noisy blow.

"Now, Sarah," an elderly gentleman said, patting her knee. "What's there to forgive? This isn't your fault. You know as well as I do that if you had tried to take your sister's Camels away, she would have made both your lives a living hell. Alva's ninety-three, for Pete's sake. That's a good run for anybody. If she wants to burn herself up along with that old recliner of hers in front of reruns of *Dr. Phil,* so what? God love her. If it kills her, let it. If you ask me, dying that way is better than dying of lung cancer any day."

"But what's Carol going to think?" Sarah asked, sniffling. "You know how she is. She always blames me for everything. She's going to say I should have done something to prevent it."

"Let her harp at you as much as she wants," the old man advised. "Just don't pay any attention. Besides, I didn't see her stepping up to the plate when Alva showed up in Phoenix needing a place to live."

"She's so much younger than Alva and I are, Roy."

Roy was already shaking his head.

"Maybe, at her age, it's about time she got over being the baby of the family," he said. "When Alva ended up on your doorstep, did Carol offer to help out? Nosiree! She didn't lift a finger. As far as she was concerned, Alva's problems were your problems and nobody else's.

"As for the cigarettes? If Carol says word one to you about that, I hope you call her on it. If she expects you to be able to take Alva's cigarettes away, maybe she should take a look in the mirror. What do you think would happen if you suggested she should give up her blasted Captain Morgan? That's not gonna happen, never in a hundred years!" He snorted. "And speaking of which," he added. "If you ask me, anyone who would swill down rum and coke night after night, year after year doesn't have much room to talk. That'll kill her just as dead as Alva's cigarettes are killing her."

It could have been a comedy routine, but it wasn't. This elderly couple and the woman's even more elderly sister were here in the hospital dealing with their own set of life-and-death issues, just like James's family and friends, and Mimi's.

They were all asking the same questions. Who would live? Who would die? Why? And who would be left to shoulder the blame? Ali didn't know the severity of Alva's wounds, but her age, like Mimi's, would count against her survival. James had youth on his side. That might mean he had a better chance of surviving, but there was no way to tell how he would be affected long-term.

As Ali silently mulled over the blended fates of the people in the room, Win and Serenity returned from their lunch break.

Noticing that a pair of new arrivals had taken over the chairs she and Win had previously occupied, Serenity gave the old folks a hard-edged stare calculated to let them know they had blundered into reserved seating and they ought to move along.

Serenity's reproof was relatively ineffective due to her stepping off the elevator with her cell phone glued to her ear. Sarah and Roy, oblivious to what Serenity considered an error in judgment, remained where they were, both of them engrossed in watching a televised baseball game on a set where the volume was now turned as high as it would go.

"I remembered something else," Serenity said into her phone as she flounced into another chair. "Call me back when you can." She closed her phone and looked at her brother. "I swear, half the time Donna doesn't seem to have her mind on the job, and I'm really tired of it. Yes, I know she's been around for years. She's familiar with the clients and she knows the business, but it's about time she figured out that she isn't indispensable. I'll bet I could find someone else to do her job in no time, and I wouldn't have to pay that new person nearly as much as I'm paying her."

"So do it," Win said, shrugging. "If Donna's not pulling her weight, get rid of her. You don't owe her anything."

The door to Mimi's room opened and Hal burst into the hallway. His face was flushed. His hair stood on end. Looking distraught, he hurried over to the nurses' station. "Where is she?"

"Who?" the charge nurse asked.

"Sister Anselm. I called the hotel to ask her to come back to the hospital. The person at the front desk told me that she never came back there after she left to go to the hospital last night."

"I'm sorry. I haven't seen her, either. Is there something I can help you with?" the nurse asked.

"It's the pain," Hal said. "It's getting worse. That one dose of morphine doesn't seem to be doing the trick, but I'm afraid to give her more than that."

"Come on," the charge nurse said, hurrying out from behind the counter. "Let me see what's going on."

They started for Mimi's room, but Serenity sprang to her feet and blocked their path.

"Don't you dare let him go back in there!" Serenity shrieked at the nurse. "Don't you see what he's doing? He's claiming she's in pain so he can slip her an overdose. You've got to stop him. Don't let him do this. He's killing her right here in front of everybody, and you're going to let him get away with it."

"Out of my way!" Hal Cooper growled. "Now!"

"Then I'm going inside, too," Serenity said.

"No," Hal replied. "You're not."

His fists were balled. He looked as though he was ready to deck her. Pushing past her, Hal and the nurse disappeared inside. Serenity seemed ready to follow, but before she could, Mark Levy left his spot in the corner and put a restraining hand on her shoulder.

"I think you need to stay out here."

"Let me go," she said furiously, trying to shake his grip. "What are you doing? Who the hell do you think you are?"

They had been in the same waiting room for hours, but Mark's presence hadn't penetrated Serenity's armor of self-absorption. From the surprised expression on her face as she peered up at him, Ali was sure she was seeing the young man for the first time.

"I'm nobody," Mark said, letting go of her arm and shrugging his narrow shoulders. "Just a friend of the family."

Ali knew that was true. He was a longtime friend of James's family, and now a very new friend of Hal Cooper's family, too. But he was a long damned way from being a nobody.

As Mark stepped away from Serenity and returned to his seat, Serenity caught sight of the bright red sign. "What's this?" she demanded.

A second nurse hurried to the door to join the one who was already there. "It's a DNR," she said. "It means no heroic measures."

"No, it doesn't," Serenity retorted. "What it really means is you're going to let him kill her."

Where's Hal? Why isn't he here? And where's the nun? Or a nurse? Or a doctor? I need them. I need someone to punch the button. I need it. Please.

"I'm here," Hal was saying overhead. "I'm sorry. I had to go get someone. I was afraid to push it again so soon. I was afraid I'd give you too much."

There's no such thing as too much, she thought. *No such thing.*

His face looks funny. Like he's going to cry. He doesn't know what to do, and that's the thing. Hal always knows what to do. The right thing to do.

Please. I want to go away. I want to go into the fog. The fog doesn't hurt like this. The fog doesn't hurt.

Hal is crying. Why? Oh wait, that's right—I know. It's because he's afraid he's going to lose me. Doesn't want to lose me, and I don't want to lose him, either. But he knows, and I know he knows. This time when I go into the cottony cloud, I may not be coming back. I'll fall into the dream and the dream will have me. Even now, it's starting. I can feel it.

But then, for only a few brief moments before the morphine took hold, she had one last glimpse of clarity, and that was when she remembered some of what had happened. She couldn't quite grasp all of it, but somehow she knew who had done this. In knowing who, she also knew why. What didn't make sense to her was that she had forgotten. How was that possible?

She knew she needed to tell someone, but in order to do that, they would have to ask her. They would have to ask the right questions, ones she could answer with a yes or a no, with one blink or two. But not right now. She was going. The fog was coming again, and she needed it. She really needed it.

Maybe later she could tell Hal what she remembered. If she still remembered.

Before the door to Mimi Cooper's hospital room closed completely, Ali had her phone in hand. She sent a text message to Sister Anselm:

Where are you? Hal Cooper is looking for you.
Things are bad here. I think we're losing Mimi.

Once Ali pressed Send, she sat with her phone open in her hand, waiting for a response, but none came. Sister Anselm had told them she was leaving for the hotel. If she had never arrived at the hotel, where was she? An uneasy feeling washed over Ali. Something was wrong. Sister Anselm was a woman of her word. If she said she was going there, that's what she would do, and she most especially would not go missing in action when a dying patient needed her.

When there was no response to her text message, Ali tried calling Sister Anselm's cell. The call went straight to voice mail. With everyone listening in, she didn't leave a message, but the fact that Sister Anselm hadn't answered either the text message or the voice call was even more worrisome.

Seeing Mark observing her, Ali closed her phone. "I'm going back to the hotel to see if I can locate Sister Anselm," she said. "In case she turns up here while I'm gone, please ask her to give Cecelia a call."

Mark nodded. "Sure thing," he said.

Ali's computer was still open and still plugged in. Knowing that carrying that and the heavy briefcase would slow her down, she turned to Mark again. "I'll only be gone a few minutes. Do you mind watching this?"

"Not at all."

Making her way through the hospital lobby, Ali was relieved to see that it was empty of media folks. The reporters and cameras had evidently moved on to the next hot story. That would change, however, once

Mimi Cooper did succumb to her injuries. Then the reporters would all come surging back.

Outside on the sidewalk the early afternoon heat was appalling. Earlier in the morning, the waiting room's droning television set had carried a local weather report. Ali seemed to remember that a smiling weatherman had reported that afternoon temperatures in the Phoenix area were expected to cross the 110-degree mark. As she hiked along the sidewalk on Camelback returning to the Ritz, Ali suspected that had already happened, and she regretted her early-morning decision to leave her Cayenne in the hotel parking lot. She wouldn't make that mistake again.

Sister Anselm can walk back and forth as much as she likes, Ali told herself. *When I go back this time, I'm bringing the car.*

By the time Ali reached the hotel entrance, rivers of sweat were dribbling into her eyes and her head felt like it was about to explode. The wig seemed to attract and hold the heat like fake grass. Ali was tempted to peel it off and leave it in her room, but she couldn't do that, either. She'd be going back to the burn unit eventually, and she couldn't afford to ditch her disguise prematurely.

Once inside the hotel, she realized that afternoon tea at the Ritz was well under way. Ali paused and looked around hopefully, thinking that perhaps Sister Anselm had simply stopped off for a bit of refreshment. There was no sign of her anywhere.

Turning on her heel, Ali approached the concierge's desk. "I'm looking for Sister Anselm," she announced.

Frowning, the concierge gave Ali an appraising look. "Who might I say is asking?"

The mat of red hair might be hot as blue blazes, but it worked—too well at times. This very same concierge had addressed her by name yesterday as her blond self. Today, as a redhead, she was a stranger and suspect.

"I'm Ali Reynolds," she said quickly, fumbling her hotel key out of her pocket. "Room three oh one. Sister Anselm is a friend of mine."

"Oh, yes, Ms. Reynolds," he said. "I'm sorry. I didn't recognize you, but yes, now I remember. You and Sister Anselm joined us for tea yesterday afternoon. I'm afraid she's not here at the moment." He glanced at his watch. "I haven't seen her since yesterday, when she left for the hospital. Have you tried calling her room?"

"She left the hospital awhile ago and said she was coming back here."

"On foot?" the concierge asked.

Ali nodded. The concierge smiled and added, "Of course, she always walks, summer or winter. She doesn't seem to mind. Perhaps she walked past me while I was busy with someone else. I can try calling her room, if you like."

"Please," Ali said.

The concierge smiled. "It's my pleasure."

When he dialed the room number, however, there was no answer. Ali turned from him and went to check with the front desk. No one there had seen Sister Anselm, either.

The worry that had been niggling at the edge of Ali's consciousness blossomed into full-blown fear. Something bad had happened to Sister Anselm on her mile-long walk from the hospital back to the hotel.

Ali turned back to the concierge. "I'll need my car right away," she said. "I don't have the ticket with me."

"It's the blue Cayenne, correct?" the concierge asked.

"Yes."

"I'll have them bring it around immediately."

Ali hurried back outside to where the parking attendants waited in the shade with a cooling mist blowing down from the ceiling of the porte cochere. She turned to the uniformed attendant who seemed to be in charge. "Did you see Sister Anselm come or go a little while ago?"

"Yes, ma'am," he said. "I did. She was just coming in the back way when a car stopped beside her. The passenger window rolled down. She spoke to someone inside the vehicle. Then she climbed inside, and they drove away."

"What kind of vehicle?" Ali asked.

"One of those new crossovers. A Honda, I think. Bright red."

"Was there a man driving, or a woman?"

"I couldn't tell. There may have been two people in the car when it stopped. Sister Anselm got in the front seat, but I think someone else was in the back."

"Which way did they go?"

"They pulled a U-turn and then left the back way. Going west toward the hospital it's easier to turn left on Twenty-fourth than it is to cross all six lanes of traffic on Camelback."

The attendant had made it all sound so routine, as though having someone drop by to give Sister Anselm a ride was an everyday occurrence

But this isn't every day, Ali thought grimly. *Sister Anselm may have thought she was getting a ride back to the hospital, but she never made it.*

When Ali's Cayenne showed up, she clambered into the driver's seat. Not wanting to betray the emotions that were roiling around inside her, she left the hotel the same way the unidentified Honda had—through the driveway at the back. Stopping at the light, Ali looked up and down Twenty-fourth. She knew that the first thing to do was go back to the hospital to make sure Sister Anselm hadn't shown up there, but if she hadn't—if someone had made off with her against her will—whoever it was had at least a forty-five-minute head start.

A few blocks to the west, just beyond Saint Gregory's, speeding traffic on Highway 51 ran north and south at sixty-plus miles per hour. If the Honda had made for that, it could be miles away from here by now, and there was no way of guessing which direction the vehicle had gone.

The light changed and Ali moved into traffic. As for who might have been at the wheel, it must have been someone known to Sister Anselm or she wouldn't have gotten into the vehicle. Or would she? Had she been forced? And if so, by whom?

That wasn't hard to figure out. Sister Anselm had spent the better part of two days with a dying woman. Hal Cooper himself had said that Mimi had moments of clarity when she emerged briefly from her morphine-induced sleep. The people who had done this were probably terrified that during one of those lucid moments Mimi might have passed the identity of her attackers along to Sister Anselm.

And there are most likely at least two of them, Ali reminded herself, *because there were two people in the vehicle that dumped Mimi's Infiniti in Gilbert.*

As Ali waited impatiently for the left-hand turn sig-
nal to allow her onto Camelback, she realized there
was a fallacy in her reasoning.

It doesn't matter if Mimi told her or not, Ali realized.
*If they think Sister Anselm knows, they need to get rid
of her before she has a chance to pass that information
along to someone else.*

"Damn!" Ali exclaimed aloud. "What the hell am I
supposed to do now?"

CHAPTER 15

Leaving the Cayenne with the hospital's parking valet, Ali raced upstairs. The waiting room of the burn unit had turned into bedlam. Serenity and Win Langley, now accompanied by Serenity's assistant, had taken over the corner of the room not currently occupied by Mark Levy. Win and Donna were both doing their best to comfort Serenity, who was once more weeping uncontrollably. A glance at Mimi's door showed the DNR sign still in evidence, which most likely meant that Mimi was still hanging on.

Hearing Serenity's sobbing, Ali couldn't help wondering if Serenity's tears didn't have more to do with her fractured relationship with her mother than it did with Mimi's impending death.

James's family, still relatively united, had taken possession of the middle of the room, including the table with the unfinished jigsaw puzzle. Mark sat apart from the rest of them, keeping to himself in the far corner, with Ali's laptop open on his lap.

Before Sarah and Roy's earlier arrival on the scene, the television set in the room had been on, but at such a low volume that no one had paid attention to whatever was showing. That had changed with Roy's arrival. He had turned the volume up to high. He sat in front of the set, still fully engrossed in his baseball game—or was it a new baseball game? Ali couldn't tell.

What was obvious, however, was that Roy was using the game to absent himself from the battle between Sarah and her recently arrived younger sister, Carol. The two of them were going at it hot and heavy over what could have been done or should have been done to keep their older sister from falling asleep with a cigarette in her hand, thus setting herself on fire.

As Ali walked past the argument to reach Mark Levy, she caught a whiff of a distinctive odor, which made her suspect that Carol had already taken a nip or two of her daily allotment of demon rum.

Mark closed the computer at her approach. "I hope you don't mind me using it," he said, handing it over. "I was checking my e-mail."

"No," Ali said. "That's fine. Did Sister Anselm come back?"

"Nope. At least she didn't come through here."

"And Hal?" Ali asked.

Mark shook his head. "He hasn't been out since you left, but you might want to check your e-mail. It sounded like several new messages came in while I was online."

Dropping into the chair next to Mark's, Ali clicked on her mail program. Her in-box showed ten new e-mails. Three of them made her hair stand on end. SRA@SOP.com. Sister Anselm writing from a Sisters of Providence Web site.

While Ali had been waiting for and expecting a text message, Sister Anselm had sent her an e-mail instead.

When Ali pushed Read, she expected a regular e-mail to appear on the screen—something complete with words and text. Instead a map popped up on her screen, a map of Scottsdale, at least one with the far northeastern edge of Scottsdale showing on the screen. There was a red dot on the Beeline Highway northeast of Scottsdale. In the upper left-hand corner was a speedometer with a reading of sixty-three miles per hour. In the upper right-hand corner was a compass showing a northeast heading.

For a moment Ali couldn't make out what was happening. What did it mean? She checked the next message. The same map appeared. In that one the pin was still on Highway 87, but a little to the north of the location in the previous message.

Suddenly Ali understood. Sister Anselm was employing one of the more exotic applications on her iPhone—she was using her navigation system to broadcast where she was. In a moving vehicle, heading north by northeast.

Weeks earlier Ali had heard Chris and B. Simpson discussing this latest add-on in iPhone technology, but she hadn't paid much attention. Now she was on full alert. Sister Anselm needed help, and she was sending out a wireless SOS, most likely to the most recently used address in her phone—Ali's. Maybe she couldn't risk attempting to leave a voice message right then for fear of being overheard, and perhaps ordinary texting was too cumbersome for some reason, but this worked. The most recent e-mail had come in a mere five minutes earlier.

Ali had been on the Beeline Highway on occasion. Once you were on it, there weren't all that many places to turn off. You either went north to Payson or south on the Apache Trail past Roosevelt Dam.

Ali glanced around the room. No one seemed to be paying any attention to her. If Mimi's children were involved in this latest plot somehow, they were doing an excellent job of giving themselves cover. If they were ever asked about it, they would be able to answer quite honestly that at the time Sister Anselm was being driven north by person or persons unknown, they had been sitting in a hospital waiting room, minding their own business, and expecting any moment that their dying mother would be pronounced dead. That would count as a foolproof alibi.

Mark leaned over the arm of his chair and peered at the map. "Hey, that's one of those new G-spot things, isn't it?" he said. "Cool."

Ali put her finger to her lips. "I'm going down to the lobby," she said aloud.

As soon as the elevator door closed behind her, Ali hit the speed dial that went directly to Sheriff Maxwell's cell phone.

"Hey, I'm in a meeting now," he said when he picked up. "Can I get back to you?"

"No! You can't," she declared. "I need to speak to you now."

"What's going on?" he asked. "You make it sound like a matter of life and death."

"It is," she said. "I think someone has kidnapped Sister Anselm."

"Kidnapped the nun?" Maxwell demanded. "Who would do that? Why?"

"The people responsible for the attack on Mimi Cooper," Ali responded. "I suspect they believe Mimi confided in her and revealed their identities."

"Damn!" Maxwell muttered, which was much the

same thing Ali had said a few minutes earlier. "You know this for sure? If so, where did it happen? If she was kidnapped in Phoenix, you'll need to contact Phoenix PD and get their people on the case."

"I don't know who has her," Ali said urgently, "but I know approximately where she is." Ali glanced at her watch. "At least I know where she was about ten minutes ago."

"Wait a minute," Maxwell said. "Hold on. Hey, guys," he said. "I'll need you to step outside so I can take this call." Moments later a door slammed shut on Maxwell's end. By the time the sheriff was back on the line with her, Ali had made her way to an unoccupied love seat in the lobby.

"Let me get this straight," Maxwell said. "You're telling me that you believe Sister Anselm has been kidnapped. You don't know that for sure, but you still think you know where she is."

"I do know where she is," Ali insisted. "She's in a vehicle headed north on the Beeline Highway."

"And you know this because . . ."

"Because she just sent me an e-mail through her navigation system," Ali said. "If you'll go back to your computer, I can forward it to you and you'll see for yourself. We need to move fast, Sheriff Maxwell. If she's not there of her own free will, and if whoever grabbed her finds her iPhone and figures out she's been sending out messages, it'll all be over."

Ali opened her computer and logged on to her Air-Card. In her new mail list, she found another message from Sister Anselm.

"Okay," Ali said. "She just sent me another one. It looks like the vehicle is north of Jake's Corner and still heading toward Payson. I'm forwarding it to you. You should have it in a few minutes."

"Okay," he said. "This is nuts, but I'll go back into my office and wait for it."

She heard the swishing sound of an outgoing message leaving her computer. Then she waited, fuming, for the forward to make its way into his mailbox. It took only a few seconds, but with Ali's heightened sense of urgency, the wait seemed interminable.

"Got it," Maxwell said. "I see it now. Where they are now is out of Maricopa County and into Gila. I can call over to Globe and talk to Sheriff Tuttle, but he's going to have the same problem we have—too much ground to cover and not enough patrol units." He paused for a moment before adding, "You really think the person who has her is the one who set the fire in Camp Verde?"

"Either the perpetrator or an accomplice."

Maxwell sighed. "Holy crap!" he exclaimed. "To get officers there in time to do any good, we probably need a helicopter. That means I'll have to call that bastard Donnelley and drag his people into this. I could call in DPS, but that'll take time, too. I'm guessing the ATF has a chopper at their disposal when needed. Let me give them a call, Ali. I'll get back to you."

Ali closed her phone and waited. It seemed to take forever. In the meantime yet another message came in from Sister Anselm. The vehicle was still moving north, but Ali worried that in that desolate and virtually uninhabited part of the state, the iPhone would lose its connection or power or both. Finally the phone rang.

"Okay," Sheriff Maxwell said. "Donnelley has dispatched several ground units. It'll take time for them to ger there. In the meantime, he has an agent named Robson on his way over to the hospital. Gary Robson. Isn't he the guy you told me about yesterday? The one who was there in the burn unit throwing his weight around?"

"Yes," Ali said. "That's the one."

"He happens to be closest to your location. He's coming by to pick up your computer. Donnelley is trying to negotiate permission for them to land an ATF helicopter on the hospital helipad long enough to pick him up."

"No," Ali said.

"Excuse me? What do you mean, 'no'? No what?"

"No, that's not going to work. Tell Agent Donnelley from me that if Agent Robson is taking my computer, he's also taking me."

"Ali," Maxwell said, making an effort to sound reasonable. "You can't do that. The ATF isn't going to let you hitch a ride with them on a tactical pursuit like this. I'm sure that would be violating at least a dozen rules and regs, to say nothing of liability issues."

"I don't care about liability," Ali returned. "Sister Anselm is sending those messages to me. I'm her lifeline. If you think I'm going to let my computer out of my hands, you're nuts. The ATF is welcome to the information on my computer, but only if they take me along. My computer and I are a package deal. I have a vest. I'll have to get it out of my car, but I have it along."

"Ali, I'm giving you an order—"

"I'm not a sworn police officer," Ali pointed out. "If you want to fire me for insubordination, be my guest. Fire away. I was happily unemployed when you dragged me out of retirement. I'll be glad to go back to that, eating bonbons and maybe learning how to play bridge. In the meantime, Sister Anselm has trusted me with her life, and I'm not going to let her down."

"Ali," Maxwell pleaded. "Be reasonable."

"My way or the highway," she said and closed her phone. She hurried over to the valet stand, gave the attendant a five, and asked him to retrieve her Kevlar vest from the back of the Cayenne. While he sprinted off to find it, Ali's cell phone rang again. This time Dave Holman's number showed in the display.

"So Sheriff Maxwell ran up the flag to you in the hope of getting me back in line?" she said.

"More or less," Dave said. "He's right, of course, Ali. You've got no business sticking your nose in all this—"

"I hung up on him and I'll hang up on you, too," Ali told him. "Sheriff Maxwell asked me to work with Sister Anselm, and that's why she's sending her messages to me. Agent Robson was here yesterday, and he didn't make a very good impression on anyone—including Sister Anselm."

"But—"

"No deal," Ali said. "Another message just came in. I don't know how many more she'll be able to send, or even if she'll be able to send them, but I'm going to be on the scene with the ATF guys or else."

"Okay," Dave said, conceding defeat. "I'll tell him. He isn't going to like it."

"Neither is Agent Robson," Ali said. "That's his problem. They'll both have to like it or lump it."

The parking attendant returned carrying Ali's vest. She slipped it on over her pink tracksuit. She also slipped off the wig and stuck it in her briefcase. She was sitting staring at her computer screen when Agent Robson appeared on the scene a few minutes later.

"Ali Reynolds?" he asked,

She looked up at him and nodded.

"I'm here for your computer."

"What?" Ali returned. "No 'please' and no 'thank you'? Just 'hand it over'?"

"This is an emergency situation—" he began.

"I'm well aware it's an emergency," she returned. "I'm the one who called it in, remember? Without me, you wouldn't even know Sister Anselm was among the missing, much less where she had gone."

"Look," he said, "Donnelley told me some garbage about your wanting to go along. That's not going to happen. The helicopter will be here any minute. If you're right and the killer has her, we don't have much time. Now give me the damned computer and show me the file so I can go."

"I don't work for you, Agent Robson. I have it on pretty good authority that Sheriff Maxwell is about to terminate my consulting agreement, too, so it turns out I don't have to take orders from him *or* from you. You might mention to Agent Donnelley that Sister Anselm has an exceptionally good working relationship with the bishop at the Catholic diocese here in Phoenix. If he wants to risk her life by not having access to my information . . ."

"Where the hell do you get off—" he began.

"That's the whole point," she said. "I'm not getting off. If my computer is going on that helicopter, so am I."

"It could be dangerous."

"So is crossing a street."

Shaking his head, Robson touched the button on his Bluetooth. "Call Agent Donnelley," he said.

Ali stood with her arms crossed and stared at him until he finally connected.

"Yeah," he said. "I talked to her. She's adamant that she's going along . . . No, she won't listen to reason . . . Yes. Okay, I'll tell her."

Just then Jake Whitman, the hospital administrator, came striding off the elevator. He nodded curtly in Ali's direction. "I'm looking for an Agent Robson."

"That would be me."

"I'm the hospital administrator. It's most unusual to have anything other than a medevac helicopter on our helipad. You need to get it out of there immediately. Come on," he added, rattling a set of keys. "I'll take you."

He started away from them, then stopped when he realized neither Agent Robson nor Ali was following. "Well," he said impatiently. "Are you two coming or not?"

As Ali stuck her computer in her briefcase, the wig, with a mind of its own, managed to tumble out on the floor.

Robson bent to pick it up. Before giving it back to her, he looked at the wig and then at Ali. "That's who you are," he said. "That's why you look familiar."

"Yes," she agreed. Then, closing her briefcase and picking up her purse, she turned to Whitman. "We're coming," she told the hospital administrator. She knew full well that Robson wouldn't go to the mat with her about any of this in front of Whitman. Cool macho dudes like Robson didn't like being seen arguing with women in public.

Whitman set a brisk pace as they followed him back into the elevator. Access to the twelfth floor required use of a key. The doors opened on a corridor with a smoothly polished floor.

"This way," he said.

The hallway ended in a pair of double doors. When

Whitman pushed open one of the doors, Ali's ears were assailed by the roar of a helicopter's engines. Her hair blew up and out in the buffeting gale from the rotating blades.

Without pausing for permission, Ali walked past Whitman and climbed into the helicopter.

"Who the hell are you?" the pilot demanded. "I was told to pick up Agent Robson."

"It turns out we've got a freeloader," Robson said, climbing in behind her. "Fasten your damned belt," he ordered her, "and keep your mouth shut. Open your computer, show me what you've got, and then stay out of my way."

You really are an overbearing jerk, Ali thought as the helicopter rose off the roof. She had worked with enough of those in her time, so she had some idea how to deal with him. Without being told and without asking permission, she clapped a set of earphones on her head, earphones with an attached microphone.

"Where to?" the pilot asked.

"I was told to head out to a road called the Beeline Highway. Northbound on that."

Nodding, the pilot put the helicopter into the air. Once they gained altitude, they set off across the city, traveling on a diagonal, pounding past Camelback Mountain, heading northeast, covering the traffic-congested roadways with surprising speed. The sun was sinking in the west. The shadow cast by the helicopter was long and skinny.

Ali waited for a few moments, taking in the sights before she spoke. "I suppose I could keep quiet, unless you'd like to know the make and color of the vehicle we're looking for."

Robson crossed his arms and glared at her. "Tell me," he said.

"A red Honda crossover," she replied. "At least that's the vehicle Sister Anselm was seen getting into outside her hotel. They might have switched into another vehicle by now and stuffed her into a trunk."

"That would be my guess." Robson's agreement surprised her.

"As hot as it is," Ali began. "How long can someone survive in an overheated car trunk?"

"Exactly," Robson said. "If we don't get to her soon, she'll be dead no matter what."

From the grim set of his mouth as he said it, Ali knew the man was totally focused on what was going on with Sister Anselm and whether it would be possible to save her.

A jerk, yes, Ali thought as she opened her computer, *but a jerk who's determined to do his job.*

Ali was relieved to see that her AirCard still worked even though they were airborne. Once she accessed it, Sister Anselm's map immediately appeared on the screen. There was also a new e-mail waiting in Ali's in-box— another message from Sister Anselm, one that was more recent than the one Ali had seen back at the hospital.

When Ali opened that one she immediately noticed that the speedometer on the screen now read fifty miles per hour. "They're slowing down," she said.

"How do you know they're slowing down?" Robson asked, leaning over to peer at the screen.

"Previously their average speed was sixty-three miles per hour. Now they're down to fifty."

"Maybe they're looking for a place to turn off," Robson said. "What's out there?"

"Not much," Ali returned. "A couple of Forest Service roads. That's about it."

"Can I see that thing?" the pilot asked.

Bypassing Agent Robson's outstretched hand, Ali handed her open computer directly to the pilot. For a minute or so, he punched commands into the keyboard. Then, satisfied with that, he punched another series of numbers into his onboard computer.

"I put in this set of coordinates," he said, handing the computer back to Ali. "That'll give us somewhere to start. If you get another one, let me know."

Nodding, Ali kept quiet while the pilot relayed the information from his computer to people on the ground. That was what they needed, she realized. People on the ground and people in the air.

"How long to get there?" Robson asked.

"Forty-five total," he said. "ETA is twenty minutes from now."

"You can't do it any faster than that?"

"If you want to disregard the laws of physics, that's up to you," the pilot told Robson, "but you and I will get along a hell of a lot better if you get used to the idea that it's going to take as long as it takes."

My sentiments exactly, Ali thought.

She was coming back. She had thought it was over, but evidently it wasn't, not quite. She was still here. Sort of. And Hal was here, too, standing next to her bed.

She needed to tell him what she remembered. If only she could speak. If only she could get rid of this damned machine that blocked her throat. Then she'd be able to tell him. Hal would know what to do. He always knew what to do.

"Win and Serenity are still outside," he said. "I can let them back in if you'd like them here. If you want to see them. I think they'd like to see you."

No, she thought. *I saw the look of shock on Win's face when he saw what I look like now. And I heard Serenity. They may think they want to see me, but they don't. I don't want them to remember me this way. I want them to remember me the way I used to be. The way I was, not the way I am now.*

Two blinks, then. Two blinks for no.

"I know there's some bad blood between you and Serenity," Hal said, "and between Serenity and me, too," he added, "but don't push them away. They're both here. They've both been here all day. Let's be kind. Let's let them in again. Please."

It was surprising to Mimi that Hal really didn't understand. Not at all. She was trying to be kind to her children just then. She didn't want them to have to suffer by seeing her this way. That was too hard on them, especially on Serenity, the one who thought she was so damned tough.

So Mimi blinked twice. Twice for no.

Hal sighed. "All right, Mimi girl," he said. "We'll do it your way. Is it time to push the button?"

Almost, but not quite. I could stay a little longer. I could stand it a little longer, if you'd just lean down and kiss me.

But he didn't do that. Instead he punched the button, and she went sliding away. And she realized as she drifted away that she still hadn't told him what she needed to say.

Because he hadn't asked. Maybe he never would.

Another e-mail showed up in Ali's in-box. Another e-mail from Sister Anselm. "They're moving at three miles per hour," she said, "and they've turned east."

"Where?" Robson asked.

"Looks like Forest Road one forty-three," Ali answered.

The pilot nodded in agreement.

"Look," Robson said. "I'm not from here. Where does it go?"

"Nowhere," the pilot answered. "Off into the Four Peaks Wilderness Area. There's nothing out there but nothing."

Ali stared at the pin on the computer with a feeling of dread. Whoever had Sister Anselm was taking her to a place where there would be no witnesses and no turning back. Even if Sister Anselm survived a ride imprisoned in an overheated trunk, she might not survive what came next. Ali's computer offered their only hope of finding her.

On TV and in the movies, pursuits were always fast and exciting. This one seemed slow as mud. Ali looked at her watch for the third time in as many minutes and wondered if it was still running. The pilot had said they were twenty minutes or so out, but if the car they were after had already turned off the highway, whatever was going to happen was going to happen soon. Sooner than they could get there. Sooner than any of the ground units could get there.

Closing her eyes, Ali murmured a small prayer. "Please keep Sister Anselm safe. Please."

Over the microphone she heard Robson talking to someone else. "Excellent," he said. "According to what I'm hearing, that road has only one way in and one way out. Have them block it and lay down spike strips. Whatever happens, the guy isn't going to get away."

"What's going on?" Ali asked.

"Units from the Gila County Sheriff's Department are still on the way, but it turns out the Arizona Department of Public Safety had a vehicle in the area. That DPS unit is already at the intersection where the forest road comes back out to the highway. The officer has blocked the road with his vehicle and is laying down tire strips on either side of where he's parked. If the bad guy tries to make a run for it and go around him, it won't work."

Ali nodded. Setting a trap to catch the guy at the intersection sounded good as far as it went, but it wasn't nearly good enough. If the guy's vehicle was stopped on the way back out to the highway, that would most likely mean whatever was going to happen to Sister Anselm would have already happened.

Too little, too late, Ali thought.

The e-mail alert sounded on Ali's computer. Another new e-mail from Sister Anselm's address had appeared in her mailbox. When she opened it, Ali's heart fell. The speedometer read zero miles per hour.

"They've stopped," she said. "The pin puts their latest position a couple of miles or so beyond the intersection."

"Crap!" Robson muttered. He turned to the pilot. "You keep flying," he said. "Can you tell me how to key in this last set of coordinates? If he dumps her there, that's the only way we're going to find her."

Ali didn't need to ask what would precede the dumping. Agent Robson knew, and so did she.

Robson held out his hand, and Ali passed the ATF agent her computer without a word of objection.

For the time being at least, Ali Reynolds and Gary Robson were both on the same side.

{ CHAPTER 16 }

The helicopter sped swiftly over a harsh desert landscape—spines of rocky ridges spiked with saguaro and dotted with low-lying grayish-green shrubs. Ali stared out of the aircraft's glass windshield at the seemingly empty desert, hoping for a glimpse of blacktop or even a sliver of dirt road—something with a moving vehicle on it that would let her know they were getting closer. Something that would give her hope that they weren't already too late.

A radio transmission laced with static came through the earphones. Ali didn't hear what was coming through the radio, but she did understand the string of obscenity-laced invective that spewed out of Gary Robson's mouth.

"What's wrong?" Ali asked.

"That was the DPS. A car moving westward started down the road toward the state patrolman who had his car parked along with the spike strips. When the driver saw that the road was blocked, he pulled a U-turn and raced back in the other direction."

"As you already mentioned, there's only one way in

and one way out," Ali said. "At least that's how it looks on the map."

"Let's hope so. A Gila County deputy is due on the scene in another five minutes. He'll probably get there at about the same time we do, or maybe a little before. The deputy is driving an SUV that'll be better suited to that kind of road than an ordinary DPS patrol car. The deputy will go after the guy, and so will we."

"Did he see what kind of vehicle?"

"It was too far away. An American sedan of some kind. That's good for us. If the road's as bad as I think it is, that should slow him down. With any kind of luck, we'll be able to lead that deputy right to him."

Ali thought of how many high-speed pursuits she had reported on during her days as a newscaster in L.A., always with the voice of the eye-in-the-sky helicopter providing the narrative. They had often lasted for hours—endless hours of stultifying boredom, punctuated by appalling crashes and spectacular spinouts, with a dozen police cars converging on the resulting wreckage. But this lonely stretch of desert wasn't a place where dozens of police cars could be summoned as backup.

Whatever happens will be up to us and that one deputy, she thought.

"If it comes down to him or us," Ali told Robson, "I'm carrying a Glock and I know how to use it."

Robson gave her an appraising look. "Don't go all Annie Oakley on me. I thought you were strictly media relations."

And I thought you were strictly a jerk, she thought, but that wasn't what she said.

"I'm wearing a vest. I'm a decent shot, and beggars

can't be choosers. I have a feeling you're going to need all the help you can get."

"Shooting someone's no joking matter," he said. "Target shooting is one thing. Shooting another human being is the very last resort."

"I know firsthand about that," she said.

Maybe there was something in her answer that told him she had done that, just as he had, too. When he finally figured that out on his own, he grimaced and gave her a grudging nod.

"All right," he said, "but not unless I say so, as in giving you a direct order, and not if we don't need the help."

Ali nodded back.

"I understand," she said. "Believe me," she told him, "Sheriff Maxwell will be furious if I end up being a part of a shooting incident outside the boundaries of Yavapai County. He specifically asked me to avoid that."

Fortunately Robson didn't ask where she carried her Glock. The discreet small-of-the-back holster she wore under her tracksuit was none of the ATF agent's business.

After that, Robson fell silent for several minutes while he stared at the ground. "There," he said pointing. "I see the road."

Ali looked where he was pointing, and she could see it, too—a silver ribbon of highway winding through an otherwise brown-and-green landscape. Soon she could see the other road, too, a dirt track leading off into the wilderness from the paved highway.

"The deputy just got there," Robson announced. "They're moving the spike strips so the deputy can get around." He turned to the pilot. "Can you take us up higher so we can see more? As slowly as he was driving when he first turned off on that, he can't have gone far. We should be able to spot him."

Obligingly, the pilot took the helicopter up.

"There," Ali said. "That plume of dust has to be him."

Nodding, Robson went back to speaking to the people on the ground. "It's looks as though he's a mile or two away, driving hell-bent for leather."

Moments later, Ali could see a green older-model car tearing up the road and spewing up a trailing cloud of dust.

"It's an old Ford Gran Torino," Robson said into the radio. "A muscle car, but that's not going to help him on this road. It looks rough. Something's going to break on that old crate and he'll be stuck."

Suddenly, as though Robson's words carried the power of psychokinesis, the fleeing vehicle stopped abruptly, slewing off to one side as though something really had broken.

"Tie rod, I'll bet," Agent Robson diagnosed. "That guy's not going anywhere."

But as they watched, a tiny man scrambled out of the vehicle and trotted back to the left rear wheel, where he squatted down to assess the damage. Then, hearing the clatter of approaching helicopter blades, he shaded his eyes with one hand and stared up at them. With barely a pause, he leaped to his feet, flung open the back door, and grabbed something from inside the vehicle. Only when he aimed the weapon at them did the people in the helicopter realize what he was doing.

"Holy shit!" Robson exclaimed. "That crazy bastard's got a rifle. He's shooting at us. Take us up! Take us up!"

The highly motivated pilot required no urging. They were rising straight up with stomach-churning speed before the words were out of Robson's mouth.

Ali didn't have to hear the sound of the shots to know they had been fired upon or to know the degree of menace involved. The man on the ground was desperate. He had no intention of being taken alive. He was armed and dangerous and prepared to fight to the death.

"Shots fired; shots fired," Robson reported over the radio. "Looks like a rifle of some kind," he said to the pilot. "We need to stay out of range."

"Tell me about it," the pilot said furiously. "What do you think I am, some kind of idiot?"

Ali was thinking about her Glock. If the guy was armed with a rifle, that meant her Glock wouldn't be much help, and neither would whatever concealed weapon Agent Robson was carrying. No doubt he was armed with a handgun, maybe even two, but up against a rifle they would be seriously outgunned.

"DPS cars have shotguns in them. They may have rifles as well. Maybe we could borrow—"

"Borrow nothing," Robson declared. "We'll bring him and whatever firepower he has along with us." He turned back to the pilot. "Fly us back to the junction," he ordered. "See if you can find a spot in this godforsaken place to set this thing down."

The pilot swung the helicopter in a tight circle, returning the way they had come. Below them they could see another towering plume of dust rising sky-

ward as a Gila County deputy roared toward the shooter's position. Since the bad guy was no longer moving,
the distance between the two vehicles was closing
fast. Robson, for his part, was trying to send out a
warning that the deputy needed to exercise caution
in approaching the scene, but due to varying frequen-
cies between agencies, no one seemed to be in direct
communication.

When Robson finished with the radio transmis-
sions, Ali touched the pilot's shoulder. "What about
the coordinates you put in from the e-mail?" she asked.
"Can you show me where that was? While you guys go
after the shooter, maybe I can find Sister Anselm."

Knowing they were out of range, the pilot nodded
and sent the helicopter into a steep dive. "There," he
said a minute or so later. "Isn't that her, there on the
left, down in that gully?"

Ali peered outside, straining to pick out details on
the ground. Finally she saw a tiny spot of something
that was bright green—not the grayish green of the
surrounding desert shrubs and prickly pear. If the figure dressed in brilliant green was Sister Anselm, she
was lying in the middle of a deep gully, stretched out
on a bed of reddish-brown sand.

"See that big rock back up by the road?" the pilot
said. "If you use that boulder as a marker and go
straight north from there, you should be able to find
her."

"Good thinking," Robson said. "You go to her and
see what you can do to help her. In the meantime, that
DPS officer and I will fly back in to give the deputy
some backup."

Ali knew he was right. From the looks of it, and

especially if Sister Anselm had been shot, they were already too late to save the nun's life, but the deputy was driving solo into an ambush.

Back at the highway, the pilot determined that the only place he could set the aircraft down was on the blacktop itself. Once they landed, Robson leaped out of the helicopter. The man didn't look like much of a sprinter, but he was. He galloped across the distance between the helicopter and the parked patrol car with surprising speed. Ali hesitated for only a moment before she, too, leaped from the helicopter. By the time Ali caught up with Robson, he and the highway patrol officer, Milton Frank, were already retrieving weapons from the DPS vehicle.

As Frank and Robson started toward the helicopter, Ali stopped them. "While you two handle the shooter, please give me your car keys, Officer Frank. We spotted the woman that man kidnapped a mile or so from here. She's lying in a gully just off the road. She may already be dead, but it's possible she's injured. I need to help her."

Frank turned to Robson. "Is she a cop?" he asked.

"Yes," Gary Robson said. "She is."

"Oh," said the officer, tossing her the keys. "Why didn't you say so? It's against regulations, but under the circumstances, I think they'll give me a pass. Do you know how to use a police radio?"

"I can figure it out."

"There's some first-aid equipment in the trunk if you need it."

"Water?" Ali asked.

"That, too. Be careful you don't run over the spike strips as you leave."

With that, he and Robson set off at a run for the helicopter. Once the aircraft was airborne again, Ali looked up and down the deserted roadway, hoping to see some sign of arriving backup, but there was none. Grabbing first one set of spike strips and then the other, she dragged them off to the side of the road and left them there. Then, as she scrambled into the patrol car, she heard the familiar text message alert coming from her cell phone.

Inserting the key in the ignition, she was tempted to ignore the message, but she didn't. When she looked at the readout, she was astonished to see the text message was from Sister Anselm. It contained one word only: "Help."

"Coming." Ali sent her one-word text message reply, then she started the patrol car's powerful engine and swung it around in a circle and then onto the rutted dirt road.

The surface of the Forest Service road had never been intended for use by ordinary passenger vehicles. The patrol car, which was fine on the highway, had a hard time managing on the primitive surface. Periodically the vehicle would scrape bottom on the low spots, and the wheel base was the wrong size to negotiate the ruts left behind by the heavier vehicles and equipment that usually traveled this way.

Over the police radio, Ali heard the sound of voices speaking urgently back and forth, but she was too preoccupied with concentrating on her driving to listen to what was being said or to guess how much of it applied to the current situation. The only thing she did manage to make out clearly was the single announcement that backup units were en route. Ali's desperate hope was that those backup units were headed her way.

The boulder the pilot had pointed out earlier turned out to be a lichen-covered monolith. Once Ali reached it, she had difficulty finding a suitable place to pull off and park. She didn't want to leave the DPS car blocking access for other arriving vehicles.

Finding a wide enough stretch of shoulder, Ali parked, took the keys, and hurried around to the trunk. Inside she found a case of bottled water, a chest labeled *First Aid,* and a lightweight survival-style blanket. She took the chest, two bottles of water, and the blanket. Not that Sister Anselm needed a blanket for heat right then. It was just the opposite. From what Ali had seen, the injured woman seemed to be baking in direct sunlight with no chance of shade. Ali hoped to use the blanket to create some shelter from the scorching sun.

Carrying the supplies, Ali raced back to the boulder. Once she left the roadway, Ali found she was in desperately rough terrain. Twenty yards or so from the road, she was standing at the edge of a deep ravine. She was shocked. The view of the scene from the helicopter had flattened the landscape. There had been no way to tell the depth of the gully, or that there was a twelve-foot, boulder-laced drop-off between the surface where Ali now stood and the spot where Sister Anselm had landed, lying still and silent, sprawled facedown in the sandy bottom.

"Sister Anselm," Ali called. "Can you hear me?"

There was no answering response, no movement.

There was no sign of footprints leading up or down the steep path, and there were none leading to or from Sister Anselm's body. She hadn't walked there or been carried there. She had been thrown there. Or pushed.

Ali was outraged. *The bastard just dropped her,* Ali thought. *He tossed her away like she was so much garbage.*

"Sister Anselm," she called. "I'm here. I'm coming as fast as I can."

Again there was no acknowledgment from the prone figure in the sand below.

Ali soon discovered that climbing down the steep bank was easier said than done. For one thing, it was eroded. Places that appeared to offer a firm foothold crumbled when she put any weight on them. Unable to manage the steep descent safely while carrying her load of supplies, she finally gave up. First she stuffed the blanket inside her tracksuit. Then, taking care to aim them in a direction where they wouldn't pose any further danger to Sister Anselm, Ali sent the water bottles and the first-aid kit tumbling down the bank.

Close to the bottom but with no visible footholds remaining, Ali finally jumped the last three feet or so, making a jarring two-point landing. The sand looked soft but it wasn't. She grunted as sharp pains radiated out from both knees, then scrabbled across the hot sand to retrieve her supplies. When she finally reached Sister Anselm's side, she knelt near her head, hoping to shield her from some of the sun's fierce heat.

"Sister Anselm," she said. "It's Ali. I'm here. Can you hear me?"

Again there was no answer.

"Please," Ali said aloud, praying again. "Please show me what to do."

For a moment, all she did was examine the extent of Sister Anselm's injuries. Her eyes were closed, her breathing shallow, her face beet red. That could have been from heatstroke or sunburn, or maybe a combination of both. Her scrubs had been torn to shreds. The pieces of bare skin that were visible were bruised and bloodied. Her right leg lay at an unnatural angle to the rest of her body. Either her leg was broken or her hip was. Her right hand, folded into a fist, appeared to be buried in the sand. Closer inspection revealed a death grip—on her iPhone. Since that wireless device had been Sister Anselm's only lifeline, Ali made no attempt to pry it loose.

"Help is coming." Ali tried to sound confident and reassuring, but even as she said the words, she knew she was lying. The kind of help that was available right now wasn't the kind of help Sister Anselm needed. If she had broken limbs or worse—if her back was broken—she would need to be airlifted from the scene in a real medevac helicopter. There was no possibility that they would be able to load her into one of the cramped seats of the ATF helicopter where Ali and Agent Robson had ridden.

Knowing she must have additional resources, Ali was reaching for her phone when Sister Anselm's eyes fluttered open. For a moment she seemed puzzled by her surroundings. Then, seeing Ali's face, she managed a tiny smile.

"You came," she croaked. "You must have gotten my message."

"I got all your messages," Ali returned. "Just a minute." Punching Redial, she called Dave's number and let out her breath when he answered after only one ring.

"What the hell's going on there?" he demanded.

"We've found Sister Anselm. She needs an air ambulance as fast as you can get one here."

"Where's here?" Dave wanted to know.

"Log on to my e-mail account," she said, giving him the name and password. "Open the last e-mail from Sister Anselm. You can get the GPS coordinates from that—or else the helicopter pilot can. They'll know they're getting close when they see a DPS car parked along the road. Tell them to take a heading north from the big boulder just to the west of the vehicle. We're down in a gully."

She could tell he was still writing. "How bad is it?" he asked.

"Bad. They'll have to put her on a stretcher. Even with one of those, I'm not sure how they'll get her up and out."

"Hanging up now," he said, "so I can call it in."

Ali turned her attention back to Sister Anselm. Her eyes were closed again.

Ali was sure the injured woman was dehydrated, but with her face sideways in the sand, there was no way to offer her a drink from one of the bottles.

Ali opened the first-aid kit and rummaged through the scrambled mess inside until she found a roll of gauze. She pulled off a hunk of that, soaked it with water from one of the bottles, and then held it to Sister Anselm's parched lips. Then she poured the water from the other bottle over Sister Anselm's hair. At the touch of the water on her skin, her eyes blinked open again.

"Water," she whispered. "Thank you."

"Suck on the gauze," Ali told her. "When you get the water out of that, I'll wet it again. Can you move?"

"No. I think my hip is broken. It hurts," she added. "Hurts like crazy, and that's good. It means my back isn't broken, and I'm alive."

Just barely, Ali thought.

She loaded the strip of gauze with another dose of water. While Sister Anselm sucked on that, Ali peered up at the sun. It was setting, but the stark line of shadow that now divided the gully in half was still a good foot and a half away from Sister Anselm's overheated body. Hoping to create some shade, Ali pulled the blanket out from under her shirt and flapped it open. By draping the blanket on her left arm and holding it out straight she was able to create a small patch of temporary shade. With her right hand, she pulled a laminated sheet of first-aid instructions out of the kit and used that as a fan.

The whole time she had been climbing down the bank and scrabbling around in the sand, she had been half listening for the sound of gunshots. Even if a shoot-out occurred a mile or more away, she expected that the sounds of weapons being fired would travel long distances in this empty landscape. Once or twice she heard what sounded like the remote clatter of the helicopter's rotating blades.

Now, though, fanning Sister Anselm's bright red face, Ali heard the sound of an approaching vehicle. Since it was clearly coming from the east, Ali realized at once that it wasn't a backup vehicle, since those would be coming from the west. The approaching vehicle was traveling fast. Ali knew that meant it had to be an SUV. No older-model sedan could make that kind of headway on the rutted road.

"More water," Sister Anselm murmured. "Please."

Giving her more water was a two-handed procedure. Ali had to let go of the blanket in order to pick up the bottle of water. After saturating the hunk of gauze again, she returned it to Sister Anselm's lips.

Ali was about to pick up the blanket again when she heard a metallic *ka-chunk*. A distinctive sound. The sound of a shotgun round being chambered. She froze.

"Where are the keys?" a man's voice said. "I want the keys!"

Ali glanced up. The man stood at the top of the bank, aiming a loaded shotgun down into the gully. Ali knew enough about shotguns to understand that, from that range, being hit by a blast from a shotgun would be fatal.

"Bring me the keys," he ordered. "Now!"

Ali realized in a split second what must have happened. Somehow the bad guy had managed to take possession of the Gila County deputy's vehicle. Had the deputy also been shot?

Far in the background, Ali heard the distant clatter of the helicopter, but what did that mean? Had the shooter somehow managed to baffle Agent Robson and the others in the helicopter with a change of vehicles? If so, by now they must have realized their error.

They were coming, but Ali knew they were too far away to provide any kind of counterforce to the man staring down from the bank with his finger clamped to the trigger of a loaded shotgun.

She stood up and faced him. He was a small man, middle-aged and balding. He had a slight paunch beneath a worn Grateful Dead T-shirt and jeans. He was the kind of man who wouldn't merit a second glance in a grocery store or post office, but with a shotgun in his hands, he commanded her absolute attention.

"Who are you?" she asked. "What do you want?"

"Insurance," he said. "You're my ticket out. Come here now or I'll kill you both."

Ali glanced down at the woman lying at her feet. Sister Anselm was helpless, and perhaps near death. Looking into the barrel of that shotgun, Ali realized that she, too, was near death. But she wasn't helpless. Her knees may have been knocking, her heart hammering wildly in her chest, but Ali was armed. Sister Anselm was not.

"Move!" he ordered.

He probably wouldn't expect that she would be carrying a weapon. It occurred to Ali that once she started climbing the bank, she might be out of his line of vision long enough to draw her Glock, but that wouldn't be easy, especially since climbing down into the gully had been a two-handed job. She suspected that climbing back up would require both hands as well.

She had no idea how long she hesitated, but it was too long for his purposes. "I mean now!" he ordered. "Move or I start shooting."

Ali didn't doubt that he meant it. She moved, plowing through the hard-packed sand and making her way toward the steep bank. Approaching it, she looked for a route that would provide some cover.

"Come up right here," he called, pointing with the barrel of his weapon.

"I can't," she said. "It's too steep. The dirt crumbles when you step on it."

She started up, grabbing at a clump of dried grass halfway up the bank to give herself some purchase. Once she pulled herself up to that, she glanced up at the bank. She could still see the shooter, which meant he could still see her as well. She needed more time, and a better route.

With her next step Ali deliberately misplaced her foot. The fragile bank gave way beneath her and she went slipping back down, all the way to the sandy bottom. It was a controlled fall. She was scratched and scraped as she fell, but she landed relatively unhurt. In the process of sliding down the bank, however, the bottom of her top had hiked up above her waist. She pulled it down quickly, hoping he hadn't seen the holster.

"Come on, come on," he screamed at her. "You can do better than that."

The sound of the helicopter was closer now, hovering far overhead, well out of range. No wonder he was growing more agitated. There was always a possibility that if he panicked, he might pull the trigger accidentally.

Trying not to think about that, Ali moved several feet down the bank and farther away from Sister Anselm before she made her next attempt to ascend. She knew she couldn't pull the same stunt twice. If she fell again, he'd probably run out of patience and start blasting away at her. She took a calming breath, trying to steady her shaking hands and trembling knees before she started back up.

This time she chose a spot just beyond the place where another massive lichen-covered boulder, not unlike the one up next to the road, had tumbled into the creek bed. She hoped the bulge of outcropping rock would give her sufficient cover to do what needed to be done.

"Get a move on!"

"I'm trying," she said.

Holding her breath, she paused behind the rock long enough to move the Glock from her small-of-the-back holster to the front of the elastic waistband on her battered pink tracksuit. She knew that wasn't necessarily the safest option, but at that point, with a dangerous killer holding a gun on her, safety was relative and her waistband provided the easiest access.

"Drop it!"

Damn! Ali thought. *He saw me.*

"I said drop it and get on the ground!" the menacing voice repeated. "Now! You're surrounded. There's no way out."

But I am on the ground, she thought.

The thought came and went in an instant before she realized what must have happened. Backup really had arrived.

Before the words to another thought could form in her head, the hot desert air exploded in a barrage of deafening gunfire. Ali's heart hammered in her chest as she flattened herself behind the rock, burying her face in the sandy bank.

She worked the Glock out of her waistband. If the shooter somehow escaped his pursuers and came her way, Ali was determined to be ready for him. If it came to that, she would pull the trigger. She wouldn't let him escape.

The first roar of the shotgun was followed by at least a dozen more shots. Listening to the firefight, Ali thought it went on for an eternity. Stray bullets ricocheted off boulders, kicking up a spray of splintery rocks and dirt. Then, as suddenly as the gun battle had begun, it ended. The sudden silence was punctuated by a terrible scream—a scream of agony—followed by more silence, almost as deafening as the gunfire had been loud.

Ali watched in horror as a bloodied figure tumbled

end over end down the bank and into the ravine. Half-way down, the shotgun separated itself from the body and went skittering off in another direction. The shooter hit the ground headfirst without doing anything to break his fall. Ali heard a fearsome crack and knew right then that his neck was broken. He tumbled twice more, finally coming to rest a half dozen feet away from Sister Anselm.

Somehow that seemed fair.

"Don't shoot," Ali called to whoever was up there as she quickly tucked her weapon back into her holster. "Sister Anselm and I are here—in the gully."

An unfamiliar male face peered down at her from the top of the ledge. "Are you all right?" he asked. "Are you coming up, or going down?"

"Down," Ali said, reversing course. "I'm sure the shooter's dead, but there's a severely wounded woman down here. She needs help. Bring more water."

Sliding on her belly back down to the creek bed, Ali knew that the pink jogging suit was a goner. She hurriedly went back to Sister Anselm's side.

The nun was still breathing, but her eyes were closed again. Despite the gunfire, she had somehow drifted back into unconsciousness. Considering her injuries, that was probably a blessing. Ali made no attempt to wake her.

In the intervening minutes the line of shade had moved several inches closer to Sister Anselm's desperately still body, but it still wasn't close enough. Picking up the fallen blanket, Ali shook the sand out of it and held it between the injured woman and the glaring sun.

For right then, that was as much as Ali could do.

CHAPTER 17

One at a time, a group of men sporting Kevlar vests with the ATF monogram printed on them came scrambling down the bank and into the gully. That meant that Agent Robson's guys were the cavalry who had ridden to the rescue, arriving first and saving the day. One of them had also fired the shots that had sent the armed gunman tumbling to his death. One agent went to check on the gunman while two more came to kneel beside Sister Anselm.

The sounds of the gunshots were still reverberating in Ali's head. Totally focused on Sister Anselm, she didn't hear her phone ringing. Instead, she felt it vibrating in the zippered pocket of her torn tracksuit. Looking down at the remains of her outfit, Ali realized that her foresight in zipping that pocket shut was probably the only thing that had kept her from losing the phone altogether.

"Hello, Dave," she said.

"Are you all right?"

"I'm fine. The shooter's dead. Sister Anselm isn't dead, but she's in bad shape."

"I know," he said. "You told me. The medevac folks are scrambling two helicopter crews. The first one should be at your location within the next twenty minutes or so."

"I already told you," Ali said. "The shooter's dead. We don't need two helicopters."

"Yes, you do," Dave answered. "One is for Sister Anselm, and the other is for Deputy Krist."

"Who's he?"

"A Gila County deputy. The guy shot him. Shot him, dragged him out of his vehicle, left him on the ground to die, and then drove off in his SUV."

Dave was most likely a hundred miles or so away from the action, but he knew far more about what had gone on than Ali, who had been directly involved. No doubt he had heard detailed reports from Agent Robson's helicopter.

"How badly is the deputy hurt?" Ali asked.

"Life-threatening," Dave replied. "That's as much as I know. Robson had his pilot put down next to him so he could drop off Officer Frank from the DPS to stay with Krist. As far as I know, Frank is still there, waiting for help to show up. Robson took off again and came back looking for you, but it sounds like his guys got there first."

"Yes, they did," Ali agreed, "and not a moment too soon. The killer had a loaded shotgun. He also had the drop on me. He demanded my car keys and threatened to shoot me and Sister Anselm if I didn't cooperate. I was in the process of doing just that when the ATF showed up."

"Just a minute," Dave said. Ali heard muttering in the background. "Sheriff Maxwell is wondering if you ended up firing your weapon."

That figured. Sheriff Maxwell had to be relieved that the shoot-out had taken place in someone else's jurisdiction. He wouldn't have to put one of his own officers on administrative duty during the ensuing investigation of an officer-involved shooting. Since this had all taken place in Gila County, it would be up to Sheriff Tuttle and the ATF to sort out whatever needed sorting. It would be someone else's media relations problem as well. For some reason, that last thought made her giggle.

"Tell him no," Ali managed, still laughing. "I didn't fire my weapon, not even once."

The sound of what was deemed to be inappropriate laughter caused some concern among the assembled ATF agents. One of the two guys kneeling next to Sister Anselm looked up at Ali. Then, after analyzing her face for a moment, he handed her a bottle of water.

"Are you all right?" he asked.

"I'm not hysterical, if that's what you're worried about," Ali assured him. "Someone just cracked a joke."

He cocked his head as though he wasn't sure whether he should believe her. "Okay," he said finally, "if you say so. But how about if you let me hold the blanket while you go sit in the shade? You look like the heat is getting to you, too."

Glad to oblige, Ali handed the blanket over to him, took the bottle of water, and then went to sit on a rock on the shady side of the gully.

"You really are all right?" Dave asked. "Your parents will have my ears for putting you in danger again."

"You didn't put me in danger. The shooter did. Do we have any idea who he is? Or, rather, was?"

Initially one of the ATF guys had checked the fallen suspect's pulse. Finding none, they left him where he had landed. Now that same agent had produced a digital camera and started diligently taking photos from every angle.

The Gila County Sheriff's Department and medical examiner would require their own sets of crime-scene photos, but the ATF would have a set as well. And although Ali was fairly certain as to the cause of death, the Gila County ME would issue the final word on that—a gunshot wound or wounds, or maybe a broken neck.

"Motor Vehicles came up with the name Thomas McGregor. That's the name listed on the registration for the Grand Torino he was driving. Records ran a check on him here and came up empty—not even so much as a speeding ticket. He evidently lived alone in a cabin outside Payson. The ATF is in the process of obtaining a search warrant and will be going to his place the moment they have the warrant in hand."

"What's his connection to all this?" Ali asked.

"No idea."

Looking up, Ali saw Agent Robson appear at the top of the bank. He hesitated for only a minute before starting down. Halfway to the bottom, he fell and slid the rest of the way on his butt, to the detriment of what had once been a carefully pressed gray suit. He walked over to Ali, dusting himself off and shedding his Kevlar vest as he came. He looked thunderous.

"Gotta go," Ali said to Dave.

To Ali's amazement, Robson threw himself down in the sand beside her. "That bastard got the drop on you? Thank God you're all right," he said.

The way he said it, Ali knew he meant every word.

"I'm fine," she said. "Your people got here just in time. Another few minutes, and things would have been pretty grim. I'm not sure what would have happened."

"I am," Robson declared. "He'd have had you in that patrol car and been screaming down the road. Krist managed to put a hole in the left rear tire of his Explorer as the guy drove off in it. He made it this far driving on the rim, but he knew he needed another vehicle in a hell of a hurry. That's where you came in. You would have given him both another vehicle and a hostage."

"Thank you," Ali said, and she meant it, too.

Robson nodded. "We've got a name," he continued. "McGregor. So far that's all we've got. We'll know more once we can execute a search warrant. We found a cell phone on the seat of his car. I've called in the number so someone can start checking his incoming and out-going calls to see where they lead. He also had a whole arsenal of weapons on the floorboard of his vehicle. He came out shooting and wasn't going to go down without a fight. We may not have a record of him, but all that means is that, whatever he's been up to, he's never been caught."

Sister Anselm moaned and stirred. Ali went over to the two officers who had taken charge of her. One was holding the blanket to shade her while the other one held her hand. At Ali's suggestion, the one officer let go of her hand long enough to offer the wounded nun another strip of water-soaked gauze.

"Did Sister Anselm say anything to you about McGregor's connection to all this?" Robson asked.

"Not so far," Ali said. It didn't seem necessary to say

that Sister Anselm was in no condition to say anything
to anybody.

"An air ambulance is en route," Robson continued.
"When it gets here, why don't you go back to the hospital with them if there's room."

"But . . ." Ali began.

Robson waved aside her objection. "I'm going to be
here at the scene for quite some time. Once my guys
get their warrant, I'll fly up to Payson and be there
when they execute it. If you stick with me, you'll be
in for twelve hours or so of crime-scene investigation
before I'll have a chance to take you back to the hospital."

An hour earlier, Ali would have thought Robson was
trying to ditch her. Maybe he still was, but it seemed
like he was letting her opt in or out of the crime-scene
situation at her discretion. She made her choice. If
the ATF media people were still in charge, she had no
reason to be there and would just be underfoot.

"Good," she said. "If the ambulance folks will take
me, I'll stick with Sister Anselm."

"They'll take you all right," Robson declared, standing up and once again attempting to dust off his now
grimy suit. "Believe me, I can make that happen."

In the absence of any local authorities, Agent Robson took charge. Both Sister Anselm and Deputy Krist
were in bad shape, but Robson declared the nun's condition to be more precarious than the wounded deputy's. When the first air ambulance arrived a few minutes later, he called for that one to take Sister Anselm
first.

As Ali had predicted, getting the injured woman
onto a stretcher and lifted up out of the gully and into

the helicopter was a difficult process. Fortunately, the trauma nurse from on board was able to start administering IV liquids as well as pain medication before they ever attempted to move her. Once they managed to get her onto a stretcher, they used a winch and a basket from the helicopter to lift her up out of the ravine. She rose into the air in a swirling storm cloud of sand. The stretcher was then transported back to the roadway, where the helicopter landed long enough for Sister Anselm to be moved from the basket and into the helicopter itself.

Following the complicated process from a distance, Ali wondered what Nadine Hazelett would have thought had she seen that. It would no doubt turn into something like "Angel of Death Ascends to Heaven."

Agent Robson gave her a ride back down to the intersection, where a stretch of state highway had been transformed into an emergency landing pad with a full contingent of cop cars and cops on hand to direct traffic around the parked aircraft.

Ali retrieved her briefcase and purse from the borrowed patrol car and remembered to hand the keys over to Agent Robson for safekeeping. Once Sister Anselm's stretcher was secure inside the aircraft, the nurse came looking for Ali.

"I understand you're accompanying the patient?" she asked.

Ali nodded.

The nurse gave Ali a cursory examination. "Come along, then," she said. "We need to go. From the looks of it, you've got some scrapes and bruises that could use some attention."

"I'm okay," Ali objected. "It's nothing serious."

"Doesn't matter," the nurse said. "We'll deliver you to the ER, too. Believe me, the paperwork will be a whole lot easier on our end if we deliver two patients to the ER instead of only one."

"Better insurance payout?" Ali asked.

The nurse nodded. "Yup," she said.

"Should I feel guilty?"

"Let the docs x-ray you and plaster you with a few bandages. You'll get a ride there, and it'll be a whole lot easier on you than waiting for one of these guys to get around to giving you a ride."

The helicopter took off the moment Ali was belted into her seat. For some reason, the ride back to Phoenix didn't take nearly as long as the ride out, and not because they were traveling any faster, either. Coming, Ali had been desperately concerned about what was happening to Sister Anselm and petrified that they would arrive too late. Now, with Sister Anselm receiving much-needed medical attention, Ali was able to relax. She closed her eyes and was astonished to find that she dozed off and didn't awaken until the drop in altitude indicated they were heading in for a landing on the hospital roof.

This time a crew of uniformed ER folks waited on the roof to take charge of the patients. Sister Anselm was wheeled off immediately. To Ali's chagrin, she was ordered onto a gurney so she could be wheeled down the wide corridor, into the elevator, and down to the ER.

Naturally, that turned into a case of hurry up and wait. She lay in a curtained cubby for the better part of an hour and a half before a young ER doc finally got around to looking in on her.

"It looks like you've taken some hard falls," he said.

"We'd better do some X-rays for starters. And I'm going to order an IV. When you're going to be out in the sun in this kind of heat, you need to be sure to stay hydrated."

Yes, Ali thought. *The next time I'm being held hostage by a crazed gunman, I'll remind him that it's his responsibility to provide the bottled water.*

She did not expect the kids to be there. She did not want them—Serenity bawling as though her heart was broken even though it wasn't and Win looking shocked. Devastated. He probably was. He had never been good at making his way in the world. He had always needed Mimi to help sort things out for him, and he must be realizing that now he would be alone. On his own. In a way he had never been.

It always surprised her that it was possible to love one child so much more than the other, but she did. Win had needed her in a way Serenity had not. She had been her daddy's girl, the apple of his eye. Serenity had *always* had her father. Winston had been his daughter's be-all and end-all. Serenity probably thought her father had never lied to her. That, of course, was wrong. Winston had lied to everyone. Lying suited him.

And that was when Mimi Cooper finally remembered the terrible words that had been flung at her in anger, in outrage. And that was when she finally understood, too, about the lie. The essential lie. The one that explained everything. Not only the lie Winston had told his wife—one of many—but the lie he had told Serenity as well.

As soon as Mimi remembered, it seemed as though she should have always known. How could she not?

The truth had been right there in front of her all this time. And if Mimi hadn't known, what about Serenity? Most likely she didn't know, either. If she had glimpsed the truth, it would have been impossible for Mimi's daughter to go on pretending that Winston Langley was the perfect father. More monster than father.

But if Serenity didn't know—if she had no idea—it was probably due to the fact that that kind of stupidity was most likely programmed into her DNA.

Like mother, like daughter, Mimi thought.

She needed Hal then, needed him desperately, right that second. Not to push the button. She understood she was beyond needing the button pushed. She needed to tell him what she knew. What she understood. What she remembered.

If only she didn't have that damned contraption in her throat. If only she could speak. If only she could say the words. Or even one word.

But then Win and Serenity moved from foreground to background, and Hal was with her again, beside her again.

"Do you need me to push the button?" he asked.

Two blinks. No. *No button.*

"Do you need something else? Is there something I can get you, something I can do?"

Hal's voice was desperate. He so wanted to do whatever it was she needed; to get her whatever it was she wanted. She could have told him to march off into hell itself, and she knew he would have gone willingly. She loved him for that. And because he had never lied to her. Not once. Not about little things and not about big things, either.

"Mimi?"

He was looking down at her, trying to suss out what was bothering her. Finally she realized that he had asked a yes or no question and she had been so busy thinking her own private, wandering thoughts that she had forgotten to answer.

One blink for yes. *Yes, I do need something.*

Please!

It took a supreme effort. For a time, Mimi wasn't even sure it was happening, but then she realized it was. Her arm, her heavily bandaged right arm, was moving. Moving from the surface of the bed where it had lain for hours, useless and unbending. It moved inexorably toward her throat. To the place where the hated ventilator invaded her body and dammed all speech.

Hal was quick to grasp the meaning. "Is it the ventilator?" he asked.

One blink. Yes.

"Is it bothering you?"

Yes.

"Do you want me to have them take it out? If I do, I don't know what will happen. Sister Anselm isn't here. If we take it out, you might die."

But of course she was going to die. Mimi knew that. It didn't matter if the ventilator stayed where it was or went away, she was going. The ventilator might make a few minutes' difference, but that was all.

"Do you want me to take it out?"

One blink. Yes.

Somewhere in the background Serenity was yelling at him. "You can't do that. If you take it out, it'll kill her."

Hal turned away from Mimi. "Get her out of here, Win," he ordered. "Get her out of here now."

For once in his life, Win Langley did the right thing. He led his hysterical sister out of the room.

Thank you, Win.

Then, just as suddenly, a nurse appeared and the ventilator was gone. It was almost like having the button pushed, only better. Breathing hurt. It hurt worse than Mimi could imagine. It felt as though her lungs were still on fire, but at least Mimi was able to move her lips.

"I love you," she told Hal wordlessly. She wanted him to know, to remember that he was the love of her life. The only real love of her life.

"I love you, too," Hal said.

He was crying now. Crying again. Crying still.

She moved her lips again, but she wasn't sure if what she was trying to say emerged as a spoken word.

But that was all she could do. Mimi had made the effort—the supreme effort. She had tried her best to tell Hal what he needed to know. But now she was gone—gone for good. She heard the steady beep of the machine morph into a squeal.

In an instant Mimi traveled far, far away from him, far from the bed and far from the button, to a distant place where she would never need the button again.

For the next two hours, Ali lay on the gurney in the ER with an IV tube feeding liquid into her arm. In the meantime she took a series of cell phone calls from concerned family members, including Leland Brooks, all of whom had been alerted to Ali's situation by the ever-helpful Dave Holman. By the time Ali had finished telling the story over and over—to her parents, to Chris, to Athena, to Sheriff Maxwell, and finally to

Leland Brooks—she was sick and tired of the whole thing, of telling the story and of hearing what all of them had to say in return.

Edie Larson went on a verbal rampage and wanted her daughter to get into some other, less dangerous kind of work. Bob Larson listened to the whole thing and then wanted to know what models of helicopters Ali had ridden in. Ali had no idea. They had gone up safely; they had come down safely. When they landed, the shiny side was up and the greasy side was down. That's all she needed to know. Chris wanted to know what a nun was doing running around with the latest wireless networking gizmo and said that he hoped to meet her someday. Athena simply said, "Way to go." Sheriff Maxwell was relieved to know that Ali hadn't been seriously injured in the incident, but Ali suspected he was even more relieved to know that she hadn't discharged her weapon. Last but not least, after hearing her out, Leland Brooks wanted to know if she needed him to bring her any additional clothing or supplies.

"I've trashed this tracksuit," she said. "It's too worn out to appear in public."

"Not to worry, madam," Leland said. "I'll see what I can do about that either tonight or first thing in the morning."

When Ali was finally released from the ER, it was with the knowledge that the X-rays had revealed no broken bones. She had bandaged cuts on both arms and her right knee, none of which had been deemed serious enough to merit stitches. She had been given a tetanus shot, a prescription for painkillers, and a verbal warning to be sure to take it easy the next few days.

It was almost ten when she finally limped out of the ER. She wanted to check on Sister Anselm, but it seemed best to go back to the hotel to clean up before presenting herself as one of Sister Anselm's visitors. As she handed her ticket stub to the parking valet at the hospital, he gave her tattered jogging suit a dubious look, but he retrieved her car without comment.

When Ali walked into the hotel lobby, the concierge hurried to greet her. "I understand you've had a difficult day, Ms. Reynolds," he said. "You have some visitors. We've upgraded them to the club level. They're upstairs in the lounge."

Going up in the elevator, Ali had no doubt who the guests in question would be—her parents, of course. They had asked her about coming to the hospital, and she had told them no. Evidently they hadn't listened. What astonished her was the idea that her parents had come to the hotel, checked in, and were prepared to spend the night.

She fully intended to go see Sister Anselm, but her parents came first. Back in her third-floor suite Ali showered and changed into her somewhat wrinkled long-sleeved pantsuit, which covered the bandages on her arms and knees as well as the darkening bruises on her legs. Then she fixed her face. It turned out she had gotten sunburned while she'd been outside scrabbling around in the wash with Sister Anselm. The jagged scar Peter Winters's fist had left on her face months earlier showed bright white against her reddened skin, and it took several layers of powder to tone it down and make it less noticeable.

With the damage concealed as well as possible, she

went in search of her parents and found them seated in the spacious club lounge, where her father was nursing a beer and her mother was sipping a cup of tea. Ten o'clock was a good three hours past Edie Larson's usual bedtime.

"What are you doing here?" Ali asked as soon as she saw them.

"Let me see," Edie said. "Would it happen to be because our daughter was almost rubbed out in a shoot-out this afternoon but she gave us strict orders not to come to the hospital? How are you? Are you okay? Is anything broken?"

"I'm fine," Ali said. "Really."

Bob Larson grinned at his daughter. "As for what are we doing here, Edie and I talked it over. We decided that since you had declared the hospital off-limits, coming to the hotel was okay."

"But what about the restaurant?" Ali said.

"We went by the Sugarloaf and put up a sign. I printed it out myself on the computer. Closed for a family emergency," Edie said. "If this doesn't count as a family emergency, I don't know what does."

The lounge attendant came over to the table where they were sitting. "May I get you something?" she asked Ali.

"A glass of merlot, please."

"And for you, sir," she said to Ali's dad. "Would you care for another beer?"

"One's my limit," Bob told her. "Otherwise the wife gets cranky."

Edie gave him a withering look. "I do no such thing," she declared. "You're welcome to drink as many of those fool things as you want."

Bob winked at the attendant. "I'll stick with one," he said. "It pays to keep her happy."

Ali's cell phone rang. There was a notice on the table asking that people refrain from using their cell phones in the lounge, but since she and her parents were the only people there and since the caller was Dave Holman, she answered anyway.

"Do you hear it?" he asked.

"Hear what?"

"ATF agents Donnelley and Robson doing their happy dance," Dave said. "It turns out Thomas McGregor was evidently the real ELF deal."

"You're kidding," Ali breathed.

"Nope," Dave continued. "McGregor has lived outside of Payson for a long time, staying under everyone's radar. When he hasn't been out on what he calls 'missions,' he's been holed up in a cabin busily documenting everything his particular fire-setting cell has been doing for the last twenty years or so—sort of an unabridged ecoterrorism history, written in longhand."

"Longhand?" Ali asked.

"Yup. McGregor's no fan of computers or electronics of any kind. He's done all his writing the old-fashioned way, with pen and ink in a pile of spiral notebooks. There are pages and pages of material, naming names and citing specific operatives involved and so forth. It's incredibly amazing stuff—invaluable stuff. Your basic ATF gold mine."

"How did he stay under the radar all this time?" Ali asked.

"By not causing trouble or calling attention to himself. He never got picked up for anything. No arrests of any kind, anywhere. He lived off the grid. He used a kerosene lamp for light and a woodstove for heat, and hand-pumped his own water from a well. The only thing that doesn't fit is the cell phone found in his possession today. It's a dead end, however. It's one of those throwaway phones that only made calls to another throwaway phone."

Ali was aware that her parents were hanging on her every word, but she had to ask. "What's McGregor's connection to Sister Anselm?"

"Good question," Dave said. "We have no idea, but on a slightly different topic, I'm afraid I have some bad news."

"What?" Ali asked.

"Sheriff Maxwell got word tonight that Mrs. Cooper didn't make it. She died a little after six this evening."

While I was downstairs in the ER, Ali thought, *and while Sister Anselm was similarly occupied in some other part of the hospital.*

"I'm sorry to hear that," Ali said, "but as bad as she was burned, she never would have recovered."

"I know," Dave agreed. "It's probably a blessing for her, and for her family. I'm sure they're relieved to know that she's not suffering anymore. And I'm sure it'll mean a lot to her husband and kids when we can tell them that we've nailed Mimi's killer.

"As for that missing painting?" Dave continued. "The arson investigators found something that looks like a piece of charred picture-frame stock and some glass with a few scraps of paper stuck to it in the other burned house up in Camp Verde. The manufacturer's number is still visible on back of the frame. The investigators are trying to trace that, but the initial reading is that it's good-quality and expensive stuff. Not from your local frame-it-yourself outlet."

"They burned up Mimi's Klee?" Ali asked. "Why would they? It's worth a fortune."

"Let's hope it's insured," Dave said.

Ali knew it was. She had spent a long time in the burn unit with Mimi's less than exemplary family. She was sure Hal would be grieving the loss of his wife and wouldn't notice the loss of the painting, valuable or not. Mimi's children were another matter. They would be looking to lay hands on any dollars available, and they wouldn't be pleased to know that if Hal Cooper was cleared of complicity, he would be free to inherit whatever Mimi had left him.

"Does Hal know about the painting?" Ali asked.

"Not yet," Dave said. "That's why I'm calling you. No one has told anyone anything. Donnelley's trying to keep a lid on this, and he's asking us to play along. There appears to be a treasure trove of names in the handwritten material they confiscated from McGregor's place. Donnelley wants to have a chance to analyze as much of that as possible before word gets out that they have it."

"In other words, Donnelley is hoping to score," Ali said.

"Big time," Dave agreed. "Robson doubts McGregor's ELF associates knew he was documenting everything he did and, as a consequence, what they did, too. ATF hopes to swoop down and bring some of those folks in for questioning before they have a chance to go to ground.

"Which is to say, they're not releasing any information about what happened earlier this afternoon, other than that there was an incident involving multiple agencies south of Payson. No names. No details. Not to anyone, including Mimi Cooper's family, because they're concerned that some of them may also have ties to ELF. Donnelley believes that the ultimate solution to Mimi's murder is going to be found in those notebooks."

"What about what happened to Sister Anselm? Who's investigating that?"

Dave sighed. "That's sort of up in the air right now. Donnelley's position is that it's not his jurisdiction or his concern, especially since he has his hands full with the ELF investigation. Sheriff Maxwell comes down in pretty much the same place. The incident started inside the Phoenix city limits and ended in Gila County. It's not his problem."

"But Sister Anselm was kidnapped because of what happened to Mimi," Ali pointed out.

"Yes."

"And they're not releasing details about what happened to her, either?"

"Not at this time."

Ali was beyond outraged. "So you're saying someone can be kidnapped off city streets in broad daylight and no one is investigating the people who did it?"

"I'm sure Phoenix PD is already working the case."

"Really," Ali said. "They haven't spoken to me, and I doubt they've spoken to Sister Anselm, either."

"There's no reason you can't call them," Dave returned. "Since you seem to know so many of the particulars, I expect they'd be interested in talking to you."

"I'm not so sure I'm interested in talking to them," Ali returned. "And what about Hal Cooper's painting? No one has spoken to him about that, either? Agent Donnelley issues a gag order and we all just shut up and let him get away with it?"

Ali's merlot had arrived and was sitting on the table. She paused to take a sip and to get her temper back under control.

"Yes," Dave said. "For right now that's what we need to do."

"That's an order?"

"Maybe not for you, but it is for me. If you want to raise an objection, how about if you do it tomorrow, after you get back home?"

"I may just do that," Ali said, "but right now, I need to go. My parents are here. I need to talk to them."

With that she closed the phone. Blaming the hang-up on her parents was just an excuse. Ali knew she was about to throw a temper tantrum. At her age, that was something best done in private.

"My goodness," Edie Larson said. "I can't imagine what Dave could have said that made you so upset. You practically hung up on him."

I didn't practically hang up on him, Ali thought. *I really hung up on him.*

It angered her to think that the vicious attack on Sister Anselm had been turned into a political football, with none of the various agencies accepting responsibility for it. That was true for ATF agents Donnelley and Robson, but it was also true for Sheriff Maxwell and Dave Holman. In order to further the ATF's investigation, everything else was being shoved onto a back burner.

"What's going on?" Edie asked when Ali didn't answer right away.

Shaking her head, Ali looked from her mother to her father. "Sometimes men drive me nuts," she said. "Present company excepted." With that, and having taken only that one sip of wine, Ali pushed her glass aside and stood up.

"I'm tired," she said. "I need to go to bed."

"Is something wrong with your wine?" Bob asked.

"No," Ali said. "It's fine. I just don't want to drink it. I'm going to my room."

"But we came all the way down here to see you . . ." Edie began.

"Now, Mother," Bob said. "Let her go." He pushed away his empty beer bottle and reached for Ali's glass of wine. "It would be a shame to let it go to waste," he said.

Edie glared at him and then shook her head. "The lady at the desk says they serve a free breakfast in here every morning. Should we meet up here?"

"Sure," Ali agreed. "That'll be fine."

"What time?"

"It'll depend on how I feel," Ali said. "Please call when you're ready."

Ali was still doing a slow burn as she went downstairs. With McGregor dead, everyone else seemed ready to pass the buck as far as Sister Anselm was concerned. Ali seemed to be the only person who was convinced that the attack on Sister Anselm had been carried out by two perpetrators rather than just one. And the fact that Sister Anselm was now in a hospital room in Saint Gregory's didn't mean she was entirely out of danger.

Ali allowed her parents to think she was on her way to bed. Instead, she went to her room and called for her car. When she left her room to head back to the hospital, Ali took her briefcase and computer along with her. After all, Ali's computer had saved Sister Anselm's life once today. Maybe it would do so again.

CHAPTER 18

By the time Ali drove back to the hospital, the valet parking stand was closed. Driving into the garage, she saw a dark-suited man with the look of a security guard standing near the garage elevator, watching everyone who came and went. For some reason, that made Ali feel better. When she exited the garage elevator in the lobby, she was relieved to see still another guard posted near the front entrance. There hadn't been a noticeable security presence at Saint Gregory's the night before, but she was glad to see one now.

Once she was in the hospital, finding Sister Anselm wasn't as easy as it should have been. No one seemed willing or able to give out any information. Having struck out everywhere else, Ali finally ventured into the waiting room outside the ICU.

As she stepped off the elevator, she was surprised to find two more rent-a-cops in black suits there as well. One stood to the right of the elevator, while the second was stationed just inside the waiting room.

The presence of the security detail probably meant that a celebrity of some kind, or maybe even

320   J.A. JANCE

a high-powered politician, was undergoing treatment in Saint Gregory's. Fortunately for them, the guards made no attempt to waylay Ali. If they had, she most likely would have given them a piece of her mind—the piece she hadn't let loose on Dave Holman.

When Ali first entered the darkened waiting room, she thought it was empty. Then a shadowy figure rose from a chair in the corner and walked toward her through the gloom.

"Please turn on the light, Edward," a man's voice said. "I'm through resting my eyes for the time being. There's no need for our fellow visitor to stumble around in the dark."

One of the guards moved at once to switch on the overhead light while Ali examined the elfin figure who had issued the order. He was tiny—only about five foot four—and he, too, wore a black suit, only his was topped by a clerical collar. His unruly mane of white hair seemed at odds with his clothing, as did his mischievous blue eyes and ready smile.

"I'm Bishop Francis Gillespie," he said, holding out his hand. "From what Sister Anselm told me, I would assume you to be Alison Reynolds. Is that correct?"

Thunderstruck, Ali nodded. "Most people call me Ali," she said.

When he clasped her hand in both of his, Ali was startled to realize that his hands weren't nearly as small as the rest of him.

"I must confess that I had a little more help in identifying you than just Sister Anselm's description," he added. "After she spoke so highly of you, I took the liberty of looking you up on the Internet. I more than half expected that if you came here tonight, you'd still be wearing that bright red wig. Sister Anselm indicated that she thought the red hair looked very fetching on you."

Ali was struggling through her memory banks, trying to remember the proper term one should use when addressing a bishop. Was she supposed to call him Your Excellency, or Reverend Gillespie, or was there something else?

"Sit down, sit down," he urged pleasantly, leading Ali to a chair.

"Sister Anselm is here now, in the ICU?"

Bishop Gillespie nodded. "Yes, they brought her up from the recovery room a few minutes ago. I spoke to the surgeon—an orthopedic guy. He says they set the leg and put in metal plates and screws to hold it in place. It was broken in more than one spot. They won't be able to schedule the hip replacement until sometime next week. No visitors but relatives," he added.

"I can't see her, then?" Ali asked.

"No," he said. "Sorry. They may let me in later, but then I have special dispensation."

Having seen Sister Anselm's damaged leg with her own eyes, Ali wasn't surprised to learn that more than one surgical procedure would be necessary to repair it. As for the fact that Sister Anselm wouldn't be allowed any visitors? That was fine with Ali.

"I'm sure you're startled to find me here," Bishop Gillespie continued, "but Sister Anselm is rather a special case. Considering the seriousness of the situation, it seemed to me that having a contingent of security guards on hand to keep an eye on her while she's recovering would be a good idea."

Ali agreed with that assessment completely. She

also liked the fact that the security guards in question appeared to take their responsibilities seriously. They seemed more than capable of handling any unexpected contingency.

"The truth is," the bishop went on, "if I had really listened to Sister's concerns—if I had been paying attention—I would have sent one of my cars and a driver to take her to and from the hospital as needed. That's what I should have done. Now we have to deal with the consequences of my negligence."

"I'm sure Sister Anselm will forgive you," Ali said.

"Yes," Bishop Gillespie agreed. "She's a very forgiving soul. But knowing she's come to grievous harm, I'm not at all sure that I shall be able to forgive myself. Then, of course, there's what happened to you today as well," he added sadly. "I understand you, too, have sustained some injuries in the process of rescuing Sister Anselm."

The man seemed so troubled that Ali didn't want to add to his burden. "Nothing serious," she said casually. "A few scrapes and bruises, but nothing's broken."

"I understand the man responsible for that dreadful attack is dead. It's difficult to imagine that kind of evil loose in the world. What sort of depraved individual would leave one poor woman to burn to death in a fire and abandon another to die in the desert? Behavior like that is entirely beyond the pale."

Ali realized that someone had been feeding Bishop Gillespie a whole lot of very accurate information that he wasn't supposed to have. Despite Agent Donnelley's embargo on information, Bishop Gillespie seemed to know almost as much about the day's events as Ali did. Under the circumstances, her best tactic seemed to be

changing the subject before she, too, ended up divulg-
ing unauthorized information.

"Have you and Sister Anselm been friends for a
long time?" she asked.

He nodded. "A very long time," he said. "Has she
told you anything about her background?"

"Some. She told me about her mission and about
how, when she's dealing with badly injured people,
she's often as concerned about healing their broken
relationships as she is their broken bodies."

Bishop Gillespie nodded sagely. "That's true," he
said. "She's forever trying to do for others what other
people once did for her."

"The nuns in France, you mean," Ali said. "Before
she became Sister Anselm."

Bishop Gillespie beamed. "So she did tell you some
of it?"

"About losing her parents and being left alone after
they died."

Bishop Gillespie nodded. "Sister Celeste, Sister
Anselm's first mother superior, recognized her natural
facility for languages and encouraged her to study as
many of them as possible. The convent saw to it that
Sister Anslem received a degree in nursing. Once she
was able to return to the U.S., she also earned a doctorate in psychology."

"She never said exactly how that happened," Ali
said. "How she came back home."

"I'm proud to say a good deal of that was my doing,"
Bishop Gillespie said. "She lived and worked in
France, speaking all those languages, but she wasn't
French any more than she was German. By then she
had given up all hope of reclaiming her birthright as

an American citizen. Yes, her family had been badly treated during the war. For her parents and her sister, Crystal City was a prison, but not for little Judith. That was her name then. As a child she had loved the relative freedom of living in the camp. She loved Texas and being out of those cold midwest winters, and she wanted desperately to come back home.

"It was Sister Anne Marie, Sister Anselm's next mother superior, who first brought her to my attention. That was during the sixties, when I went to Rome as a special envoy to Vatican Two. Sister Anselm was dispatched there to serve as a translator. By then she could speak several additional languages, including fluent Italian and, I'm told, credible Latin as well," he added with a chuckle. "She made a big impression on me at the time, but it took another fifteen years before I was able to help negotiate her return to this country, first to California and now here. I was also able to help her regain her lost citizenship, so she is now free to travel wherever I need her to go on an American passport."

"Why are you telling me all this?" Ali asked.

"Because I want you to know what a treasure she is," Bishop Gillespie said, "and because I want you to help me."

"Help you do what?"

"You may have wondered what Sister Anselm was doing with the latest GPS/networking applications on her iPhone. Those are my doing as well, I'm afraid. When she's at home, she stays in Jerome, in Saint Bernadette's, a convent that specializes in treating troubled nuns, but when she's on the road . . ."

Ali knew from reading Nadine Hazelett's article

that Sister Anselm's home convent was in Jerome, but she knew nothing of Saint Bernadette's

"Wait a minute," Ali interrupted. "What's this about troubled nuns?"

"Back when Jerome was a busy mining community, there was a parochial school there. That shut down when the mines did, but the building itself was still in good shape, as was the convent. Since the diocese couldn't find a suitable buyer at the time, we ended up keeping it. A few years ago we remodeled the place and turned it into a rehab facility.

"It turns out nuns have the same kinds of difficulties everyone else has—anger management issues, substance-abuse issues." Bishop Gillespie smiled and shrugged. "You name it, we've got it. With a doctorate in psychology, Sister Anselm helps out there with the sessions when she's home, but when she's on the road, it's important for me to be able to stay in touch with her, and with some of my other special emissaries as well.

"As I said earlier, over the past several days Sister Anselm had e-mailed me some of her concerns," Bishop Gillespie continued. "She felt that even in a hospital setting, Mimi Cooper might still be in danger—that the people responsible for the attack on her life might attempt to strike again. She was also concerned that due to working so closely with Mimi, she, too, might be targeted. It turns out she was all too right about that," he added regretfully. "What do you think?"

Bishop Gillespie's direct question put Ali on the spot. "I was there," she said finally. "I know that the man who died this afternoon, Thomas McGregor, is the person most directly responsible for what happened to Sister Anselm, but I don't believe that he acted alone."

"Why?" Bishop Gillespie asked. "Who else do you think might be involved?"

"I've been told there may have been two people in the vehicle that picked Sister Anselm up this morning, supposedly under the guise of giving her a lift to the hospital. The parking attendant at the hotel told me that vehicle was red. The vehicle McGregor was driving this afternoon, the one he abandoned in the desert, was green."

Bishop Gillespie nodded thoughtfully. "All right," he said. "That makes sense. Two vehicles; two people. It's my understanding, Ms. Reynolds, that you were with Sister Anselm at the time she was rescued. Was she able to tell you anything about the identity of her attackers?"

Ali shook her head. "No, she was in bad shape by the time I found her, but if she recognized her attacker, she didn't pass that information along to me. She wasn't able to."

"I'm quite confident she would have, had she been able," Bishop Gillespie said, patting Ali's hand. "She trusts you implicitly."

"I'm not sure why," Ali said.

"Sister Anselm is a very good judge of character," he said. "That's one of the reasons she's good at her job."

"What about her e-mails to you?" Ali asked. "Did she give you any theories about who might have been behind that initial attack on Mimi Cooper? And did you know Mimi Cooper died earlier this evening?" Ali added as an afterthought.

"Yes, I know," Bishop Gillespie replied. "I was

made aware of Mimi's passing. As for Sister Anselm's suspicions? She had several interesting takes on the situation. She was quite certain the victim's spouse, Mr. Cooper, was in no way responsible.

"Sister Anselm found the son and the daughter to be quite contemptible, individually and collectively, but she also regarded them both as relatively inef fectual. She didn't believe either of them would have the intestinal fortitude to plan or carry out this kind of horrific action. Still, she said there was something insidiously personal about the attack."

"Yes," Ali agreed. "Which brings us back to Thomas McGregor. I'm sure he holds the key to everything—to what happened to Sister Anselm today as well as to the attack on Mimi Cooper on Monday."

"What is Sheriff Maxwell's department doing to make those connections?" Bishop Gillespie asked, then held up a cautioning hand. "Please understand that I wouldn't be at all offended if you're not autho- rized to tell me. This is, after all, an ongoing investi- gation."

Except it isn't, Ali thought. Dave had already told her that Sheriff Maxwell was deferring to Agent in Charge Donnelley.

"As far as I know," Ali said, "no one in Phoenix has initiated any kind of investigation into the matter of Sister Anselm's abduction."

"That's not entirely true," Bishop Gillespie said with a smile. "I reported it myself. Phoenix is the kidnap capital of the world at the moment, but most of the ones that happen here are drug-related and involve people being held for ransom. A non- drug-related kidnapping with no ransom demand, a recovered victim, and a dead perpetrator isn't high on anyone's list of priorities."

That was Ali's take on the situation as well, but she didn't comment aloud.

"It's unfortunate," Bishop Gillespie continued, "but that's the way it is. Yes, the person who tried to murder Sister Anselm earlier today, the trigger man as it were, may be dead, but the person or persons who set him on that evil path is not. My main concern and my main reason for becoming involved is to protect Sister Anselm from suffering any further harm. To do that may require some coloring outside the lines, as my mother used to say. That's where you come in."

"Me?" Ali echoed. "How?"

"I know from the online research we did on you that you're acquainted with a certain young man up in Sedona, a very useful young man by the name of B. Simpson."

Ali's jaw literally dropped. She didn't expect Bishop Gillespie to know about B., or Ali's relationship to him, but clearly the bishop was a talented interrogator, and there was no reason to deny it.

"Yes," she said.

"I suspect that a request for help coming directly from me might not rate high on Mr. Simpson's to-do list. I believe you might have a better in with him."

"Possibly," Ali said. "What kind of help do you need?"

"I was informed that Mr. McGregor's having a cell phone with him was something of an anomaly."

Ali nodded. "That's my understanding as well."

"At the moment I happen to have two phone numbers in my possession," he said. "One is the number of the phone Mr. McGregor was using, and the other is the number of the phone that was used to call him numerous times in the last week or so. I won't mention how it is that I came to have access to those numbers. That would be indiscreet. I was told that since they're from disposable phones, there is no way they can be traced, but I happen to know better. I believe that if someone as resourceful as Mr. Simpson were to apply himself to this problem, he might do a great deal to give us some answers, and we need answers, Ms. Reynolds. We need answers in the very worst way."

With that, Bishop Gillespie reached into his vest pocket and extracted a single piece of paper. When he held it out to Ali, she hesitated, but only for a moment. It seemed clear to her that no one else was looking out for Sister Anselm right then. In that regard, Bishop Gillespie was the only game in town.

"Thank you," he said when she took it. "I'll only be here for another hour or so, but my people will be here twenty-four/seven. There are these two here in the waiting room, two in the lobby, one outside in the parking garage, and one roving about. That is to say that you needn't trouble yourself about Sister Anselm's safety so long as she's here. I'm more concerned about her safety once she leaves the hospital."

"Yes," Ali said, slipping the paper into her own pocket.

"Don't worry about getting in touch with me," Bishop Gillespie added. "I've taken the liberty of writing my cell phone number on that slip of paper as well—down at the bottom of the page. Feel free to call me. Anytime."

"Yes, Your Excellency," she managed.

"None of that," he said, waving a hand dismissively. "Just call me Father," he said. "That works."

Riding down in the elevator, Ali reflected on what she'd heard. With Bishop Gillespie's support, Sister Anselm had devoted her life to repaying a long-ago act of Christian charity. Unfortunately, more than half a century later, that repayment effort had resulted in an unsuccessful attempt on Sister Anselm's life.

It was after midnight when Ali stepped off the elevator in the hospital lobby. At first she thought the place was deserted, but before she could make it into the garage elevator, a man came hurrying after her, calling out, "Hey, Ali. Wait up."

Wishing she had the red wig on her head instead of in her briefcase, Ali turned to face the man who trotted after her. He turned out to be none other than the ELF-specializing investigative reporter, Kelly Green.

"How is she?" he wanted to know.

"How is who?" she returned.

The garage elevator door opened. She stepped on. So did he.

"You know who I mean," he said. "That nun they call the Angel of Death. I believe she had been looking after Mimi Cooper."

Ali simply stared at him and said nothing while Kelly rushed on. "I understand that McGregor guy, the one who got killed earlier today and who allegedly started the fire in Camp Verde, is someone with long-term connections to ELF. What about this injured nun? What's her connection? I'm working on a book on the Earth Liberation Front, you see," he explained. "Anything you could tell me would be greatly appreciated."

"I'm not authorized to talk about this, and neither is anybody else," she said curtly. Stepping around him, she exited into the garage. She was grateful to see one of Bishop Gillespie's security guards watching from the far side of the building.

"I could make it worth your while," Kelly said with an ingratiating smile.

Ali was not impressed.

"Is that how it worked with Devon?" she asked. "You slipped him a little something now and then as a bribe in exchange for his feeding you information that allowed you to scoop everyone else?"

Green's smile faded. "That wasn't what I meant," he said.

It was exactly what he meant, and they both knew it.

"With Devon off on administrative leave, who's your source inside the department these days?" Ali asked.

"I don't have one," Green said quickly. "The stuff about McGregor came from the media relations folks over at the ATF."

"No," Ali said, "it didn't. No information on this afternoon's incident has been released to anyone, not officially at any rate, and if it leaks out before Agent Donnelley is ready, I'm going to let him and anyone else who is interested know that you're the most likely source."

Green looked shocked. "If you do that, I'll be locked out of the loop. I won't be able to do my research—"

"Exactly," Ali said. "So who told you about Sister Anselm and Thomas McGregor?"

"I never reveal my confidential sources," he declared.

"Maybe so," Ali returned, "but if you don't tell me, I'll see to it that you don't have any sources left, confidential or otherwise. As for that book you're supposedly working on? It won't be much of a blockbuster if you no longer have access to any of the official information coming from inside the various investigative organizations."

"You wouldn't do that," he said.

"Try me," she said, pulling out her phone. "I happen to have Agent Robson's phone number right here. If I let him know you're leaking information about what went on this afternoon, you'll be history."

"But I didn't," he whined. "I haven't told anybody."

"You told me," she said. "That counts as telling."

For several long moments she waited while Kelly Green shifted uncomfortably from one foot to the other. Once, when Chris was four, Ali had caught her son telling fibs. She remembered his doing the same thing, shifting guiltily back and forth from one foot to the other under his mother's unflinching gaze. Eventually Chris had told the truth, and so did Kelly.

"Devon," he said finally. "Even though he's been on leave, he's still been helping me."

"How?" Ali asked. "Who's giving him information?"

"I don't know," Kelly said. "I never ask. It's none of my business."

"It happens that it *is* my business," Ali returned. "I'm currently in charge of media relations at the Yavapai County Sheriff's Department, and I want to know. Someone is feeding Devon the information he's giving you, and I want to know who that person is."

"I don't know how to find out . . ." Kelly began.

"You're an investigative journalist," Ali said. "Figure

it out, and then let me know. If I don't have the person's name by nine tomorrow morning, I'm going straight to Donnelley. I guarantee you, he won't be happy. He'll make sure you're hamstrung as far as information from the ATF is concerned."

She handed him a business card with her phone number printed on it. "Call me," she added. "Before nine."

With that she turned and walked away. She heard him mutter the B-word in her direction as she moved out of earshot, but that didn't bother her. She had been called worse on occasion.

And will be again, she thought.

CHAPTER 19

Driving out of the garage, Ali wondered how long Devon Ryan had been using his position as media relations officer as his own private moneymaking concession. Even though he was supposedly off on leave, clearly he still had access to enough information that he was able to maintain a stream of income. So who was helping him? It seemed apparent to Ali that it wasn't Sally Laird Harrison. She may have had an affair with the guy, but right this minute, she too was off work on administrative leave, so she wasn't a logical source of information.

By offering Ali money, Kelly Green showed that he was only too willing to pay to play. She wondered if threatening him with exposure would be enough to force him to name names. Ali hoped so. She knew that if the information on Thomas McGregor got out prematurely, Agent in Chief Donnelley would come looking for her, wanting her head on a platter. She needed to be prepared to hand him someone else's. Two heads, rather than one—Devon Ryan's and the one belonging to whoever was helping him.

Then, of course, there was the other side of the
coin—Bishop Gillespie. He, too, had been made privy
to what should have been confidential details of the
investigation. Who were his sources?

Ali drove up to the hotel entrance, parked, and
handed her key over to the attendant. As she started
toward the door, she almost collided with Hal Cooper.
He was walking back into the lobby with a dog on a
leash—a tiny white dog not much bigger than a bag of
coffee.

"Maggie?" Ali asked.

Hal nodded absently. For a moment Ali wondered if
he even recognized her.

"She needed to go out, and so did I," he explained.
From the aroma of cigarette smoke lingering on his
clothing, Ali knew he'd gone out for a smoke. "I haven't
had a cigarette in years," he added. "Tonight I needed
one."

"I'm so sorry about your wife," Ali said.

He looked at her and nodded sadly. "Thank you," he
said. "I'm sorry, I don't believe I know you."

The red wig was still working, even in its absence.

"I was doing some work with Sister Anselm," she
said. "Up on the burn unit."

"I see," he sighed. "I kept hoping she'd make it—
that she'd pull through somehow. I can't imagine what
I'm going to do without her. What we're going to do
without her," he added despairingly, looking down at
the tiny dog. "When I go off on my next trip and have
to be gone for three or four days, who'll take care of
Maggie?"

Those were the first questions people always asked
when someone died—how would the survivors cope?

How would they go on in a world suddenly bereft? Who would do all the things the missing loved one used to do?

It occurred to Ali that if Hal Cooper had been the kind of no-good fortune hunter Serenity thought he was, he would have already stopped thinking about having to go to work. If the missing Klee was insured for anything near what Serenity had said, Ali suspected that Hal Cooper could now afford to give up flying for a living. It also occurred to her that he was lost and needed to talk to someone.

"Would you care to stop off for a drink?" Ali asked.

"That would be nice," he said after a moment's hesitation. "I doubt I'll be able to sleep."

Ali ushered him into the lobby, which was almost deserted. He sat down at a corner table and lifted Maggie into his lap. "What would you like?" Ali asked.

"Scotch," he said. "Single malt. Neat."

"Have you had anything to eat?"

Hal shook his head.

"You should eat," Ali said. She went into the bar and placed an order for chicken wings and fries along with the drinks—Scotch for him and straight tonic for her. While she waited for the bartender to pour the drinks, she realized that DNA was what had brought her here. That's what her mother always did for grieving people—she fed them. Wings and fries weren't exactly Edie's signature tuna casserole, but they would fill the bill.

After all, wasn't that exactly what she had done for Athena the night before—taken her food?

For the first time, Ali realized that her parents hadn't mentioned anything about an expected great-grandchild, and that when she had spoken to Chris and Athena earlier, neither of them had mentioned it, either.

It shamed Ali to think that she had been so caught up in her own concerns that she hadn't brought up the subject. What had happened when Athena had told Chris she was pregnant? Had she somehow managed to convince him that the two of them wouldn't be able to handle caring for a baby? Ali was half sick when she came back to the table with the drinks. But seeing Hal sitting there, grieving, Ali forced herself to switch gears.

"You said you worked with Sister Anselm," Hal said when she set his Scotch in front of him. "What happened to her? I expected her to be there for Mimi and me this afternoon. I can't believe she just deserted us like that."

Gag order or not, it was time someone told this man what had really happened, so Ali did. She told him all of it—about Sister Anselm being lured into a kidnapper's vehicle and being left in the desert to die by the same man suspected of murdering Mimi Cooper. Because the charge was murder now that Mimi was dead.

Hal listened to what Ali had to say in stricken silence. "I don't understand any of this," he said when she finished. "None of it makes sense. Mimi didn't have an enemy in the world, and she would never have been mixed up with those Earth Liberation people. That just wasn't her."

"Tell me about the painting," Ali said.

"The painting?" Hal asked, as though he weren't quite paying attention.

"The Paul Klee," Ali supplied. "The one you said is missing from your house."

"Oh, that. Mimi did plan to sell it eventually," he said. "In fact, she had it reframed last year for that very reason—as a preparation for selling it. I never much liked the piece, and I wouldn't have bothered reframing it, but I still wonder if maybe it hasn't found its way into one of Serenity's galleries. I don't trust that woman, and I don't think she'd be above trying to sell it behind her mother's back."

"It's insured?" Ali asked.

"Yes, for something like $750,000, but that's probably less than it would bring at auction. At least that's what I was led to believe."

"You have a record for the reframing?"

"I suppose so," Hal said. "Somewhere. Mimi always kept meticulous records of everything, including the vet bills." He patted Maggie while the dog continued to snooze in his lap. "I don't understand," he said. "Why are you interested in the reframing job?"

"Because investigators found a piece of frame stock in the burned-out wreckage of one of the houses in Camp Verde."

Hal was aghast. "They burned the painting, too?"

Ali nodded. The bartender emerged from the bar long enough to deliver their food, napkins, and silverware. Hal ordered another drink. Ali did not. For a long time after the bartender left the table, Hal stared after him.

"Why would someone hurt her?" he asked. "Mimi was a wonderful person. A lovely person. She wouldn't hurt a fly, and yet someone did this to her—murdered her and destroyed her prize possession, because that's what that painting amounted to. I don't understand."

"I do," Ali said. "What it means is you were wrong a

little while ago when you said Mimi had no enemies. She did—at least one."

"She never said a word to me about it."

"Maybe she didn't know about it, either, and that's why she didn't mention it to you. Tell me, who was there in Mimi's room this afternoon?"

"Win and Serenity and me. Surely her own children wouldn't do something so despicable."

"I don't think so," Ali said. *And neither does Sister Anselm.* "There is the art connection."

Hal nodded. Absently he tried one of the wings. By then, noticing the food on the table, Maggie had roused herself. She was sitting up and taking notice.

"Too hot for you, little girl," Hal said to the dog. "Try a bit of french fry."

Ali watched as the tiny dog downed one morsel of potato and then pleaded for more.

"So it was just the three of you in the room?"

"Not at the end," Hal said, swallowing hard. "Then it was just Mimi and me. Serenity was acting like a jerk and Mimi wanted her out of there. So Win took her back to the waiting room. I know Sister Anselm kept hoping that she'd be able to tell us something about what happened. At first she didn't remember anything at all. Right at the end, I think she was starting to remember, and she wanted to tell me. That's why she wanted the ventilator out. So she could talk. So she could say something."

"Did she?" Ali asked.

"She tried. She only managed one word," Hal said. "She said, 'Donna.' That's what makes me think she really had started remembering what happened. Donna Carson, Serenity's personal assistant, was the last person who came by to see Mimi that day, the day she disappeared. The problem is, that's all Mimi managed. Before she could say anything more, she was gone."

Donna, Ali thought. Maybe that name wasn't just part of what Mimi remembered or wanted to say. Maybe it was exactly what she intended and needed to say.

"Tell me about Donna," Ali said.

Hal favored Ali with a puzzled look and then fed Maggie another bit of french fry. He let his breath out in a long, ragged sigh. "Let's see. She's been around the galleries for a long time," he said. "I think she first went to work for Mimi's first husband, Winston, when she was still in high school, and worked for him the whole time she was in college and since then, too. She was Winston's personal assistant for a while. Now she's Serenity's."

"In other words," Ali said, "a long-term family retainer."

"Exactly," Hal agreed. "I don't remember all the details. It seems like Donna's family had some kind of difficulties, and Mimi and her husband took her in, looked after her, saw to it that she got an education."

Ali was busy filtering everything Hal said about Donna Carson through the sum total of everything she had seen and heard during her endless hours in the burn-unit waiting room, trying to examine everything she had learned with her heart as well as her brain.

For example, Ali knew that Donna wasn't necessarily on the best of terms with Serenity Langley, her current boss. Ali recalled that Donna had left out some of the telling details—details about the missing painting—when she had reported events to Serenity over the phone. And what was it Serenity had said to her brother, Win, about Donna? Something to the effect that she knew the art and she knew the customers but that she wasn't irreplaceable.

"Do you happen to know what Donna's major was in college?" Ali asked.

"Art history, I believe," Hal said, "but I'm not sure. Don't quote me on that."

Ali felt her heartbeat quicken. What she had right then was little more than a spiderweb of tiny facts and innuendos, but she knew how strong spiderweb fibers could be when they were used to trap unsuspecting insects, and Ali was busy constructing her own spiderweb.

An art history major would know the worth of that Paul Klee. So would someone who had worked for years in the Langley art galleries. What was it Hal had said about Winston Langley being a chronic womanizer? Donna Carson was a dish now; Ali could easily imagine what a gorgeous bit of womanhood she might have been back in her teens and twenties.

What if Winston had betrayed Donna in the same way he had betrayed Mimi, by taking up with someone else? After all, wasn't that what womanizers did, go from one unsuspecting victim to another?

Suddenly Ali was struck by another thought. Maybe Winston Langley hadn't betrayed Donna at all. Maybe Winston's plan had been for them to be together eventually, a plan that was inalterably derailed when Winston died before his divorce from Mimi became final. Good for Mimi; bad for Donna. Sort of like what had happened to Ali—good for Ali, bad for April, the young woman who had planned on being Paul Grayson's second wife.

"Do you have any idea where Donna lives?" Ali asked.

Hal Cooper had been staring off into space, sipping his drink and woolgathering. He seemed startled when Ali's question drew him back into the present.

"I seem to remember that she bought a condo, or maybe a town house, up in Paradise Valley. I don't know where, exactly," Hal added. "I've never been there. Had no call to go, but it seems like it wasn't that far for her to come when Serenity needed her to keep an eye on Mimi."

That was another strand to add to the web. Donna was the last person known to have seen Mimi on the day she disappeared. There had been no sign of forced entry. Whoever had taken Mimi and the priceless painting had been let into the house by someone.

Ali did her best to contain her excitement. The bartender poked his head out the door. "Last call," he said.

"Nothing for me," Ali said. "Just the bill."

Hal pushed his empty glass away, put Maggie down on the floor, and stood.

"It was very kind of you to listen to my blabbing on and on tonight," he said. "My mother is flying in tomorrow morning, and tomorrow I'll be busy making funeral arrangements, but tonight I really needed to talk. You were a handy target. I hope I wasn't too much of a burden."

After billing their tab to her room, Ali reached out, took Hal's free hand, and shook it. "I didn't mind, Mr. Cooper," she said. "You weren't a burden at all."

Ali exited the elevator on floor three while Hal and Maggie rode on up to twelve. By the time the door closed behind her, Ali had her cell phone out and was punching in B. Simpson's number. Yes, it was the middle of the night, but those were B.'s prime working hours.

"Are you all right?" he said when he answered the phone. "I talked to your folks. They told me some of what happened this afternoon. I figured you'd get back to me when you could."

"I'm a little battered and bruised," she said. "Nothing serious."

"That's not what your mother said."

"Mothers tend to exaggerate," she told him.

"To what do I owe the honor of this call? It's late for you—or is it early? I can't tell which."

"Late," she said, "but I need your help, and so does Bishop Frances Gillespie."

"As in the local bishop?" B. asked after a pause. "Of the Phoenix Catholic diocese?"

"The very one," Ali said.

"What does he need?"

She explained the telephone-tracing problem.

"That's no big thing," B. said when she finished. "As long as I have the phone numbers, it shouldn't be that difficult to triangulate the calls and create a cluster map of where they came from and where they went. That's the wonderful thing about phone calls. They have a point of origin and a point of destination. Knowing those two things can often tell you a whole lot. What else?"

"Can you search Maricopa County property records for a Donna Carson? I believe she owns a town house in Paradise Valley. Anything else you can give me on Donna would be terrific."

"Do you want this to be official information, or unofficial?"

"Whatever you can find without a court order," Ali said. "School transcripts, property ownership, motor vehicles. If this person turns out to be who I think she is, I don't want to have done anything that might come back on the sheriff's department and muddy the water."

"Okay," B. said. "I'll do my best to keep our noses clean. By the way, I think I found your Mr. Yarnov, the Russian art collector. Mr. Vladimir Yarnov. If he's done something bad, he won't be easy to catch. He's a former arms dealer who took his money and an extensive art collection and decamped to Venezuela before the Russian economy went south along with everyone else's. I understand he lives like a king in a beachfront mansion outside La Guaira, near Caracas. It turns out his private collection is thought to contain several Paul Klees."

"You're right," Ali agreed. "Sounds like Vladimir is our guy."

"Let me see what else I can find for you. Do you want me to call later tonight, or in the morning?"

"Morning," Ali said. "I'm running on empty."

"Good," he said. "I'll work the night shift. You get some sleep."

On the bed in the bedroom part of her suite, Ali found a Nordstrom bag that hadn't been there before. Wrapped in tissue inside the box was a brand-new jogging suit—the same make and model as her pink one, but this one was navy blue.

A card was enclosed. "Hope this fills the bill. L.B."

Leland Brooks rides again, Ali thought. *That man is a wonder and a marvel.*

She was asleep the moment her head hit the pillow, and she was dead to the world until the phone on her bedside table rang at 7 a.m.

"It's not much of a breakfast," Edie Larson grumbled, "but your father and I are here in the lounge. The coffee is good, and there's plenty of it."

When Ali tried to get out of bed, she discovered that the parts of her that had gone slipping and sliding down the wall of the gully the day before were stiff and sore, and when she looked at her face in the bathroom mirror, the scar, still accentuated by the sunburn, stood out on her face. B. had told her once that he thought the scar gave her character. She did what she could to fix her face, then peeled the price tags off the new blue tracksuit and wore that upstairs to breakfast.

In the club lounge Ali discovered that the pickings weren't nearly as grim as Edie had implied. As far as Bob and Edie were concerned, anything less than a cooked-to-order breakfast was something of a hardship. Ali helped herself to a bowl of fresh raspberries, a few slices of salmon, some cream cheese, and a bagel. Then she joined her parents at a small table, where her mother had already poured Ali a cup of coffee.

"I hope you had a better night's sleep than we did," Edie said. "Your father turned the air-conditioning down so low I was afraid we were going to freeze to death by morning."

"I was hoping she'd cuddle up to get warm," Bob said with a grin.

"I slept fine," Ali said. *Fine, but not long.*

"What's on your agenda for today?" Edie asked. "Since we're both here, your father and I plan to check out some of the restaurant supply places. I did what you said and asked him about that big-screen TV. What he really wants is a new stove in the restaurant."

That sounded like even less of a gift than the outdoor barbecue, but Bob Larson was nodding enthusiastically.

"Some things you can order from a catalog," Edie continued, "but with something as important as a stove, he likes to see it up close and personal before he forks over his credit card. You can join us if you want, but I don't know how much fun it'll be."

Ali was glad to know the Father's Day question was settled. As far as her going along? Ali had gone restaurant equipment shopping with her parents on other occasions. This was an invitation that didn't require much thought.

"I'm working," Ali said. "I need to stop by and find out if they've moved Sister Anselm out of the ICU so I can see her. After that I expect to pack, check out of the hotel, and head back home."

Ali excused herself soon after that. Down in her room, Ali turned on her computer and logged on. A few moments later, she was looking at the Web site for Winston Langley Galleries. It was interesting that even though the man was dead, his name was still a part of the company's identity. There was a separate page for each of the several branches, and a group photo of the personnel at each. There, front and center in the photo from the Scottsdale office, was the smiling face of Donna Carson.

Ali had been upstairs with her parents when she

realized that most of the time when Donna had been
in the burn-unit waiting room, Sister Anselm had not.
Bookmarking that page, Ali hurried down to the hotel
business office and printed off a color copy. The reso-
lution wasn't perfect, but it was clear enough. Taking
the printed photo as well as her computer, she called
for her car with the full intention of showing the picture to Sister Anselm.

Her phone rang as she walked through the lobby to
pick up her car. "Hey," B. said. "I think I've got something for you."

"What's that?"

"Donna Carson bought a condo in Paradise Valley five years ago. Paid minimum down. It's currently
listed for sale for fifteen thousand less than she paid
for it originally. Which means she's trying to sell it in
a hurry.

"That's not all," B. continued. "I've come up with
an ELF connection. Donna's parents got a divorce
when she was a sophomore in high school. Her
mother got full custody, and the father disappeared
into the great beyond. Then, during Donna's junior
year, her mother hooked up with some off-the-wall
people and ended up getting arrested for arson. She
was part of a group of people who torched a bunch of
houses that were under construction on the outskirts
of Santa Barbara. They didn't call the organization
ELF back then. That name came later. The mother,
Leah Lynette Carson, was sentenced to five to ten,
but she never got out. She died of breast cancer while
she was still in prison."

"So maybe Donna stayed in touch with some of
those folks from her mother's past."

"If you look at the ages, they work," B. said. "It could be that Thomas McGregor and Donna's mother were an item way back then. Here's the real kicker," he said. "I googled the location of phone calls placed to Thomas McGregor's phone from the other one. Guess what? You can tell Bishop Gillespie for me that five of those calls originated through a cell phone tower three blocks from Donna Carson's town house in Paradise Valley, and some of them came and went within blocks of Saint Gregory's—when both phones were within blocks of the hospital."

Ali felt goose bumps spring up on her leg. "We've got her, don't we?"

"Maybe not close enough to cover all the probable-cause bases, but we're close."

"Thanks," Ali said. "You have no idea."

"You're welcome," B. said. "I'm going to grab a nap. I've got some meetings later today."

He hung up as the parking valet handed Ali her key. She looked around, hoping to see the man who had told her about the red crossover. She wanted to show him the picture. Unfortunately today was his day off.

She climbed into the Cayenne, but instead of driving off, she sat there, thinking.

So Donna had connections to someone from ELF. She must have gotten him to set the fire, but why? What did she have against Mimi? And why burn up that valuable painting? What was the point in that?

Suddenly Ali knew. She didn't know how she knew, but she did. It all made sense. There had to be two paintings—the real one and a fake. The real one could be sold to the highest bidder, while insurance coverage would pay for the one destroyed in the fire. That meant that for someone, the Camp Verde fire was going to be a big win-win.

Ali knew that there were times when owners of valuable art made their own copies of various pieces, thus enabling them to display the copy while keeping the real work safely stored in a vault. She doubted that was what had happened here. Had Mimi taken that kind of precaution, surely she would have told her husband. That meant the switch had been done without Mimi's knowledge or consent. So who was behind it? Was that big win for Donna alone, or was Mimi's son or daughter also involved?

Bounding back out of the vehicle, Ali tossed the keys back to the valet, raced inside, and made straight for the nearest house phone.

"Hal Cooper, please," she said when the operator picked up.

Ali was afraid she'd be told he had already checked out, but he hadn't. "Hello," Hal said. He sounded groggy, as though she had awakened him out of a sound sleep.

"It's Ali," she said urgently. "Ali Reynolds. We spoke last night. In the lobby."

"Oh, yes. Of course. What time is it? Eight-thirty? I should have been up a long time ago."

"I need to ask you something, Mr. Cooper. Tell me about your wife's missing painting. When did Mimi have the reframing done?"

"I don't remember exactly. Sometime last summer, I think. After we got married. Why?"

"Who did it?"

"I don't know that, either, but I'm sure I can find out. I believe Serenity handled the job. She has lots of connections with framers and the like. I seem to remember that she sent Donna over to pick it up. Why?"

So the reframing was done last summer, Ali thought. *Now Donna Carson is beating a path out of town and taking a big loss on selling her condo in the process. Interesting.*

"Tell me something else," Ali said. "How long had Mimi had trouble with cataracts?"

"For a couple of years, I suppose," Hal said. "Since before I met her. She didn't want to have the surgery and kept putting it off. Why are you asking about Mimi's cataracts? What's this all about?"

"I'm not sure myself," Ali said, "but right now I need to run. Please give me your cell phone number so I can reach you if I need to."

She jotted down the number. Then, instead of going back to her car, she made her way to an empty couch in the far corner of the lobby. Once there, she pulled out her phone and called Dave Holman's number.

"Good morning," he said. "I hope we're on better terms this morning."

"Maybe," Ali said. "I wasn't at my best last night."

"Are you feeling all right? Your dad said you got banged up pretty bad."

On the one hand it was nice to know Dave cared enough to be checking with her parents. On the other hand, it was a little provoking.

"I'm fine, really," Ali said. "I was about to go over to the hospital to check on Sister Anselm. She was in the ICU last night, and I didn't see her."

Had Ali been doing full disclosure, she might have mentioned Sister Anselm's other visitor, Bishop Gillespie, and what he had asked of her, but she didn't. Instead she got straight to the point about the painting.

"I have a question. Who's handling the Camp Verde arson investigation?"

"ATF," Dave said. "Who did you think?"

"Do you have a name and phone number?"

"Why? What's going on?" Dave sounded suspicious.

"I'm working a hunch here. If it pans out, I'll let you know. If it doesn't, I won't have to listen to your telling me you told me so."

He laughed. "Am I that bad?"

"No," she said. "Most of the time you're not."

"Hang on. Let me look through what's come in so far." He paused, then said, "Okay. Here it is. The chief arson investigator is a guy named Sam Torrance. I've got a phone number here. Do you want it?"

"Please."

That was the next number Ali dialed. "Torrance here," he said.

"Detective Holman gave me your number," she said. "I'm Ali Reynolds with the Yavapai County Sheriff's Department."

That was true insofar as it went. She didn't mention exactly what she *did* for the sheriff's department, and Agent Torrance didn't ask. The fact that she had his cell phone number seemed to lend her some credibility, but he didn't care to hang around making small talk, either.

"Look," he said. "I'm busy as hell right now. If you could call back—"

"I have a question," Ali interrupted. "Just one—about that piece of charred picture frame stock you found in the ashes yesterday?"

"What about it?"

Ali knew from the sudden shift in his voice that she now had Sam Torrance's undivided attention.

"I understand there were some scraps of paper found as well."

"Yes, ma'am," Torrance said. "I was told this was supposedly some supervaluable name-brand piece of art, right? Wrong. It's nothing but a cheap copy. Done on old paper, so it looks real— until you see the pixels under a microscope, which one of my lab techs was able to do on one of the paper fragments this morning. I forget what they call that technique. Starts with the letter *G*. Just a minute. It's right on the tip of my tongue. *Giclée*. That's it. They do it with ink-jet printers. My first guess would be that someone's trying to rip off an insurance company."

"That's my guess, too," Ali said, "and someone else besides."

On that score they may have already succeeded, she thought, but she didn't say that aloud.

Ali understood in that moment that the switch most likely had been made months earlier, at a time when Mimi, the person who had loved the painting best, was being plagued with cataracts and was in no position to notice the difference. The person responsible must have known that once Mimi decided to put the picture up for sale, the jig would be up. By destroying the fake painting, the theft of the real one might never have been discovered.

"Thank you, Agent Torrance," Ali said. "I have Agent Robson's number right here. I believe I'll give him a call."

Before she could dial, though, her phone rang. The number in the readout wasn't one she recognized.

"Kelly Green here," he said. "Sorry to be calling so close to the wire."

Ali looked at her watch. She had been so busy she hadn't noticed that the nine o'clock deadline she had given Green was rapidly approaching.

"I just got off the phone with Devon. I managed to weasel the information out of him. You won't tell him I told you, will you?"

That depends, Ali thought, *but that doesn't mean I won't tell Sheriff Maxwell.* "Who is it?" she asked.

"His girlfriend," Green said quickly.

"That's impossible," Ali said. "She's not even working right now. How would she have access?"

"Beats me. All I know is, he said that Holly was keeping him in the know."

Holly, Ali thought. *Holly Mesina? As in Sally Laird Harrison's best friend?*

That meant that Devon was cheating on his wife *and* his girlfriend. Ali wasn't entirely surprised. It made perfect sense.

"Are we good, then?" Kelly was saying.

"You kept your part of the bargain, so here's some free advice," Ali told him. "If I were you, I'd keep away from Devon Ryan. I have a feeling he isn't going to be much use to you after this."

{ CHAPTER 20 }

Instead of heading for the hospital, Ali called Dave back. "Okay," she said. "Here's the deal. I have a photo of the person I think may be responsible for kidnapping Sister Anselm. She's most likely the same person who hired McGregor to set the fire in Camp Verde."

"Wait a minute," Dave said. "You're supposed to be media relations. Who turned you into a detective?"

"Wanting to do something for Sister Anselm," she said. "As far as I can tell, no one else is particularly interested."

"Who's the suspect?" Dave asked. "Serenity Langley, by any chance?"

"She may be involved, but for right now the one I'm looking at is Donna Carson."

"Serenity's personal assistant?"

"That's right. I was going to show the photo to Sister Anselm first, but now that I have reason to believe I'm on the right track, I don't want to do anything that will screw things up. That's why I'm calling you. What should I do?"

"If you want the victim's ID to hold up in court, don't show that photo to Sister Anselm until you have an official mug shot photo lineup to go with it."

"How do I get one of those?" Ali asked.

"You may be in luck on that score. I just got off the phone with Detective Maria Salazar," Dave said. "She's an investigator assigned to Phoenix PD's Kidnapping Unit. She said the Sister Anselm kidnapping was reported to them late yesterday by someone from the Phoenix Diocese. She just left there. Now she's on her way to the hospital to speak to Sister Anselm, if she's up to it. She wants to speak to you as well. I told her that you have a reasonably comprehensive record of what went on in the waiting room the past couple of days. She asked me to tell you that she'd like a hard copy of that file. I'd like to have a copy, too," he added.

"I want to reread it myself," Ali said. "I don't remember for sure, but I don't recall a time when both Sister Anselm and Donna were in the waiting room at the same time. They may have been for a little while yesterday morning, but there was so much going on, Sister Anselm might not have noticed."

"You're saying Donna might have known who Sister Anselm was, but the reverse wasn't necessarily true."

"Yes," Ali said. "I'll e-mail your copy, but since I'll most likely see Detective Salazar, I'll print hers out."

"Good," Dave said, "but don't edit them. Send and print them as is, typos and all. If you start editing, you might end up leaving out something important."

Ali e-mailed a copy of the file to Dave, then returned to the business center to print out the thirty-five-page single-spaced document. While the copies were being made, she called Agent Robson. It turned out the ATF agent had already spoken to Dave. Now that things were falling into place, he seemed to have a noticeable interest in being cooperative.

"I'm up in Payson," he said. "I've got a whole team reading through Thomas McGregor's opus to see what we can find. One of the most interesting things we've discovered so far is the name of a friend of his, Leah Lynette Langley Carson—Donna Carson's mother, and Winston Langley's sister."

Ali was stunned. *If Donna was Serenity and Win Langley's cousin, why hadn't anyone mentioned it?*

Robson went on. "Twenty-five years ago Donna's mother and McGregor were an item. He claimed he talked Leah into being involved in one of their 'actions,' as they called them then. She got caught; he didn't. The prosecutor offered Leah a plea deal—a lighter sentence if she'd rat out her cohorts, which she refused to do. She ended up receiving a sentence of five to ten for first-degree arson, first offense. The thing is, it turned out to be a life sentence after all. She died in prison three years later."

"Of breast cancer," Ali added.

She understood her misstep at once. Robson was giving her information he had gleaned from Thomas McGregor's notebooks. Ali knew about Donna's mother from B. Simpson's capable research. But rather than asking about how Ali had come into possession of that bit of knowledge, Robson continued.

"So this may be some kind of payback," he said. "I don't know if Donna stayed in touch with McGregor all these years or if she tracked him down recently. We may learn that in one of the later notebooks. For now, I'm operating under the assumption that Donna

may have gone looking for his help when she wanted
to put out a hit on Mimi Cooper. Most likely she had
learned that Mimi had decided to go ahead and sell
the painting."

"If she had done that," Ali said, "everyone would
have figured out that her supposedly original Paul Klee
was a fake."

"Which explains why that one had to be destroyed,"
Robson said. "It's a good thing Torrance's people were
able to retrieve a few scraps of identifiable paper ash."

Ali had seen the utter destruction of the burned-
out houses. It had seemed unlikely to her that anything identifiable could have been found inside.

"How did that happen?" she asked.

"McGregor detailed all of that in one of his last
notebook entries. He had Mimi in the trunk, the gas
cans in the backseat, and the picture in the front seat
with him. He got so busy doing everything else that
he forgot about the picture until he was almost ready
to take off. He ran back and tossed it into the second
house at the last minute. It landed just inside the door,
but since that's where the firefighters first attacked the
fire, that part of the house didn't burn as thoroughly
as the rest."

"He wrote this stuff down?" Ali asked. "Why?"

"Ego," Robson said. "He had ultimate bragging
rights. He was with ELF before ELF was ELF, and
he documented everything that got near him. He had
already made up his mind that he was never going
to be taken alive or go to jail. That's in the notebooks as well. He was determined that his life's work
would survive him—that everyone would know what
he had done. Once word about the notebooks gets

out, McGregor's going to get his wish," Robson said. "Posthumously, and in spades."

"What about the other people involved?" Ali asked.

"They'll be going down, too. We won't be able to convict on just his say-so, but the notebooks give us a good jumping-off place in terms of who, where, and when. It looks like a number of them have lived respectable lives—with bland, ordinary façades that kept them from ever coming to our attention. Now that they're actively under suspicion, however, I have no doubt we'll find corroborating forensic evidence. It's a lot easier to find a needle in a haystack when you've got a line on the right needle."

Someone spoke to Robson in the background. "Sorry," he said to her. "Have to go."

Ali rang off and finished collating and stapling her two sets of documents. In looking over the hard copy, she had found some typos that she wished she'd taken the time to correct, but that was the problem—time. There wasn't any.

After stuffing the burn-unit transcripts into her briefcase, Ali went back down to the lobby. Halfway to the door, a woman rose from a chair and cut her off. "Ms. Reynolds?"

Ali nodded as the woman quickly produced an ID wallet, complete with a Phoenix PD badge.

"Detective Maria Salazar, I presume," Ali said.

The woman, fairly tall and clearly Hispanic, smiled and nodded. "Word gets around, doesn't it?" she said. "I would have called ahead, but it's a matter of some urgency."

"What can I do for you?" Ali asked.

"I've just come from Bishop Gillespie's office," the

detective said. "Naturally he's quite concerned about what happened to Sister Anselm. Believe me, if Bishop Gillespie is concerned, our department is concerned."

"Naturally," Ali agreed.

"Most of the kidnapping unit has spent the last night trying to free a drug dealer from the hands of the people he ripped off. They grabbed him during a carjacking yesterday afternoon. It took until five o'clock this morning to bring that one to a close. As a consequence, we haven't had much time to deal with the Sister Anselm situation, which appears to be quite different from our usual cases. But we're dealing with it now. In the meantime, Bishop Gillespie has had some of his people working on the problem as well. That's where you come in."

"How?"

"Donna Carson is in the process of selling her condo. She listed it for fifteen thousand dollars less than she paid for it originally. She's about to accept an offer that will mean a fifty thousand loss."

"In other words, a fire sale," Ali said.

"An unfortunate choice of words," Detective Salazar returned with a half smile, "because this *is* a fire sale of sorts. The point is, she's on her way out of town in a hell of a hurry. The closing is scheduled for half an hour from now, then she's due to fly out of town later this afternoon. First stop is L.A. Second stop is Caracas, Venezuela. The U.S. has no extradition agreement with Venezuela."

"So unless you stop her today . . ." Ali began.

"At this point, we don't have probable cause to arrest her. We're working on that," Detective Salazar said, "but we have enough for a sit-down. I'm told by two separate people, Detective Holman from Yavapai County and Bishop Gillespie, that you know more about this situation than anyone else. So I'm asking you to go along on the interview. You can brief me on the way in far less time than it'll take me to read through those transcripts."

"If I'm in on this and the ATF isn't, Agent Donnelley will have a fit," Ali said.

"They might," Detective Salazar agreed, "but as far as I know, both Agent in Charge Donnelley and Agent Robson are up in Payson right now. Donna Carson is due at the airport in a little under two hours. Do you have a vest?"

"Yes," Ali said, hefting her briefcase.

She had stuffed the vest in the briefcase along with the wig when the admitting clerk had returned her goods to her as she was leaving the ER the night before. Fortunately, it was still there.

"Good girl," Detective Salazar said. "Come on. I'll drive. I've already programmed the escrow agent's address into my GPS."

The escrow office was in a newly constructed office building at the corner of Scottsdale Road and Indian School. On the way there, Ali told Maria Salazar everything she knew, or thought she knew, about Donna Carson, including the fact that it seemed that Donna was Winston Langley's niece, and Ali's own private suspicion that even though Donna was Winston's blood relation, she might have been one of his sexual conquests.

"I suppose that would make sense," Detective Salazar allowed. "Powerful men often go looking for people who, for one reason or another, can't fight back. If you look at the Langley family history, though, growing up, Winston was the fair-haired boy to Leah's black sheep. She's the one who ran away from home as a teenager, got herself knocked up, and got married—in that order. That was also when her parents disowned her."

"Being an upright local banker and having a juvenile delinquent for a daughter probably didn't mix too well."

Detective Salazar nodded. "Later on, after Leah's divorce, she went right on making bad decisions. She got caught up in a gang of arsonists and went to prison. At that point, Winston stepped up and took his niece under his wing. He saw to it that she got an education; gave her a job."

In exchange for what? Ali wondered.

"There was no mention of Donna's being a relative in any of the discussions I heard," Ali said. "When Serenity talked about her it was as a long-term employee, but not as a relative. There was even some mention about letting her go."

"In other words," Maria Salazar said, pulling into a parking garage, "Donna's a charity case. She's the poor relation who's allowed to have a job, but she's also expected to know her place in the family pecking order. Sounds like a possible motive to me."

Ali and Maria Salazar exited the unmarked Crown Victoria.

"So here's how we're going to play it," Detective Salazar said as they walked through the lobby and toward the elevator. "So far Donnelley has done an incredible job of keeping the lid on all this. McGregor's ID has not yet been given out, pending notification of next of kin. Your involvement has yet to be made public, either. Did Donna ever see you in the waiting room?"

"She may have," Ali said, "but I looked different."

Detective Salazar smiled again. "Right," she said, "I heard. The infamous red wig."

"Most of the people in the room assumed I was part of another patient's group of visitors," Ali added. "Nobody there paid much attention to me. There's a good chance Donna didn't, either."

"Let's hope," Detective Salazar said. "Now, as far as the interview is concerned, she's only a person of interest, but you and I are going to pretend that McGregor gave her up. We'll see what that gets us. With any kind of luck, we'll be able to provoke her into doing something stupid. By the way, are you carrying?"

Ali nodded. "I doubt your supervisors know I'm doing an armed ride-along on this one."

"Don't worry about my supervisors," Maria Salazar said. "Bishop Gillespie has the ability to pull any number of strings. I believe he's already pulled several."

Ali believed it, too.

They rode the elevator in silence. Arriving at the sixth floor, they found their way through a maze of corridors to the office marked *Pan American Escrow*. While they were still outside in the hallway, Maria Salazar produced a tiny tape recorder. After switching it on and re-stowing it in her pocket, the detective pushed open the door and flashed her badge in the direction of the young woman seated at the reception desk.

"We're here to see Donna Carson," she said brusquely.

"I'm sorry. She's involved in a signing. Her escrow officer has asked that they not be disturbed."

"This is police business," Maria insisted. "Which way?"

The receptionist capitulated. She pointed. "That way," she said. "The conference room at the end of the hall."

The conference room telephone was ringing as Ali and Detective Salazar reached the door. Before anyone had a chance to answer, Maria flung open the door and marched inside with Ali on her heels.

The escrow officer's name tag identified her as Louise Wilson. She and Donna Carson were seated side by side at a large conference table. Two separate stacks of documents were spread out in front of them. Louise was just reaching out to answer the ringing phone when Detective Salazar stopped her.

"Don't bother," the detective said. "That's just your receptionist calling to let you know we were on our way."

After two more rings the phone fell silent.

"Who are you?" Louise demanded. "I don't know who you are or what you think you're doing. I'm calling the police!"

"We are the police," Detective Salazar responded, flashing her badge. Then she turned her attention to Donna Carson. "Is this her?" she asked Ali.

"Yes," Ali said.

Now it was Donna's turn to object. "Who are you?" she demanded, looking from Detective Salazar to Ali. Her face revealed no sign of recognition as far as Ali was concerned. "What do you want?

"You're Donna Elizabeth Carson?" Detective Salazar confirmed.

"Yes, I am, but can't you see we're busy here?"

The escrow officer stuffed the two stacks of documents into a file folder. "Just give me a minute, Ms. Carson," she said. "I'll get rid of them."

"No, you won't," Detective Salazar said. "We're not going anywhere." She pointed at a chair. "Sit," she ordered. Without further objection, the escrow officer sat.

"What's this all about?" Donna asked.

"It's about two attempted homicides that occurred northeast of here yesterday afternoon. You're a person of interest in those two cases, Ms. Carson, along with another incident that happened earlier this week in Camp Verde. We need you to tell us where you were yesterday afternoon, and what you were doing."

Donna paled slightly. "This is ridiculous," she said, rising. "I was at work yesterday afternoon. My employer's mother was in the hospital, where she died early yesterday evening. I spent most of the afternoon there with them. Serenity Langley will verify I was there, so will her brother."

"Sit," Maria said again, this time pointing a finger at Donna Carson. With a put-upon sigh she, too, subsided into her chair.

"That would be at Saint Gregory's Hospital?" Maria asked.

"Yes," Donna said. "The burn unit. On the eighth floor."

"So are you acquainted with Sister Anselm, a Sister of Providence who was working as a patient advocate there?"

Donna shook her head. "I might have seen her. I'm sure I've heard the name, but I don't believe I ever met her."

There was the tiniest tremor in the corner of her

eyes when she gave that answer. Ali suspected that Donna was telling the truth, sort of. Perhaps she and Sister Anselm had never been formally introduced, but Donna Carson knew who Sister Anselm was and what she did.

"I suppose we should read her her rights," Maria said casually to Ali. "Just in case she turns into a suspect."

"Right," Ali said agreeably. "Just in case."

Maria recited the Miranda warning from memory. Ali waited until the Mirandizing was complete. Ali expected Donna to demand an attorney at that point. When she didn't, Ali posed another question.

"What did you do with Mimi Cooper's watercolor?" she asked. "We know what happened to the fake Paul Klee. What happened to the real one?"

"What painting?" Donna demanded in return. "I don't have any idea what painting you mean."

"Yes, you do," Ali insisted. "You stole Mimi's Klee months ago, when you took it out for reframing. You replaced it with a fake. The two house fires in Camp Verde were supposed to get rid of the evidence. So what's your connection to Thomas McGregor?" Ali asked. "How did you persuade him to help you?"

Donna had been warned that anything she said could be held against her, but apparently she wasn't listening.

"I didn't have to persuade him," she said dismissively. "He offered to help me. He wanted to help me. He hated those people as much as I do."

A hint of a smile twitched at the corners of Detective Salazar's mouth, but she said nothing.

"What people did he hate?" Ali continued. "Sister Anselm? Mimi Cooper? What did they ever do to you, or to him? You still haven't said what you did with the real Paul Kloc. Where is it?"

"It's on its way somewhere you'll never find it," Donna answered. "You'll never get it back. Neither will Serenity or Win. It's mine. All mine."

Donna sounded like a petulant little girl, frustrated because she hadn't been allowed to have her own way and had been forced to share some beloved toy. She didn't sound the least bit like someone capable of planning and executing a cold-blooded murder.

But if she's damaged goods, Ali thought, *if her uncle took advantage of her . . .*

Ali decided to tackle that delicate subject head-on.

"Why did you do this?" she asked. "Why are you lashing out at Winston Langley's family? Is it because your uncle molested you? Was he your lover?"

For a moment Donna stared at Ali in openmouthed amazement. "My lover!" Donna exclaimed. "Are you kidding? That bastard was never my lover."

Ali and Maria exchanged looks. If Donna Carson and Winston Langley hadn't been lovers . . .

"And he wasn't my damned uncle, either," Donna declared, trembling as outrage overtook her. "Oh, he played the good uncle, all right, the beneficent uncle. But he was my father—my biological father! He raped his own sister and convinced their parents that she was the wild one! She ran away and found someone who married her and gave me his name. Those are the names on my birth certificate, you know—Leah Lynette Carson and John David Carson."

Ali was appalled by the whole idea. "You're saying Winston Langley was your father, and that he raped his own sister?" she repeated.

"Yes."

"What about your mother's parents?"

"What about them? I never even met them until after my mother went to prison. That's when Winston came riding to the rescue, playing the part of the generous uncle. And all this time, that's what I thought he was."

"Your mother never told you what happened?"

"Tom McGregor was the only person who ever told me the truth. Winston didn't, not even when he was dying, and his goody-goody bitch of a wife didn't tell me, either, although she knew. She claimed she didn't, but she must have. As far as the world was concerned, Winston Langley was this really good guy—the magnanimous uncle who stepped up to the plate to help out his poor, deprived, and orphaned niece by seeing to it that I got an education and by giving me a job. All I had to do was keep my mouth shut about my mother. She was the bad seed, and the less said about her the better.

"So I went along with the program. I was the charity case. I wore Serenity's cast-off clothing, but I had a place to live and food to eat. That was the price I was prepared to pay as long as I was an orphan. But it turns out I wasn't an orphan at all. Once Tom told me the truth, I realized how badly I've been cheated—by Winston and Mimi and by Serenity and Win, too.

"What I've earned in paychecks over the years is a drop in the bucket compared to what Win and Serenity got when Winston died. I'm expected to bow and scrape and do whatever Serenity says, while she treats me like dirt. But then, she can afford to. She had access to her share of Winston's estate, and mine, too."

"That painting belonged to Mimi," Ali put in. "How does stealing it even the score with her dead husband?"

"It didn't," Donna said. "Not nearly. All three of them got way more than I did."

"Tell us about Tom McGregor," Detective Salazar suggested. "What brought him into the picture?"

"He reached out to me after he saw Winston Langley's obituary in one of the Phoenix papers," Donna answered. "He didn't think it was fair that the story said Winston had a son and a daughter when Tom knew it should have been a son and two daughters."

"When did you first hear from him?"

"A little over a year ago. He said his conscience was bothering him and that he owed it to my mother to set the record straight. When he first told me, I didn't believe it, either, but then I had some DNA testing done. You're cops. DNA doesn't lie, does it?"

"So you convinced Tom McGregor to help you," Ali asked.

"I already told you. He offered to help me."

"Why kidnap Sister Anselm? What did you have against her?"

"Because Tom blew it the first time around. Mimi was supposed to be dead, but she wasn't. I was afraid she'd tell someone that I was involved before I had a chance to get away."

"You're right," Ali said. "She did tell someone."

"The nun?" Donna asked.

"No," Ali told her. "She told her husband."

"Tell me about your mother's involvement with Tom McGregor," Maria Salazar urged.

"He was lonely," Donna said. "She loved him and he loved her. He told me that he never got over her, and that he felt responsible for what happened to her. Not that she died, but that she died in prison. He said that once he'd evened the score with my mother once he'd repaid what he owed her by helping me— he didn't care what happened. He said he was done and that chapter was finished. I'm not sure what he meant."

Ali did. He was referring to all those handwritten notebooks—and to his suicide by cop.

The escrow officer, who had been listening to this whole exchange in slack-jawed amazement, rose to her feet.

"I shouldn't be here," she said. "I need to go."

"But what about the papers?" Donna objected. "If I don't sign them, I don't get the money."

"No one is getting any money today," the woman said. "Under the circumstances, the closing can't proceed. I'm sorry."

She stood up to walk away. Before she made it out the door, Maria Salazar stopped her. "I understand Ms. Carson was leaving town today. Where were you expected to send the proceeds from the sale?"

Louise looked as though she was ready to object. "I can get a warrant," Detective Salazar told her, "but it would be easier all around if you'd just tell me."

Biting back a comment, the escrow officer opened the file and shuffled through the papers. Finally she settled on one.

"Here it is," she said. "Once we received the funds, we were to make a wire transfer to an account in Caracas, Venezuela. It's a joint account, registered to Ms. Carson and a Mr. Vladimir Yarnov."

"Vladimir wanted the painting and I wanted him,"

Donna Carson explained. "I was going to give it to him. For a wedding present."

"Too bad for him, Ms. Carson, because I don't believe there's going to be a wedding," Detective Salazar said. "We're done here. You're under arrest. Hands behind your back."

The whole process left Ali stunned. Winston Langley had set in motion an avalanche of evil that had overwhelmed everyone in its path. He had raped his own sister and let her parents throw Leah to the wolves. He had betrayed his wife in life, and he had continued to betray her in death, leaving her to die a horrible death that left behind a truly bereft husband and an equally bereft cockapoo.

Tom McGregor, the arsonist who had personally started the fatal blaze, was dead as well, gunned down in a hail of gunfire before he could hurt anyone else. Two innocent bystanders—Sister Anselm and Gila County Deputy Guy Krist—had come away from their encounters with these people gravely injured.

Without a further word of objection, Donna Carson stood and placed her hands behind her back while Detective Salazar snapped the cuffs into place.

And that's how it all ends, Ali thought. *Not with a bang, but a whimper.*

CHAPTER 21

To Ali's surprise, Donna Carson never did stop talking. In the year since she had learned the truth about Winston Langley's family and her own, she had built up a lifetime's worth of resentment that all came gushing out. She had spent the better part of that year wallowing in unreasoning hatred and plotting her revenge, all the while maintaining the façade that nothing had changed. It had been Serenity's casual order for Donna to look in on Mimi that had put the last pieces in place.

Donna spilled out her story with no attempt to minimize her culpability and with zero regard to how her words might impact a legal defense in a court of law. Her defense attorney would have a mountain of self-incrimination to overcome if Donna's case ever made it as far as a trial, but as long as Detective Salazar and Ali kept asking questions, Donna kept answering them, both in the car on the way to the precinct and later in an interview room at Phoenix PD.

Listening to Donna's tale of woe, Ali couldn't help but compare what had happened to her to what had happened to Judith Becker. Both of them had been disowned and dispossessed—but Judith Becker had responded to the loss of both her parents as well as the loss of her country by turning her horrendous losses into a blessing for others.

Donna had done the opposite. She had lost her mother, the man she had always believed to be her father, and her biological father as well. She had turned the injustice of what happened to her into an excuse to inflict incredible harm on others.

Ali looked on as Donna was being booked. As the booking officer inventoried the items in her purse, Ali saw that there were two diamond rings tied inside in a small felt bag. The diamond on one was a rock, while the other was much more modest.

Mimi's missing rings, Ali thought, making a mental note to pass that information along to Detective Salazar.

The purse also contained a whole series of documents—Donna's passport, along with preprinted boarding passes for both her Phoenix-to-L.A. flight and the one from L.A. to Caracas. Tucked into her wallet was a FedEx receipt for a package Donna had shipped to herself in care of her hotel, the Caracas Hilton. For import duty purposes the document listed the contents of the package as a "framed art print" with an insured value of $50.

"I'm guessing that's an original and that it's stolen goods," Detective Salazar said.

While she went off in search of a warrant that would allow the package to be intercepted and returned, Ali was left alone in the interview room with Donna. Sitting across the table from this dangerous woman, Ali was a little concerned that her weapons—her Glock and her Taser—had been placed in a locker before she entered the small, mirrored room.

As the silence deepened around them Ali asked one final question

"What would have happened if you had come to Mimi and Serenity and Win and told them what you had learned?"

"You mean would they have made some provision for me?" Donna asked bitterly. "Like that's going to happen. For one thing, Winston Langley's money is mostly gone. Win has a gambling problem. He ran through his inheritance like it was water. As for Serenity? She's convinced that she has a great head for business, but she doesn't, not like her father did. The galleries are all losing money. She's been keeping them afloat with her inheritance. Once that's gone, so are the galleries. Where would that leave me? A third of nothing is nothing."

"In other words, since whatever was left of Winston's estate belonged to Mimi, you went after that."

"Why wouldn't I? She wasn't going to give me any of it. After all, she's no relation to me—no blood relation."

"Not enough of a relation to talk to, but enough of a relation to murder," Ali said.

"I guess," Donna said with a shrug.

That was when Ali realized that Donna simply didn't care. The fact that other people had been hurt or killed meant nothing to her. Less than nothing.

For the remainder of the fifteen minutes Detective Salazar was gone, Ali and Donna sat in the room in absolute silence.

Earlier, no one had been paying attention to what had happened to Sister Anselm and Mimi Cooper. Now everyone was.

Ali spent most of the rest of the day being debriefed

by a series of agencies about what had happened. The Fountain Hills marshals wanted access to the information that would allow them to sort out what had happened to Mimi Cooper. Phoenix PD wanted to know details about what had happened to Sister Anselm, an incident that had started in their jurisdiction and ended in someone else's. But over all this, Agent in Charge Donnelley's media embargo still held sway.

Donna Carson's name wasn't being released to the media because she had yet to be charged. Tom McGregor's name still wasn't being released pending notification of next of kin, who most likely didn't exist. And Sister Anselm's name and medical information were being withheld as well.

The real reason behind all the interagency silence was Agent in Charge Donnelley. Tom McGregor's handwritten notebooks counted as a major break in the ATF's long battle with the Earth Liberation Front, and Donnelley wanted things kept quiet long enough to gather warrants and to bring some of the people named in those notebooks in for questioning.

It was late afternoon before Ali finally headed back to the hotel. Since her phone had been turned off most of the day, her voice mailbox was brimming with messages. Several were from B. Simpson, but those all said he was in a series of meetings and would call again later.

One message was from her mother. "Dad and I bought a stove," Edie said. "Used, not new, but your father loves it. It'll be delivered next week, in time for Father's Day. See you at home."

Another message was from Bishop Gillespie. "I understand you were on hand today when Donna Carson was arrested. Good work. Sister Anselm seems to be recovering. She asked that you please stop by when you can, but you might want to use that wig again. It looks like the hospital lobby is full of reporters."

That one made Ali smile, not because of the wig suggestion but because Bishop Gillespie seemed to have excellent sources of information. The question was, were those sources inside Phoenix PD, or were they inside the ATF, maybe even Agent Donnelley himself? Was it possible the agent in charge and Bishop Gillespie were pals?

Ali took the bishop's suggestion seriously. After showering and putting on clean clothes, she donned the wig and drove back over to the hospital. Camera vans too tall to make it inside the garage were parked outside, and she appreciated the media alert warning.

She also noted that even though Donna Carson's arrest and Tom McGregor's death should have lowered the threat toward Sister Anselm, Bishop Gillespie's security detail was still very much in evidence—in the garage, in the lobby, and in the waiting room on the orthopedic floor.

When Ali pushed open the door to Sister Anselm's room, she discovered Bishop Gillespie himself seated next to Sister Anselm's bed. He was reading to her from a notebook Ali recognized—Mimi Cooper's guest log.

When Ali appeared in the doorway, he pushed his reading glasses to the top of his head. "So here's the woman of the hour," he announced with a smile. "Ali Reynolds herself. It turns out we were just talking about you. Sister Anselm has been asleep most of the day, and I've only now been bringing her up to date. I told her that an arrest has been made, but I'm unable to tell her much more than that."

Standing at the bedside, Ali could see Sister Anselm's face was sunburned to the point of peeling. "How are you?" Ali asked.

"Better than I would have been without you," Sister Anselm said. "How can I ever thank you?"

"I believe you've been paying that one forward all your life," Ali said with a smile.

She pulled up another chair, and for the next half hour, Ali gave Sister Anselm and Bishop Gillespie the highlights of what she knew. When she saw Sister Anselm was fading, Ali excused herself. Rather than pushing the Down elevator button she pushed Up and went to the eighth floor. A new patient or two had been admitted. The burn-unit waiting room was crowded with a whole new collection of worried family members, but in the far corner, Ali spotted a single familiar face—Mark Levy. He looked bone weary, but his face brightened when he saw her.

"Hey," he said. "I didn't think I'd see you again."

"I came back to thank you for the help you gave me earlier."

"You're welcome," Mark said with a shrug, "but it wasn't that much."

"It was," Ali said. "How's James?"

"Better," Mark said. "They're starting the skin grafts. That's good news. His parents even let me go in to see him once today. He was sleeping, but still. Visitors are limited to family members only. I think his mother said I was his brother."

"Good," Ali said. "You act like a brother."

Mark was silent for a moment before adding, "I

guess you heard that the woman in eight fourteen didn't make it."

Ali nodded. "I heard," she said.

"Neither did the woman in eight twelve. Her name was Alva. She was smoking in a chair and fell asleep, and now she's dead, too. I don't think I could work in a place like this," Mark added. "It would be too hard."

"You're right," Ali agreed. "It is that."

Her phone rang while she was riding down in the elevator.

"I don't believe it," B. Simpson said. "You finally answered the phone. Where are you?"

"Leaving the hospital," she said. "I'm on my way back to the hotel."

"Great," B. said. "I'm here, too."

"Where?"

"At the hotel."

"My hotel?" Ali asked.

He laughed. "Yes, your hotel. I had meetings in Phoenix today. I thought I'd stop by and see if I can take you to dinner. Morton's is right out front. We don't have a reservation, but I'm betting they can fit us in."

"Did I tell you I was staying at the Ritz?" she asked.

B. laughed. "When I couldn't reach you, I weaseled the information out of your parents. What about dinner?"

That was typical. Now that Ali's romance with Dave Holman was pretty much off the table, Edie was promoting another possible candidate, but however B. had found his way to the Ritz, his invitation to go to dinner was a welcome one. Ali was hungry. It had been a long time since breakfast.

"Good," she said. "I'll be there in a few minutes."

B. was waiting in the lobby when she arrived. "Congrats," he said, standing up to give her a hug. "I hear you and Detective Salazar saved the day."

"How do you know that?" Ali asked. "The news hasn't exactly been disseminated to the media."

"I heard it from a friend of yours," B. said. "I expect he'll be a friend of mine as well—or at least a client. Bishop Gillespie plans to hire High Noon Enterprises to keep track of diocese-owned computers. If any of the people who work for him are messing around with online porn, Gillespie wants to know about it. That man is something," B. added admiringly. "If he weren't a bishop, I think he'd make a wonderful hacker."

That made Ali laugh.

"Are you ready to go to dinner?"

"I'll go upstairs and drop off my briefcase," she said. Up in her suite, she combed her hair and freshened her makeup. When she rejoined him downstairs, they walked across the driveway to the restaurant.

Even though Morton's was crowded at that hour, the maître d' showed them to a corner booth. Once seated, they ordered drinks and exchanged stories about all that had happened in the previous several days.

"It sounds like you've really made a name for yourself," he said finally. "I know this thing with the sheriff's department was supposed to be temporary, but will you stay on?"

"I don't know," Ali said seriously. "There's a lot more going on in Gordon Maxwell's department than meets the eye. If I end up being the one who delivers the bad news to him, he may not want me hanging around any longer. You know what happens to bearers of bad news."

"Do you want to talk about it?"

"No," Ali said. "Not yet. I haven't decided what to do."

"I see," B. said.

Ali was gratified that he let it go at that. He understood she wasn't ready to discuss it, and she liked the fact that he didn't quiz her about it anymore, that he was at ease with her not telling him what she wasn't prepared to tell.

They had a great time at dinner. The food was wonderful; so was the service. They laughed. They talked. Only when their waiter dropped off the bill did B.'s smile disappear.

"This has really been fun," he said. "Thank you for coming. I finally figured out that the only way I'd ever be able to take you to dinner was if we were both out of town. You're worried about the age thing, aren't you?"

He had her cold on that one. He was attractive. He was interesting. He had money and a marital history of his own. The problem was that for Ali the age difference had always been the one major drawback to their having anything other than a professional relationship.

Tonight, at dinner, sitting there chatting and eating and enjoying themselves, Ali had noticed that no one noticed them or paid them the least bit of attention. They were simply two people out on the town, having fun. If some of their fellow diners or the waitstaff were busy calculating the difference in their ages, it didn't show.

The last time B. had asked her out, Ali had said no. This time she had said yes. Why? Was it because she was hungry? Partly, but to be honest, she had to admit that after meeting Hal Cooper and seeing his devotion to his beloved wife, the fifteen-year age difference between Ali Reynolds and B. Simpson no longer seemed to be such an insurmountable barrier.

"Yes," she said finally, in answer to his question. "I have been worried about that in the past, but maybe I'm not so worried about it anymore. Would you like to walk me home?"

"Sure," he said with a grin. "Door-to-door service."

Once in the hotel elevator, he pressed the button for the third floor without having to ask. "How did you do that?" Ali asked. "How do you know I'm on the third floor? What did you do, bribe the desk clerk? Hack into the hotel's registration system?"

"Nothing as underhanded as that," B. said. "I asked your mother."

"That figures," Ali said with a laugh. At the door to her suite, Ali pulled out her room key and plugged it into the slot. B. opened the door and held it for her.

"Don't you want to come in?" she asked. "For a nightcap, maybe?"

They both knew she wasn't talking about a drink.

"You don't have to do that," B. said. "I have my own room."

"So?" Ali asked. "Nobody says you have to use it."

With that, she led him inside.

When Ali awakened in bed the next morning, lying next to B. Simpson, she was surprised to realize that she felt happier than she had in a very long time. She slipped out of bed and was showered, dressed, and packed before she ever woke him up.

"Okay, sleepyhead," she said. "Time to wake up. I

need to check out and go to work. And you need to check out, too, or else you need to go to your own room."

It turned out that it took longer for her to boot him out of her bed than she had expected. Ali also had to dress again and redo her makeup, but by the time she drove away from the Ritz, she was incredibly light-hearted. She didn't know what would happen in the future. Was this relationship with B. Simpson merely a passing fancy—a bit of mutual attraction by two lonely people—or would it turn into something more serious?

What she did know was that the two of them had been good together. They'd had fun—uncomplicated, glorious fun, more fun than she'd had in years, which explained why Ali felt so alive. Once Dave Holman had retreated into his fatherhood duties, Ali had pretty much put the possibility of romance out of her head.

B. Simpson's appearance on the scene was forcing her to rethink that position.

That morning, though, instead of heading home for Sedona, Ali drove straight to Prescott to handle some unfinished business. Arriving at the office on Gurley Street, she asked to speak to Sheriff Maxwell, only to discover he was out for the day—down in Phoenix for a major ATF press conference announcing a break-through and several arrests in Arizona- and California-based cells of the ELF network.

It took a while for Ali to track down the information she needed. Once she had it in hand, she left the department and drove to Devon Ryan's place, several blocks away. She found him in the front yard of a mod-est bungalow, standing on a ladder, painting the wood trim on the front soffit.

"How's it going?" she asked, walking up the side-walk.

Devon turned and looked down at her. "Oh," he said. "It's you. Did you stop by hoping to pick up some media relations pointers?"

Arrogant jerk, Ali thought.

"Not exactly," she said. "I came by to see how things were going with you and Holly."

He put down his paintbrush and then stepped down from the ladder. "Holly?" he said "Holly who?"

"That would be Holly Mesina," Ali said. "Sally's good friend Holly. When she started giving me such a ration, I thought she hated my guts because she and Sally were such pals, but that isn't it at all, is it?"

"I don't know what you're talking about," Devon said. "If Holly's said something about me, she's proba-bly just making up stories."

"I doubt that," Ali said. "Does Sally know that you've been screwing around with Holly behind her back, and does your wife know about either of them? If not, I'll be happy to tell them both."

The stricken look on Devon's face was priceless.

"You wouldn't."

"Actually," Ali said, "I would. I have some experi-ence with cheating spouses. I was married to a man just like you—a cheat and a bully and a coward. If I tell your wife, I know exactly how she'll feel, because I've been there."

"If you tell her—" he began.

"What?" Ali asked before he could put the threat into words. "What exactly will you do? I already know way too much about you. I also have a theory about who lifted that missing evidence from the evidence room and blamed it on Sally. It was too complicated having two of your girlfriends working in the same office. They might have started comparing notes and figured out what a worthless creep you are."

"You can't prove that," Devon objected. "You can't prove any of it."

"I can if I have to."

"How?"

"Kelly Green, I know all about your cozy little relationship with him. If you don't go to Sheriff Maxwell with all this, I will, and so will Mr. Green."

For a moment, Devon said nothing aloud, but his face told the whole story. Ali had him between a rock and a hard place and he knew it.

"What do you want?" he said finally.

"I want Sally Harrison to get her job back," Ali said. "Her daughter is sick. She needs the insurance coverage."

"What about me?" Devon whined. "What about my family?"

"Maybe you should have thought about them before you started collecting payoffs from people like Kelly Green for doing your job. Sheriff Maxwell is down in Phoenix today. I'll give you until tomorrow to turn in your resignation and take responsibility for your actions. If you don't do it by noon tomorrow, I'm going to him with everything I know. The only question in my mind is whether you'll take Holly down with you. I have an idea about the kind of guy you are, so it might be a good idea for Holly to start polishing up her résumé."

When Ali finally made it back home that night, Leland Brooks came out to carry her suitcases in from the car.

"What's for dinner?" Ali asked.

"I didn't know about tonight, so I have a casserole in the fridge."

"What about tomorrow night?" she asked. "I'm thinking we'll be having company."

"What would you like?"

"How about lamb chops?" she said. "Asparagus, and some of your potatoes au gratin."

"For how many?" Leland asked.

"Two," she said. "B. Simpson and me. And for the time being, I'd like that kept quiet, especially from my mother, and from Chris."

"Of course, madam," Leland said, nodding. "I understand completely."

Ali was sure he did.

"One more thing," Ali said. "I'd like you to drive down to Phoenix this week, go to Best Buy, and pick up one of those fifty-two-inch flat-screen TVs for my dad for Father's Day. I'm sure Chris will be glad to get some of his friends to help you install it."

"Absolutely, madam," Leland said. "With pleasure. But speaking of Chris, he dropped by a little while ago and left a puzzling message that has something to do with Father's Day as well. He said for me to tell you to please not mention 'you know what,' I believed he called it, because he and Athena are planning to unveil the surprise to your parents on Father's Day."

Ali got it. She was thrilled, but she managed to restrain herself from giving Leland a swift hug. Hugs weren't necessarily a good thing as far as Leland was concerned.

"Thank you," Ali said. "That's very good news."

Sam wandered into the bedroom while Ali was changing clothes. "So did you miss me?" Ali asked.

Broken tail in the air, the cat wandered away without answering.

When Ali's alarm went off the next morning, she was still sound asleep, but she dragged herself out of bed. Sheriff Maxwell called while she was in the process of putting on her makeup.

"Everyone is suitably impressed," he said. "That includes Agent in Charge Donnelley."

"Good," Ali said. "I'm glad to hear it."

"I've had an interesting call from the Catholic bishop down in Phoenix, saying what a splendid job you did with Sister Anselm. Bishop Gillespie couldn't say enough good things about how you saved Sister Anselm out in the desert. That was a little outside your assigned duties—as was the situation with Donna Carson. So you're on Phoenix PD's good side, too."

"Okay," Ali said. "I'm hearing all this good news, and I'm waiting for the 'but.'"

"What 'but'?" Gordon Maxwell said. "There is no 'but.' Well, maybe a little one."

"What's that?"

"I may have hired you under false pretenses."

"How's that?"

"I told you the job was temporary because I expected Devon Ryan would be coming back any minute. It turns out he isn't. He turned in his letter of resignation this morning. Internal Affairs was looking into some possible charges against him, but now that he's leaving we'll let that go. It'll keep my department from having more of a black mark than it already has."

Which will also be good for Sheriff Gordon Maxwell, Ali thought. Some of that Internal Affairs fallout might well have blown back on the sheriff himself.

"What about Sally Harrison?" she asked. "Is she getting her job back?"

"You knew about all of that, too?" Sheriff Maxwell asked. "About the two of them carrying on?"

Well, duh! Ali thought.

"Yes," she said. "I knew. Did Devon say anything to you about Holly Mesina?"

"I'm not sure why, but it turns out she's quitting, too," Sheriff Maxwell said. "It's too bad, but under the circumstances it's probably just as well. I'll be better off with fewer people on the payroll."

"Yes," Ali agreed. "I'm sure you will."

"So, getting back to what I was saying before. With Devon not coming back, will you stay on for the time being?"

"For the time being," Ali told him. "Unless something better comes along."

"Good," Sheriff Maxwell said. "That's just what I wanted to hear. What are you doing for the next month?"

"What do you mean?"

"Someone just dropped out of the upcoming police academy training class down in Peoria. When I heard they had an opening, I asked them to hold it for me long enough to check with you. How about it? Will you go? The media relations job will be here waiting for you once you graduate."

Ali thought about it, but not for long.

"My mother will have a fit," she said, "but I can't think of anything else I'd rather do."

Keep reading for an excerpt of

CREDIBLE THREAT

The newest mystery featuring Ali Reynolds

Available March 2020 from Gallery Books

PROLOGUE

On a mid-March afternoon as the sun drifted down over Piestewa Peak to the west, Rachel Higgins wrapped her sweater a little closer around her body and took another sip of her vodka tonic. Snowbirds might be running around dressed in Bermuda shorts, Hawaiian shirts, flip-flops, and sandals, but for Rachel—a Phoenix native and true desert dweller—mid-March still counted as winter. Even so, she wasn't ready to go inside, not just yet. For one thing, there was nothing to go in for other than another evening of mindless viewing of whatever empty-headed crap happened to be on TV. No, she was better off staying outside for a while longer, savoring the luscious perfume of orange blossoms from her neighbor's trees, an aroma that seemed to intensify each day as afternoon turned to evening.

Rachel had long since become immune to the rumble of rush hour traffic on State Route 51 and Highway 101 in the near distance. When Rachel and her husband, Rich, had bought the place on Menadota Drive, the mountain formerly known as Squaw Peak had not yet been renamed Piestewa Peak in honor of Lori Piestewa. Lori was the young Hopi woman who had become the first Native American woman ever to die in combat, back when her convoy was ambushed in 2003 during the Iraq War. At the time Rachel and Rich had moved to the neighborhood, both Loop 101 and Route 51 had barely been a gleam in the eye of some crazed highway engineer. Now the name Squaw Peak was no more, and what had once been a serenely quiet desert landscape was overwhelmed by the unrelenting roar of 24/7 traffic.

This had been their dream home back then—one of the first houses to be built in a new subdivision. The new house was a far cry from the modest bungalow off 7th Avenue and Indian School that had been their first home. No, this one was spacious inside and out. Rich had told her at the time that this lot on a corner of the cul-de-sac would be plenty big enough for a pool, and five years later they had one. At the time it had seemed as though their family life was coming to order at last.

Rich had just been given an amazing promotion as an engineer at the Salt River Project that had made their purchase of the new place financially feasible. As for Rachel? At age twenty-five, after years of trying, she had managed to get pregnant. On the day they moved into their new house, their son David had been a babe in arms.

Rachel had been ecstatic with the way things were turning out. She'd never wanted to be anything other than a housewife and mother. That's why she'd majored in Home-Ec in college. *Was that major even an option these days?* she wondered. Rachel didn't know, but that's exactly what Rich had wanted back then—a stay-at-home housewife and mother—and Rachel had settled into the job with enthusiasm.

Rachel's father, Max, had been an accountant—a mousy little man with a propensity for letting people walk all over him. Her mother had been glad to spend his CPA earnings, all the while calling him a milquetoast behind his back. Naturally Rachel had gone looking for something different from that, and Rich Higgins had turned out to be her father's polar opposite. He had been a big, burly "my way or the highway" kind of guy. Which may have worked all right to begin with, but what happens when the guy calling the shots loses his way? What are you supposed to do then?

In their family, Rich had always been the sole breadwinner, and he hadn't bothered consulting her when he'd accepted an employer-offered buy-out at age sixty. Starting his pension then meant it was far less than they had counted on. And because his leaving was considered a voluntary separation, he didn't qualify for unemployment benefits, either.

Realizing how tight money was becoming, Rachel had offered to try getting a job, but Rich nixed that idea completely. It was fine for Rachel to volunteer here and there, but no wife of his was going to work outside the home. They would survive on the money he brought home come hell or high water. It was the way it had always been, and that was the way it would be in the future.

And what had Rachel done about that? Absolutely nothing. At age fifty she had morphed into a female version of her father. She had let Rich have his way and had gone along with that edict. Besides, when it came to entering the work force at her age, what could she do? Office work? Hardly. She was no typist. She could manage their home computer well enough to find things on the Internet when she needed to and to send out occasional e-mail, but she was definitely not computer literate. And when it came to typing, she was of the hunt-and-peck variety. She could have looked for a job as a sales clerk, she supposed, but she couldn't imagine standing behind a cash register for eight hours a day scanning other people's groceries at Safeway or A.J. Bayless.

In the end, it had been far easier to be complicit and simply go with the flow. She and Rich had made their bed together, and now they were lying in it. Except that wasn't entirely true. They slept in separate bedrooms now. Rachel had the master, and Rich slept down the hall in the room that had once been David's. They woke at different times and went to sleep at different times. The meals they ate together were generally eaten in silence. They were more like roommates now than they were husband and wife. Was Rich as unhappy as Rachel was? Maybe, but it wasn't something they talked about because they mostly didn't talk.

At this point, Rachel was bored. She'd had a few flirtations here and there, but the relationships had never gone beyond that. Dealing with one man was quite enough, thank you very much! Had she thought about getting a divorce? Not really. For one thing, despite the fact that neither she nor Rich had attended Mass in years, she still regarded herself as a Catholic, meaning that divorce was out of the question. She would do the same thing her mother had done, which is to say, she would stick it out to the bitter end.

Once Rich's Social Security income started coming in, that too was lower than it would have been had he started collecting benefits later. As they gradually depleted their savings and their financial situation deteriorated, they were forced to cut one corner after another, and that's when Rachel's resentment about that early buy-out began to simmer beneath the surface. She looked after the house, read the books she dragged home from the library each week, read her on-line newspapers, watched TV, and otherwise lived the life of a hermit—or at least the life of a hermit's wife.

The shabby cars they drove—her aging Mercedes and his

Cadillac Escalade—were ten and fifteen years old respectively but at least they still worked. Years of being parked in full sunlight out in the driveway meant that their exterior paint jobs had faded away to powder, and the interiors were rugged with drooping head rests and sun-damaged upholstery. Buying a new car for either one of them was simply out of the question.

As the mandatory belt-tightening continued, things Rachel had always taken for granted as part of her social life simply went away—restaurant meals, golf outings, gatherings with friends, going to movies, standing appointments at her favorite nail salon. It had been a real blow to her when she'd been forced to let her long-time cleaning lady go. They still had a yard man and a pool guy, but only because the homeowner's association would have come after them if they'd let those items slide, and Rich simply refused to do the work himself. He was too busy—making bird houses!

With mourning doves cooing in the background, Rachel thought about how things had been at the beginning when they had first moved here as opposed to how things were now. Their house had been among the first ones built when the new development had been carved out of open desert. Once they moved in, Rachel soon discovered that the creatures who had been the original inhabitants of the area were none too happy about ceding their territory to these infringing interlopers.

As a little one, David had never been allowed to play outside alone without having his eagle-eyed mother watching over him. Rachel had been forced to use a hoe to dispatch more than one rattlesnake that had somehow managed to slither into their yard. There had always been a plethora of centipedes and scorpions hanging around as well, but Rachel had signed on to protect her child from all comers, and that's exactly what she did.

When it came time for David to go to school, she had cheerfully donned her chauffeur's hat and driven him back and forth to a small, newly established parochial school at St. Bartholomew's Church on Shea Boulevard several miles to the south. She'd driven him everywhere he needed to go—to Boy Scout meetings and Little League games and swim lessons because that's what she'd signed up for—to raise her son; to take care of him; to see that he thrived. And then . . . She shook her head. How on earth could it all have gone so terribly wrong?

The doorbell rang just then. Later Rachel would think of that sound as something her high school drama coach, Miss Reavis, would have referred to as a "knocking within." At a critical point in a play, someone from offstage announces his arrival with a sound of some kind. Once that character appears, he brings with him some bit of compelling information that will propel the drama to its final conclusion. Eventually Rachel would come to realize that's exactly what that doorbell had been—the tipping point that had turned everything in her life upside down, but at the time it was nothing more than an unwelcome intrusion on her solitary afternoon cocktail.

There was no question about Rich emerging from his workshop to answer the door. Even if he'd heard the bell, he wouldn't have bestirred himself from behind his workbench to bother. And that was Rachel's initial reaction, too—that she would simply ignore the ringing bell until this unwelcome visitor gave up and went away. After all, how important could it be?

In the old days, a caller this late in the afternoon might have been a paperboy out collecting from customers on his route, but Rich had stopped subscribing to paper-and-ink newspapers long ago. Since this was March, it might be one of the Brownies from up the street, peddling Girl Scout cookies. Or it might even be some political hack out canvassing the neighborhood, looking for votes in an upcoming municipal election.

The doorbell rang again, but still Rachel didn't move. After a minute or so, it rang a third time. Obviously whoever was at the door wasn't giving up and going away. They probably assumed that, with two cars parked in the driveway, someone had to be home. Only then did Rachel finally go inside to answer. In the front entryway, she paused long enough to use the peephole. What she saw was a heavily tattooed young woman wearing jeans and a T-shirt and holding a banker's box. She looked to be twenty-something, so she was most definitely not hawking Girl Scout cookies.

Once Rachel unlatched the deadbolt and security chain, she swung the door open. "Yes?"

"Are you Mrs. Higgins?"

"I am," Rachel responded.

"David Higgins's mother?"

"Yes," Rachel replied. "I'm David's mother. Who are you and what do you want?"

"My name's Tonya Bounds," the young woman said. "My dad was John Bounds, and I came to give you this."

She held out the box, but Rachel made no move to accept it.

"Who's John Bounds?" she asked.

"After my folks divorced, my father took in boarders for a while," Tonya answered. "I'm guessing your son must have rented a room from him at one time or another. My father died a couple of months ago. My boyfriend and I have been helping my mom get the house ready to sell. The place was a mess. We found this box in a corner of the garage with your son's name on it. Inside was a copy of his obituary. I found your address, but the phone had been disconnected."

"Yes," Rachel said, "we gave up having a landline years ago."

"I didn't know if you still lived at the same address, but since it's on my way home, I decided to take a chance and try dropping by to give it to you."

"What's in it?" Rachel asked.

Tonya shrugged. "Not much, just random stuff David left behind, and I'm not even sure why my dad bothered saving it. There's a comb and brush, some clothing, and a pair of shoes, along with some odds and ends—a class ring, a pin from Disneyland, a school yearbook, and a little notebook that looks like he used as a journal or diary."

Relenting, Rachel reached out and took the box. When she did so, she found it to be a lot lighter than she'd expected.

"Thank you for going to the trouble of tracking us down to deliver it."

"You're welcome," Tonya said with a smile. "Like I said. Your address was on my way. I live just south of the Scottsdale city limits in Tempe."

"If you don't mind my asking, what did your father die of?"

Tonya's smile faded and she shrugged. "An overdose," she answered bleakly. "What else? That's what caused Mom and Dad to split up in the first place. Dad was in and out of treatment time and again. He lasted longer than anyone thought he would, but still . . ." She paused for a moment before adding, "But then I guess you know that drill."

Rachel nodded. She had tried getting David into treatment several times, too, always to no avail. "I guess I do," she agreed, "and it's no fun. So sorry for your loss."

Tonya turned to go. Rachel remained on the front porch long enough to watch the young woman drive away, before going back inside, closing and bolting the door behind her. Initially Rachel started toward the kitchen with the box before changing her mind and heading for her bedroom instead.

David's untimely death was what had plunged Rich into his pit of despair, and to this day, even the mention of his son's name was often enough to provoke a relapse. Rather than leaving the box out in the open, Rachel tucked it away in a corner of her closet and shut the door. When she returned to the kitchen, she was surprised to find Rich there, making himself a bologna sandwich.

The way things were those days, Rachel no longer bothered with cooking nutritious meals. Chances were, Rich wouldn't be interested in eating them anyway. Instead, they subsisted on a steady diet of cold cereal and sandwiches. Rachel's natural metabolism was still serving her in good stead. Rich's was not. In the past seven years he had gained at least fifty pounds, probably more. She hadn't said anything about it. If he didn't care, why should she?

"Who was that at the door?" he asked.

She wanted to say, *why didn't you answer the damned door yourself*, but she didn't. "Magazine salesman," she replied, lying to him without the slightest hesitation. "I told him we didn't want any."

"Good," he said. "We sure as hell don't."

With that he collected his sandwich and a bottle of Bud Light and returned to the garage without bothering to clean up his mess. Rachel did so because that's what she always did—cleaned up after him. And then, rather than make herself a sandwich, she poured another vodka tonic. Before she would be able to face the contents of David's box, she'd need some of what her mother had always referred to as "Dutch courage."

It wasn't until much later that night, after Rich had retreated to his room without a word to Rachel and after his TV set was blaring behind his closed door, when Rachel, more than slightly drunk, finally meandered down the hall to her own room where she closed the door, pulled the banker's box out of the closet, and moved it to her bed.

When she removed the lid, the first thing she saw, of course, was the obituary along with the printed program from the funeral home—the one that had been handed out to people attending the service. That meant that Tonya's father had been enough of a friend that he had gone to the funeral, but Rachel had been in so much pain at the time that she had no real recollection of that day—not of the service itself or of the people who had bothered showing up. John Bounds may have lived and died a druggie, but he had been kind enough to preserve David's paltry collection of belongings, and Rachel was grateful to him for that.

Just under the yellowed newspaper clipping and funeral program was David's moth-eaten letterman's jacket from Scottsdale's St. Francis of Assisi High School. David had been an outstanding athlete. He had lettered in basketball and swimming all four years. He'd played point guard on the both the JV and varsity basketball teams and had been captain of the swim team his senior year when St. Francis had walked away with the state championship. He'd been smart, too. He should have gone on to school, but he hadn't. Rachel had never understood why he had simply turned his back on the idea of going to college, but he had. The night when he had told his parents that he had no intention of going on to college, father and son had gotten into a terrible row.

"Do you have any idea what you're doing?" a livid Rich had demanded. "Don't you care anything about your future?"

"No," David had replied. "I don't."

He had packed up his things that very night and moved out of the house. He had never gone on to school. He had held a series of menial jobs, but mostly he had hung out and done drugs, drifting deeper and deeper into that world until there was no turning back. A heartbroken Rachel had tried reaching out to him from time to time, to no avail. Rich had not. Once David was dead, Rachel had the advantage of having already processed some of her grief. Rich, on the other hand, had been utterly grief stricken. Paralyzed with guilt and unable to cope at work or at home, he had fallen into a downward spiral and had been stuck there ever since.

Rachel unfolded the jacket and held it up to her face, hoping that some trace of David's scent had lingered in the material. It had not. All she smelled was dust with just a hint of motor oil in the background. Laying the jacket aside, she returned to the box. Next up were a few shirts, two worn pairs of Levis, and a broken down pair of Nike's. At the bottom of the box she found the odds and ends Tonya had mentioned— the pin and the class ring as well as a copy of the St. Francis High School yearbook for 2001, the *Clarion*.

Two thousand and one had been David's senior year, and the swim team had been the center of his existence. Since St. Francis had walked off with the state swimming competition title that year, it was hardly surprising that when she put it in her lap, the book opened almost of its own accord to the sports section near the back and to a page that featured the swim team. The shock of what she saw there took Rachel's breath away. The page featured a full-page photo of the ten members of the team along with their coach, Father Paul Needham. The boys, grinning for the camera, all wore their swim suits. As for the priest? He was fully dressed, but above his white dog collar, every feature of his face had been blacked out with a Sharpie.

In that instant and despite all the vodka she'd consumed, Rachel found herself stone-cold sober because, for the first time in all these years, she finally had some inkling of the reality of what had happened to her son. And that's when the tears came. She and Rich had wanted only the best for David. That was why he had attended parochial schools. That was why they had coughed up the tuition so he could attend St. Francis High, and yet all their good intentions had backfired on them. In wanting to give David everything, they had given him worse than nothing. Rich and Rachel had failed their son, and the Catholic church had failed the whole family.

The storm of tears that followed rocked Rachel to her core. At last, spent with weeping, she dried her tears, repacked the banker's box with David's things, and then steeled herself for the grim task ahead. One way or another she would have her revenge. Someone needed to be held responsible, and if God wouldn't smite them, she would.

CHAPTER 1

On a bright Monday morning in late June, Ali Reynolds and her husband, B. Simpson, sat drinking coffee on the patio outside the master bedroom of their Sedona home.

"Okay," he said. "The party's over, so time's up. Are you coming to London with me or not?"

The party in question had been a garden-party homecoming event for current and past recipients of Amelia Dougherty Askins scholarships. As a high school senior at Cottonwood High, Ali had been one of the first students to be awarded one of the Verde Valley–based scholarships, and it had enabled her to do something she might not otherwise have been able to do—attend college. She'd gotten a degree in journalism that had allowed her to pursue an award-winning career as a television newscaster. When that had fallen apart, she had returned home to Sedona to regroup. Sometime later, she had found herself in charge of the scholarship program from which she herself had once benefited.

Yesterday's afternoon tea had been in the works long before Alexandra Munsey, one of Ali's good friends from her news anchor days in LA, had been brutally murdered in her home outside San Bernardino. In the aftermath of Alex's death, Ali, along with several members of B.'s cyber security firm, High Noon Enterprises, had been sucked into the vortex of a homicide investigation.

Alex and Ali had both led complicated past lives. Maybe that was part of what had created such a strong bond between them. Both of their lives had crashed and burned at about the same time and they had both reinvented themselves afterwards. At the time of her death, Alex had been on the cusp of a blossoming literary career. The novel that had been published within days of her death had been a huge success and had hit the *New York Times* bestseller list several weeks in a row. That was one of the reasons her homicide had hit Ali so hard. Alex's death had forever denied her the critical and literary accolades she had so richly deserved.

As for Alex's killers? Hannah Gilchrist, one of the people responsible, was dead of natural causes. The other conspirators were either already incarcerated on other charges or in jail awaiting trial, but Ali knew that it would take years of court proceedings before justice was finally served—if ever. Even so, there would be no eye for an eye here. No matter what the final outcome was in some California courtroom, nothing would ever bring Alex Munsey back. She would never live to see her precious grandson grow up, graduate from high school, go off to college, marry, or have a child of his own. She would never have the opportunity to write and publish another book. No, her untimely death had destroyed all those potential outcomes, and the unbearable finality of that was wearing Ali down.

Weeks earlier she had risen to the challenge, traveled to LA, and stood up to speak at Alex's funeral, but back home it had been all she could do to go through with the party. The food had been catered by one of the scholarship fund's food science graduates, and B.'s and Ali's new majordomo, Alonzo Rivera, had sorted out most of the physical details. Still, it had taken real effort on Ali's part to simply dress up, put on a happy face, and go forth to welcome her guests. Once the party had ended, late in the afternoon, she had been ready to collapse.

B. was due to attend an international cyber security conference in London at the end of the week, and days earlier, he had invited Ali to come along with the added incentive that they'd be able to see a play or two in the West End and maybe spend a couple of days hiking in the Cotswolds once the conference ended.

"Come on," he had said. "It'll be good for what ails you. We've got a full team on board to look after things in your absence."

If B. had expected an enthusiastic affirmative, it wasn't forthcoming. "Maybe," she had said. "Let me get through the garden party first."

"I just checked with BA," B. added. "There are still a couple of first class seats on my flight. Shall I book one for you?"

Ali had stalled him on the subject earlier, but now with the party in the rearview mirror, it was time for her to give him a final answer.

"All right," she agreed reluctantly. "I'll come along, but I'm not sure I'll be very good company. When do we leave?"

"Wednesday," he replied, "Wednesday afternoon."

"Sorry," she said after a thoughtful pause. "I guess I'm acting like an ungrateful, spoiled brat."

"You are," B. agreed with a smile while reaching across the table to take her hand. "But at least you're my spoiled brat, and one who's been through one hell of an ordeal."

"Thank you," she said. "And maybe a trip is exactly what's needed."

CHAPTER 2

On a Monday morning in late June, Francis Gillespie, Archbishop of the Phoenix Archdiocese, fled the air-conditioned chill of his study for the welcome warmth of his shaded outdoor patio. The perimeter of the property was lined by an impenetrable wall of oleanders that had grown to be twenty feet tall. Beyond the wall to the back, the craggy red expanse of Camelback Mountain loomed large against a hazy blue sky. To the front, the hedge shielded the property from the roar of city traffic rushing past on Lincoln Drive East. Inside that green barrier, the manicured grounds of his residence constituted a whole other world.

The archbishop loved sitting here on the patio, surveying his lush domain. Because the residence had its own private well, water was not an issue. There was grass, plenty of hearty, thick-bladed grass. There were raised flower beds scattered here and there, all of them alive with riots of vivid color from blooming petunias and snapdragons. Most of the palm trees in the city and on neighboring properties had been stripped of their skirts, but that wasn't the case here. Every year the gardener came to him begging to be allowed to strip off the palm trees' masses of hanging dead limbs, and each year the archbishop overruled him. Those dead leaves provided habitats for any number of flying creatures—a flicker or two, a woodpecker, and squadrons of bats. Several rock dove resided there along with a pair of house finches that migrated back and forth between the trees and the bubbling fountain at the foot of the patio.

The archbishop had taken his old bones outside to warm them in the summer heat, and he had brought his work with him. His Holiness at the Vatican may have taken strong positions on things like climate change and reducing carbon footprints, but Archbishop Gillespie had seen no reduction in the amount of tree-based paperwork that flowed like a gigantic river in and out of the Holy See. After being sidelined by ill health for the better part of two months, the archbishop regarded the incoming missives as more of a flood than a river.

In late March, something the archbishop had tried to pass off as a minor cold had soon morphed into a full blown case of bronchial pneumonia. He had spent close to three weeks in the ICU at the Mayo Clinic Hospital and another four weeks confined to their rehab facility. The doctors had warned him that at his age—closer to eighty-eight than to eighty-seven—he was lucky to still be "on the right side of the grass." As an exceedingly young doctor had told him, his recovery would be a "long, slow process."

That was certainly proving to be true. To his dismay, Francis was still having to depend on a walker to get around, and the previous night, while trying to push his way through another pile of paperwork, he'd fallen asleep at his desk and had awakened a full three hours later. He was making better progress in the paperwork department now, but with a noon-time appointment looming, he wasn't going to come close to getting to the bottom of the pile.

At that moment the patio slider opened and Father Daniel McCray, Archbishop Gillespie's private secretary for the past fifteen years, stepped outside.

"Excuse me, Your Grace, but one of your luncheon guests has arrived and would like a word."

Father McCray and Archbishop Gillespie had worked together on a daily basis for a decade and a half. Although the archbishop might have welcomed a bit of informality between them, Father McCray was careful to maintain the proper amount of distance and decorum.

Archbishop Gillespie removed his reading glasses and set his paperwork aside. Back when he'd been a parish priest, his flock had been his parishioners. Once he was appointed Archbishop of the Phoenix Diocese, his flock had become the priests and nuns who did the hands-on work of spreading the gospel. Some archbishops tended to isolate themselves and stay far above the fray. That was not Archbishop Gillespie's *modus operandi*.

He understood the essential loneliness of living a godly life. A shepherd is there to guide and protect his sheep, not to befriend them, so priests were always set apart from their parishioners As both a bishop and archbishop, Francis Gillespie had loved the camaraderie of meeting with others of his own ilk—men who knew both the joys and burdens of doing God's work. As a young priest he had formed close friendships with several of the men he'd met at church gatherings, one of whom was now a cardinal.

Francis wasn't a political animal. At the time of his appointment, there had been two warring factions inside the Phoenix Archdiocese. Considered to be a natural outsider, he had been promoted from within for that exact reason—because he wasn't a member of either clique. He had risen through the priesthood by dint of being both smart and direct. If he saw a problem, he didn't care to sit around endlessly jawing about it; he wanted to fix it. As a consequence, early in his tenure as archbishop he had made himself available to his flock by hosting monthly luncheons for the priests in his diocese. The gatherings, held in his residence, were certainly not mandatory but they were always widely attended, as much for the delicious food provided by Father Andrew, the archbishop's cook, as for the fellowship provided by simply being together.

The archbishop's luncheons were customarily held on the last Monday of the month—Mondays being the one day of the week when priests might reasonably take a day off. The luncheons allowed his far-flung clerics to socialize and come to know one another. For Francis Gillespie, the gatherings allowed him to keep his finger on the pulse of his flock. Since the previous two luncheons had been scrapped due to his illness, the expectation was that this one would be especially well attended, and Father Andrew had been cooking up a storm for days.

"Which priest?" Archbishop Gillespie asked.

"Father Winston from Prescott," was the reply.

Father Jonathan Winston was one of the newer priests in Archbishop Gillespie's fold. He was an Iraq War veteran who had gone to seminary and joined the priesthood after three separate deployments to the Middle East. In addition to serving as the priest at St. Mary's in Prescott, Father Winston did a good deal of chaplaincy work at his local VA Hospital. He and the archbishop had carried on many long conversations on how best to serve veterans dealing with PTSD.

"Have Father Winston come out here then," Francis told Father McCray. "Once I've had a chance to hear what's on his mind, the two of us will go in to the luncheon together."

"Very well," Father McCray replied, nodding his assent. He disappeared through the slider and returned a few moments later with Father Winston following on his heels. Once he had delivered the newcomer into Archbishop Gillespie's presence, Father McCray disappeared inside.

With the exception of his white collar, Father Winston was dressed all in black, and it occurred to the archbishop that perhaps the younger man wouldn't find the outside heat nearly as comfortable as Francis did.

"Your Grace," Father Winston said, holding out his hand, "it's good to see that you're on the mend."

"Mending, but not altogether one hundred percent at this point," the archbishop replied, waving in the general direction of his much-despised walker. "I'm still having to use that confounded thing."

"We've missed you," Father Winston said.

"Thank you," the archbishop said. "I've missed you, too. Have a seat," he added, "and tell me what's on your mind."

Seating himself at the round patio table, Father Winston withdrew something from his pocket and handed it over. Looking down, Father Gillespie saw a standard offertory envelope. There were places where parishioners could write in their names, addresses, and phone numbers along with the amount of their offering. Those lines had all been left blank.

"What's this?" Archbishop Gillespie asked.

"It showed up in the collection plate yesterday when the deacon in charge was sorting the banking deposit. Take a look inside."

Archbishop Gillespie opened the envelope and pulled out a folded three-by-five card. On it, handwritten in ink, was the following message:

HEY HEY, HO HO.

ARCHBISHOP GILLESPIE HAS TO GO!

Looking up from the message, the archbishop smiled. "I'm sure this reflects the feelings of any number of folks around here who are of the opinion that I'm well past my sell-by date."

Father Winston didn't smile in return. "It sounds like a threat to me," he said. "And the fact that it was anonymous . . ."

"I doubt it's as serious as all that," Archbishop Gillespie advised. "What is it they call people like that—the ones who post all kinds of awful things on the Internet under the mask of anonymity?"

"You mean trolls?" Father Winston asked.

"That's it exactly—trolls. Trolls used to hide out under bridges. Now they hide out behind computer screens or, as in this case, behind an offertory envelope, where they can be totally anonymous and feel perfectly free to say all kinds of appalling things. Hidden behind a curtain like that, they can spit out all kinds of nonsense that they'd never have gumption enough to say directly to someone's face. If I were you, Father Winston, I wouldn't give this message another moment's thought."

With that, the archbishop returned the card to the envelope and slipped it into his pocket. Then he gathered his papers and rose to his feet. "It's getting hot out here. What say we go inside and see what Father Andrew has been up to. He told me at breakfast that he's outdone himself today."

For the remainder of the day, Archbishop Gillespie followed his own advice and didn't give the handwritten missive another thought. It wasn't until he was emptying his pockets in preparation for going to bed that evening when he came across the envelope again. He studied it for a moment before slipping it, unopened, into the top drawer of his dresser.

Father Winston was a priest who'd had firsthand experience with war. He'd been in combat. He'd done tough things and seen worse. No wonder he was suspicious and maybe even a bit paranoid. But that wasn't Francis Gillespie's worldview.

"It's nothing," he said aloud, closing the dresser drawer with a thump. "It's nothing at all."

Unfortunately, he was wrong about that. The message that had been dropped into the collection plate at St. Mary's in Prescott was anything but nothing. It may have been the first threat Archbishop Gillespie received, but it was certainly not the last. Although the wording would be different, they would all be similar in nature and dropped off in collection plates in churches scattered all over the archdiocese. And each time Francis Gillespie added a new one to the growing collection in his dresser drawer, he was forced to draw one simple conclusion. Someone was after him, and whoever it was wouldn't quit until he was gone.